where the night ends

MELISSA TOPPEN

Editing and Interior Design by

Silla Webb at Masque of the Red Pen

Cover Design by

Judi Perkins at Concierge Literary Designs

Where the Night Ends
Playlist

Dive- Ed Sheeran
Untouchable- Taylor Swift
Fall For You- Leela James
The Cure- Lady Gaga
Shadows- Sabrina Carpenter
Make Me- Noah Cyrus
Force of Nature- Bea Miller
Sledgehammer- Fifth Harmony
How Would You Feel- Ed Sheeran
Come Wake Me Up- Rascal Flatts
Catch Me- Demi Lovato
Every Little Thing- Carly Pearce
Heavy- Linkin Park
Song #3- Stone Sour
Space- Lindsay Ell
River of Tears- Alessia Cara
Fix a Heart- Demi Lovato
Say Something- A Great Big World
Lost in California- Little Big Town
Tell Me How- Paramore
Sweet Creature- Harry Styles

True love, especially first love,
can be so tumultuous and passionate
that it feels like a violent journey.

-Holliday Grainger

TESS

"Come on Tess, you have to come," my best friend Courtney whines from the edge of my bed where she's currently sitting, giving me her best pout. "You know I need you there."

She's spent the better part of the last hour trying to convince me to come to a party that I have no desire to go to. But like most things, Courtney rarely ever lets me off easy. It's been the story of our entire friendship dating all the way back to the second grade.

"I think you'll be just fine without me. Besides, you already said Bree was going," I remind her, turning my attention back to my closet.

"You know Bree will be so far up Blake's ass the whole time I probably won't even see her. I need you," she reiterates.

Of course, I know she's right. Bree, the third part of our little gang, is what some might classify as well, to put it frankly, a slut. She's one of those girls who chases love like it's the only thing in the world that will make her happy which makes her a bit flakey in the friendship department.

We both love her in spite of that, though. Because well, she's Bree, and there's no one in the world like her.

"Then why even go?" I snag the yellow sundress Courtney wants to borrow, pulling it from the hanger before turning back in her direction.

"Because it's the biggest party of the summer, not to mention the last, and everyone who is anyone is going to be there," she says for the hundredth time since she told me about the party last week.

"That's what you said about the party last month, too," I remind her, dropping the sundress into her lap.

Because we're very close in size, we spend more time borrowing each other's outfits than wearing things of our own. I would be lying if I said my self-esteem doesn't take a bit of a nose dive every time Courtney walks out in one of my outfits making it look ten times better than I ever could.

She's all curves and boobs whereas I'm—well, not. Where things cling to her body in all the right places, the same outfit looks more like a sack on me. Of course, in normal girl fashion, she complains about every inch of her body, even though she knows she's gorgeous. With dark eyes and long dark wavy hair, Courtney is the embodiment of what every teenage girl wishes she looked like. There's no way she can't see what everyone else does.

Unlike me...

I'm more of a plain Jane. I don't go out of my way to look overly done up. I typically keep my long, light brown hair natural, letting it hang straight down my back. Makeup to me consists of a little mascara and some clear lip gloss, and while I love wearing sundresses and cute tops, I never wear anything too revealing—not that I have much to show off anyway.

I wouldn't say I'm shy necessarily—just a lot more modest than my two promiscuous best friends. While they're all about boys and having fun, I'm more worried about staying on track to get into Columbia. Considering it's one of the hardest colleges to get into, I can't afford to get too distracted.

"Yeah, but this is different," Courtney huffs, pulling me back to the topic at hand. "Sebastian Baxter throws the best parties in all of the school. And since his parents' are in London, you know this one is going to be a doozy."

"Remind me again how we got invited to this party? Neither of us is even friends with Sebastian."

"No, but Ant is," she says, referring to her current boy toy, and one of Rockfield High's most popular athletes, Anthony Treadway. "You know they play football together." She gives me a knowing smirk.

"Ah yes, how could I forget? The golden boys. The dynamic duo. Eggs and spam and all that jazz." I roll my eyes, having never cared much for anything sports related.

"Says the girl who's been infatuated with Sebastian since he moved here our freshman year." She narrows her eyes at me.

"That was two years ago, Court. I've been over that forever," I lie, knowing that even when my ex-boyfriend Dylan and I were dating I harbored a massive crush on the infamous Sebastian Baxter.

Not that I ever stood a chance of even catching his attention. He's a year older than me—a soon to be senior—and if there's one person in the school who's more popular than Ant it's Sebastian. Which means he's constantly surrounded by girls—all the time.

"Come on, Tess, you never do anything with me anymore. Ever since you and Dylan broke up you've been hiding out in your bedroom." She tries a different angle with me.

"This has nothing to do with Dylan," I immediately object.

"That's what you've said all summer, and yet you refuse to go anywhere you think he might be."

"He cheated on me, Court, or do I need to remind you of that? "The sting of everything he put me through pushes Sebastian completely out of my mind. "Why would I want to subject myself to a night of watching him flaunt his new girlfriend in my face? No thank you. I'll be just fine right here."

"I thought you said it didn't have anything to do with Dylan." She quirks an eyebrow at me.

"It doesn't, but it certainly doesn't help matters."

"So what then? You're just going to sit around here all night watching re-runs of whatever lame ass television show you pretend to find interesting while the rest of your high school years pass you by?"

"Don't mind if I do." I plop down at my desk that sits in the corner of my bedroom, swiveling my chair around to face her.

"You're letting him win, you realize this, right?" she challenges.

"There's no winning or losing here, Court. I've already lost. He made sure of that when he shacked up with Taylor Davies, and the whole school knew about it before me."

I don't mention the fact that he made sure to include that I'm a stuck-up prude virgin to the rumor mill. Virgin, yes. Prude or stuck up—not in the least. I want to experience all the things my friends already have. I want to know what all the fuss is about. But I also refuse to just give it away to the first guy who looks my way. Dylan clearly didn't understand this, hence why six months into our relationship he found himself a girl who was willing to open her legs without a second thought.

Being my first real relationship, I didn't take our break up well. I think it was more about how humiliated I felt than it was the actual fact of losing him. I won't lie and say I'm not jealous of how quickly he moved on or hurt by how easily he dropped me, but it's more about my own pride now than anything else.

"Screw Dylan!" Courtney throws her hands up in frustration. "You should be out there showing him all the reasons why he epically fucked up and not sitting here letting him think that he got the last laugh."

"And I'm supposed to do that how? By dressing up and prancing around like everything is great?" I cross my arms in front of myself.

"That's exactly what you're supposed to do. Fake it till you make it, Tess. You, of all people, should understand that. You're the one who preached it to me for months after my parents' split up. If it wasn't for you, I'd have been a hot mess. But you didn't let me wallow. You didn't let me sit around feeling sorry for myself. You forced me to get out of the house. And if it wasn't for that, I never would have met Ant," she says.

"And how's that working out for you?" I question sarcastically.

"What's that supposed to mean?"

"I'm just saying, Court, you've spent all summer following him around like a lost pup, and the boy hasn't even had the decency to make you his official girlfriend. I think it's pretty safe to say he's stringing you along."

"Oh, so now not only are you in the business of being a sorry sap, but you're also determined to tear everyone else

9

down with you?" she snaps, my choice of words clearly hitting a sensitive subject with her.

I can tell by the look on her face that I've crossed the line. She's right, who am I to piss on other people's parades. If their arrangement works for her then who am I to judge?

"I'm sorry, Court. I don't know why I said that."

"Look, I get that things haven't been easy for you these past few weeks, but the best way to get over it is to get back out there. Which is why you're coming to this party with me," she states matter of fact. "Now get your ass back in that closet and find something to wear that will have Dylan questioning why he ever let you go."

"I don't think a cute outfit will make a difference. Besides, I don't care what he thinks anymore. He made his choice."

"Then show him you don't care and come with me. I'm not taking no for an answer."

"I don't know," I waver, thinking over everything she's just said.

"Please, Tess." She sticks out her lower lip. "I'm not above begging."

Truth be told, a night out doesn't sound like the end of the world. Courtney's right, ever since Dylan and I broke up I've been hiding out. But that doesn't mean the thought of seeing him doesn't make me nauseous. Like she said, everyone who's anyone will be there, and Dylan never misses out on a good party. I know with complete certainty that if I go there, I will most definitely see him.

It's one thing to know I'll have to see him in the hallways when school starts next week. It's another thing completely to have to face him in a social setting.

I weigh the pros and the cons in my head. If I don't go, it will only further solidify to Dylan and the rest of my friends and classmates that I'm still hung up on what he did to me. And while that's somewhat true, it doesn't mean I want him to know that.

"Fine." I finally cave, knowing there's no way she's going to let me get out of this anyway.

She squeals in delight and instantly jumps up, making a beeline for my closet

"But I'm picking out my own outfit," I quickly add, knowing if I leave it up to her she'll have me dressed like a teenager in heat.

"Spoilsport," she whines when I join her in front of my closet.

***

I've never been to Sebastian's house. From what I've heard it's something to be seen but nothing could've prepared me for the expansive property that is laid out before me. By the time Courtney maneuvers the long driveway up, I feel like we've entered an entirely different world. House is an understatement. This place is more like a mansion.

Sitting on a large wooded lot, there isn't a neighbor around for miles. No wonder everyone says this is the best place to party—it's likely you could have a live band outside and not a soul would know what was happening.

"You ready?" Courtney gives me a reassuring smile seconds after killing the engine to her small Civic.

I'm still not entirely sure why I let her talk me into this.

"As I'll ever be." I let out a slow exhale before reaching for the door handle.

The driveway is lined with cars. The front of the property looks more like a parking lot to a busy mall than the front entrance of a house. Courtney joins me at the back of the car, and together we make the remainder of the walk up toward the house. The music coming from inside pumps so loud I feel like we're already surrounded by it before we even reach the huge front porch that wraps around the entire house.

Several people are lounging out front, beer bottles and cups in hands. Busy chatter dances around us as Courtney eyes me excitedly before pushing her way inside.

The music hits us like a tidal wave, the sound so loud my first thought is to plug my ears. Court senses my unease and immediately bats my hand away.

"Live a little," she mouths over the heavy thump of the bass, shimmying her way through the crowded foyer to an enormous sitting area that's almost the size of the small one story where I live with my mom.

"Tessa Wilson, you fucking bitch." I hear Bree before I see her. Her arms drape around my neck from behind just seconds before I feel her lips against my cheek. "Muah." She makes a spectacle out of the whole ordeal in true Bree fashion.

"How the hell did you get this tight ass out of the house?" she asks Courtney, sliding up next to me.

"Good to see you didn't waste any time," I tease, pointing out her inebriated state.

"When in Rome," she announces, holding up the red solo cup in her hand.

Bree is a spitfire, wild and fierce. Her red shoulder-length bob and dark lined eyes are just some of the ways

12

she displays her defiance. While she acts tough and in control, only those of us who really know Bree know that deep down she's just a product of a really bad past.

"Are we in Rome? Because the last time I checked we're still in Rockfield," I reply dryly.

"You can take the sour sap out of the house, but you can't make her any more fun." She pouts before laying a hard smack to my jean-covered backside.

"Remind me again why we're friends with her?" I ask Courtney over the music, hitching my thumb in Bree's direction.

"You know you bitches love me," she screams in response, downing the remaining contents of her cup.

"I'm gonna go find Ant. You okay for a second?" Courtney asks, gesturing around the room.

"She's fine. All she needs is a drink and a hot piece." Bree knocks her hip against mine.

"Leave me with this one and who knows where I'll end up," I say to Courtney, shaking my head on a laugh as I allow Bree to link her arm through mine and drag me out of the room.

We weave through several people crowding the hallway and then into the large gourmet kitchen. There's only a handful of people inside, refilling drinks and grabbing snacks. Thankfully the music isn't quite so loud on this side of the house and while I can still hear it, it's not the only thing I can hear.

Two kegs are set up along the large island in the middle of the room, and there is just about every variety of liquor lining the top of it. Bree refills her cup from the keg before pouring me a drink, shoving it in my hand the moment it's full.

"Cheers, bitch." She smiles, tapping her cup against mine before taking a long drink.

I take a small sip, trying my best not to cringe. I've never been a fan of beer. I'm not much of a drinker normally. That's more Bree's style than mine. Not that I'm opposed to having a good time, I just don't like to get too inebriated. I know how some of these parties go down.

"Where's Blake?" I finally ask, surprised to find them not attached at the hip. He rarely lets Bree out of his sight which in my opinion is a little weird, but she seems to like it so I don't give her a hard time about it.

As if he can sense my question, he appears in the doorway of the kitchen not seconds later, his eyes bloodshot and glazed over.

"Where the fuck have you been?" He approaches Bree, purpose in every step.

Blake is not what you would classify as a big guy, but there is something very intimidating about him— possessive even. I can see the attraction for Bree; she's always had a thing for the bad boys, and Blake is definitely that.

"Babe." Bree smiles, pulling him to her the moment he reaches us. "I was looking for you, and I found Tess instead." He barely acknowledges my presence before he leans in and says something to Bree, his voice low enough that I can't hear his words.

A wide smile slides across my friend's face and just like that, I know I've lost her.

"I'll be back, Tess, okay?" she half promises seconds before Blake is leading her out of the room.

Well, there goes hanging out with my friends tonight. Not like I didn't know this would happen. This is what always happens, which is why I usually avoid these types of situations.

Knowing there's nothing I can do about it now, I down the beer in my hand, hoping to somewhat calm my nerves, and then toss my cup in the trashcan. Deciding to go hunt down Court, I'd rather play the third wheel than stand around by myself, I head back in the direction of the living room.

A few of the girls I know from school stop me on my way, asking about my summer and making small talk. By the time I reach the living area a good thirty minutes have passed, and yet by the amount of people now crowding the space, you would think I'd been gone two hours.

Pushing my way through the crowded room, I find myself entering another living space, this one even larger than the last. I swear the ceilings are thirty feet high. There's a table set up in the middle of the room where some of the football players are playing beer pong, drunk girls giggling and watching them with lust-filled eyes.

I really must have lost that teenager trait somewhere along the way. Maybe it's because of how my mom raised me, maybe it's because deep down I'm just a really good girl, but either way I feel like I exist on an entirely different planet than most of these people.

I ignore the twist in my stomach that tells me I should leave and push further into the room in search of Court. It takes me a while to finally find her, spotting her through a wall of windows along the back that give a perfect view of the pool where she, Ant, and several other people seem to have migrated.

I'm seconds away from going out to join them but stop dead in my tracks when I realize that not feet from where Courtney is sitting, her legs hanging over the edge of the pool, is Dylan and Taylor. Of course, you'd have to know what they look like really well to even know it's them, considering they're practically swallowing each other's heads.

I swallow down the bile that rises in my throat and quickly spin on my heel, taking off up a flight of stairs along the back wall, just needing a second to compose myself.

When I reach the landing at the top, I turn left down a long corridor, desperately needing a bathroom to hide away in for a few minutes.

Why did I come here?

Why did I ever think this would be fun?

The further down the hallway I go, the quieter my surroundings become. It's a testament to just how big this house is. I can still hear the thump of the bass and the voices that filter through the house, but it's nothing like being downstairs in the thick of it.

When I come across a double glass door that opens up to an empty second story balcony, I quietly slip outside. Closing the door behind me, I make my way to the edge of the balcony, looking out at the thickly wooded landscape that seems worlds away from the other side of the house where all the action is.

Taking a deep breath, I let it out slowly, feeling my anxiety start to slip away.

"Enjoying the party?" I hear his voice before I see him, startled by the sudden awareness that washes over me.

Tiny pinpricks pepper my skin as I turn, finally spotting him hidden in the shadows of the house.

Sebastian.

SEBASTIAN

I've been hiding out on this balcony for the better part of thirty minutes, trying to escape the chaos that always seems to surround me. Sometimes I feel like I can't fucking breathe.

I've got it good, I know that. I'm not in the business of complaining or playing the woe is me card. I know just about every asshole in school wishes he could be me. But being me isn't as great as they all seem to think it is.

I'm so lost in my thoughts that it takes me several moments to register the petite, little thing that stumbles out into my sanctuary, completely unaware of my presence.

My gut instinct is to tell her to fuck off. But for some reason, I don't say a word.

I watch her cross the balcony, gripping the railing as she looks out over the woods that surround about ninety percent of the property. Her slender shoulders slouch inward as she takes a deep breath and lets it out slowly.

I can't help but let my eyes wander the length of her.

She's rather thin, there's no doubt about that. But there's also something really sexy about her too, the way her long hair grazes across her lower back. The way her skinny jeans cling to her backside just right. The way her purple tank top has chunks of material missing up the sides revealing tiny slivers of perfect ivory skin. My groin tightens just looking at her.

"Enjoying the party?" I don't know how long it takes me to find my voice, but as soon as I do, her entire body goes rigid.

She turns, her eyes wide in surprise as she finally spots me sitting in the corner

legs crossed in front of myself, a bottle of Jack hanging from my fingers.

"Oh god, you scared me." She lays a hand on her chest.

Fuck me. She's even prettier than I thought.

I'm certain I've seen her before, but I can't pinpoint how I know her. Then again, keeping girls straight has never been one of my strong suits.

"My apologies." I tip my chin, taking a long pull of whiskey, my eyes never leaving hers.

"I didn't realize you were out here," she says, a slight tremble in her voice. "I didn't mean to intrude." She stutters over her words. "I'll just go."

Before she even takes one step, my voice sounds again.

"Don't." My statement doesn't just surprise me, it seems to catch her off guard as well.

"Are you sure?" I can tell every part of her is itching to take off, and this has me more than a little fucking intrigued. It's definitely not the reaction I'm used to getting.

If she was like most of the girls who are here tonight, she'd already be in my lap just hoping to get one night with the captain of the football team so she could brag about it to all her friends.

And they say I'm the whore…

It's not my fault girls throw themselves at me constantly. Even knowing what they know about me—my no relationship rule—they still keep coming out of the woodwork to try to be the one to change me.

Good fucking luck.

Some thing's simply can't be fixed.

"I'm sure," I finally answer after a long moment of silence. "Here." I snake my leg around the chair next to me and pull it out, gesturing for her to take a seat.

She slowly makes her way toward me, her eyes full of hesitation as she finally takes the seat next to me. She immediately knots her hands in her lap, her eyes looking anywhere but at me. I don't think she could look any more uncomfortable if she tried. I don't know why but this knowledge only eggs me on more.

"Drink?" I hold up the bottle of Jack, offering it to her.

"No thank you." She shakes her head, her blue eyes finally meeting mine.

"You don't like whiskey?" I arch a brow at her.

"I'm just not much of a drinker." She shrugs.

"I see. So you come to a party with no intention of drinking and then end up hiding out upstairs where you think no one will find you?" I question, just trying to figure this girl out.

"I had a beer just a few minutes ago." She seems offended by my statement.

"I meant no insult. Just seems like maybe this isn't your scene," I observe.

"Well, you're not wrong there. But not because I'm some goodie-two-shoes or anything," she quickly adds. "I just don't get the whole party atmosphere. Why anyone wants to get so drunk they end up hooking up with someone they don't even like or they spend half the night puking in the bushes, is just beyond me."

"What was that you said about not being a goodie-two-shoes?" I tease, just wanting to keep her going.

I'm mesmerized by her mouth, those full, pouty lips that I can't stop myself from imaging around my...

I clear my throat, trying to shake off the thought.

"You're so funny," she says sarcastically, rolling her eyes seconds before snagging the bottle of Jack from my hands. "I bet this little routine works on all the ladies," she spews, lifting the bottle to her lips and taking a long pull.

I'm pretty impressed when she swallows it down like a champ and doesn't even grimace after the fact.

Okay, now I'm really intrigued.

"Trust me." I smile when she hands the whiskey back to me. "If I was trying to work you over, you'd know it," I promise, narrowing my eyes at her.

"Is that so?" She arches a brow.

"Don't get me wrong, you're cute and all, but I usually go for girls with more..." I think over my words for a moment before adding, "experience."

Truth be told, she's totally doing it for me right now. But I can tell she's one who needs to be challenged, and so I'm going to do just that.

"So you want a slut who won't think twice about letting you stick your junk inside her." Her choice of words has me fighting back laughter.

"My junk?" I chuckle, shaking my head.

"Oh, shut up." She once again snags the bottle of Jack from my hands, taking two long drinks before handing it back to me. "Junk sounds better than dick or penis." She crinkles her nose, and it's about the cutest fucking thing I've ever seen.

My junk, as she so eloquently called it, instantly stirs to life.

"You're quite the contradiction, you realize this, right?" I sit forward, resting my elbows on my knees.

"How's that?"

"You don't like parties and yet here you are. You don't like drinking and yet I've watched you hit this bottle like a pro. You call my man parts junk and then spit out words like dick and penis without even blushing. I'm just trying to keep up here."

"Not everyone is so black and white." She throws me a sideway glance.

"In my world, they are." I blow out a breath, looking off into the distance.

"Well, maybe you should explore people outside of *your* world because it sounds like you're missing out," she states matter of fact, her blue eyes cutting right through me.

"How is it I've never met you before?" I ask, not entirely sure that I haven't.

"I think it's more remembering me rather than meeting me," she confirms my suspicion. "Dylan Thompson." The name instantly makes everything crystal clear.

"You're Tess," I say, already putting it all together.

"Wow. All I have to do is say his name and you know instantly who I am. Looks like he really did put me on the map," she grinds out, snagging the bottle of whiskey once again.

"You know, for someone who doesn't drink, you sure are going to town on that bottle." I chuckle.

"What do you care? I bet you love when girls get drunk and throw themselves at you," she bites, hurt and anger lacing her voice as she takes another drink.

"Does that mean you're going to throw yourself at me later?" I arch a brow, my statement bringing a small smile to her lips.

"You wish," she quips, taking another drink before handing the bottle back to me. I instantly take another long pull before answering,

"So what if I do?" I ask, my question seeming to confuse her.

"What if you do what?" she finally asks when I make no attempt to elaborate.

"Wish that you would throw yourself at me."

Her head instantly falls back, and I swear to God the sweetest fucking sound I've ever heard flows from her mouth. Fuck me, even her laugh makes me hard.

"In case you haven't heard the rumors, I'm a prude bitch who won't give it up," she quickly adds, looking down at her hands which are once again knotted in her lap.

"That only makes the victory that much sweeter. It would have been a damn shame had you given it to the likes of Dylan Thompson. Fucking douche bag. I find it hard to believe you even dated a guy like that to begin with."

"Well, he wasn't a douche bag to me—at least not in the beginning. I guess I'm not the best judge of character. If I was I probably wouldn't still be sitting out here with you."

"Ouch." I flatten my hand over my heart. "What's that supposed to mean?"

"You're Sebastian Baxter. Star quarterback and captain of the football team. You're rich and gorgeous and can quite literally have anyone you want." She swallows hard. "I know you go through girls like you're running a marathon, never actually dating a single one. And I know with complete certainty that the little smirk you're wearing right now is probably one of your deal sealers, but trust me when I say, you can save it. I'm not like the girls you usually surround yourself with."

"I'm realizing this," I observe, never taking my eyes off her. "But you made one fatal error in that little rant of yours." I lean forward, my leg brushing against hers.

"What's that?" I don't miss the way her voice catches or how she tenses at my nearness. She may play like she's immune to my charms, but her body says something else completely different.

"You said I can quite literally have any girl I want," I remind her, giving her a knowing look.

"Man…" She shakes her head slowly back and forth. "You are good." She smiles like she's figuring me out, and I'd be lying if I said it wasn't a bit of a slap to my ego.

"Thank you." I grin, not letting her see the effect her words have on me.

"That wasn't actually a compliment," she challenges.

I swear I think I could go back and forth with this girl all night.

"Do you want to get out of here?" I ask, abruptly standing.

"What?" My unexpected action clearly catches her off guard.

"Let's get out of here," I repeat, extending my hand to her. She looks back and forth between my hand and face several times before finally responding.

"You want to leave your own party?"

"Trust me when I say, this is the last fucking place I want to be." I smile, my hand still out waiting for her to take it. "Come on."

I can see the hesitation, the inner battle going on behind those innocent blue eyes.

"I don't know if that's such a good idea," she finally answers, standing on her own accord.

I let my hand fall to my side, a smile playing on the corners of my mouth.

"Do you always do that?"

"Do what?" She eyes me curiously.

"Question everything. I bet you've never done anything spontaneous a day in your life." I chuckle. "You say no before you even know what's being offered."

"Fine. Then what's being offered?" She crosses her arms in front of herself.

I shrug. "How about we just see where the night ends."

"That's all you got?" She shakes her head on a laugh. "See where the night ends? How many girls actually fall for that?"

"I wouldn't know," I answer truthfully. "It's not a line I can say I've regularly used."

"Is that so?" She stares back at me, her gaze unwavering.

"It is." I grab the whiskey, tucking the half empty bottle under my arm. "I normally know what's to come when I sneak off somewhere with a girl. But with you, I don't know, I kind of like not knowing."

"Because I'm not attractive enough to make a move on, is that it?"

"Now, I didn't say that." I let my eyes trace down her small five-foot frame.

"I just don't know about you," she admits, clearly still hesitant.

I can't say I blame her. I know the reputation I've made for myself. I wouldn't be surprised if she told me to go fuck myself.

"I promise to be on my best behavior." I cross an X over my heart with my index finger. "Come on." I close my fingers around her hand, not missing the way her eyes widen at the contact. "Just take a walk with me."

"Fine." She finally concedes. "But if you try any funny business…" she warns.

"You have my word." I smile, leading her inside.

When we reach the bottom of the stairwell that opens up to the main floor, I readjust our hands, intertwining my fingers with hers.

She looks up at me questioningly, but I only wink and tug her along next to me, nodding to a few people who call my name as we cross through the family room and out the back doors that lead to the pool.

I can feel her tense next to me the moment we step outside, and it doesn't take me long to figure out why. I spot Dylan just seconds before he sees us. He's got Taylor spread across his lap in one of the lounge chairs, his mouth leaving her neck the moment he registers our presence.

I pay him absolutely no mind, and while it takes everything in me not to swing Tess around and lay a kiss on her mouth right in front of him, I refrain, knowing that probably wouldn't go over too well with her.

I'm honestly a little surprised when she stops, tightening her grip on my hand as she speaks to the girl currently up on Ant's nuts.

"We're going to go for a walk," she tells the dark-eyed brunette who seems more than a little excited by this news.

"You two have fun," she immediately responds, earning an eye roll from Tess.

"A friend of yours?" I ask as we start to walk away.

"She's the only reason I'm even here tonight." She peers up at me through thick lashes.

Fuck me—I've only just met this girl and already I know I'm in fucking trouble.

"Remind me to thank her later," I tease, quickening my strides.

TESS

Sebastian Baxter is holding my hand.

Sebastian Baxter… The undisputed hottest guy in school is choosing to spend time with me over indulging in one of the many girls here tonight that I'm sure are eager to warm his bed. I suddenly feel like I'm living in an alternate reality.

Sebastian leads me down a long, wooded trail that after several yards opens up to reveal a stunning lake view. The sight of the full moon beaming off the water is beautiful, and for the first time since Sebastian opened his mouth and made his presence known on the balcony, I feel myself starting to relax.

To say that going off on my own with a guy who has a reputation like Sebastian's is out of character for me would be the understatement of the year, but something about the way those hazel eyes look at me has rendered my resolve nonexistent.

"Sebastian, this is incredible," I find myself saying without even meaning to.

I can't help it. Not when we approach a long dock that stretches out into the water, two layback lounge chairs positioned at the end. This place is like a dream. Everything is so still and peaceful, the noise from the house a distant memory.

"This is probably my favorite spot." He throws me a sideways smile, his hand not releasing mine until we reach the chairs.

"I can see why," I admit, taking the seat he gestures to, pulling my legs up in front of myself as I watch him claim the seat next to me.

"Sometimes the world just gets too chaotic." He lay back in his seat, feet stretched out in front of him, and arms behind his head as he stares up at the star-filled sky. "This is the only place that makes me feel—normal," he admits, the vulnerability in his tone taking me by surprise.

"And here I had you pegged for some hot shot who had everything he ever wanted," I tease, mirroring his action as I lie back in my own chair and focus my gaze upward.

"Trust me, Tessa; my life's far from perfect." The use of my full name does something unexplainable to me. It sounds so different coming off his lips.

But I also can't deny the spark of anger that lights deep in my belly. Some people just have no idea how good they have it.

"Then enlighten me. What more could you possibly want?" I ask, gesturing around. "You've got money and all the perks that come along with it. You're an incredible athlete and will no doubt be able to play for any college you want. Every guy wants to be you. Every girl wants to be with you. Forgive me for saying this, but if you don't see how incredibly good you've got it, maybe you should look a little harder."

"What was it you said to me earlier—that people aren't always so black and white?" He turns his gaze toward me.

28

I can feel his eyes burning into the side of my face, but I keep my eyes focused on the sky. "I think you'd be surprised to learn that I'm probably furthest from the person you think I am."

"Sounds like a bunch of talk to me." I shrug.

"And you would know this how?" The playfulness in his voice pulls my gaze to him. I suck in a hard breath when I see him staring at me with a look I can't quite describe—like he can see right through my façade to the weak, scared girl beneath.

"Action, Mr. Baxter. Action." I grin when his eyes widen, a hint of mischief behind them. "Words are easy, meaningless. But action. Action is what makes you who you are."

"And what do my actions show you?" He rolls to his side, his eyes now locked solely on me.

"That you're cocky and arrogant. That you don't have to wonder if you're good enough—on the football field or off—you know you are. That you devalue girls to nothing more than what they can give you in bed. That you have the world at your feet and yet have no appreciation for it. You walk around like you own the world, Sebastian. That doesn't strike me as someone who doesn't believe they have it all."

I expect my words to offend him, piss him off even, so when a slow smile creeps across his handsome face I'm left wondering once again if I have just completely misjudged him.

"I like you," he finally speaks after several long moments.

"Um. Thank you?" I say more as a question than a statement.

"I mean it, Tess. Do you have any idea how long it's been since someone has told me exactly what they think of me? It's fucking refreshing." His smile widens. "Keep going."

"Keep going?" I look at him like he has five heads.

"I like this game." He runs a hand through his perfect sun-kissed blond hair, his hazel eyes never leaving mine.

"Are we playing a game?" I question, suddenly more nervous than ever.

"You tell me," he challenges, that damn smile still etched across his perfect face.

I look at him for several long moments, silence stretching between us. I'm not sure what to say to that. I've never had someone make me feel so twisted up inside, and I have to admit as much as I hate that it's Sebastian making me feel this way, it also feels good just to feel something.

"Can I ask you something?" he asks, reaching between our chairs to retrieve the bottle of whiskey he brought with him.

"Okay." I stretch out, butterflies swimming wildly in my stomach.

"Is what Dylan said about you true?" His question is like a slap back to reality, but I try to hold my composure and not let him see just how affected I am by it.

"You'll need to be more specific. Last time I checked he had quite a few things to say," I grind out.

"Have you really never slept with anyone before?" he asks, his question a little shocking but surprisingly not unexpected.

"Are you seriously asking me if I'm a virgin right now?" I cock a brow, not sure what he's getting at.

"A guy likes to know these things." He clearly finds humor in my reaction.

"Why, so you can up your game and try to be the one to rob me of my virtue." I grab the whiskey bottle from his hands before he can even get it to his lips.

Taking a long pull, I ignore the burn—loving the warmth that spreads through my body as I shove the bottle back into his hand.

"I don't rob virtue." He chuckles. "It's given to me."

"Well if you think I'm giving it to you, you're barking up the wrong tree." I cross my arms over my chest and look back up at the sky.

"So then it's true?" I can hear the smile in his voice.

"Oh my God. Yes, it's true. Are you happy now?" I throw my hands up in the air as I push into an upright position, my gaze once again going to the handsome and yet infuriating man next to me.

"Quite." He smiles, relaxing back in his chair, the bottle of Jack still in his hand.

"Typical." I shake my head, mirroring his action as I lean back.

"Despite what you may believe, Tess, I'm not as bad as you think I am. I don't make it my mission to just fuck girls. I can't help it if they throw themselves at me. Who am I to discriminate? If a girl wants me and knows what I'm offering, then that's on her. I don't lie, and I don't waste my time wooing a girl I only have an interest in fucking. If I'm gonna make the effort it's gonna be for someone worth more than that."

I turn my head to the side, taking in his sincere expression as he stares up at the stars.

"So is this you wooing me then?" I tease, just trying to lighten the mood back up.

I never intended for it to get so heavy, but here recently that seems to be my specialty. Maybe I should actually listen to Courtney and Bree when they tell me I need to lighten up a little.

"Maybe." He shrugs, giving me a grin that makes my heart do flips inside my chest. "How I'm doing so far?"

"I give you a three out of ten," I tease.

"Damn, sounds like I need to step up my game." The grin turns into a full smile, showing off his perfectly straight white teeth.

God, I swear I could spend forever looking at that smile.

I've spent two years harboring a secret crush on this guy and now that he's here next to me, surprising me in ways I never thought possible, I want him even more. I think that scares me more than anything. Because with a guy like Sebastian Baxter, nothing is guaranteed.

"I guess so." I can't stop myself from playing right into his hands. What can I say? I'm not nearly as immune to Sebastian as I pretend to be. I think even the strongest girl would buckle under those gorgeous hazels and perfect smile.

"So, Tessa, tell me what it will take to win you over?"

I ignore the giddy feeling that's swimming through me and try to keep my composure.

"I don't think you can handle a girl like me." I give him a smirk, not sure where all this fire is suddenly coming from.

It's Sebastian. It has to be. He makes me feel a way that no one has ever made me feel before—and we haven't done anything but spend the last half an hour bantering back and forth. How does he do it?

"Considering you seem to know everything about me, I would've thought you would've picked up that I'm not someone who backs away from a challenge," he warns.

"So I'm a challenge to you, is that it?" I quip.

"Among other things." He snags his bottom lip between his teeth, and I swear it lights a fire under my skin.

"Care to enlighten me?" I can't stop smiling now, no matter how hard I try to fight it.

"All in due time, pretty girl. All in due time."

"That's all I get?" I object when he settles back into his chair and looks up at the sky.

"It's all about where the night ends, Tess—never how it begins."

"Are we talking in riddles now?" I question, sinking further into my chair, my eyes never leaving the side of his face.

"I'm just saying, I've got all night to change your mind. One night is all I need."

"You sound pretty sure of yourself. Who's to say I'm not getting ready to get up and leave right now. In case you missed it, there's a pretty kick ass party going on right through those woods." I point behind me.

"If there's one thing I do not lack in this world, Tess, it's confidence." When he flips his gaze back to me, I swear my entire stomach bottoms out. "And if you were going to leave, you would've done it already. So why don't you do us both a favor and stop pretending like you're not enjoying every minute of this as much as I am."

"You're something else, you know that?" My lips betray me once more, the stupid smile pulling them up giving away exactly what he's doing to me.

"You have no idea," he promises.

"So, if you're planning to keep me out here all night, the least you can do is stop playing your little games. I see right through you," I counter.

"I think you'll be surprised to find you don't know me nearly as well as you think you do. But because I don't feel up for getting into that tonight, why don't you tell me more about you." He lifts the bottle of Jack to his lips, taking a long pull before offering me the bottle.

I take it, drinking more than I should before passing it back to him, only now truly realizing the buzz running through my veins. I wouldn't say I'm drunk,

not by a long shot, but I'm certainly feeling the effects more than I've been letting on.

"I'm pretty boring," I admit, keeping my gaze on the sky.

"Now why do I find that hard to believe?" I can hear the smile in his voice, but I keep my focus off him. I need to keep a semi-clear head, and when I look at him I swear everything goes wonky.

"You shouldn't, it's true." I shrug.

"Well, let's say for argument's sake that you're wrong."

"I'm not, but by all means—ask away." I sigh.

"How about we just start with the basics. You know: childhood, your home life, favorite kind of music. You get the idea."

"So you can see just how boring I actually am. Okay," I concede. "I've lived here my whole life. It's just me and Mom, has been since I was little."

"Your dad?" he asks before I can keep going.

"Died when I was six, car accident."

"I'm sorry," he offers, his voice softer than before.

"I don't really remember him. My mom rarely talks about him. I think it's easier for her to pretend like he never existed. I don't know. I never really understood it." I pause, letting the moment settle around us. "Anyway, my mom is a pediatric nurse for Sanderson General in Montgomery," I say, referring to the next town over. "She works third shift and a lot of twelve hour days, so sometimes I'll go a handful of days without seeing her because of the way our schedules work."

"Sounds lonely," he observes, rolling to his side to look at me.

I hesitate for only a moment before doing the same, loving the way his hazel eyes hold mine so intently.

"It's not so bad. I have Courtney and Bree, who are more like my sisters than my best friends."

"Is that why they ditched you tonight?" There's no insult in his tone, he just seems genuinely curious.

"That's just how we are. When I need them, they're always there. And they know I'm a big girl and can take care of myself. Besides, they love to have fun, and I don't want to be the Debbie Downer who holds them back."

"Sounds like they don't deserve you."

"They do," I instantly object. "More than you can know."

"Fair enough." He takes my answer for what it is. "Keep going," he encourages.

"You're not bored yet?" I ask, tucking a hand under my cheek.

"Not even a little bit." He smiles.

"Fine." I let out a deep breath, trying to figure out where to go next. "Let's see. I love indie music. I'm a sucker for old television shows. And if I could, I'd spend every second of every day losing myself in a book—preferably a thriller or something dark and demented."

"You're kidding me, right?" He laughs like he can't believe it.

"What?" I question playfully.

"You look so sweet and innocent."

"What does that have to do with anything?"

"I just never expected you to be someone who liked—well, any of the things you just listed."

"Guess it goes to show you can't judge a book by its cover," I remind him.

"You realize that goes both ways." He narrows his gaze at me.

"Okay then, prove me wrong," I suggest. "Tell me something about you that will surprise me."

"Truth?" he asks.

"Truth."

"I hate parties," he says, his admission not what I expected.

"Really?" I question, gesturing back up toward the house.

"I know. I know." He chuckles. "That's just more of a fuck you to my parents'. Figure if they're going to pretend like I don't exist, I might as well show them I damn well do."

"Sebastian." My voice wavers as I stare back at the boy I always thought to be so confident, wondering now if we aren't more alike than I would have ever guessed.

"It's fine," he quickly interjects. "It's been this way my entire life. I'm used to it."

"But," I start.

"It's fine. Really," he cuts me off, clearly not wanting to linger on the topic.

As much as I want to push, I let it go. I know how hard it can be to talk about things you're not used to sharing with anybody.

I change the topic to safer ground, asking him more about football and if he has any idea where he wants to go to college since he's getting ready to start senior year. The conversation flows from there and by well into the night, I've learned so much more about him than I ever expected to know.

How he loves football because it's the only place he feels like he truly belongs.

How he misses California tremendously and how hard it was for him to leave. How he plans to move back there someday.

How he can't wait for college and while LSU is his dream school, he doesn't even really care where he attends as long as he gets to play football.

We talk for hours, both of us curled on our sides in opposite chairs, facing each other. We talk until time no longer seems relevant and everything else just kind of slips away.

I don't know at what point we fall silent, existing in a comfortable space where neither of us feels the need for words.

All I remember is staring at Sebastian until I physically couldn't hold my eyes open any longer, wondering if I would wake up tomorrow and find that all of this was just some crazy dream.

Sebastian said it only takes one night to change everything; he couldn't have been more right. Because after just one night everything feels different.

TESS

I feel my body start to warm. The sensation starts on my face and then slowly spreads over the remainder of my body. It's like a soothing cocoon basking me in its warmth and comfort. But the feeling is fleeting, quickly replaced by heat that sears my skin.

My eyes shoot open and I immediately squint, the bright sun blazing down on me making it difficult for my eyes to adjust or my mind to process where exactly I am. I roll to the side, trying to avoid the harsh rays, and my eyes instantly lock with Sebastian's.

He's lying in the same position as last night, curled on his side facing me, his hazel eyes bloodshot and heavy. A slow smile pulls up the corners of his mouth as he gauges my reaction—the shock and disbelief I feel probably written plain as day across my face.

"Do you have any idea how beautiful you are?" My heart immediately kicks into overdrive, beating frantically against my ribs.

I open my mouth, but nothing comes out. My throat is so dry I doubt I could speak clearly even if my mind would cooperate.

Am I still dreaming?

It takes me several long moments to gather my thoughts enough to blink, breaking the connection that seems to be mounting between us.

Rolling onto my back, I swallow down the thick knot in my throat and push into a sitting position, looking out over the beautiful water that sparkles under the bright morning sun.

"What time is it?" I finally manage to speak, my voice hoarse.

"Not sure." I feel Sebastian shift in the chair next to me.

"I don't even remember falling asleep," I admit, tucking my chin against my shoulder as I look back to where he's now lying on his back, his hands tucked behind his head.

The look in his eyes causes my skin to flush, and I immediately look away.

"I should call Courtney." I reach for my phone in the back pocket of my jeans, not surprised when the clock on the screen reads just after six thirty in the morning. I can tell from the position of the sun that it hasn't been up long.

Normally I would be a walking zombie—given that I couldn't have slept more than a couple of hours—but I feel wide awake. The second I opened my eyes to see Sebastian staring back at me was like I had picked up a live wire, and my body is still feeling the effects of the shock.

I swipe the screen and see a couple missed calls and a few texts from Courtney. I don't know how, but I guess I must have accidentally switched my ringer off.

"Shit," I mutter under my breath, reading her messages.

Courtney: When you get back to the house, call me.

Courtney: Can you text me so I know you're good?

Then about an hour later—

Courtney: I swear to God you better have a good reason for not calling me.

Courtney: You can thank Ant for me not coming after you. He assures me that Sebastian will not hurt you, but mark my words, if he does, I will chop his dick off. And his balls, too.

I stifle a laugh, the vision of Courtney chasing after Sebastian one I can't help but picture. It's something she totally would do.

The last message came in about four o'clock this morning.

Courtney: Me and Ant are crashing in one of the spare rooms. Come find me when you're done doing whatever it is you two are off doing.

"Everything okay?" I turn to see Sebastian now sitting upright, the green in his eyes so prominent under the morning sun that for a moment I completely lose my train of thought.

"I should head up to the house," I finally blurt. "Courtney's been messaging me all night. She's probably ready to murder me." I throw him a nervous smile, not sure why all of sudden my stomach feels like it's taken flight.

"I'll walk you up." He doesn't hesitate, pushing to his feet so quickly that he's reaching out to help me up before I've even moved.

"Thank you," I say, allowing him to pull me to my feet.

I move to take one step and stumble, nearly face-planting into his hard chest.

"Whoa, you okay there?" He sets his hands on my shoulders to steady me.

40

"Think I might still be feeling the whiskey," I lie, just needing an excuse to cover my blunder.

"Well, considering you drank a third of the bottle last night, that doesn't surprise me," he teases, draping an arm over my shoulder and tucking me into his side.

"I think I can manage to walk now," I reply dryly, making no attempt to step out his embrace.

"Well, I think I'll keep you close just in case." He winks down at me, the action causing heat to spread from my face all the way to my toes.

I'm quickly learning why Sebastian Baxter has the reputation he does. You have to have skin made of steel not to feel the effects of him everywhere. There's something so consuming about him—so raw and sexy. In just one night he's made my body feels things it never has before, and he's barely even touched me.

I remain tucked against him as we make the walk through the woods and back toward the house. The proof that a party took place here last night is everywhere. Just in the pool area alone there are enough bottles, cups, and trash to account for most of the student body, and that's before we even make it inside.

Sebastian releases his hold on me just feet before we reach the back door. I feel the loss of him instantly, but at the same time, I'm thankful for the opportunity to compose my thoughts. It's hard to breathe, let alone think, with his hard body next to mine and his faint cologne intoxicating my senses.

Just when I reach for the door, I feel Sebastian's hand on my backside, my phone emerging between his fingers seconds later.

"What are you doing?" I spin in his direction, reaching for my phone.

"Hang on." He smiles, holding the device out of my reach as his fingers quickly move across the screen. "There," he adds just seconds later, reaching around me to slide the phone back into my pocket.

I don't miss the way his fingers linger there for a moment or the tight knot that forms in my lower belly when they do.

For a moment, I almost swear he's going to kiss me—his eyes locked on mine, his lips in a firm, hard line like he's trying to fight against himself—but then a sound in the distance breaks the moment, and we both turn toward the disruption.

"Davis, what the fuck, man?" Sebastian starts just seconds before the tall, brawny guy leans over into the bushes and loses his stomach.

"On that note," he quickly adds, pulling the door open, and ushering me inside. The incident with my phone long forgotten.

If I thought outside was bad, it's nothing compared to the mess that litters the beautiful interior of the home. Like the pool area, there are bottles, cups, and trash across every surface. A lot of the décor looks misplaced, and most of the couch pillows and cushions are strewn across the floor.

Two girls are fast asleep on one couch, a guy I don't recognize on the opposite one, and then a handful of people scattered across the floor—all passed out cold.

Sebastian pays no attention to the mess, like it's an everyday occurrence, and casually leads me around the chaos and into the kitchen. He doesn't say a word as he crosses toward the refrigerator, retrieving two bottles of water before appearing from behind the massive stainless-steel door.

"Your house. Um, do you want me to stick around and help you clean up?" I ask, taking the bottle of water he extends to me.

"Nah. Sonya will be here in a little bit." He shrugs, draining over half the contents of his water bottle in one swift pull.

"Sonya?" I question, twisting the cap off my own bottle and taking a sip, the cool liquid instantly soothing my dry throat.

"Housekeeper," he replies, quickly finishing off the remainder of his water.

"Of course." I shake my head, suddenly reminded of how very far apart our lives actually are.

It's fun to pretend that Sebastian would ever be the kind of guy to settle down with a girl like me, but if I'm being honest, that's all I've been doing all night—pretending.

He's the star quarterback—rich and handsome and well, a bit of a man whore. I'm just me. Plain old Tessa Wilson. I have nothing to offer a guy like Sebastian.

"You okay?" He must sense the shift in the air between us, but I do my best to brush it off.

"Yeah, fine. I should probably find Courtney, though. Her parents think she's at my house, and my mom will be home from work soon," I lie, knowing my mom got off work two hours ago and is likely at home fast asleep.

She thinks I'm at Courtney's and since I don't typically lie, she would never expect me to be anywhere other than exactly where I said I would be. And in my defense, Courtney's house is where I planned to be right now; clearly the night worked out differently than I expected it to.

"Ant usually sleeps up in one of the guest rooms." He tosses his empty bottle of water onto the island and snags my hand. "I'll take you up there. Hopefully, he's decent. I've seen his bare ass more times than I care to admit." He's joking, I'm sure, but I can't help but wonder how many of those times he was with a girl that wasn't Courtney.

It just solidifies that I am way out of my league with guys like this.

I try to let myself enjoy the feeling of Sebastian's warm hand wrapped around mine as he leads me up the stairs, knowing that it's going to be short-lived. I don't belong in Sebastian's world any more than he belongs in mine. We couldn't be more different. Hell, we practically exist on entirely different planets.

When we reach the second floor, Sebastian walks right into the first bedroom without even knocking. I follow him inside, not surprised to see a sleeping Courtney draped over Anthony. Both appear to be naked but luckily have a sheet covering all the important stuff.

When Sebastian releases my hand, I choose to stay back toward the doorway rather than follow him further into the room. They may be covered but that doesn't mean I want to get all up in their business.

"Ant." Sebastian nudges the side of the bed with his leg the moment he reaches it. "Ant," he repeats, nudging it harder.

Anthony's head instantly pops up and he looks around, dazed and disoriented.

"What the fuck, dude?" he questions, rubbing his eyes with the backs of his hands as he sits up, the sheet falling dangerously low down his toned body. I keep my eyes averted, purposely not looking directly at him.

44

"Tess has gotta go." Sebastian gestures toward me and then points to Courtney who stirs in the bed next to Ant.

"Court." Ant nudges her with his arm, which seems to fully wake her. She pushes up on her elbows, a wide smile on her face when she finds me standing by the door.

"Hello there, sunshine," she says before giving into a big yawn. "Good to see I don't have to cut any dicks off today." Her eyes dart to Sebastian who seems a bit confused by her statement. "Or do I?" She lifts a brow at me.

"Oh my God, you're ridiculous." I shake my head, honestly a little embarrassed by my loud mouth friend. "We gotta go. Mom should be home soon." I give her a look I know only she will pick up on.

Thankfully Courtney and I have established our own little language over the years, and she understands me instantly.

"Okay, give me a sec to get dressed." She yawns again, clutching the sheet to her chest as she sits up. I give her a thankful smile and step backward out of the room.

"We'll wait downstairs," I hear Sebastian say just moments before joining me in the hall, pulling the door shut behind him.

Silence stretches between us as Sebastian leads me through the expansive house and then out onto the front porch. The morning air is so warm and inviting, but it does little to calm the nervous jitter of my heart.

I take a deep inhale, trying to steady myself. I just need to get out of here. Away from this house and this intoxicating boy who keeps looking at me in a way that makes me feel things I shouldn't be feeling. Not with him.

Don't get me wrong, last night will probably go down as one of the highlights of my high school life, but that doesn't mean it will be any more than that. Dylan did enough to show me that I'm not ready for what comes along with dating at this age. Especially with someone as *experienced* as Sebastian.

I'd be lying if I said I didn't want that with him, though. You'd have to be blind not to be physically stunned by him. But I can't afford the distraction or the heartbreak that I know will follow if I let myself even entertain the idea that there could be an *us*.

And what's to say he even wants that to begin with?

I spent the entire night with him, and he didn't even make one move. Not one. Given his reputation, I think it's safe to say he's not into me like that. Otherwise, I doubt we would have spent the entire night just talking.

But then what about this morning? What about waking up to find him looking at me the way he was? And then there was the beautiful comment, the one I've been trying to dismiss since the moment it left his lips.

I'm not sure what would be worse—fighting to keep myself from drowning in the ocean that is Sebastian Baxter, or just letting myself be swept under and see where the waves take me.

"Can I see you later?" Sebastian's voice pulls me back to where he's standing next to me on the porch, his large hands wrapped around the banister as he leans forward, his gaze locked on the side of my face.

"What?" The word just falls from my lips without me meaning for it to.

"Later." His mouth pulls up in a smile. "Are you busy?"

"Um, I'm not sure yet," I stutter, my words dying off as Courtney steps outside, interrupting the moment. "I guess I should get going. Last night was fun." I give him the best smile I can muster before grabbing Courtney's arm and practically dragging her off the porch.

I'm afraid that if I stay even a moment longer I'm going to give into the pull of the tide and let him drag me under.

"I'm going to call you later, Tessa Wilson," Sebastian yells after me, laughter in his voice as if he can sense my need to escape him.

As much as I want to ignore his statement and just make it to Courtney's car unscathed, I can't stop myself from turning around. I also can't hide the wide smile that stretches across my face when I look up to see that sexy as sin look in his eyes.

"I'm not going to hold my breath," I call back, taking one last look at the breathtaking smile on his face before turning and disappearing down the driveway.

TESS

"Spill." It leaves Courtney's mouth the instant she slides into the driver's seat next to me.

"There's nothing to spill." I shrug, buckling my seat belt.

"Bullshit, Tess. You spent the entire night with Sebastian Baxter, of all people, and you actually expect me to believe that not one thing happened." She gives me a disbelieving look as she starts the car and pops it into reverse, backing out before switching it into drive.

"That's exactly what I expect you to believe because it's the truth."

I don't know why but I feel like admitting anything about the way Sebastian made me feel both last night and this morning is an admission of weakness, and I'm not ready to swallow that just yet.

"Seriously, Tess."

"I'm being serious. We just talked."

"You just talked?" She glances at me for a moment before pulling out onto the road.

"Honestly," I tack on for good measure.

"Wow." She shakes her head, a small laugh escaping her lips.

"Wow, what? Why are you laughing at me?" I cross my arms over my chest.

"I'm not laughing *at* you, Tess. I'm just having a hard time wrapping my head around the fact that you just spent the entire night with the school's sexiest and most sought-after guy, and you still managed to walk away a virgin."

"Did you seriously think I would sleep with him?" I turn wide eyes on her, but her gaze remains on the road.

"I sure as hell hoped you would." She smiles, giving me a quick sideways glance. "But no, I didn't think you would sleep with him. But I did hope you'd at least have fooled around—you know, get back on the horse—show Dylan he doesn't have the power over you like he thinks he does." She pauses. "Though I will say, his face when you left with Sebastian was priceless."

This piques my interest immediately.

"What do you mean?"

"Oh, he was pissed. You could see it all over his face. And so could Taylor. They left shortly after. I wouldn't be surprised if she dumps his ass over the way he was talking to her when they left."

"Wait, how was he talking to her?"

"He was just being a huge ass. You know Dylan. Anyway, I overheard her say something about him being jealous—referring to you and Sebastian—and he snapped at her, said he wanted to leave. It was so obvious how bothered he was by the whole thing. I rather enjoyed watching the show." She smiles at the memory.

"I don't understand. Why would Dylan care if I went anywhere with Sebastian?" I ask, already knowing the answer.

"Because he's not over you. Duh," Courtney says exactly what I'm thinking—but it doesn't help lessen the confusion I feel.

"But he broke up with me."

"Yeah, but I think he thought you'd crumble and beg for him to come back to you. Clearly his little plan backfired."

"I don't know what planet he's living on, but in what world does a girl beg for a guy to take her back after he cheats on her?" I grind out.

"You'd be surprised," Court responds instantly.

"I don't understand the rules here." I let out a frustrated sigh. "Just when I think I have even a small grasp on this growing up thing, everything shifts."

"Look, Dylan is an ass. He's always been an ass. And he should be the last person you're thinking about right now." She slows the car as we enter town. "You just spent the night with Sebastian Baxter—so why are we wasting our time talking about Dylan? I want to know more about your night."

"I've already told you, nothing happened."

"But you did spend the entire night talking, yes?"

"Yes."

"O-k-a-y," she stretches out, waiting for me to say more.

"Okay what?"

"Oh my god, Tess. Do I have to force everything out of you? Can't a best friend just get some juicy insight into the sexy as sin, Sebastian Baxter, without having to beg?" she whines dramatically.

"I mean, we just talked. I don't get what you want to know."

"Was he nice to you?" she asks.

50

"Very," I admit, resting my head against the headrest.

"Did he seem—I don't know—interested?"

"I mean, I guess. He did hold my hand both last night and this morning. And he listened when I talked—like he really wanted to know what I had to say. And then this morning." I stop, the memory causing heat to flush my face.

I can still see him lying there, his eyes locked on mine. *"Do you have any idea how beautiful you are?"* My chest tightens, a feeling I don't quite understand settling in the pit of my stomach.

"What? What happened this morning?" Courtney pushes.

"Well, when I woke up, he was watching me."

"Watching you?" she questions. "Like, what do you mean?"

"I mean—he was laying on his side watching me. I don't know if he watched me sleep the entire time or if he just happened to be watching me when I woke up, but the way he was looking at me... I don't know, Court. No one's ever looked at me like that before."

"And—did he say anything?"

"He asked me if I had any idea how beautiful I am."

"What!?" Courtney practically screams next to me. "Why didn't you start with that?" She smacks the steering wheel. "Holy shit, Tess. Sebastian fucking Baxter is totally into you."

"What? No, he's not." Even though it seems unlikely, I can't deny that he was throwing some serious vibes my way.

"He totally is," she insists. "And—he said he was going to call you later," she reminds me.

"He doesn't even have my number." The image of him stealing my phone flashes through my mind. "Shit."

"Shit what?"

"He stole my phone earlier." I lean forward, sliding the device from my back pocket.

Unlocking the screen, I go into my contacts. It only takes a quick glance to see that his name isn't in there. My list isn't all that expansive.

"What?" My best friend bounces anxiously beside me.

"I thought maybe he added his number, but it's not in here."

"Go to your outgoing calls," she suggests.

Sure enough, there's an outgoing call right around the time he took my phone.

"See." She looks over at the device in my hand when she stops at a red light. "He totally called himself from your phone so he would have your number."

"You don't think he'll actually call, do you?" I feel panic start to creep in, my earlier fear returning.

As attracted as I am to Sebastian—because trust me, I am—I think I'm even more scared of him.

"Um, hell yes I do." Courtney breaks into my bout of self-doubt.

"And you think I should answer?" I stare at my phone, feeling the car slow to a stop. It isn't until I look up that I see Courtney has parked on the side of the road in front of my house.

"What's going on, Tess?" She turns in her seat, knowing me well enough to know that I'm about to have an internal meltdown.

"I just." I sigh. "I'm not really cut out for someone like Sebastian," I vocalize my fear. "Even if by some crazy twist of fate he's actually interested in me that way, I don't think I would hold his interest for long."

"Stop doing that!" Courtney scolds. "Stop overthinking every single moment that happens in your life. Sometimes you just have to take the bull by its horns, Tess, and ride that motherfucker as long as you can."

"That's easy for you to say, you're not afraid to climb on top of the bull."

"And you shouldn't be either," she interrupts. "Look, the most popular boy in school just spent the entire night with you. Not only that, he took your number and told you he was going to call you later. You should be excited. Not sitting here looking like you're about to vomit all over my car." She sighs, shaking her head. "Do you like him?"

"I don't know."

"Tess, this is me." She holds a hand to her chest. "Do you like him?"

"I do," I admit, hating to even say it out loud.

"Then just see where it takes you okay? I know you're in the business of doubting yourself at every turn, but I'm telling you right now—if Sebastian saw even a fraction of the girl I know you are, he's already falling in love."

"I don't know that I would go that far." I laugh, shoving Courtney's shoulder when she leans into me and bats her eyes.

"Embrace it, Tess. I promise if you let your hair down, I think you'll find you enjoy the wind in it." She winks. "Now get the hell out of my car. Go get some sleep. And call me later."

"Yes, ma'am." I reach for the handle, pushing the door open before climbing out.

"And, Tess." Courtney waits until I turn around before continuing, "For what it's worth, I think you and Sebastian would be totally smoking hot together." She grins, wide and excited. "Just imagine. You and Sebastian, me and Ant—

we'd be like the most popular foursome in all of school."

"Just what I've always wanted," I say sarcastically, laughing when Courtney flips me off seconds after I shut the door.

"Love you, bitch," she calls through the open window.

"Love you more." I throw her small wave before turning around and heading inside.

***

I wake with a start, my head swimming the second I open my eyes. I wish I could say that the first person who pops into my head isn't Sebastian, but that wouldn't be the truth. I stare up at my ceiling, recalling all the events of last night over and over in my head.

It isn't until I hear noise coming from the kitchen that I snap out of my fog and look over at the clock. At first I think I'm seeing things—there's no way it's three o'clock in the afternoon. Reaching for my phone, the time is confirmed the second I tap on the screen.

Dropping it back onto my nightstand, I groan, stretching my arms above my head. I must have been exhausted, considering I crashed within thirty minutes of Courtney dropping me off and am just now waking up.

Peeling myself out of bed, I cross the small space of my room and step out into the hallway. The sound of my mom rustling around in the kitchen is more prominent now and I set off in her direction, assuming she's probably making something to eat before work.

My stomach rumbles at the thought. God, when is the last time I ate something? Now that I think about it, it's been nearly twenty-four hours. No wonder I feel so famished.

"There she is." I barely make it around the corner before my mom speaks. She's standing at the stove, clad in pink scrubs, her shoulder length brown hair pulled back in a small ponytail, stirring something in the pan in front of her that smells an awful lot like chicken stir fry. "I was starting to wonder if you were ever going to get up."

"Sorry. Court and I stayed up late watching some weird movie." I don't feel the need to be specific, my mom isn't much of a television person. Well, except for watching re-runs of *Friends*—that she could do for hours.

"What time did you get in?"

"Around eight. Court had to work, so she brought me home early." I hate being deceitful, but I'm not lying entirely. Courtney really does have to work today, just not until later this afternoon.

"Speaking of that, have you decided when you want to go car shopping?" my mom asks, glancing over her shoulder at me.

I've had my license for about six months now, but due to limited funds I haven't been able to get a car. I've saved up quite a bit over the last two years from my summer job at the mall, but I'm not sure I have enough to buy anything worth a crap.

"I think I'll just ride with Courtney this year." I shrug. "I'd rather save the money and be able to add to it next year's paychecks so I can buy something that will actually last me more than a few months."

"I think that's smart. You'll want something reliable when you go off to college." She rests the spoon on the side of the pan and turns toward me. "How did I get a daughter as responsible as you?" Her blue eyes that match mine shine with pride.

"Good parenting?" I question, humor lacing my voice.

"Good answer." My mom smiles big and wide, cupping my cheek for a moment before stepping past me. "Are you hungry?" she asks, returning from the pantry with a box of instant rice.

"Starving."

"I just need to make the rice," she says, grabbing a pot from the counter before heading to the sink to fill it with water.

"What time do you have to be at work?" I ask, claiming her place at the stove where my suspicions are confirmed—chicken and vegetable stir fry, one of my favs.

"I have to be there at five. I'm working sixteen tonight." She joins me at the stove, placing the pot of water on the back burner.

"You work too much," I tell her.

"That may be true, but you're not the only one saving." She bumps her hip with mine.

I'm not stupid, I know that the main reason she's picking up all these extra hours is because she's trying to save for my college tuition, and that's hard to do when she provides the sole income for our household. She won't accept a penny of the money I make even though there have been times I've offered.

She would never tell me that's what she's saving for outright because she doesn't want to make me feel guilty. She's just that kind of mom. Selfless, giving—I know there isn't a thing she wouldn't do for me. I just wish I got more time with her than I do. I'd take time over money any day.

Where the Night Ends

We spend the next hour cooking, eating, and then cleaning up the kitchen. Mom leaves for work shortly after which leaves me all alone on a Saturday night. Normally I'd be working too, but Wednesday was my last day at *Ophelia's,* the small clothing boutique where I've worked the last couple summers. I never work during the school year, that's a rule of my mom's. She wants me to focus on school work—to her there's nothing more important than a solid education.

She would know. She spent six years in school—four in nursing, two additional getting her practitioner license. She does pretty well for herself, too. While we live modestly and don't have the kind of money Sebastian's family has, I've never really wanted for anything. My mom always makes sure I have the clothes I want and nice things, but there's also things she can't afford on only one income; like a car for her sixteen-year-old daughter.

Not that I mind. I take pride in being able to do things for myself. It's always been me and my mom. I like to think that we're in this together. I think a lot of that stems from my dad passing away when I was so young. In some weird way, I've always felt like I need to take care of my mom, even though she's never acted like she needed it.

She's strong and independent. I like to think I'm like her in that regard, though I'm not entirely sure that's true.

I try to keep myself busy over the next couple hours by folding some laundry and taking a shower. I do everything in my power to keep my mind from wandering to Sebastian, but despite my best efforts, it's all it seems to want to think about.

I keep checking my phone—making sure the volume is all the way up—

wondering if he'll call.

I dress in my most comfortable pajamas—pink and white striped bottoms with a white tank top. After letting it air dry most of the way, I finish drying my hair with the blow dryer before tying it up into a messy knot on top of my head.

By eight o'clock I've accepted that Sebastian isn't going to call and decide to try to distract myself with a movie. There's nothing really good on any of the channels, so after several minutes of surfing, I finally decide on renting the new Kevin Hart comedy. I could use a good laugh right about now.

I no more than hit the purchase button on the remote when a firm knock sounds against my front door. Not sure who it could be, I toss the fluffy red throw across my lap to the side and climb to my feet.

Another knock sounds just as I reach the front door. Knowing better than to just open it, especially being home alone, I peek out of the small glass inserts that surround the door frame.

Who I see on the other side has my heart clamoring inside my chest.

I expected to see Courtney or at the very least Bree—both of whom are known to just show up at my house at all hours of the night and day. There's a reason we call each other's houses our second homes. So when Sebastian's tall frame and handsome face comes into view, for a moment I think I'm imagining things.

Certainly, this isn't real—right?

Why would—how could—I just can't seem to make sense of it.

My body acts on autopilot, unlocking the door before my mind even has a chance to process what it's doing. There's a small voice in the back of my head, questioning

58

every movement, but I'm powerless to stop myself. It's like my body knows exactly what it wants—to be near Sebastian—and my mind doesn't get a say in the matter.

I've convinced myself that the events that took place last night were simply exaggerated—that I made something out of nothing. But when the door swings open between us and those hazel eyes meet mine, I know with complete certainty that what I felt last night, what I've felt all day, is in fact real. Very real.

One quirk of his lips and my knees nearly buckle underneath me… Oh god, I'm in so much trouble.

TESS

"Hey." Sebastian rocks back on his heels, shoving his hands into the pockets of his jeans as he stares back at me, a twinkle of mischief in his eyes.

I swear I feel like I've entered some alternate reality.

There's no way Sebastian Baxter is standing on my front porch right now. And yet, here he is—right in front of me—looking so handsome in his dark jeans and gray tee, his hair pushed back haphazardly like he's run his hands through it several times throughout the day.

He's so good looking it should be a sin. No one should be this sexy. And yet he is. Every inch of him is perfection and I hate that with just a smile, my heart beats a little harder.

"Hey." I don't try to hide my confusion over his unexpected visit. "What are you doing here, Sebastian?"

"I wanted to see you." He shrugs, a smirk playing on the corner of his mouth.

I swear if I could bottle up this moment and keep it forever I would. God, what is he doing to me right now?

"How did you even know where I lived?" The moment the question leaves my lips I know the answer.

"Courtney," we both say in unison, his smirk turning into a full smile.

Butterflies erupt in my stomach, and I'm suddenly painfully aware of how ridiculous I probably look.

As if he can somehow read my mind, he adds, "Cute pajamas."

I nervously fidget with the bottom of my tank, thanking the heavens that I had enough forethought to put on a bra.

"I wasn't expecting company," I finally manage to squeak out.

"Well, now that you have it are you going to invite me in?"

Could he be any surer of himself? His confidence oozes from every orifice of his body, and I desperately want to soak it in—know what it's like to feel that good in your own skin.

"I'm still trying to decide." I eye him warily.

"Anything I can do to sway your decision?" He steps forward, his tall frame now towering over me.

I wish I could say that I'm immune to his charms, that the nearness of his body doesn't stir something deep inside of me—a wanting I didn't even know I could feel, but that wouldn't be the truth.

"I-uh my mom's not home. I don't think she'd approve of you being here." I regret it the moment I say it.

Stupid, Tess. Seriously. You're mom's not home. That's the best you got?

"I'll be good." He tips my chin up with the back of his hand so that I'm looking up at him. "You can trust me," he offers with a humored grin.

"It's not you I'm worried about," I mumble under my breath a little too loudly, realizing my mistake almost instantly.

His eyes sparkle with humor, but he chooses not to address the statement we both know he heard. Instead, he slides past me into the house, giving me no choice but to follow him inside.

"When does your mom get home?" he asks, looking around the small space that equates to about one sixteenth of his house.

"Not until morning," I say, feeling like he already knew the answer to that long before he got here—especially if Courtney had anything to do with it.

I make a mental note to give her a piece of my mind later. I can't believe she would send Sebastian here and not even give me a heads up. *Some friend.*

"Popcorn?" Sebastian inhales, turning in the foyer to face me.

"I was getting ready to watch a movie."

"Perfect." He kicks off his shoes, sliding them against the wall with his foot.

"What are you doing?" I can't keep the smile from my voice.

"Getting comfy," he says like it should be obvious. "What movie are we watching?"

"We?" I choke out.

"Yes, we. I'm here, aren't I? I think that means I'm joining you." He turns, heading into the living room without waiting for me to respond.

Unlike Sebastian's house, he doesn't have to go far to find the room he's looking for. The living room sits right off the foyer and given the paused movie on the screen and the bowl of popcorn on the coffee table, it's pretty obvious where I was planning to watch said movie.

Flopping down where I was sitting just moments earlier, he stretches his arm along the back of the couch and throws me a wide grin when I stop in the doorway.

"Are you just gonna stand there checking me out all night, or are we gonna watch a movie already?" he teases, patting the cushion next to him.

"Do you always show up uninvited and just make yourself at home?" I ask as he props his feet up on the coffee table, his long legs stretched out in front of him.

He thinks on that for a moment, humor etched in his features.

"Yep." He finally concedes, patting the couch again.

I laugh, I can't help it. He's so damn endearing. Shaking my head, I cross the room, taking the seat on the opposite end of the couch.

"You know," he leans forward and snags the popcorn. "If you sit all the way over there you can't reach this." He shakes the bowl before setting it in his lap.

I let out a frustrated sigh and then scoot closer, secretly dying to get as close to him as I can. Not that I would ever admit it out loud.

Taking the middle cushion, I pull my legs up, tucking them underneath myself. "Happy?" I roll my eyes, leaning forward to grab the remote.

"Very." He smiles at me, his eyes holding my gaze for a long moment before he grabs a handful of popcorn and shoves it into his mouth.

"You're something else." I try to keep the smile off my face but fail miserably.

"I do my best." He smiles around a full mouth.

I don't know what to do, what to say, how to act. I'm such a ball of nervous energy that I feel like I might bounce out of my seat at any moment.

"Are you going to hit play on that?" he questions, his eyes darting between me and the remote.

"I'm working on it," I huff, embarrassed that he seems to know just how distracted he's making me.

"Well work faster," he teases, nodding in approval when I finally manage to get my fingers to work and the movie kicks on.

I wish I could say I calmed down, that eventually I settled in and lost myself in the movie, but I didn't. Not even a little bit. I couldn't focus on anything except Sebastian. How he laughed next to me. How about halfway into the movie, after the popcorn was pretty much gone, his hand found its way to mine and didn't leave it for the next hour—the pad of his thumb tracing circles along the back of my hand. How I kept feeling his eyes on the side of my face instead of on the television screen where they should have been.

I've never watched a movie before and had no idea what actually happened by the end of it. It's Sebastian. He's intoxicating and distracting and demands to be the center of attention no matter what's going on. And he doesn't even have to try—it's just him.

"I gotta admit, I didn't peg you as a Kevin Hart fan." He finally breaks the silence just as the end credits start to roll.

"Why?" I ask, stretching—my pretty obvious play off at pulling my hand away.

"You just seem, I don't know, kind of serious." He shrugs.

"I do?" I question, wondering what kind of impression I'm giving him here.

"A little, yeah." He chuckles, clearly amused by my reaction to his statement.

"Well, I'm not," I blurt defensively.

"No?" He smiles, shifting his body toward me.

"I mean, okay, I'm a little serious." I sigh. "But not to the point that I don't know how to laugh or have a good time. I'm just serious when I need to be."

"And right now is one of those times?" he challenges.

"What?" I can't keep the defensiveness out of my voice.

Is this why he came here—to make me feel worse about myself than I already do?

"See—there," he points out, that damn grin firmly placed on his handsome face. "You're so easy to rile up."

"I am not," I huff, even though I know he's right.

"You're adorable." His comment isn't patronizing the way I expect it to be; in fact, the way he says it coupled with the way he's looking at me reads quite the opposite.

My heart beats against my ribs like a sledgehammer.

"I am?" I don't know why the question leaves my lips. I wish I could take it back, stuff it away, but then Sebastian nods slowly, his tongue darting out to trace along his bottom lip.

I'm fascinated by the action, my eyes glued to his mouth, wondering what his lips would feel like pressed against mine.

He laughs lightly which causes a deep blush to flood my face. Something about his expression tells me he knows exactly where my mind has gone, and it's both frustrating and sexy.

"You're more than just adorable, Tess." He reaches out, sliding his fingers across my jaw. "And what makes you even more beautiful is that you have no idea just how breathtaking you are." My breath catches when his thumb crosses my bottom lip.

I swear my stomach is a mass of butterflies and something else that I'm not quite sure I've ever felt before. I squeeze my legs together, trying to dull the unfamiliar ache I feel.

"I-I'm not like those other girls, Sebastian," I blurt nervously.

"And what other girls would you be referring to?" he asks, his gaze locked on mine.

"The kind that sleep with you." It takes everything in me to force it out. "If you think you can come over here and sweet talk your way into my pants, you're wrong. It takes a lot more than that to win me over."

"I think that might be the point." His comment surprises me, but I'm too far gone to respond.

I can feel him inching toward me, his hazel eyes dark. I swear everything stands still as I wait. And I wait. And I wait. He stops so close to my face I can feel the heat of his breath on my cheek.

"I'm going to kiss you now, Tess," he whispers, not moving an inch.

It takes me a moment to realize he's waiting for me to say yes.

"Okay." It's less than a whisper and then his lips are on mine. Hot and firm, pressing against me so gently I almost whimper.

This is not what I expected at all. Not from someone like Sebastian. When he opens his mouth, tracing his tongue across the seam of my lips, I immediately open to him. His tongue darts out, seeking mine and he groans deep into my mouth when he finds it.

The ache in my lower belly explodes into an inferno, my breathing ragged and less controlled the deeper the kiss goes.

I feel like I'm at a tipping point—my feet are hanging off the edge and only a very thin string is holding me in place, keeping me from tumbling over the side. But I want to jump. I want to spread my arms and dive into the unknown. And I want it with Sebastian.

"Tess." He's the first to break the kiss, my name a strangled groan from his lips before he pulls back completely.

Like being doused in cold water, my actions suddenly become clear, and embarrassment becomes the most prominent feeling I have.

"I'm sorry." I hold my hand over my lips that now feel so different somehow.

"Don't do that." He gently pulls my hand away. "Don't kiss me like that and then apologize afterward. I want you to mean it. God…" He pulls me back to him. "I don't know what you're doing to me, Tessa Wilson, but I want you to keep doing it." He kisses me again, this time a small peck, followed by another and then another, before pulling back again.

"Fuck." He looks at me for another long moment and then pushes to his feet. "I should probably go."

"Wait, why?" I question, his abrupt movement catching me off guard.

"Because, Tess." He lets out a long exhale and then turns, looking down at me. "You said it yourself—you're not like the other girls. And I like that about you. But I'm also a guy, and right now I want nothing more than to take you to your bedroom and do really bad things to you."

"Like what?" I push to my feet, not sure where in the hell my words are coming from.

"Things you're not ready for, let's leave it at that."

I want to challenge him. Ask him how he knows I'm not ready, but deep down I know he's right. It's easy to get lost in the excitement and the thrill of it all, but as the rational part of me slowly returns, so does my voice of reason.

Sebastian kisses the top of my head and then takes off into the foyer, stopping to slip on his shoes. I walk him to the door, not really sure what to say or what to do.

"Thanks for tonight, Tess. I needed this." He pulls me against his chest, my arms going around his taut frame.

I close my eyes and inhale deeply, having never smelled anyone who smells quite like Sebastian. Unlike Dylan, Sebastian is more man than boy, and his scent reflects that—musky and masculine.

"Me, too," I admit, having not realized how much until this very moment.

"Can I call you tomorrow?" he asks, pulling back to look down at me.

"I'd like that," I answer truthfully.

The smile I get in return nearly takes my breath away. My god, he's even more handsome than I realized before. It's one thing to check Sebastian out from a distance, it's quite another to be so up close and personal with him.

It's almost inconceivable that a guy like this would ever waste his time on a girl like me and yet, here he is. Looking at me like I'm all he sees, and here I am feeling like I'm seconds away from melting into a puddle at his feet.

TESS

"Well, here we go." Courtney joins me in front of the car, and together we make our way toward the high school building for our first day of junior year.

I'd be lying if I said I wasn't nervous, but I think it's more about seeing Sebastian than it is about starting school again. I always have first day jitters, but this is something else entirely.

Even after what happened on Saturday, I still wasn't one hundred percent convinced I'd hear from Sebastian on Sunday. But as promised, he called me; it was shortly after dinner, and we talked for nearly two hours.

When we hung up he left me only with an *"I'll see you tomorrow, Tess."* His sultry voice making me wish it was already tomorrow.

Now it is, and I'm walking into school with an entire swarm of butterflies in my stomach flapping so wildly it's a wonder I'm able to keep myself securely on the ground.

We meet up with Bree, whose locker is just a couple down from mine, and then walk together toward our homeroom classes. Courtney and Bree were lucky enough to end up in the same homeroom where I was not.

I bid my two best friends goodbye before making my way four doors down to where my homeroom class is located. The room is already packed and bustling with excited students catching up with friends.

I head for the empty desk in the far front corner, saying hello to some of my classmates as I pass by. Unfortunately, because I spent so much time in the hallway with Court and Bree, the bell rings before I even make it all the way to my desk.

Mr. Johnson is still in the hallway, ushering some last-minute arrivals through the door, so I quickly take my seat. While he's distracted, I take a quick moment to check my phone, wanting to make sure it's on silent before class starts. Sliding the device from the back pocket of my skinny jeans, my breath catches in my throat the moment I see a text message from Sebastian.

Sebastian: I hope you have a good first day.

Looking up to see Mr. Johnson entering the room, I quickly lock the device and shove it back into my pocket without having a chance to text Sebastian back.

The first part of the morning goes by in a blur. While I'm familiar with the building, there's still some classroom searching that takes place on the first day, especially given that half the classes on my schedule are spread over the four different wings of school making it somewhat difficult to make it from one class to the next in the short three minutes that's allotted between bells.

By the time third period rolls around, I've managed to be late to all three classes, stumbling into Advanced Chemistry nearly two full minutes after the bell because I got turned around having never really been to the east wing before.

There are only two seats open, and I immediately opt for the one in the row closest to me about halfway toward the back. I hate drawing any attention to myself and considering my late arrival, pretty much everyone in the class watches me until I finally claim my desk.

I've barely gotten my notebook open before I hear snickering coming from behind me. Because of my rushed entrance, I didn't really pay much attention to who was sitting around me, but knowing it probably has nothing to do with me, I choose to ignore it and turn my attention forward.

It's not long before the girls are giggling again, talking in hushed whispers. Mr. Merlock is either completely oblivious to it or chooses to ignore it, but considering they're sitting right behind me, it's a far more challenging task for me, but I manage to shut them out for most of the class. That is until I hear Sebastian's name. That's when my ears perk up, and I really start listening.

"Are you sure that's her? He would never hook up with her. Look at her. She's so—boring." The hair on the back of my neck stands up as a fresh set of goose bumps spread across my skin.

"Maybe he did it out of pity. You know, so people would think they hooked up," the second girl responds.

"Oh, you're probably right. Sebastian really is so sweet, taking on such pathetic charity cases. I wonder if she actually believed he was giving her the time of day, or if she knew all along it was just a rouse."

"Poor thing. She probably thought it was real." This causes both the girls behind me to break into a fit of giggles once again.

It takes everything in me not to turn around and say something. I want to so bad. I want to tell them that not only did we spend an incredible night together on Friday, but that he came to my house Saturday and we spent hours on the phone Sunday, but I know better than to open that can of worms. It would probably just egg them on more.

I wish I could say I'm a thick-skinned person and their words don't poke me like little needles being jabbed into my skin, but that's simply not the case.

By the time the bell rings, I'm so on edge I feel like I'm gonna crawl out of my own skin. Grabbing my stuff off my desk, I hightail it toward the door before I do something I'll regret, like slapping tweedle dee and tweedle dumb right across their catty faces with my chemistry book.

I'm in such a rush to get away from the entire situation that I narrowly miss running into Dylan as I turn the corner in my attempt to flee. He jumps, startled by our near collision, and then recognition flashes across his face.

"Sorry." I avoid his gaze as I attempt to step around him.

I get all of two steps before his voice halts my movements.

"So, Sebastian Baxter huh?" The disdain dripping from each word has me slowly turning around.

He looks like his normal put together self. Dark hair short and styled, his decent built frame dressed in his usual jeans and sports tee. But it's his eyes that throw me off. The deep brown color not as soft as I once thought it to be. There's an edge to him I never really noticed while we were together.

Did he always look at me like that?

"What?" I finally question, my pulse drumming against my neck.

"You know, I actually felt bad for what I did to you," he says, his nose snarled. "But then you go and pull some shit like this."

"What are you talking about?" I don't try to hide my confusion.

"Six months, Tess. We were together for six months, and still, you weren't ready. One night at Sebastian Baxter's house and you're offering it up like it's a free meal service that everyone is entitled to but me."

His words are like a slap across the face, and I rear back from their impact.

This is the first interaction I've had with Dylan since our breakup, and he has the nerve to come at me about Sebastian after what he did with Taylor. Anger boils deep in my chest, and I have to physically restrain myself from exploding.

"So what if I did?" I find myself lying just to hurt him. "You're the one who cheated on me, you broke up with me remember?"

"So you go and fuck the biggest player in school to get back at me?" His voice booms around me, and only then do I realize the eyes that have stopped to watch this little altercation.

"Fuck you, Dylan!" I seethe, surprising even myself. "Fuck you!" I repeat before spinning around and practically running down the hallway, leaving him standing in what I can only guess is complete shock.

I've never stood up to Dylan before, not like that. I'd be lying if I said it didn't feel good. It did. It felt better than good—amazing might be a better word for it. I just wish there weren't so many people around listening to him spew his lies.

Between the girls in Chemistry and Dylan's little hallway outburst, it's only a matter of time before the whole school thinks I screwed Sebastian Baxter.

***

The downfall to being in all advanced classes is that I rarely get to see my friends throughout the day. And with the day I've had, I could use a little detox time with Bree and Courtney. Luckily, like the last two years, we have the same lunch period. After grabbing a salad and yogurt from the lunch line, I make my way across the cafeteria to the far right side where Courtney, Bree, and I have sat every lunch period since freshman year.

As I get close to the table, for a moment I question if I've got the right spot. Our ten-person round table that usually sits around five girls and the occasional boy Bree is dating, is now packed full of guys and girls alike.

I hesitate before I spot Courtney who holds her hand up in a half wave the moment she sees me. I nod, surprised to find Ant sitting next to her. But the real shock is who is sitting on the other side of him.

A flood of heat washes over my face when those brilliant hazel eyes meet mine, and a slow smile spreads across Sebastian's face. It doesn't take me long to realize that there is only one seat open and it's between Sebastian and Marissa, a mutual friend of our group.

I take a deep breath and head around the table, fully aware of how Sebastian's eyes never lose sight of me, following my every move until I finally claim the seat next to him.

74

"Bout time your ass showed up." Bree throws a French fry at me from across the table. It skids across the surface and ends up somewhere on the floor behind me.

"My class schedule is insane this year." I try my best to remain casual despite feeling like I'm going to bounce out of my seat with nervous energy.

"Well, that's what you get for being such an overachiever," she teases, turning toward Blake when he grumbles something under his breath.

"Hey." Sebastian gently nudges his shoulder against mine, pulling my gaze away from Bree.

"Hey." I have trouble speaking around the knot in my throat.

It's one thing to play pretend with Sebastian—to exist with him outside of school—but being here with him next to me feels almost like some cheesy teenage RomCom.

"You didn't text me back this morning."

"Sorry. I meant to. I just got really busy," I croak out, my throat dry.

"I guess I can give you a free pass this time," he teases, his mouth pulling up on one side.

"What are you doing over here anyway?" I try to push past my nerves, quickly adding, "Slumming it today?"

Sebastian always sits at the long table next to the windows where most of the football team and cheerleaders tend to congregate. To say I'm shocked to see him over here in my neck of the woods is the understatement of the year.

Not that my group of friends isn't popular. I mean, Bree and Courtney are hands-down two of the prettiest girls in school, but we are definitely not part of *his* crowd.

"More like I upgraded." His response brings an immediate smile to my face. I swear if he was sitting any

75

closer he could probably hear my heart thumping inside my chest.

I'm seconds away from spitting back some smart ass comment but can't get the words out before I hear—"You two are just too cute together," come from one of the girls at the table.

I look up to find Trisha, one of Courtney's good friends, sitting caddy corner from us looking directly at me. Heat creeps up my neck, spreading to my cheeks when I realize she's talking about me and Sebastian.

"Oh, we're not..." I start, the words sticking on my tongue.

"Thank you." I hear Sebastian say next to me, officially cutting me off.

I turn wide eyes on him, shock probably etched in every feature of my face.

"Though I think it's more Tess making me look good than anything," he adds, his words meant for Trisha but his gaze never leaving mine.

"What are you doing?" I grind out under my breath so only he can hear me.

"What?" He gives me an innocent, knowing smile. "I'm just telling the people how smitten I am with you." His tone is low, but I have no doubt that anyone who cares enough to listen can hear him.

"Is that what you're doing?" I question, trying to fight the smile his words bring to my lips.

"I mean, I'm trying, but you're getting all squeamish on me." There's humor in his voice but truth to his words.

Squeamish is exactly how I would describe it. I hate being put on display and right now, that's exactly how I feel knowing that every set of eyes at our table and probably several other tables are locked on the little show Sebastian is putting on.

"Dear god, just kiss her already," I hear Bree groan.

I'm seconds away from telling her where she can take her comment when Sebastian's words render me speechless.

"Don't mind if I do," he says as his face lowers toward mine.

At first, I think he's just going to kiss my cheek or something, but when he tips my face up my entire body freezes. My reaction time isn't quick enough, and before I can even process his movements his lips are on mine, soft and smooth.

He keeps it PG, his mouth lingering on mine just long enough to get the reaction out of me he wants. I feel like I'm in a trance, lost in some hypnotic spell that Sebastian has cast over me.

Pulling back, he stares at me for a long moment. Time seems to slow down as those hazel eyes burn deeply into mine. Eyes that I'm sure hold more truths than the man they belong to will ever dare admit.

I know everyone sees Sebastian as the player, the football star, the unattainable heartthrob, and so did I for the longest time. But having spent these last few days getting to know him better, it's clear to see there's so much more to him than I originally thought.

I hear one of the girl's sigh and then Ant groans, "Dude, we're all trying to eat." His words instantly break the moment, and my embarrassment spreads.

I immediately look away, wishing the floor would open up and swallow me whole.

It's so easy to get lost in Sebastian's charm that sometimes I forget that there's an entire world going on around us.

"Stop being an ass," I hear Courtney say seconds before she changes the subject, addressing the rumor that Mr. Johnson, my homeroom teacher, is sleeping with the married Mrs. Spellman from the Math department.

Silently thanking my best friend for knowing exactly how to draw the attention away from me, I spend the next twenty minutes trying to force down at least a little of my lunch. It's not the easiest thing to do, especially when a certain gorgeous senior won't stop staring at me.

He remains completely at ease like he doesn't have a care in the world; meanwhile, I feel like a pressurized ball of nerves that's going to explode at any moment, spewing my contents all over the lunch table in front of me.

By the time the bell rings, signaling the end of our lunch period, I'm both disappointed that my time with Sebastian is over and yet so relieved at the same time. Maybe once I get away from him this weird knot that's formed in the pit of my stomach will go away, though I'm not entirely sure it will.

"Let me walk you to your next class," Sebastian offers as we drop off our trays and make our way out of the cafeteria.

"And draw even more attention to us?" I question. "I think you put on enough of a show back there." I gesture back to the table we just left. "Keep it up, and people might actually think you like me or something," I joke nervously.

"And that's an issue?" he questions with a smirk, taking my hand before leading me across the aisle and down the far left hallway, not stopping until we reach what I can only assume is his locker.

"I mean, I get it. You need to show off your charity work." I shrug, humor lacing my words as I lean against the locker next to his. "Whatever it is we're doing here though, I'd like to survive it with as much of my reputation intact as possible."

"And being with me tarnishes that reputation?" he questions, cocking his head to the side as he pulls two books from his locker and tucks them under his arm before closing it.

"They think I'm sleeping with you, which doesn't speak very highly of me."

"So it's a bad thing if people think we're having sex?" he questions like the statement couldn't sound more ridiculous.

"It's a bad thing if people view me as just another one of your conquests." The humor dies away as my true feelings boil to the surface. "Look, I like you, Sebastian. I really do. But if this is some screwed up game you're playing to screw the uptight virgin, I'd appreciate it if you'd just not waste my time. I'm not interested in being just another girl in the long line of people you've slept with."

I don't expect my words to come out as harshly as they do, but the situation in chemistry class coupled with my altercation with Dylan seems to be weighing heavier on me than I initially thought. And while Sebastian has been nothing but amazing to me, I can't help but be hesitant and suspicious; who wouldn't be in my situation?

The last thing I expect is for Sebastian to find humor in my rant, so when he tips his head back and a full belly laugh erupts from his throat, I stand completely dumbfounded, not at all sure what the hell is happening.

"God, you're something else." He shakes his head, laughter still lacing his words. "Are you done now? Did you get it all off your chest?"

"I'm serious, Sebastian." I cross my arms in front of myself.

He steps closer. "You really need to learn how to just go with the flow, Tess. Not everything has to be so life altering. So people talk, who cares."

"I care."

"Well, you shouldn't." He reaches out and tucks a strand of hair behind my ear, his hand lingering on my cheek for a moment longer before it returns to his side.

"Come on, we're gonna be late." And with that, he loops his arm through mine and drags me alongside him, effectively ending our conversation.

TESS

Who knew that one display of public affection in a crowded cafeteria could create so much buzz. I mean seriously, do people have nothing better to do than worry about who Sebastian Baxter is hooking up with?

I feel like every pair of eyes is on me as I make my way out of school at the end of the day. Maybe part of it is just me being paranoid, but I know for certain that's not entirely the case. I had four different girls come up to me between the last two periods of the day wanting to know if Sebastian and I were dating.

I wanted to say yes, more than I thought I would. But instead, I settled for a shrug and non-committal response like *"we're just hanging out."*

To say it's been an exciting first day is putting it mildly. I don't think I've ever gotten so much attention in my life, and truthfully, I'm not sure I like it. I mean, Sebastian I like. But I'm starting to feel a bit overwhelmed by what it might mean to be a part of his world.

All I want is to climb in Courtney's car and whine to her and Bree about the day I've had, but my plans are immediately thwarted when I see Sebastian leaning against

Courtney's passenger side door, his muscular arms crossed in front of him.

My heart instantly kicks into overdrive, pumping so hard and fast it's a wonder I don't go into cardiac arrest.

"There she is." He smiles, pulling me into his arms without an ounce of hesitation.

The heaviness of the day melts away the moment his scent invades my nostrils, and I feel the firmness of his chest against my cheek. I thought I needed Courtney and Bree, but maybe this was what I needed all along. Sebastian has this unique ability to make the outside world seem so insignificant.

"What are you up to now?" I pull back and peer up at him, his dazzling smile even more prominent in the bright afternoon sunlight.

"I was hoping I could give you a ride home." He tucks my hair behind my ear, something I'm learning he does a lot.

"I usually ride with Courtney." I gesture to the car behind him as I take a step backward.

"I'm aware, but usually doesn't mean always." He winks. "Come on." He drops an arm over my shoulder, leading me away from the car.

"I should probably wait and tell Courtney," I try to object.

"Already did." He smiles down at me before turning his attention forward.

"Awfully presumptuous of you, Mr. Baxter; what if I didn't want you to take me home?"

"You do," he states matter of fact, humor lacing his voice.

"You're confident," I deadpan.

Seconds later his incredible laugh flutters around me. I swear I could record the sound of it and listen to it all day, every day. It's the most amazing thing I've ever heard.

"And you, Ms. Wilson, are a pain in my ass," he teases.

I'm ready to respond with some witty retort but end up changing gears when Sebastian stops next to a fancy black sports car.

"I thought you drove a Jeep?" I question, knowing that's what he was driving Saturday when he came to my house.

"I do." He pulls the passenger door open and takes my book bag, waiting until I'm planted inside before dropping the bag onto the floorboard between my feet and closing the door.

"Then whose car is this?" I ask when he climbs into the driver's seat next to me.

"Mine."

"Yours?" I blanch. "You have a sports car and a Jeep? I can't even afford a beater and here you have two vehicles that probably cost more than the house I live in."

"Half." He chuckles next to me.

"Half?"

"Half of the cost of your house." He grins, clearly just messing with me.

"Wow. You really are spoiled." I snap my seatbelt, turning my gaze out the windshield.

Sebastian is silent next to me for a couple seconds before he finally speaks again, and I'm instantly surprised by the vulnerability in his voice.

"Your mom shows you love by spending time with you, being your mom. My parents do it with possessions. Anything they can give me to keep me happy, so long as they don't have to lift a finger in the parenting department."

"I'm sorry. I shouldn't have said the thing about you being spoiled." I immediately feel guilty over my statement and my assumption. I take his hand that's resting on the gearshift between us and give it a squeeze.

"Don't be. It's what everyone thinks." He shrugs, giving me a quick sideways glance.

"Does that bother you? That people view you a certain way?"

"Not really." He shakes his head, his focus remaining on the road. "It comes with the territory."

"What territory is that?" I ask.

"Being the hottest, richest guy in school." His words drip with playfulness, but that doesn't stop me from rearing back and slapping his chest.

"Owe." He laughs, rubbing the spot where my hand connected. "Such violence. I see I'm not the only one who has everyone fooled."

"I have no idea what you're talking about." I cross my arms over my chest and stare out the window, a huge smile on my face.

"I gotta say, you play the good girl routine well, but I'm starting to see through your façade."

"I *am* a good girl," I object, looking back in his direction to see a smug smile on his handsome face.

"Okay," he says disbelieving, nodding his head.

"I am," I insist.

"Says the girl who can drink whiskey straight from the bottle like a champ and kisses like a porn star."

"Did you just compare me to a porn star?" I'm not sure whether to laugh or be offended.

"Relax, it was a compliment." He chuckles. "I just meant, you're a phenomenal kisser." He grins, his eyes catching mine for a brief moment before returning to the road. "And you do this little moan—it's like you're a starving woman and my mouth is the most delicious meal you've ever tasted. It's seriously so hot. You play like you're this innocent little thing, but I think deep down you've got one hell of an untapped wild side."

"I think you have me confused with someone else," I offer.

"You may think I don't see you Tessa Wilson- but I do. I see everything." He winks at me seconds before pulling the car to a stop on the street outside my house.

"Well…" I hesitate, not really sure what to do. "Thank you for the ride." I move to grab my bag, but Sebastian catches my arm before I reach it.

Tugging me toward him, the next thing I feel is his warm lips against mine. He kisses me gently, dragging his tongue along my bottom lip before sliding it inside of my mouth.

Like being invaded by a body snatcher, something else takes over and I feel crazed, lustful. I deepen the kiss, my fingers tangling in his short hair as I try desperately to control the overwhelming urges I feel taking over.

By the time we part I'm breathless, my chest heaving up and down as I ride out the high Sebastian's touch sparks inside me.

"See." He smiles against my mouth. "My little minx." He kisses me again, this time a gentle press of his lips to mine before he pulls back, his hazel eyes dark and hooded.

I can tell he wants me, maybe even more than I want him, and the thought is dizzying. Sebastian makes me feel a way I've never felt before. Wild and untamed. And while I love the feeling, it's also terrifying at the same time.

"I should probably go," I finally blurt. "My mom is home today. It's Monday, her one consistent off night each week. We always spend Monday's together."

"Can I call you later?"

"You better." I smile, grabbing my bag before quickly exiting the car.

I manage to make it up to the front porch before turning back. Sebastian is still sitting on the curb, his eyes glued to me. I throw him a little wave over my shoulder, my heart doing acrobats in my chest as I stick my key in the lock and push my way inside.

I take slow calculated breaths, trying to calm my rapid pulse, before sneaking a peek out of the vertical panes of glass that line the sides of the front door. I do it just in time to see the back of Sebastian's car as he drives away. I stare at the place where he was just parked for what seems like forever before my mother's voice causes me to jump in surprise.

"Who's the boy?" she asks, pulling my attention to where she's leaning against the doorway of the living room watching me.

"What?" I question, unable to stop the smile from spreading across my lips.

"You know, the one who put that there." She points to my mouth. "The black sports car. Who is he?"

"Sebastian Baxter." I sigh.

"Well, it looks like this Sebastian Baxter really knows how to lay on the charm." She gives me a knowing look, and I swear I smile wider.

"He's so... I don't even know how to describe it." Nervous laughter bubbles from my chest.

I've never been one to keep much from my mom. In the boys department we've always had open communication, but telling her too much about Sebastian right now almost feels premature.

I mean, she knew everything about Dylan as it happened, and even though it took me a while to see through him, my mom never cared for the boy. Guess she could see something I couldn't. But Sebastian, I think she'd like him. I mean, I could be wrong, but I can't see how anyone could not. He's just so damn charming. But it's still so new and I don't want to jinx it, as dumb as that sounds.

"Uh oh," mom teases, giving me a knowing look.

"It's nothing." I blow it off, slinging my book bag over my shoulder. "I've got lots of homework to do," I say, wasting no time taking off down the hall toward my room.

"Okay, but I want to hear more later. Dinner will be ready in about an hour," mom calls after me. I swear I hear her chuckle when I shut the door without a word, but I'm too far gone to worry about what she thinks at the current moment.

Pressing my back against the door, I let my mind wander back to the scene that unfolded in the car just moments ago. The way Sebastian kissed me, the way he looked at me—his eyes so full of longing. I swear my heart is still trying to find a normal rhythm.

I smile, touching my fingers to my lips as I think about lunch and how he kissed me without caring who saw. I don't know why but I had convinced myself that whatever this thing is we started Friday would come to end when we got back to school, but that no longer seems to be the case.

My chest swells as I think about all the girls who would kill to be in my shoes right now. They're all probably sick with jealousy and you know what—I can't blame them. Sebastian Baxter is special. And I'm not talking about his money or his popularity—he, as a person, is special. There's something about him. This endearing quality that makes it impossible not to like him.

I'm so lost in thought that I jump slightly when my phone buzzes in my back pocket. Pulling it from my jeans, I immediately answer when I see Courtney's name flashing across the screen.

"Hey," I get out breathlessly, still unable to wipe the stupid smile off my face.

"Holy shit, Tess. Holy shit. Holy shit. You and Sebastian. Oh my god, I think I'm going to die," my best friend rambles. "You owe me so big for making you go to that party. I about died when he kissed you at lunch. God, he's so fucking hot. I bet he's an amazing kisser. Tell me everything that happened. Wait, is he still there?"

I laugh, knowing there's no sense in answering any questions other than the last one she asked.

"No, he just dropped me off. Monday, remember?"

"That's right. Mom day," she says, knowing my schedule probably better than anyone. "So how was the ride home? Did you guys talk more? What's going on? Is it like official yet?"

"Are you going to continue to ask me five hundred questions in a row, or are you going to give me a chance to answer?" I chuckle, collapsing down on my bed, and staring up at the ceiling.

"Sorry. I'm just freaking out for you. I mean, Sebastian Baxter, Tess. He's only the hottest guy in school. Well, besides Ant of course," she quickly tacks on. "So... Tell me. I'm dying over here."

"There's nothing really to tell," I admit, having already filled her in on the events of this past weekend.

I think she, like me, was curious if things would continue with school starting back up, or if everything would kind of go back to normal. Again, we're not unpopular by any stretch, but Sebastian is on a completely different level, and even though Courtney was convinced he liked me, she didn't know how school would change the dynamics between us; nor did I.

"Bullshit. Sebastian Baxter doesn't just kiss anyone in the middle of the cafeteria. Now spill."

"I'm serious, Court. We're just—I don't know—going with the flow. He hasn't said anything about actually dating, and I'm not going to bring it up. I mean, I like him—a lot, but it's only been four days."

"And, I knew I wanted to date Ant after an hour." She laughs.

"Do I want to *date* Sebastian?" I say as a question. "I mean, I think I'd have to be dead not to want that. He's very charming and well…"

"So hot," Courtney adds.

"Yes, and that." I chuckle. "But there's more to him than that. I don't know, I feel like I haven't even scratched the surface with him yet and already I'm finding it hard to keep my thoughts straight when I'm with him. He makes me feel—god, I don't even know," I say, trying to find the right words. "But I don't want to move too fast either. The last thing I want is another repeat of the Dylan fiasco."

"Sebastian is not Dylan. Don't let that douche bag ruin every other guy for you just because he couldn't keep it in his pants."

Melissa Toppen

"I know, Court. I'm just worried that there will be certain expectations with Sebastian. What if I'm not ready?"

"Maybe you're not yet. But trust me, eventually, you will be. And when that time comes you'll be glad if it's with someone like Sebastian. At least he knows what he's doing. Nothing worse than losing your virginity to another virgin, trust me I know. It's like two people who've never played chess before trying to play a match in the dark."

I laugh at her analogy. Only Courtney would describe her first sexual experience as playing chess. She doesn't even know what the chess pieces are called. If I had to guess she probably has never even seen the game played. Then again, maybe that's why she's used that as her comparison.

"Yeah, but that also means I'm subject to being compared to every other girl he's been with before." I sigh, shaking off the thought. "Whatever, it doesn't matter anyway. It's not like I'm just going to hop in bed with him after four days of hanging out," I say, ignoring the voice in my head that tells me that's exactly what I want to do.

"Well, you better snatch his ass up before long. Ant and I have a bet going that you're going to be the first girl Sebastian has officially dated since he moved here from California, and I've got fifty bucks and a blowjob on the line."

"What?" I snort in disbelief.

"If you and Sebastian become official, Ant owes me...Well, you don't want to know what." She giggles. "But if you don't then I owe Ant fifty dollars and a blowjob. Not that I mind that second part."

90

"Gross." I shake my head, not wanting to envision that picture at all. "And why would you bet on something like whether or not we'll start dating?"

"It's Ant's fault. He says there's no way you'll break Sebastian's no relationship rule, and I disagree."

"Wait—his what?"

"His no relationship rule. Tell me you knew about that. You'd have to be living under a rock not to know that Sebastian has a strict no dating rule."

"Well then, apparently I've been living under a boulder because I had no idea. I mean, obviously, I've never seen him officially date anyone, but I had no idea it was some weird rule of his," I say, feeling a bit of my happiness deflate. "And if that's the case, you shouldn't have bet in my favor because I seriously doubt a guy like Sebastian is going to change his rules for a girl like me."

"I think you'd be surprised," Courtney sings confidently. "Trust me, I can read people a hell of a lot better than Anthony. He may know Sebastian, but I know boys and I'm telling you—the way he looks at you—he's definitely interested in more than just a hookup. When he smiles at you, dear god, even I melt a little. I'm telling you, girl, as long as you don't do anything to screw it up, that boy is going to be yours."

"Do I want him to be mine?" I ask like I'm asking her permission.

"Um... duh," she says dramatically followed by a long pause. "Hey, I gotta go, Ant is beeping in. Talk soon. Love you."

"Love you, too." I barely get the words out before the line goes dead.

Tossing the phone down on the bed next to me, I let out a deep exhale and let Courtney's words sink in.

Sebastian has a no dating rule?

He looks at me a certain way? Why have I not noticed? Then again, maybe I have. I mean, I feel it don't I—the connection between us, the chemistry. But what if this is all just a game to him? What if this really is just some elaborate scheme to get me into bed? It's not like things like that don't happen on the daily. And while yes, he could have any girl he wants, what's the fun in that? Don't boys like him get off on the chase, conquering the unconquerable? After all, isn't that kind of what Dylan was doing?

I shake the thought away. Courtney's right, I can't let what Dylan did effect the way I see Sebastian. I'll never know unless I try, right? And god knows I want to, more than anything I've ever wanted before.

And while yes, this no relationship rule is a bit of a shock, it's also something that could very easily change. Who knows, maybe I'll be the first girl to ever get to call Sebastian Baxter her boyfriend.

Now isn't that a thought…

TESS

"Tess." I hear Dylan's voice before I see him, the little hairs on the back of my neck standing up the moment I register it's him.

Of course, he would choose today—the mother of bad days—to come add the big ole cherry on top of my mounting Sundae. Friday's are usually my favorite day of the week, but Friday has not been my friend today. Quite the opposite actually.

It started this morning with a group of girls who were clearly talking about me in Math class. They made a point to make sure I could hear what they were saying about how Sebastian was just with me to fuck me, and how stupid I was to think the show he was putting on was actually real. One even went as far to say that he had called her the previous night, and they had a good laugh at my expense.

I tried to brush it under the rug—girls being girls—but I'd be lying if I said the seed of doubt hadn't been planted and continued to sprout throughout the remainder of the day.

Sarah Jordan cornered me in the locker room after fifth-period gym and asked me if I had any idea how stupid I looked walking around on Sebastian's arm like what we had going on was actually real. And then she had the audacity to laugh right in my face like I was the punch line of an extremely funny joke.

Now granted, Sarah and her group of teenage bullies aren't in the majority, but it still feels like the entire school is against me suddenly.

I take a deep breath and calmly close my locker before finally turning toward Dylan, not surprised to find him leaning against the locker next to mine, arms crossed like he always used to do when he was waiting for me to get my things so he could walk with me to class.

The vision causes an odd sensation to run through me. A sense of déjà vu, if you will, and it takes me a second to snap back to present day.

"What do you want, Dylan?" I ask, swinging my bag over my shoulder.

"I was hoping we could talk for a minute," he says, voice soft.

"About?" I don't buy into his nice act, tapping my foot against the floor like I couldn't be more impatient.

"I wanted to apologize for the other day." His words calm my annoyance a bit, but there's still this nagging feeling—like an involuntary tick, like I know something is coming.

"O-k-a-y," I draw out, giving him a chance to continue.

"It was wrong of me to come at you about Sebastian the way I did. You didn't do anything wrong, and this isn't your fault."

"I'm sorry, what's not my fault?" I cock my head to the side, my eyebrows pulling together in confusion.

"Sebastian gets off on landing girls like you. I can't fault you for falling for his act. You wouldn't be the first. I just hope you know you don't have to sleep with someone like Sebastian to get even with me. You've made your point."

"Wait, I'm confused." I hold a hand up between us.

"I know. My actions have been all over the place these last few months, but I get it now. I made a huge mistake the day I let you go," he quickly continues.

"Wait, what?" My mind can't seem to catch up to what he's actually getting to.

"I want you back, Tess. I want us back," he says, reaching out to trail his fingers lightly down my forearm. The contact causes my whole body to tense. "I fucked up and I'm really sorry, but I'm ready to move on—with you."

"With me? Dylan, do you even hear yourself?" I try to control the anger that flares in my voice. "You cheated on me, remember?"

"I know, and I just apologized for it."

"You think an apology is just going to fix it? You humiliated me, Dylan. Not only did you cheat on me, you made sure everyone in school knew *why* you were doing it."

"I made a mistake." He shrugs like it's no big deal.

"You made a mistake," I repeat his words, disbelief evident in my tone.

"Yeah, I did. I'm entitled to make a mistake, Tess. Not everyone is as perfect as you are," he grinds out.

"I'm far from perfect. The difference between you and me is that I actually care who my actions hurt, and I would never intentionally hurt or embarrass someone the way you did me. It's called common courtesy. Perhaps you should try it sometime." I turn, completely over this conversation.

"Where are you going?" Dylan grabs my arm and spins me back toward him. "I'm not done."

"Well, I am." I jerk my arm out of his grasp.

"I'm trying to fucking apologize here, Tess." His voice echoes around us and I know, like the other day, we've gathered a small audience of students who haven't yet left for the day.

"Well, I don't want your apology," I say through clenched teeth.

"So what then, you're just going to walk away from everything we had *for him*." He points down the hall at nothing in particular.

"I'm walking away for me. Because I deserve better than you, Dylan." I don't miss the way his eyes widen like I've just slapped him right across the face.

I wish I was that kind of person because slapping him is exactly what I want to do right now. Why can't he just leave me alone?

"Just wait—I give it two weeks and you'll be crawling back," he warns. "You think things are going to end differently with a guy like him. Good fucking luck. When he fucks you and then dumps you, don't come crying to me. This is the only chance I'm going to give you."

"Thanks, but no thanks." I give him the biggest 'fuck you' smile I can muster before spinning on my heel and storming off down the hallway.

By the time I reach the parking lot, my hands are shaking and the adrenaline of what just happened seems to catch up to me. I'm so mad I swear fumes are going to start shooting straight out of my ears.

The nerve of him—does he really know so little about me that he thought he could intimidate me into getting back together with him?

I want to scream so bad that it feels like my chest is going to explode.

"Tess." I vaguely hear my name, but I'm too far gone to care. "Tess." I hear again but I keep walking, my face straight ahead just needing to get the hell away from everything and everyone before I lose it.

Don't do it, Tess.

Don't you dare cry.

Even as I think it the tears are already forming and spilling down my cheeks within seconds. I veer left, leaving the school parking lot on foot with every intention of walking home, but then I hear his voice again—Sebastian—seconds before his hand closes down on my shoulder and eases me to a stop.

"Tess." He hesitantly steps around me, tipping my face upward when I refuse to look at him. "Tess. What the hell is going on?" he questions, his voice full of concern.

"I just need you to leave me alone, Sebastian." I refuse to meet his gaze.

"What happened?" he repeats, this time his voice taking on a hard edge.

"You happened," I snap, directing my anger at the completely wrong person. "You, and your bullshit happened. It's been a week and already I've been talked about, laughed at, and ridiculed more than I ever have in my entire life." I throw my hands up, spinning in the opposite direction.

Sebastian is back in front of me within seconds, his forehead drawn together in concern.

"What you mean? You haven't said anything." He once again tips my chin up when I try not to look at him.

If I'm being honest, it's because I'm ashamed. He's the last person who deserves my anger and yet here I am, placing all the blame on him when in reality he's one of the best things in my life right now.

"Because I don't like playing these stupid games." I swipe angrily at my tears. "Are you aware that I've been told at least ten times since Monday that you're only hanging out with me because I'm a challenge? That once you sleep with me you'll never speak to me again."

"Who's saying that?"

"Everyone's saying it." I cross my arms defensively in front of myself.

"Have I given you any reason to believe that's what my intentions are?" he asks, his voice so soft it makes it hard to not break into another fit of tears.

"No, then again, you really haven't said anything to me at all," I argue for no reason other than just to argue.

"Have my *actions* said to you that's what I'm after—to get you into my bed?" He reaches out, tucking my hair behind my ear. "Because if that's the case, tell me now. I never want you to feel like I expect something from you, Tess. I don't. I just like being around you. People talk, who gives a shit. At the end of the day, it doesn't change anything between us." His hand lingers on my jaw. "You can't control everything and everyone around you. You have to learn to let go a little."

"That's easy for you to say." I push past the rush of heat his touch causes. "Not everything is so easy, Sebastian. Maybe it is for you, but it's not for me. You've probably never had to work for anything a day in your life.

Some of us don't have the luxury of just going with the flow."

"What are you saying, Tess?" he questions. "That you don't want to hang out with me because it's too hard?"

"Look, this was fun, but I need to refocus. I can't afford this distraction. I can't be listening to people snicker behind me because they don't think I'm good enough for you when I should be paying attention to the teacher. I can't afford to be late for class because I'm hiding in the bathroom stall waiting for the girls who are talking about me to leave. And I can't continue to have my ex-boyfriend causing scenes in the middle of the hallway because he's now convinced himself we should get back together. I just—it's too much, Sebastian."

"Wait, causing scenes how?" He ignores everything else I said and hones in on the Dylan thing.

"It's—it's nothing." I sigh. "Just forget about it."

"It's not nothing. If Dylan is giving you shit, I need to know about it."

"Why? What are you going to do?" I question, throwing my hands up in defeat.

"I'm going to teach him what happens when he messes with something that's mine." The possessiveness in his voice has my body reacting in ways I never expected.

"Yours?" I manage to push the word out. "You hardly know me."

"I know enough to know I don't want anyone else to have you."

"What are you saying, Sebastian?" The clear shake in my voice gives away how much his words affect me.

"I'm in, Tess." He takes my face in his hands. "Look at me, I'm in. What more do I have to do to show you that I like you—I mean, I really fucking like you, Tess. You're not like any other girl in this school. I haven't been able to stop thinking about you since you walked out onto that balcony. You want to shut them all up, be my girlfriend."

"Sebastian," I start, but he cuts me off.

"I'm not asking for them, I'm asking for me. Showing them all they're wrong is just an added bonus." A small smile spreads across his mouth. "What do you say, Tess? Will you be my girlfriend?"

Everything about the moment is so sickeningly sweet that it almost doesn't feel real. The way his gaze is locked on mine, his hands holding my face, his words dancing around me. I wish I could say I stand even a chance against him, but it should be pretty obvious by this point that I don't.

"I thought you didn't do relationships?" I see the humor flash across his face the moment the words leave my mouth.

"Correction—I didn't do relationships. It would appear as though that is no longer the case."

"You're serious?" I ask, surprised to find my own smile making an appearance.

"I've never been more serious," he says, leaning in closer. "So, Tessa Wilson, is that a yes?" he whispers against my lips, waiting until I nod before closing the remaining distance between us.

He kisses me softly, and yet there's a sense of urgency as his lips work against mine. By the time we part several moments later we're both a little breathless, and my mind is once again complete mush.

"Come on." Sebastian turns, dropping an arm over my shoulder. "I gotta drive my *girlfriend* home." He smirks, leading me back toward the school parking lot.

"I think that sounds good," I say, snuggling into his side.

"Which part?" he asks, looking down at me with a wide smile.

"The girlfriend part."

I hate how incredibly giddy I probably seem, but I can't help it. Sebastian just pulls so many emotions from me all at once that I have a hard time keeping them all under wraps.

"Well good, because I intend to keep calling you that." He winks, pulling open the Jeep door for me the moment we reach it.

Instead of closing the door like I expect him to, he leans in through the doorframe and kisses me again, snapping my seatbelt in the process.

"Now that I'm your girlfriend, you feel the need to buckle me in?" I giggle against his mouth.

"Gotta make sure my girl is safe," he teases, kissing me again.

"You do this for all your girlfriends?" I ask, brushing my lips against his.

"Well, considering you're the first." He pulls back and winks before giving me the cutest smile.

I don't say anything. I can't. Instead, I watch him step back, shut the door, and cross in front of the Jeep before climbing into the driver's seat. As soon as he's buckled he reaches for my hand, lifting it to his mouth where he places a gentle kiss on the back before resting them in his lap, forcing me to lean slightly into him—which I think is the point.

I can't help the small laugh that escapes my lips as he starts the Jeep and slowly pulls out of his parking spot.

"Something funny?" he questions, his voice playful.

"You're not at all what I expected you to be." I find the words leaving my mouth without actually meaning to say them.

"How so?"

"I don't know, I just always thought you were some conceited asshole," I admit on a shrug. "I never expected you to be so—nice," I admit, a little embarrassed.

"So you've thought about me before last weekend?" he questions, throwing a knowing glance my way.

"I didn't say that," I object, laughter in my voice.

"Oh, but you did. When you said you expected me to be a certain way- which means you've at least thought about what I'd be like. So tell me, Tess, how long has this obsession of yours been going on?" He chuckles, tightening his grip on my hand.

"Obsession?" I blurt. "Can I take back that thing I said about you not being conceded?"

"Nope." He shakes his head. "No take backs."

"And to answer your question, since freshman year," I admit, loving the way his eyes widen at my statement. "Well, your sophomore year," I correct.

"So you..." He lets the beginning of the question hang there.

"Have had a huge crush on you since the first time I saw you two years ago," I admit, looking out the window instead of at him.

"Why didn't you ever say anything?" he asks like it should be that simple.

"Um, because you're Sebastian Baxter," I retort.

"What's that supposed to mean?"

"It means that I didn't believe I had a snail's chance in hell with you," I say dryly, surprised when Sebastian laughs, the action vibrating from deep within his chest.

"Why are you laughing at me?" I ask dramatically, pretending to be offended.

"A snail's chance in hell?" He gives me a sideways glance, fighting off his laughter.

"What?"

"Who says shit like that?" He tries to hide his amusement, but it's written all over his face.

"Well, I do apparently," I huff, crinkling my nose at him as he pulls into the spot in front of my house, managing to put the Jeep into park without letting go of my hand.

He shifts toward me, his demeanor changing so rapidly it takes me a moment to catch up.

"God, you're so damn beautiful," he breathes, the dynamic between us shifting so dramatically I feel like I'm suffering from a case of whiplash.

Heat creeps up my neck and into my cheeks.

There's no way this is real. It's all I can think as those gorgeous hazel eyes hold my gaze. I'm transfixed, mesmerized, and for the life of me, I can't look away.

I find myself uttering my next words without a second thought.

"Do you want to come inside?"

The look that flashes across his face is like a kid on Christmas morning, his smile stretching from ear to ear.

"Okay, but only if you promise to keep your hands to yourself," he warns.

"Why?" I ask innocently, loving this little game we suddenly seem to be playing.

"Because I can't be held responsible for my actions if you touch me, Tess," he says, his voice almost strained.

"I promise to be gentle." I wink, quickly exiting the Jeep before he can even get a response out.

I have no idea where any of that came from, and a nervous knot instantly forms in the pit of my stomach. A part of me is very aware that I'm playing with fire, and yet the other part of me wants to test out the heat—see how close I can get without getting burned. Or maybe I want to just give up and let the flames engulf me altogether.

Lord knows when Sebastian steps up next to me on the porch and looks at me like he's seconds away from devouring me right here on the spot, that's exactly what I want to do. Hell, I'm already holding the match in my hand, ready to set us ablaze.

TESS

It's been a week since I officially became Sebastian Baxter's girlfriend. I wish I could say that slapping a title on what we're doing helped alleviate some of the unwanted attention I've been receiving, but that's simply not the case.

I have learned to somewhat tune out the noise over the last few days. Sebastian was right when he said *people will talk.* I can't control what they say any more than I can control the weather. So I'm trying my best to not let it get to me.

Obviously, sometimes that's easier said than done, but being with Sebastian makes it bearable—worth it even.

When I let the outside noise seep in, I find myself uncertain of more than just our relationship. But all it takes is one smile from his lips and all of that just melts away. It's scary how hard I've fallen for him—and how fast.

I wasn't sure what would come along with being Sebastian's girlfriend, but so far, I've been more than just a little surprised by him. I know he's used to having sex, though we have yet to really discuss the details of his past, so I somewhat expected sex to be something he pursued harder. So far it's been quite the opposite.

I'm the one unable to control myself, and he's the voice of reason. On two different occasions now we've been alone, and both times he's limited it to just kissing despite my effort to push for more. I don't know what it is. It's like when he touches me my mind goes all wonky and everything else just flies out the window.

Last night, while we were home alone in my bedroom, I was sure he was going to take things a step further, but as soon as the make-out session got too heated he made some excuse about a family dinner and high tailed it out of my house. I called him afterward only to have my suspicions confirmed—there was no family dinner.

"I don't want to rush this, Tess. Sex is sex, and I've done it all before. I'm not looking for just another hookup," he had said. "But I'm also a guy, and I only have so much restraint. Do I want to have sex with you?" He had laughed. "It's all I think about—when I'm in the shower, when I'm lying in bed at night, when I was hovering over you in your bedroom and you were looking up at me with those big blue eyes. Fuck, Tess. You have no idea how much I want you. That's why I had to leave. I don't trust myself not to think with the wrong head." Even remembering his words causes my skin to prickle.

What he said next affected an entirely different organ. "But you mean more to me than just sex, and I want to make sure you're one hundred percent ready before we even think about crossing that line."

I swear he steals a little bit more of my heart with every second that passes. I can't help but wonder how long until he's consumed the entire thing completely. I'd be lying if I said I wasn't scared. I'm terrified. But I'm also really, really happy.

Sebastian makes me feel things I've only ever read about in books and seen in movies. I didn't know it was possible to feel so strongly about another person, especially one that I've only really known for about two weeks.

"Tess." I hear Courtney's voice seconds before my bedroom door pushes open and she appears in the doorway.

"Hey." I look up from where I'm sitting on the edge of the bed slipping my shoes on. "I thought you were gonna call me when you were on your way."

Courtney's gone all out for tonight's football game, wearing a white fitted t-shirt with *Blue Devils* printed across the front in blue lettering, her dark hair is piled on top of her head with white and blue ribbon sticking out everywhere.

"I forgot." She shrugs. "What's your mom doing home anyway?" she asks, knowing that my mom is usually at the hospital this late in the evening and was clearly the one who answered the door.

"They're rotating her days off each week now. Apparently, it's a new thing they just started. She'll still be off on Monday, but the other days will be different each week."

"I can't remember the last time she was home on a Friday night," Court observes.

"Probably because it's never happened." I snort, double knotting my shoe strings before standing. "So, how do I look?" I question, holding my arms out so Courtney can get a good look at me.

"Like a girl who's never been to a high school football game before." She laughs, shaking her head at me.

"Why, what's wrong with it?" I look down at my red top and jeans.

"Well, for one the team we're playing's colors are red and black." She chuckles. "Do you not have a Rockfield shirt?"

"You already know I don't," I state dryly, knowing Court probably knows what's in my closet better than I do.

"Well, you can't wear that." She shakes her head, crossing the room toward my closet. She rummages inside for less than twenty seconds before emerging with a blue tank top, throwing the shirt at me. "Here. This is better than nothing. But I gotta say, Tess, if you're gonna date a football player you might want to invest in some school apparel."

"I'll get right on that," I answer in a way that says I probably won't.

I quickly change out of my red top into the blue tank, holding my hands out again once I'm finished. "There. Better?"

"Much." She nods in approval. "I've got some spare ribbon in the car. I can do your hair when we get there."

"I don't think that's necessary." I shake my head, looking from her hair to her face and then back again.

"You look at me like I'm crazy now, just wait until you see what some of the other students do," she warns.

"Hey, girls." My mom appears in my doorway before Courtney can say more.

"Hey, Mom." I smile, grabbing the thin sweater laying over the back of my desk chair and draping it across my arm. Late August in Connecticut is warm, but some nights tend to get a little chilly.

"Just about time for the big game, huh?" She smiles, leaning inside the doorway, crossing her arms in front of her petite frame.

"It's not a *big* game, Mom," I object, hating how annoyingly excited she's been since I asked her yesterday if I could go. "It's just a game."

"Ignore her, Mrs. W," Court interjects. "It's not just a game." She pins her gaze on me. "It's the first game of the season."

"And..."

"And the first game is always one of the biggest, second only to homecoming of course."

"I just can't believe she actually agreed to go," my mom chimes in. "Football games were one of my favorite things to do at your age. I remember we used to paint our faces and wear the most ridiculous outfits." She smiles at the memory.

"Tess just needs to get there and see it all in action. I think she'll really get into the spirit once she sees Sebastian out on the field. Money says the first time that hot shot quarterback boyfriend of hers throws a touchdown I won't be able to get her to sit down," she says to my mom like I'm not standing right next to her.

"I wouldn't hold your breath," I say, knowing that's not likely to happen.

"We'll see." She smiles.

"Speaking of Sebastian, when am I going to get to meet him?" my mom asks as she follows us out of my room and into the living room. "Considering you're not supposed to ride in a car with anyone I haven't met, and I know for a fact he's driven you home at least a couple different times," she reminds me.

I'm honestly surprised this is the first time she's mentioning this fact.

"I know," I say, ignoring the way Courtney's gaze sweeps to my face giving me a look that says—*if she only knew.*

Obviously, my mom has no clue that Sebastian has been here a few times while she was at work, and even though I feel bad for keeping things from her, I also have no intention of telling her.

"He's really busy with football practice right now," I add.

"Well maybe he can come over for dinner Monday," She suggests.

"I will ask, okay?" It's more to pacify her than anything.

"Okay." She doesn't push the issue, though I know this conversation is far from over.

Honestly, my mom is pretty amazing, and I think Sebastian will love her. And I'm certain she'll love him as well. I don't think anyone is immune to the charms of Sebastian Baxter, adults included. But I don't want to put any added pressure on our still very new relationship, so if I can stall for a few more weeks then that's what I plan to do. Lord knows I'm in no rush to meet Sebastian's parents, though I'd be lying if I said I wasn't at least a little curious.

"Here, let me give you a few dollars in case you guys decide to go out to eat or something before you head home." My mom stops us just shy of the door, grabbing a twenty out of her purse that's sitting on the coffee table before extending the bill to me.

"Thanks, Mom." I stuff the money into the back pocket of my jeans.

"You girls have fun, okay." She follows Courtney and me to the door, holding it open until we are both outside on the porch. "And don't be home too late," she adds on.

"We won't. Love you."

"Love you, too." She blows a kiss. "You girls be safe."

"We will." Courtney's the one to answer this time, waiting until my mom is out of earshot before adding, "Safe, but maybe not good." She laughs, shimmying her hips as she crosses around her car to the driver's side.

"You are so ridiculous." I laugh, shaking my head as I slide into the passenger seat.

"You say that now. You just wait until you see Sebastian in his uniform. You may be a virgin still, but I don't think you will be for long. Especially when you see how those tight white pants cling to his…" She gestures between her legs.

"Oh my god, shut up." I smack her arm.

She laughs, throwing me a teasing sideways glance before taking off down the street.

***

Within ten minutes of leaving my house, we are walking through the parking lot toward the high school football stadium. Because I live so close to the school it takes no time at all to get here.

It wouldn't even have taken us this long if it wasn't for Courtney insisting she braid the blue and white ribbon into my hair once we arrived. And while I fought her every step of the way, I have to admit that the way she pulled all my hair into a side braid and weaved the ribbon through it looks pretty amazing.

My stomach flutters with nervous energy as we pay and make our way into the bustling stadium. The space is filled with classmates and parents alike, nearly every one of them wearing something *Blue Devils* related.

Okay, so maybe Courtney was right. I may need to invest in some school apparel if this is what my Friday nights are going to look like for the next several weeks.

Court weaves her arm through mine and pulls me toward the bleachers, but instead of going up into the stands like most everyone else, we stop directly in front of them, next to the fence where the cheerleaders are gathering on the track that wraps around the entire field.

"Court," I say uncomfortably when I catch two cheerleaders specifically giving me a dirty look, one whispering something to the other.

"Don't worry about those bitches," she says loud enough for them to hear her. "They're just jealous because Sebastian wasn't interested in any of their skanky asses."

God love Courtney. She's so unapologetic.

"Oh, don't worry, honey," one of the cheerleaders, Sarah Brock, retorts. "I've already been there and done that."

"Awe, good for you. So tell me what happens next? Because clearly, he didn't care enough about what you were offering to keep you around," Courtney taunts, slowly raising her middle finger to flip Sarah off.

"Courtney," I grind out next to her, growing more uncomfortable by the second, "please stop." I plead under my breath.

"You have to put these catty bitches in their place, Tess. Don't let them walk all over you just because they're jealous of what you have." She says the last part significantly louder than the rest, but Sarah and the rest of the cheerleaders have now moved far enough from us that none of them heard her.

"Yeah, I'll remember that," I retort. "Where's Bree anyway?" I ask, swiveling to look behind us.

The stands are packed full of people, but it looks like the majority of students have all congregated on the right side. And boy was Courtney right about what people wear. Tons of people have painted their faces or are wearing handmade shirts and hats in support of the team. Several boys in the front row don't even have shirts on at all. Instead, their entire torsos are painted blue and each one has a different letter painted across their chest in white so that when they all stand together it reads *BLUE DEVILS*.

I never knew how into this people got.

"I talked to her a little while ago. She said she was coming with Blake. Oh, oh, here they come." Courtney pulls my attention back to the field just as the football team erupts from the locker rooms, a blur of blue jerseys as they pass through the banner the cheerleaders are holding.

"Ahhh there's Ant. God, look how hot." Courtney sighs next to me, but I'm too preoccupied looking for Sebastian to really pay attention.

It takes only a few seconds to locate him and the moment I do, my heart goes haywire. He looks impossibly sexy in his uniform. I mean, he always looks mouthwatering, but seeing him like this—his broad shoulders accentuated by shoulder pads and his lean waist defined by tight white football pants. I have to use the back of my hand to wipe my mouth in fear that I might actually be drooling.

I watch him run onto the field, his helmet hanging loosely from his fingers as he circles back around and approaches the bench just a few feet down from where we're standing. Like an electric current that singes every time we're near each other, he looks up, his eyes finding me instantly.

I watch the smile spread across his face seconds before he's taking off in my direction. I ignore the glares I know are being thrown my way from the cheerleaders who have reclaimed their position to my right and give Sebastian my full focus.

"You're here." He stops directly in front of me, the fence barely reaching his chest whereas I can practically rest my chin against the top.

"Where else would I be?" I giggle when he drops his arms over the fence and pulls me into his chest, my feet leaving the ground.

"Fuck, you look good." He smiles, kissing me good and hard for the entire stadium to see.

Someone screams, "Go Tessa," behind us, and I laugh against his mouth.

"Baxter, what do you think you're doing? Get over here?" Coach Jones hollers.

"Uh oh. Busted." Sebastian chuckles, pressing his lips to mine once more before gently setting me to my feet. "I'm getting my good luck on, Coach," he retorts loud enough for the coach to hear him without ever taking his eyes off of me.

"You better get out there, hot shot," I say, smiling like a damn idiot. I can't help it. He makes me so happy I swear I feel like I'm going to burst open and rainbows are going to start flying out of me.

"Stay here. That way I can look over here while I'm on the field and see my girl cheering me on." He tips my chin up with the back of his hand.

"Go. Fight. Win," I say playfully, waving an imaginary pompom in my hand.

The way he smiles at me does more than just make my knees go weak—

it makes my entire body tremble. If melting were a thing, I promise I would be a puddle right now. Nothing can describe how it feels to have someone like Sebastian Baxter look at you the way he's looking at me right now.

"Dinner after?" he asks, backing away from the fence.

"You're buying," I call back, blowing him a kiss just seconds before he takes off toward his team.

"You two are sickening." Courtney fakes annoyance, reminding me that she's still standing next to me.

"Shut up." I don't even attempt to wipe the smile off my face. I have a feeling it's not going anywhere anytime soon anyway.

TESS

"So, what did you think?" Courtney asks as I follow her out to the parking lot.

"It was amazing," I say, still not down from the high I feel after watching Sebastian lead his team to a 35-0 shutout victory.

To say he's amazing would never do that boy justice. I don't know that I've ever seen someone so naturally talented before. The way he commanded that team, the field, all of it—it's comparable to how he controls my heart—effortless.

"See, I knew you'd love it." She gives me her typical *I told you so* face—lips pursed, eyes narrowed.

"How could I not?" I stop next to Courtney's car but make no attempt to climb inside.

We're not leaving yet anyway. We told the boys we'd meet them out here after they got changed so we could all ride over to the restaurant together.

"Sebastian was incredible out there. To see the entire stadium cheering for *my* boyfriend…" I hold my hand over my chest, words failing me.

"*Our* boyfriends," Courtney adds, and it takes several beats for me to catch on to what she's saying.

"Wait—you're official?" I squeak, beyond excited for my best friend who has put up with enough of her fair share from Ant over the past few weeks.

"As of ten minutes ago." Her smile is so wide it practically stretches from ear to ear.

"That's what he whispered to you as he was leaving the field?" I question.

Even though Sebastian had stopped by to lay a celebratory kiss to my lips and I was a bit pre-occupied, I still managed to pick up on the quick interaction that took place between Court and Ant, leaving my confident friend looking rather winded. I was too distracted at the time to address it, but now I can see why for a brief moment she looked like she might faint. She probably thought this day would never come. Lord knows I didn't.

Don't get me wrong, Ant seems like an okay guy, and I know that Sebastian is really close to him, but the way he's been stringing Court along has put a bit of a bad taste in my mouth where he's concerned. Maybe now he can redeem himself.

Courtney nods excitedly, biting down on her bottom lip.

"Congratulations." I immediately pull her in for a hug. "I'm so happy for you," I say over her shoulder before releasing her and taking a step back. "It's about time."

"Girl, you're telling me." She blows out a breath. "I was starting to believe this was my life, chasing after a guy who had no intention of taking things to the next level. I've gotta be honest, I was nearing my breaking point."

"I could tell," I respond truthfully.

I know Courtney better than anyone, and while some may be blinded by her tough exterior, I know that deep down she's just as sensitive as me—maybe even more so—though she would never admit it.

"This is so amazing. Look at us, dating best friends who are also both stars on the football team. This is going to be one hell of a school year," she practically sings. "We can double date, go to homecoming together, spend our weekends hanging at Sebastian's. Then there's prom, of course."

"You're getting a little ahead of yourself there aren't ya?" I laugh, shaking my head. "Sebastian and I are so new; I don't know that I'd be making plans for prom when school just started."

"Shut up, you two are going to be together forever." She swipes her hand through the air.

"Cause that's not premature or anything." I roll my eyes at her, even though deep down a part of me feels like I could do forever with Sebastian.

"Whatever. You're crazy about that boy, and he's just as crazy about you. Look at you." She points to the smile on my face that's always there anytime we talk about Sebastian. "You're already head over heels, and you probably don't even know it."

"It's only been two weeks." I try to deny my feelings even though I know she's got me spot on.

"People fall in love after an hour."

"Yeah, in the movies," I retort.

"Go ahead, deny it all you want. You forget I know you. I'm not saying you're ready to start writing wedding vows or anything, but you're definitely falling for him."

"So what if I am? You're just as into Ant."

"The difference between you and me is that I own that shit, too. Hell yes, I'm into Anthony. Have you seen that boy? Besides, he's killer in bed." She wiggles her eyebrows at me.

"Here we go." I laugh. "It always comes back to sex."

"Because sex is very important. Just wait, you'll see." Her gaze flips behind me and an instant smile takes over her face.

I know the boys are heading our way before I even turn around and see them approaching. The second I do, I swear all the wind leaves my body. Sebastian is dressed in a plain white tee with dark jeans, his blond hair still wet from the shower, a cocky smile pulling up one side of his mouth as he closes the distance between us.

"There's my girl," he says, swooping me up the second he reaches me. Once again, my feet leave the ground as he secures me against his chest. "You miss me?"

"Miss you? I just saw you fifteen minutes ago." I giggle when he drops his face to my neck and breathes in. "God, you smell good." He pulls back and something intense flashes through his eyes.

My stomach bottoms out, and that tight coil in my lower belly returns with a vengeance. One look—that's all it ever takes with Sebastian.

"So do you." I run a hand through his messy wet hair.

"Are you two about done yet?" We both turn our heads toward Ant's voice. He's standing next to Court, arm draped across her shoulders, looking at us like we couldn't be any more annoying.

"Not quite," Sebastian answers, his eyes back on me. "Why don't you ride with Courtney, and Tess and I will meet you guys at *Perchatellies*?" he suggests, lowering me to my feet but not taking his gaze off me.

"If it means I don't have to watch you two, hell yes. Come on, Court," I hear him say, followed by the opening of a car door.

"We'll see you there, Tess," Courtney calls out, and this time I give her my attention, nodding, and throwing her a small wave before Sebastian is leading me toward the back of the parking lot.

"So, how was it?" he asks, looking down at me as we make our way to his Jeep. "Your first game I mean?"

"Incredible." I smile up at him. "You were *incredible*."

"Well, I had some motivation." He winks, pulling open the passenger side door of the Jeep the second we reach it. He waits until I'm firmly planted inside before shutting it and crossing to the driver's side.

"Did you now?" I continue the conversation as soon as he's settled in next to me.

"Hell yes. I had the most beautiful girl in the whole school cheering me on, and I had to make her proud."

"Really, sounds like a pretty lucky girl," I tease.

"Not nearly as lucky as I am." He throws me a wink as he backs the Jeep out of its parking spot.

"I think that depends on who you ask." I wait until he's pulling out of the parking lot before responding. "And I was—proud of you I mean. You were amazing out there. I've never seen anything like it."

"I love it." He shrugs, his gaze focused on the road.

"Do you think you might want to try to go pro one day?" I ask, not missing the way he shifts next to me.

"I don't know. I doubt it. I mean, I love the game and I definitely want to play college ball, but I'm not sure I love it enough to try to make it a career. The life of a pro athlete is too uncertain."

"Then why play college ball? Isn't that usually the end goal? To play pro?" I ask, just wanting to understand better.

"Not always. A lot of players do it to help pay tuition. Playing college ball gives me the freedom to go to school where I want and not where my parents' think I should go. If I get a scholarship to play ball then it takes away all their power."

"Where do they want you to go?"

"Ivy league. My father thinks that's the only way to get a good education. But I don't agree, and I have no desire to follow in his footsteps."

"So where do you want to go?" I ask, for the first time realizing just how short our time together actually is.

It's nearly September. Sebastian will graduate in May and then comes college. I, on the other hand, am stuck here for another year at least.

"I want to go somewhere South. I've applied to LSU and Miami so far, but I think I'll also submit to Georgia and Alabama just in case my first two choices don't work out."

"Why South?"

"Because they have amazing football and educational programs. I mean, there's more colleges, they're all over the country, but I've always pictured myself playing at LSU; that's my top pick."

"Well, they'd be crazy not to want you," I say, ignoring the sudden heavy feeling in the pit of my stomach.

"Thank you." He throws me a sideways smile, reaching over to squeeze my thigh. "What about you, you know where you want to go to school after you graduate next year?" he asks.

"Columbia," I answer without hesitation.

"Wow. Just like that. Not an ounce of hesitation." He chuckles.

"I've always wanted to live in New York. I've known for as long as I can remember that, that's where I want to go school. My dad went to Columbia. It's how he met my mom. She was a nursing student and doing her clinical hours at the hospital not far from campus. My dad came into the ER needing stitches in his knee after he busted it open jumping off a second story landing at a frat party." I chuckle at the story my mom has told me at least a hundred times.

"Sounds like he was my kinda guy." Sebastian picks up my hand and kisses the back of it. "So Columbia it is..."

"Well, if I can get in."

"You will."

"How do you know?" I ask, my eyes locked on the side of Sebastian's face.

He slows the vehicle, pulling into the parking lot of *Perchatellies*, not bothering to answer my question until he's parked. He shuts off the engine before turning toward me.

"Because if there's one thing I've learned in the short time I've known you it's that you are extremely smart and driven. If you say Columbia is where you're going, I have no doubt that's exactly where you'll end up."

"I wish I shared your optimism." I force a smile.

"There you go again." He reaches over and tugs on the end of my braid. "Always doubting yourself."

"Sorry." I blow out a breath, knowing he's right. It's something I know I need to work on.

"One day, Tessa Wilson, you're going to see what the rest of the world does, and I hope like hell I'm around when that day comes."

"Planning on going somewhere?" I cock my head to the side, eyes questioning.

"Not a fucking chance." He smiles, leaning forward to press a kiss to my mouth.

Per usual, the second our lips meet, what was meant to be a quick, innocent kiss morphs into something else entirely. It's like there's this live wire that dances between us, and the second we connect we spark an electrical current that's impossible to break.

I shift in my seat, seconds away from crawling into Sebastian's lap when a loud knock sounds against the driver's side window.

Like being doused in cold water, we instantly break apart, both of your gazes turning toward the window.

"Let's go," I hear Ant, followed by another pound.

"We're coming," Sebastian hollers back before his gaze once again locks on me. "Remind me again why the hell I'm friends with that douche bag," Sebastian groans, sliding his thumb against my now semi-swollen bottom lip.

"I don't know." I barely get the words out, my pulse still vibrating through me. "But we should probably go," I say, resisting the urge to suck his thumb into my mouth.

What the hell is wrong with me?

"Yeah, you're probably right. To be continued…"

"To be continued," I agree, pushing open the passenger door and climbing out.

The second my feet hit the pavement I spot Court and Ant waiting at the back the Jeep, arms draped around each other.

I smile at my friend, loving how happy she looks.

"Who else is meeting us here?" I hear Sebastian ask just as I step around the Jeep and join them.

"I think most of the team—looks like a few are already here." Ant gestures to all the cars in the parking lot of the old family-owned pizza parlor. "You guys ready?"

"Yes." I'm the first one to answer, taking Sebastian's hand when he offers it to me.

We follow Ant and Court through the parking lot and then inside the small restaurant which is bustling with high school students, most wearing still wearing their Blue Devils attire.

The second Sebastian steps through the door, voices pull us in every direction.

"There he is."

"Great game tonight, Sebastian."

"You looked incredible out there tonight, Sebastian."

He just nods and smiles like it's an everyday occurrence for him. Meanwhile, I'm shrinking smaller and smaller behind him as he leads me through the restaurant. He finally stops at the far corner booth where a couple guys from the team are sitting along with Bree, who I'm instantly surprised to see.

"What the hell?" Courtney gets to her before me. "I thought you were joining us for the game."

"Sorry, something came up." She shrugs, patting the booth next to her. I immediately slide in, feeling Sebastian's hand on my leg the moment he settles next to me.

"Where's Blake?" I ask, watching something flash across her face before her carefree smile once again falls back into place.

"He had to take off." She shrugs, taking a drink from the soda glass in front of her.

"You okay?" I lower my voice, knowing something's off.

"Yeah, I'm fine. We just got a little *preoccupied.*" She says it in a way that I know instantly means they were having sex. "Anyway, we missed the game and instead of taking me home I asked him to drop me here. Since I bailed on the game, thought I'd at least come hang out for dinner."

"And he decided not to come?" I question, knowing how Blake can be.

I don't know why but the thought of him dropping her off where all the football players are hanging out and not accompanying her inside doesn't quite sit right with me. He rarely lets her go anywhere without being glued to his side. It doesn't seem like the healthiest relationship, but anytime anyone says anything about it Bree jumps to Blake's defense.

Courtney and I have gotten to the point now where we just keep our mouths shut. If Bree is happy then that's all that matters anyway. Though more and more recently, she hasn't really seemed all that happy.

"Wasn't feeling well." She shrugs, quickly changing the subject. "So tell me about the game. Sebastian, I hear you were on fire tonight." She directs her attention to where Sebastian is sitting next to me.

"I did okay." He leans inward, knocking his shoulder against mine.

"Yeah, okay as in he threw four of the five touchdowns tonight." I roll my eyes at him.

"Always talking me up." He smiles, dropping a kiss to my temple. "Keep this up, and I might end up with a big head."

"Might?" I tease.

"You two…" Bree shakes her head, pulling my attention back to her.

"Why do people keep saying that?" I question, looking at Sebastian for answers. "You two, like we have some kind of disease."

"Maybe because y'all are sickeningly sweet together." Bree pretends to gag.

"Oh, whatever." I laugh, shoving her shoulder.

"I'm serious. You two are like the poster children for a fucking teenage

Hallmark movie." She rolls her eyes playfully.

I'm seconds away from spitting back some half ass attempt at a rebuttal when the waitress appears. By the time we're all done ordering and she leaves again, an entirely new conversation is going on around the table.

From there, the rest of the evening went on much like the first. Various people came to our table, talking to Sebastian and some of the other players about the game. A few random girls stopped by and much to my surprise, every time a new one showed up, Sebastian inched closer to me. By the end of the night, we were practically sitting on each other's laps, not that I minded.

Bree only stayed about an hour. After excusing herself to take a phone call, she disappeared shortly after. Court and Ant seemed like they were in their own little world for most of the night, which was totally fine by me because it meant I got more Sebastian time.

While I was nervous for my first night out in public as Sebastian's girlfriend, I have to admit I liked the attention of being on his arm more than I thought I would. Unlike at school, most of the people who surrounded us for a good portion of the night were actual friends of Sebastian's and as such, accepted me with no more than an introduction.

126

It was like being Sebastian's girlfriend was an automatic acceptance into the cool kid's club. The whole night was kind of surreal.

By the time Courtney and I arrived back at my house just after eleven, I kind of felt like the entire experience was just some weird dream, and I'd wake up tomorrow having realized that none of it actually happened.

That's what being with Sebastian is like—one big dream. And it's a dream I never, ever, want to wake up from.

Twelve

TESS

"Tess." The second I hear Dylan's voice behind me my entire body tenses.

It's been three weeks since our last altercation—the one that resulted in me becoming Sebastian's girlfriend. And while that day ended way better than it started, that doesn't mean I'm in any rush to go another round with my ex.

"What do you want, Dylan?" I sigh, shutting my locker before turning toward him.

He's standing just a couple feet to my right, hands shoved in the pockets of his jeans. Normally I might have swooned a little bit at the sight of him; Dylan has always been good looking, but the face that once made my heart beat faster now only makes my stomach turn.

I guess having things put into perspective will do that for you. He may be attractive, but that's where his pleasantries end. And he has nothing on Sebastian, who always looks like he just stepped out of a magazine.

"I was hoping we could talk." His voice is soft, hesitant even, and it instantly causes a nervous knot to form in the pit of my stomach.

"About?" I go for annoyance.

I mean, I am annoyed. Annoyed that he can't just go away and leave me in peace. Annoyed that he waited until I was interested in someone else before even offering a semblance of an apology—which was ruined when he continued to speak. Annoyed that he thinks I owe him anything after everything he put me through.

"Us." He says it like it should be obvious.

A weird cackle escapes my throat, and I look at Dylan for a long moment, slinging my book bag over my shoulder.

"There is no us, Dylan. Or did you forget that now that Taylor isn't up your ass?" Even I'm shocked by how smooth the statement leaves my mouth. Normally I'd stutter and stammer, my nerves getting the better of me.

Not anymore… I'm done letting this asshole walk all over me.

Tess—one. Dylan—zero.

Damn, I like this.

"Come on. Don't be like that." He wastes no time coming after me when I push past him down the hallway, heading for the exit.

"Be like what, Dylan?" I spit, keeping my gaze focused ahead. "Don't stand up for myself. Don't hold a grudge when you completely screwed me over and made me look an idiot. What exactly don't you want me to be like, Dylan? Huh? Tell me because I sure as hell would like to know," I hammer out, not stopping until I've pushed my way outside, Dylan right on my heels.

"Tess." He abruptly stops as soon as we reach the parking lot and for whatever reason I find myself stopping with him. "I'm sorry, okay." His gaze drops to the ground the moment I turn toward him.

"You're sorry?" The question is riddled with attitude, but I can feel my anger waning. I've never been one to stay mad at people.

"I fucked up, Tess. I fucked up bad." He takes a step toward me and then another, closing the distance between us. "I miss you."

When he reaches for me I take a full step back, holding my hand out between us.

"You should have thought about that, Dylan." I stand my ground. "I'm with Sebastian now. And even if I wasn't, there's no way I'd ever take you back."

"He's just going to hurt you," he threatens.

"Like you did?" I snarl. "He wouldn't do that."

"How the fuck do you know? Just because he's whispering sweet nothings into your ear doesn't mean he doesn't have a hidden agenda. Come on, Tess, open your fucking eyes. He's using you."

"Go fuck yourself, Dylan." I spin back around, done with this whole situation.

I'm so mad that when his hand wraps around my forearm seconds later preventing me from walking away, I have to physically restrain myself from swinging around and hitting him.

"Why the fuck are you so quick to pass judgment on me, and yet you won't even look at all the shit *he's* pulled?"

"Because he's never hurt me," I grind out, ripping my arm away. "My answer is no, Dylan. I'm not going to give you a second chance. I'm not interested in hearing any more of your half-assed apologies. I'm done. Do you hear me? Done!" I practically scream in his face.

"You fucking bitch. You think he's so different, do you? Just wait. It's gonna be an epic fucking show when you finally realize what everyone else already knows—he's only with you to fuck you."

"Why do you even care?" I can't control the tremble in my voice. "My life doesn't concern you anymore. Leave me alone, Dylan. For the last time, just leave me alone."

He's pushing me toward my breaking point, and the look on his face tells me he knows exactly what he's doing. And what's worse—he's enjoying watching me come unraveled.

"You're such a fucking…" It's all he gets out before a fist comes out of nowhere connecting with Dylan's jaw, causing his head to snap back.

He falls to the ground, his eyes wide in surprise. It all happens so quickly I barely have time to process any of it.

Sebastian is on top of Dylan in a second, punching him so hard that blood instantly spurts from Dylan's nose and mouth, staining the concrete below him. He tries to fight back, but Sebastian is too strong, too quick, and Dylan's efforts are pointless.

I open my mouth, try to tell Sebastian to stop, but I'm not entirely sure any words come out. I can feel eyes on us everywhere, but I can't seem to make myself move.

Do something, Tess!

"Sebastian." I finally find my voice, gripping his shoulder in an effort to pull him off of Dylan.

"You motherfucker," he seethes, laying another hard blow to the side of Dylan's face.

"Sebastian." I try again, his entire body tensing this time. He freezes with his fist still extended in the air. "Please stop."

His face turns toward me, the rage in his eyes softening the moment he registers my face.

"Stop." I mouth.

He looks at me for another long moment and then looks back down at Dylan who's holding his nose, trying to control the blood pouring from it.

At first, I think he might hit him again, but instead, he leans down—his voice so low I have to strain to hear it.

"If you even so much as look at Tess again I will fucking kill you. Do you understand me?" He waits until Dylan nods furiously before climbing off him, but the action is too late.

Teachers swarm our position, one swooping down to help Dylan while two others back Sebastian away, telling him to calm down.

I look back and forth between the two of them, wondering how in the hell something so small turned into something this big. Dylan just wanted to talk. I should've just said no and walked away. Instead, I stood there and let him get me riled up. I should've known he'd intentionally push my buttons.

Then again, I never expected Sebastian to see the altercation, let alone jump in and do something about it. I watch helplessly as the two teachers lead Sebastian back into the school; if I had to guess I'd say he's headed straight for the principal's office. He doesn't look at me even once, disappearing inside seconds later with his head tilted toward the ground.

Dylan is helped to his feet and ushered inside after him; they'll no doubt take him to the nurse first. His face looks like someone stomped on it with a big combat boot over and over again.

My stomach twists violently as the events seem to catch up with me, and if it weren't for Bree showing up just at the right moment, I might have lost the contents of my stomach all over the school's parking lot.

"Are you okay?" She immediately pulls me into her arms.

"You saw?" I tremble in her embrace, the adrenaline pumping through my veins catching up to me.

"I did." She slides her hand over my hair in a soothing gesture. "What the hell happened?" She finally pulls back, her hands on my shoulders as she looks at me.

"I don't know," I answer truthfully. "I don't even know where Sebastian came from. It was like he appeared out of thin air." I shake my head, trying to clear the fog. "Dylan was being Dylan, taking jabs at me just because he can. The next thing I know he's on the ground and Sebastian is on top of him beating the hell out of him." Tears spill from my eyes, and I swipe at them angrily. "What's going to happen to him?"

"Sebastian?" Bree questions, continuing when I nod. "He's probably looking at a few days suspension at least. Probably won't be allowed to play in the next few games either. Man…" She blows out a breath.

"He won't be allowed to play?" I question, guilt knocking into me like a round of bullets hitting me in all the right places.

"Let's just wait and see, okay?" She drops her arm over my shoulder and leads me back toward the school. "Come on. I'll wait with you."

***

"Are you fucking kidding me right now, Sebastian?" His father's voice practically vibrates the office windows next to where Bree and I are sitting.

I knew who he was the second he entered the room. Tall and broad, like Sebastian, with edged features and the same medium blond hair. But unlike Sebastian—whose eyes are kind and smile is easy—his father is hardened and stern.

I've been sitting here for the last thirty minutes waiting to find out what's going to happen. The second Sebastian's dad walked in looking like he was ready to kill someone, I knew it was going to be bad. But I never expected to witness him talk to his son the way he is right now.

"Do you have any idea how bad this looks to colleges? You're not a fucking child. Why would you do something so stupid?"

In the entire time he's been in there, I have yet to hear Sebastian say one word. Either his responses are quiet or he simply isn't answering, which one it is I'm not sure.

Bree sits next to me, her hand wrapped around mine. She squeezes a little tighter every time Sebastian's father speaks, like somehow that's going to make it better.

My stomach has been twisted in the same ugly knot since everything happened and seems to get harder and harder with each minute that passes.

I tried to talk to Ms. Shamin, the vice principal, to tell her what happened, but she wasn't interested in hearing what I had to say. According to her, Sebastian attacked Dylan unprovoked and would receive the punishment the principal felt appropriate.

Dylan, though just as guilty in my mind, was in her office for less than three minutes before he was excused to go home. I didn't have to ask if he got into trouble too, I already knew he hadn't, which only makes this whole situation that much worse.

Sebastian's in there right now getting screamed at and probably suspended—if not kicked off the football team—

and here I sit, the one who's responsible for it all, helpless to do anything.

I jump when the office door swings open without warning and Mr. Baxter comes storming out, his pressed suit tight against his flexed shoulders. Sebastian follows shortly after, his eyes widening when they land on my face. Clearly, he hadn't expected me to stay.

I stand, seconds away from saying something when Sebastian gives his head a quick shake, as if to tell me not to, before following his father out of the office.

The pressure in my chest constricts my ability to breathe freely, and for a moment I struggle to pull in a breath.

"He's gonna be okay," Bree says, standing next to me.

Flipping my gaze toward her, I manage to suck in a deep inhale and let it out slowly.

"Come on, let's get out of here. There's nothing more we can do here." She links her arm through mine and leads me out of the office without another word.

I wish we would've waited a few minutes longer because when I look up to see Sebastian following his father down the empty hallway, his head lowered in defeat, I feel like someone has just hit me in the chest with a baseball bat.

It takes everything in me not to run to him. I want to tell him I'm sorry. I want to make sure he's okay. I want to pull him against me and tell him that nothing his father said is true. But I can't do any of those things at the risk of just making the situation worse.

So instead of going after them, I allow Bree to lead me in the opposite direction where we exit on the other side of the building.

Courtney pulls up to the curb just as we step outside into the warm afternoon sun. I look at Bree who smiles reassuringly and tugs me toward the car. I don't have to ask, I know she must have text Courtney and asked her to come back and get us. My two best friends are nothing if not dependable.

The ride home is a bit of a blur. I'm too worried about Sebastian to really participate in the conversation. I only half listen to Bree filling Courtney in on what happened. I offer a yeah or a nod when asked but offer nothing more.

The five-minute drive feels like it takes forever and yet no time at all. All I want to do is call Sebastian but I know that even if I do, he's not likely to answer.

"Tess, did you hear me?" I register Courtney's voice, turning my head to where she's sitting next to me in the driver's seat.

"What?"

"Do you want us to come in for a while? Keep you company?" she repeats since clearly, I didn't hear her the first time.

"No, that's okay." I reach for the door handle. "I just wanna be alone right now if that's okay."

"Of course." She nods. "I'll talk to Ant, see if he hears anything. Let us know as soon as you talk to Sebastian."

"I will," I agree, pushing the door open.

"And, Tess." Court stops me before I even get one leg out of the car. "None of this is your fault. Dylan had an ass beating coming. Don't beat yourself up over this like I know you probably will."

"Then why even tell me not to if you already know I'm going to?" I ask, feeling something other than dread and sadness for the first time since this whole situation spiraled out of control.

"Honestly, I have no freaking clue." She laughs. "Call me later, okay?"

"I will." I climb out of the car. "And thank you," I say, turning around just as Bree climbs into the front seat.

"Anytime, you needy bitch." She gives me a wide smile, her normal demeanor slipping back into place.

That's one of the things I love the most about Bree. She can be serious when she needs to be but as soon as the moment passes, she's back to her spitfire, crazy ass self.

"And you better call me, too," She calls after me through the open window as I turn to walk away.

"You know I will." I throw a half wave before jogging up to the front door and pushing my way inside.

The moment the lock latches behind me, I press my back to the door and let out a slow breath, fighting back the tears that once again threaten to spill.

"Tess." I hear my mom's voice seconds before she appears in the living room, concern taking over her face the second she sees me. "What happened? What's wrong?"

That's all it takes before I fall apart into a blubbering mess.

Mom jumps into action, quickly pulling me into her side and leading me to the couch. I should've known that one look at my mother and I would fall apart. She's always been the one person I can't hide my emotions from.

I spend the next half hour telling her everything that happened. By the time I'm done I expect her to tell me she doesn't want me seeing Sebastian anymore, so what she says instead has my jaw almost hitting the floor.

"Sounds like Dylan got what was coming to him."

"Mom!" I can't hide the shock from my voice.

"What? You don't agree?" She smiles, tucking my hair over my shoulder.

"I mean, I do. Obviously. But aren't you supposed to say something like— violence is never the answer, or nothing was ever solved from fighting or some other parental nonsense."

"Would it matter if I did?" She pulls me close, resting her head against mine. "Bottom line, Sebastian was protecting my baby. And that will never be frowned upon in my book," she says, turning her face to kiss my temple.

"So you're not going to make me stop seeing him?" I question, turning to look at her.

"Make you stop seeing him?" She gawks. "I'd be more likely to award him with some kind of medal."

This pulls the first smile from me since I walked through the front door.

"Now stop procrastinating and invite that boy over for dinner. I think after today I should at least get to meet him already," she adds, bumping her shoulder against mine.

"You're a pretty perfect mom, you know that?"

"It's easy when you have a pretty perfect daughter." She smiles, abruptly standing from the couch. "Now go, text that boy and find out if everything is okay, and I'm gonna go order us some Chinese food before I have to get ready for work."

"Hey, Mom," I call just as she reaches the foyer, "thank you."

She offers nothing more than a nod and a warm smile, but it does so much to calm the earthquake inside of me.

It's not lost on me how lucky I am to have her. The thought once again brings Sebastian to the forefront of my mind. The way his father spoke to him— the clearly dysfunctional dynamic of their relationship—it makes me sad to think that this is what he deals with on a daily basis.

My mom has never spoken to me the way his father did today. And while I don't remember much about my own father, I can't see him being the type of man who would do that either, otherwise, my mom never would've married him.

I don't know what I would do if I didn't have my mom to fall back on, which in turn makes me wonder—who does Sebastian have?

SEBASTIAN

"Why the fuck do you think he does shit like this?" My father's voice echoes through the house.

I can see him now. Pacing back and forth in his study, my mom sitting in the corner chair with her nose turned in the air like he's to blame for everything and she's never done anything wrong in her life.

They're fucking delusional—both of them.

If I could strive to be one thing in life it would be to be the polar opposite of both of my parents'. There's a reason I want complete control over my future, because any future where they're involved in is a future I don't want to be a part of.

I've spent too many years trying to please them, be the son I thought they wanted. Not anymore. Hell, I don't give a shit if they hate me at this point, which given their current argument I would guess is a distinct possibility.

"You tell me, you're his father." My mom's voice comes out calm but laced with bitterness. I'm sure it's killing her to even be sitting in the same room as the man she's married to.

Why they're still together is beyond me. I can't imagine staying with someone I couldn't stand to be around for more than five minutes.

Tess's face instantly flashes through my mind, and the sickening feeling in my stomach tightens. The way she looked at me as I was leaving the office, like she didn't know whether to be sorry or feel sorry for me. I hate that I put that look there. I hate that I made her feel like she was somehow responsible for the way I went at Dylan.

Truth be told, I really didn't think it through.

I saw him grab her arm and all I saw was red. I don't even know what they were saying to each other when I reared back and cocked him right in the face. Once the first contact was made, I couldn't stop.

All I could think is that he hurt her, he continues to try to hurt her, and all I wanted to do was hurt him in return.

I don't regret fucking up his face for even a second, but I do regret how it all went down and how I left Tess standing in that office like she was seconds away from bursting into tears.

Had my father not taken my phone the second we left school, I would've already called her to reassure her that none of this was her fault. I know she's probably blaming herself, and it fucking kills me that I can't do anything to reassure her right now.

"Don't pin this on me!" my father roars, pulling me back to the argument taking place in the next room over. "You're his mother. You're the one who couldn't wait to have children when in all reality you just wanted to tighten the fucking noose around my neck."

"As if you're any better. Traveling all the time, disappearing with your little whores for days on end. Do you blame me for never wanting to be here?"

"Because you want for so much. Why the fuck did I move my firm halfway across the country? Why did I buy you this big expensive house? So you could spend all *my* money going to spas and fucking spirit retreats that are more like male-themed whore houses. Fuck all your problems away, do they?"

"Fuck you, Jonathan. You did this for you. Don't for one second pretend like this wasn't all about you. I didn't want to come here. Sebastian didn't want to come here. But we did anyway. *You* dragged us halfway across the country for what *you* could get out of it. Let's not pretend like it was for any other reason." My mother's voice never changes.

Happy or sad, mad or elated—she always has the same dry tone. I think it's because she doesn't actually feel real emotion anymore. Trust me—if you knew even the half of the shit show that is this family, you'd know I'm right.

"Watch your mouth, Lydia. You may think you're untouchable, but this is still my fucking house."

"*Our* house," she corrects him calmly, not missing a beat.

"Well, if you want it to stay that way you better do something about *your* son," he retorts, a snarl in his voice.

"I don't know what you want me to do with him."

I know my father told me to stay put, but at this point, I have no desire to listen to this shit any longer. They'll probably be at this for hours anyway. That's typically how it goes. They'll spend weeks not speaking to one another and then once they are forced to be in the same room together, everything boils over.

Making a beeline for the foyer, I grab my car keys from the side table before pushing my way through the door.

The alarm beeps twice the second it swings open, and I wait for a moment to make sure no one heard it. True to his nature, my father is too busy continuing his lecture to my mother about what an awful son she's raised to even notice.

Quietly closing the door behind me, I hop in the black Alfa Romeo my dad bought me less than three months ago—another attempt to keep me happy and quiet. I guess he figures if he gives me whatever I want that it will somehow make up for the fact that he's a sorry ass excuse for a dad.

I usually prefer my Jeep anyway, but considering it's still sitting in the school parking lot where my father insisted we leave it, I don't really have a choice. I'm sure it will be back in the driveway before morning. My father will no doubt send one of his minions over to pick it up.

The second I slide behind the wheel, I fire the engine to life and take off like a bat out of hell. The further I get away from this fucking house the better.

I know exactly where I'm going without even thinking about it—because there's only one person I want to see.

Tess.

***

The sun has started to set, casting an orange glow over Tess' small white ranch. I've been sitting outside, two houses down from her house for over an hour now. I'm considering sneaking around the back of the house and knocking on her bedroom window just as her mom comes out the front door and climbs into her car.

Thank fuck.

Yes, I could've just gone up and knocked on the door, but considering I haven't officially met her mom, and after everything that happened today, I thought it best to wait.

Besides, for all I know, she's already banned Tess from seeing me ever again. Not that I'd blame her. I have a tendency to fuck up everything good in my life. Why would my relationship with Tess be any different?

The first girl I've ever really cared about and less than a month into it I'm already showing my true colors.

I wish I could say I'm not that guy—the guy who loses his temper and reacts rashly—but I am. This is *not* the first time that I've acted first and asked questions later.

Letting out a slow breath, I climb out of the car as soon as I see Tess' mom's taillights disappear around the corner. Shoving my hands in my pockets, I make my way up to her front door—staring at the chipped paint for a long moment before finally working up the nerve to knock.

The door opens seconds later and the look on Tess' face nearly knocks me back a few steps. Her pale face is flush, and there's a sense of immense relief that washes over me when her eyes glaze over and a wide smile spreads across her mouth.

"Took you long enough." Her arms are around my neck before I can even form a response, and fuck me if she doesn't feel perfect pressed up against me.

"I'm sorry," I mutter into her hair, inhaling her sweet scent. "I wanted to wait until your mom was gone," I explain, pulling back to cup her face. "I can't imagine she's very happy with me right now."

"Are you kidding?" Tess giggles, and I swear to god it's my favorite sound in the whole world. My god, the things this girl is doing to me. "She is far from mad at you. Between you and me, she never cared for Dylan."

I kiss her right there on the spot for no other reason than I just want to feel her lips pressed against mine.

She melts into my body like she always does, not an ounce of hesitation. I can't describe what that does to me, knowing that what she witnessed earlier today didn't change the way her body responds to me.

I was worried she'd be scared of me or hesitant at least. I can't imagine watching me go crazy like that was easy for her. Hell, if it wasn't for her stopping me, I might have actually killed the fucker.

Backing her into the foyer, I kick the door closed and continue my assault on her mouth, never wanting to stop kissing her, but all too soon she's pulling back, looking up at me with those big blue eyes that make it hard for me to think straight.

"Before I forget, Mom wanted me to invite you over for dinner Monday."

"Meeting the mom," I tease, rubbing my nose against hers. "Does that mean you're planning on keeping me around?"

"Just try and get rid of me." She crinkles her nose adorably before wrapping her hand around the back of my neck and pulling my mouth back down to hers.

"Not a chance," I say between kisses.

"So is that a yes then?" She giggles.

"Hell yes," I mutter against her lips before adding, "I'm so sorry."

"Don't apologize." She pulls back slightly.

"I have to, Tess. I don't know what came over me," I try to explain but she places two fingers over my mouth, silencing me.

"It's okay. I don't care about how or why it happened. I just need to know that you're alright."

145

And just like that, she chips another piece of my protective wall away.

"Me? I'm more worried about you." I cup her face in my hands. "I saw how scared you were in the office. I'm so fucking sorry that I frightened you."

"I wasn't scared of you. I was scared for you. Your dad—he's a bit…"

"Of an asshole." I snort, letting my hands fall away. "Trust me, I know."

"I was going to say intimidating but yes, asshole will work." She grins. "Are you hungry? Mom ordered a ton of Chinese food, but I wasn't hungry at the time."

"Starving." I smile, allowing her to lead me into the kitchen.

***

"Is he always like that?" Tess speaks after several minutes of silence, her fingers mindlessly tracing circles across my stomach.

"My father?" I question, looking down to where her head is lying against my chest, her tiny frame tucked perfectly against mine.

"The way he talked to you." She says it almost apologetically, like she's sorry for even bringing it up again.

It's almost one in the morning, and neither of us have spoken about what happened today beyond the small discussion when I first arrived. Instead of making me feel worse about everything, she's actually made it her mission to make me feel better.

After stuffing me full of Chinese food, we snuggled up on the couch and watched reruns of *Family Guy* for a good three hours, laughing and joking like nothing even happened.

It was just after midnight when we finally made our way to bed. I had every intention of leaving and letting her get some sleep, but Tess insisted I stay and sneak out in the morning. She said she didn't want to be alone, and truthfully neither did I.

That was over an hour ago and since then we've been laying in her bed, limbs tangled together, talking about everything and yet nothing at all at the same time.

"He's not the easiest man to live with, that's for sure," I finally respond after a few long seconds, not really sure what else to say.

"What about your mom?"

"She's not any better. In fact, she might be a little worse. I mean, she doesn't yell at me or tell me what a disappointment I am like my father, but sometimes I think her silence says so much more." I let out a slow breath, not missing the way Tess' grip on me tightens.

"I'm sorry." Her voice is so soft I almost don't hear the words.

"Don't be." I continue to run my fingers through her hair as I speak. "It could be worse."

"How could it be worse?" she asks, looking up at me.

"I could be poor," I joke, laughing when she lays a hard smack to my chest.

"I can't believe you just said that." She squeals when I shift in the bed and she ends up pinned on her back beneath me.

"Would you have preferred I lied to you?" I grin down at her.

"No," she answers seriously, her breath catching when I slowly lower my face to hers and plant a slow lingering kiss to her mouth.

My body once again stirs to attention, and I'm not the only one who's aware of it. When I pull back Tess is looking up at me, gaze hooded, her chest rising and falling at a rapid pace.

"Do you have any idea what you do to me?" I whisper, hovering inches from her face.

"Show me," she challenges, and I damn near lose my shit right on the spot.

It would be so easy for me to take her the way I've taken countless girls before her, but I can tell by the hesitation she tries to hide that she's not there yet. And honestly, that's okay. I mean, it's fucking torture—don't get me wrong. But I can't imagine a sweeter torture than one that I know will end with me getting to claim this girl in a way no one ever has before.

"Not yet." I kiss her again, grinding myself down on top of her.

"Please," she whimpers into my mouth.

"Soon, I promise. But not until you're ready."

"I am ready," she huffs, growing frustrated beneath me.

"No, you're not," I reassure her, trying to stay strong for both of us. "And I'm not going to lose you because you felt rushed into something you weren't ready for." "You're not going to lose me. I want this, Sebastian. I want you."

"God, you're killing me right now." I take a deep breath trying to hold my composure. "Let me ask you something." I hesitate for a brief moment before trailing my hand down the side of her petite body, stopping on her hip. "How far have you gone before?"

Her cheeks instantly flush; even in the dim lighting filtering in through the hallway I can see it. She looks away, unable to meet my gaze.

"Look at me," I challenge, waiting until her eyes meet mine before continuing, "There's nothing to be ashamed of. Tell me the truth."

"Nothing. I've never done anything." She shakes her head from side to side.

"Never?" I ask, both turned on and completely floored by this knowledge. I thought for sure she at least had *some* experience.

"Never." She bites her bottom lip, kneading it between her teeth nervously.

"But Dylan, you must have done something." The last thing I want to do is talk about that douche bag while we're in her bed having such an intimate conversation, but I need to know.

"We just kissed. That's it. It just never felt right with him." She lets out a shaky breath before continuing, "It feels right with you. Please, Sebastian, I want you to be my first—for everything."

"Everything?" I question. "You mean you've never even…" I let the statement hang, my jaw going slack when she shakes her head no.

"I want all my firsts to be with you."

I swear to god I almost come undone.

I shake my head and take a steady inhale. I've never been one to enact control over a situation before, and I have to say—it's fucking hard. Especially with her small body withering beneath me, begging to be taken.

"Make love to me, Sebastian." Her eyes plead right along with her words, but no matter how much I want to, I know it's too soon.

Tess isn't just any other girl, and I have no intention of treating her as such. When I take her—and I will—I want to know that there will not be one ounce of regret over it the next day.

"I will... Soon," I promise. "But not yet." The disappointment plays across every inch of her beautiful face. "But," I quickly add, "there is a first I could take care of in the meantime." I slide my body to the side so I'm positioned next to her.

I graze my fingers slowly up her leg, hesitating for only a second before sliding them up her loose-fitting shorts and then along the seam of her panties. Her eyes widen and her breathing quickens when she realizes what I'm doing, but she doesn't hesitate, spreading her legs wider for me.

"Just close your eyes and breathe, baby," I whisper, nearly losing it the moment my fingers brush against her bare, untouched skin.

TESS

The alarm clock next to my bed wakes me abruptly. Swatting at it until I manage to hit *snooze*, I collapse back down onto my pillow feeling groggy and disoriented. Just as I start to give way to the drowsiness that threatens to pull me back under, everything hits me all at once and my eyes shoot open.

Sebastian. His fingers—the way he touched me, the way he kissed me, the undeniable pleasure he showed me. Pleasure I didn't even know I could feel.

I dart upright, my eyes going directly to where Sebastian was lying next to me when I drifted off to sleep just a few short hours ago. I place my hand on the sheet as I look around the room, wondering how long ago he left. Considering the warmth of the spot he occupied most of the night, I'd say it wasn't all that long ago.

Smiling, I pull the blanket up to my chin, remembering how it felt to open myself up to him in a way I never had before, remembering the things he said as he brought me to the brink and then forced me over the edge. It felt like fireworks had exploded inside of me.

If he can do that with just his fingers, I can only imagine how other parts of him will feel.

My face heats at the thought.

"Tess." I jump when I hear my mother's voice seconds before she opens my bedroom door. Having not realized she was home yet, I quickly try to gain some composure. "Hey, you better get up or you're going to be late for school," she says, peeking her head inside my room.

"Okay." I nod several times in concession, a nervous tick of mine. "I'm getting up now."

"I'm gonna head to bed if you don't need anything." She hesitates in the doorway, and for a moment I feel like maybe she can tell. Maybe she can see on my face what I was up to in this very room just hours ago.

"I'm good." I force a smile. "You get some sleep."

"Okay, honey. Have a good day at school. I love you."

"Love you, Mom." I let out a heavy exhale the moment the door latches between us.

My earlier elation deflates drastically when I remember that I won't get to see Sebastian at school today, or the next four days after today for that matter. He received five days suspension and is being benched for the next two games for his fight with Dylan.

It makes me nervous to have to go back today without him there. I know there's bound to be a ton of talk going on over what happened, and since it was all centered around me, once again I'm going to be surrounded by unwanted attention. Though if I'm being honest, I'm starting to get used to it. I've accepted that it just comes along with dating someone like Sebastian.

Finally managing to pull myself out of my warm bed and into the shower, it only takes me about thirty minutes before I'm on my way out the front door, a cold pop tart and bottle of OJ in hand. Because it took me so long to get going, I don't have enough time to do my normal morning routine which usually consists of me sitting at the kitchen table eating Cinnamon Toast Crunch—one of my biggest weaknesses.

Checking my phone as I lock up the house, I'm seconds away from texting Courtney to see where she is when Sebastian's car pulls up in front of my house.

My body instantly floods with heat when he steps out of the driver's side door, pushes his aviator sunglasses down onto the bridge of his nose, and gives me a smile that nearly causes my knees to buckle.

I hesitate for only a moment before heading toward him.

"What are you doing here?" I question, trying to shake off the blush I can feel creeping its way up my neck and onto my cheeks.

I'm not embarrassed about what happened last night, but I definitely feel a little nervous about being around Sebastian. More so because I'm worried about what he thinks of me now.

"There was no way I was going to get through this day without seeing you first." He's on me in five seconds flat, pushing my hair over my shoulder before cupping my face in hands. "Fuck, you're even more beautiful now that I've felt you come apart on my hand." He grins mischievously before lowering his mouth to mine, kissing away both my doubts and my embarrassment.

In fact, by the time he finally releases me, my mind is only thinking about one thing—*doing it again.*

"Come on." He pulls back, wrapping his hand around mine as he leads me to the car. "Let me drive you to school." He opens the door, moving to the side to give me room to get in.

"Oh, um Courtney should be here any minute," I say, remembering the text I was about send her.

"She's not coming." His smile widens. "I called her this morning and told her I was taking you."

"A bit presumptuous don't you think." I cross my arms in front of myself, making no attempt to move. "What if I don't want you to take me?" I tease.

"Get your gorgeous ass in the car, Tess," he says slowly, a seductive warning laced with his words. "Or I will put you in it." His eyes sparkle with mischief, and I get the feeling he would like nothing more than to exert that kind of dominance over me, and so would I.

It takes everything in me not to play into his threat just to see what he'll do, but knowing I need to get to school I refrain.

"Okay," I huff playfully before ducking under his arm and climbing into the car. I wait until he's seated next to me, his large hand engulfing my small one, before commenting on the statement he made earlier. "You said to get through today, what's happening today?" I ask, admiring his profile as he stares out the windshield, his gaze locked on the road.

"I get to go to work with my father." He throws me a look that says it's the last thing he wants to be doing.

"And I'm guessing after everything we talked about, this is not a good thing," I observe.

"This is about the farthest from good you can get. My father is unbearable at home, but in the office, he's a hundred times worse. It's his job to pick people apart, tear them down bit by bit, and he does it to me every chance he gets. It got so bad the last time I went into his office that his secretary, Joanne, stepped in and stood up for me. Needless to say, she is no longer employed with *Baxter and Lawson*."

"That's awful. I'm so sorry. This is all my fault. I should've just kept walking when Dylan said he needed to talk. Then none of this would be happening. You would be going to school with me instead of having to subject yourself to such abuse."

"I don't know that I'd call it abuse." He seems slightly amused by my comment.

"It is abuse, Sebastian."

"It's fine, Tess. His words stopped hurting me a long time ago. Trust me, I'll be fine. Besides, you didn't cause this, I did. You did nothing wrong."

"Well then, why do I feel like all of this could have been avoided if I had made a different choice?"

"We all could've made different choices, Tess. Yes, you could've chosen to walk away. But I also could've chosen not to knock his teeth down his throat." He throws me a sideways glance and smiles.

"You didn't mention having to go to work with your father last night when we were talking," I observe, going back to our original conversation.

"That punishment got handed down when I arrived home at six this morning."

"Now I feel even worse," I say, knowing he only stayed last night because I asked him to.

"Don't." He shakes his head. "I wouldn't change last night for anything. I'd work with my father a hundred times over if it meant I could do it all over again." He winks, and once again the heat rushes to my cheeks.

Pull it together, Tess. This man has had his hands… Okay, nope—that's only making me blush harder.

"So what will you be doing today?" I clear my throat, choosing to ignore his comment at the risk of further embarrassing myself. He smiles, telling me he knows exactly what I'm doing, but is good enough of a sport not to call me on it.

"Other than being my father's bitch," he answers, chuckling when I grimace. "I'm kidding. He'll probably stick me in the copy room all day or have me doing some bullshit paperwork. Either way, I'll survive."

Slowing the car and pulling it up to the curb about a block from school, he throws the car in park and turns in his seat to face me.

"This is as far as I can go. I'm not allowed on school property until next Wednesday." He reaches into the center console and grabs a pair of keys. "I need you to do me a favor," he says, tucking the keys into my hand. "Drive Jessie back to your house for me."

"Jessie?" I ask, confused.

"The Jeep." He laughs at the obvious bewilderment on my face.

"Your Jeep's name is Jessie? How did I not know that before now?" I can't help but laugh at how ridiculously cute he is.

He shrugs. "It never came up."

"And I can't—drive Jessie, I mean."

"Why not? You have your license, right?"

"I do."

"Then what's the problem?" he asks, reaching out to tuck a chunk of hair behind my ear, his hand lingering on the side of my face.

"I don't have insurance and well—it's really nice, and I'd never forgive myself if I wrecked it."

156

"The car has insurance so it's legal. Besides, it's not like my father can't afford to fix it on the off chance that you do wreck it. In which case, I'd be much more worried about you than Jessie." He leans forward, pressing his lips to my forehead. "So will you do it for me?" he asks, pulling back just enough to leave a couple inches between us. "I hate the thought of her sitting here for the next week, and my father is trying to make a point by not sending someone after her." He sighs. "He knows how much I love that Jeep, so to further solidify the control he has over me, he's refused to let me have it back until my suspension is up. I'd feel much better knowing that *my* girl is taking care of her for me."

"When you put it that way." I nearly melt in my seat at the way he says *my girl.*

"You'll do it?" His face lights up, his smile so handsome I can't help but lean in and kiss him.

"I'll do it," I murmur against his mouth before pulling back. "But you have to promise me you won't be upset if something happens to her."

"I promise." He grabs my chin between his thumb and index finger and guides my lips back to his, kissing me slow and lazily like neither of us have anywhere we need to be.

"I'm gonna be late for school," I whine, finally managing to pull myself away from his intoxicating mouth.

"Fine." He secures the keys to his Jeep in my hand. "Can I come by again tonight?" he asks, not letting my hand go until I shake my head yes.

"Mom goes to work at six. You can come see me and Jessie any time after that." I smile, kissing him one last time before quickly exiting the car, knowing if I don't do it soon I may never leave.

"Tess." Sebastian rolls down the window and hollers after me just as I reach the other side of the street. "Make sure to miss me today."

"I already do," I call back, the happiness that spreads across his face at my words damn near knocking the wind out of me.

I've got it so bad. I can't even pretend anymore.

Blowing him a kiss, I have to physically force myself to turn back around and keep walking when all I really want to do is run back across the street and never leave his side.

It only takes me about three minutes to make it to the high school building. I spot Jessie, the Jeep, in her normal spot looking as shiny as ever. I have to stop myself from waving at her, sort of feeling like she's more person than car all of a sudden.

Silently telling her that I'll see her after school, I tuck the keys in the front pocket of my jeans. In some weird way having them on me makes me feel closer to Sebastian, though I can't really explain why.

***

I feel lost most of the day. Even though Sebastian and I have zero classes together, I can feel his absence in every classroom I enter. It's sad to think that just him being at school has such a huge impact on how I feel.

Lunch was even worse, though I did manage to turn it around about halfway in when I decided to share with Court and Bree a small snippet of last night's events. I had meant to keep it between the three of us, but that quickly went out the window when Courtney gasped and then loudly said, "You finally had your first *O*."

To say I was embarrassed is the understatement of the year, but luckily only Ant was close enough to hear her, and he seemed just as uncomfortable as I did by her outburst.

I have to be honest, I haven't been a big Anthony fan since him and Courtney started hanging out, but I think he might actually be managing to grow on me a bit. I mean, if Sebastian likes him how can I not?

Stopping by my locker on my way to sixth period, I check my phone for the hundredth time today, an immense relief washing over me when I see I have a message from Sebastian.

Sebastian: By the time this week is over I'm going to be a master at answering phones and scheduling appointments. You wouldn't believe some of the stories I've heard today. No wonder lawyers are in such high demand.

Me: Sounds like your day isn't as bad as you thought???

Sebastian: Oh no, it still sucks. But thinking of you makes it a hell of a lot better.

Me: I miss you.

Sebastian: I miss you—and my new... friend. I think she likes me.

I laugh out loud, covering my mouth to muffle the sound as my classmates pass by with no knowledge of the slow burn that has suddenly erupted in my lower belly.

Me: Your friend? Is that what you're calling her?

Sebastian: Well I'd call her something else, but I have a feeling even using the word friend has that cute blush spreading across your cheeks. Tell me I'm wrong.

I smile, knowing if I looked in the mirror right now my face would be beet red.

Me: I can't, that would be lying.

Sebastian: I knew it!

Me: No one likes a gloater.

Sebastian: You like everything about me.

I'm seconds away from telling him he's actually right yet again when another message immediately follows.

Sebastian: Shit. Gotta go. My sorry excuse for a father is back in the office, and he doesn't know I managed to sneak my phone from his study this morning. Ooops.

Me: I hope the rest of your day isn't awful. I can't wait to see you later.

Without even meaning to, my fingers type out another message and press send before I can think it through enough to stop myself.

Me: And neither can your new friend ;)

I smile, completely surprised by my own brazen behavior. Stuffing my phone back into my locker, I quickly close it and spin the combination lock before taking off down the hallway, knowing I'm going to have to haul ass if I hope to make it to class on time.

TESS

"Are you really that nervous for me to meet this boy?" My mom chuckles behind where I'm pacing in the living room waiting for Sebastian to knock.

Because of his suspension and the fact that his father decided to crack down on him going anywhere after the night he stayed over, we had to delay him coming over for dinner by a week. In fact, this is the first time he's been here since the day after his and Dylan's fight.

I'm so glad to have the whole suspension incident behind us. Sebastian is officially back at school, and things have since returned to normal. Well, as normal as they can be when you're dealing with someone like Sebastian. And right now, I'm wishing this was behind us as well.

Don't get me wrong. I want Sebastian to meet my mom. I really do. But it just feels like such a huge step, and I'm worried she might scare him off. I mean, she's amazing, of course, but she can also be very protective of me which sometimes doesn't always come across the nicest.

"No," I finally answer my mom after several seconds. "Yes." I stop pacing and turn toward her. "He's really important, Mom."

"Trust me, I know he is." She smiles when a knock sounds on the front door. "I'll play nice. I promise." She closes her hand around the knob and yanks it open before I can say anything else.

"You must be Sebastian." Her smile widens, and she steps aside to let him enter. "Please, come on in. Tess is over here nervously pacing. I think she thinks I'm gonna embarrass her," she teases, closing the door behind him.

Sebastian steps into the foyer, looking so handsome in dark jeans and a black polo—his normally unruly hair combed back away from his face—that it takes everything in me to keep the drool from pooling out of the sides of my mouth. My god, this boy is perfect.

As if reading my mind, a slow smile plays on the corner of his lips as he takes in my reaction. Offering me nothing more than a wink, he turns his attention back to my mother, handing her a beautiful arrangement of wild flowers I hadn't even noticed he was holding until this very moment.

"These are for you. Thank you for having me over, Mrs. Wilson."

I have to choke back a laugh at how formal he seems. Of course, he's probably used to having to behave a certain way around adults, considering his father hosts a lot of professional gatherings at their house that Sebastian is forced to attend.

"Oh, how thoughtful. And please, call me Elizabeth." My mom takes the flowers, looking at me with wide eyes as if to say *Oh my god, he's so cute—and sweet. You did good, kiddo.* Even though she doesn't say a word of that, I know that if Sebastian weren't here to witness it, that's exactly what she would be saying to me right now.

"I'm going to go put these in water. Sebastian, please make yourself at home."

"Thank you." He gives her another one of his famous smiles, waiting until she disappears inside the kitchen before closing the distance between us. "I missed you," he says, tipping my chin up and placing a soft kiss to my lips the second he reaches me.

"I missed you more." I smile up at him, my earlier nervousness evaporating.

I should've known there was no reason to worry. Everyone who meets Sebastian loves him. How can you not? He's gorgeous, smart, well spoken, and so damn charming you can't help but be mesmerized by him.

"Not possible, Tess." He winks, turning his attention back to my mom as she reenters the room.

***

It's been two hours since Sebastian arrived, and I swear this night could not have gone any better if I had dreamt it up. Sebastian won over my mom just as he did me, with absolutely no effort.

About halfway through my mom's homemade lasagna, I had to sit back and take it all in for a moment. It was strange how natural it all felt—me, my mom, and Sebastian all sitting around the kitchen table laughing and talking like we'd done it a million times before.

I knew within minutes that my mom more than approved of Sebastian, and I didn't realize until that moment how badly I needed that approval. Knowing she supports our relationship makes me feel like I can be with Sebastian more freely.

And that's so important because there's something else I realized today as I watched my mom and Sebastian's interaction with each other. Something I think I've known for a while now and maybe just let myself admit…

I'm head over heels, undeniably consumed by everything that Sebastian is. His smile, his touch, the way he says my name. I love every single thing about him.

I've fallen in love with Sebastian Baxter.

I'm so in love with him that I'm terrified by the power of it, and yet it's all I want to feel. I want to bathe myself in the weight of that love and hold onto it for dear life because now that I've experienced it, I never want to let it go.

"You're awfully quiet tonight." Sebastian knocks his shoulder with mine as we walk side by side down the sidewalk toward where Jessie the Jeep is parked on the street.

"Just thinking, I guess."

"Oh yeah, about what?" he asks.

"You," I answer truthfully.

"Tell me more." He laughs, pulling me into his chest the moment we reach the street.

"My mom loves you." I look up into those incredible hazel eyes and wonder how on earth I ever got so lucky.

Another whoosh of uncertainty sweeps through me. The kind of uncertainty I feel anytime I let myself think too long on how or why Sebastian chose me. I push it down, refusing to let my own insecurities ruin this perfect night.

"She's amazing." He grins down at me, rubbing the pad of his thumb across my bottom lip. "She's everything I wish my own mother was."

"I'm sorry." I don't know what else to say.

I *am* sorry. Sorry that he doesn't know the true love of a parent. Sorry that he was born to people who don't deserve a son like him. Sorry that he's missed out on the kind of love my mother shows me every single day.

"Don't be. I'll just borrow your mom." He kisses me gently, his touch like fire to my chilled skin.

"I think I'd be willing to share, under one condition of course," I tease, pulling back to look up at him.

"Name it."

"You have to promise not to break my heart."

I don't mean to say it. The words sort of just tumble out, my heart speaking rather than my mind. I try to formulate words to cover my blunder, but my brain can't seem to conjure anything up quickly enough.

"That's one promise I'm confident I can keep." He grins, his reaction calm and understanding. "I'm all the way in with you, Tess. A hundred percent. You're all I care about, you have to know that. I would never—I will never, intentionally hurt you, ever."

"I'm all the way in with you too, you know?" The look he gives me has my knees feeling like they might give out under my weight.

"Tess," he breathes, dropping his forehead to mine, his hands resting on each side of my neck. "Fuck, I love you."

My entire body freezes at his words.

How is it possible that he just expressed the exact emotion I had settled on just earlier this evening? Certain I heard him wrong, I stare blankly into his eyes waiting for some indication that I'm not hearing things.

"Did you hear me, Tess?" He pulls back, his hands sliding up to cup my cheeks. "I'm in love with you."

Tears instantly fill my eyes, and I struggle to form words. This moment couldn't be more beautiful, and here I go ruining it because I can't seem to get my brain to work.

"You do?" It takes me a second to realize it's my voice that extends between us.

"I do." He smiles, his gaze holding mine intently.

Closing my eyes, I take a moment to compose myself before opening them again. His bright hazels are still locked on mine, something in them I'm convinced I've never seen before.

"I love you too, Sebastian," I finally manage to push out, not missing the relief that floods his face when I do.

It didn't dawn on me that he'd been waiting for a response.

Seconds later his mouth is closing down on mine, and it's not lost on me that this kiss feels different—more passionate, more intimate—than any kiss we've shared up until this moment.

It's like he's trying to prove to me with his kiss that his love is real, and I'm reassuring him with mine that I already know. I know he loves me. In some weird way, I think I've known it for quite some time. The way he looks at me is unlike any other person has ever looked at me before—like I'm his world.

It's both incredible and overwhelming, but it's something I wouldn't give back for anything in the entire world.

I love this man, and he loves me.

I can't imagine life gets any better than this.

"Wait, so tell me again how he said it." Courtney's sitting on top of my bed, legs crossed in front of herself while Bree lounges next her.

"I've already told you like five times." I plop down on the foot of my bed and let out an audible sigh.

"I know, but I want to hear it again." She smiles dreamily at me. "It's not every day that the school's hottest guy confesses his love to one of my best friends. I need to bottle this shit up so I can revisit it for years to come. It's like a fucking fairy-tale."

I laugh. Only Courtney would pair the word *fucking* and *fairy-tale* together in the same sentence.

"It kind of was like a fairy-tale," I admit, pulling my legs up to my chest and wrapping my arms around them.

"Oh my god, look at that smile." Courtney nudges Bree who seems a bit off tonight. "I give it another week and our girl will finally join the land of non-virginity." She bounces excitedly, shaking the entire bed.

"One step at a time." I laugh, not bothering to tell them that it's been on my mind a lot here recently—especially after the things Sebastian said to me this past Monday.

"I don't know what you're waiting for," Bree finally chimes in, seeming to snap out of her fog a bit. "It's just sex."

"Not everyone is quite as casual about it, though," I remind her, knowing Bree and I are on opposite sides of the spectrum when it comes to anything sex related.

While she uses sex as a way to feel connected to another person, I'd rather share a deeper connection than physical before giving that part of myself. Call me old fashioned, but I think you should love the person you're *sleeping* with.

I know a lot of it has to do with Bree's past. She was sexually abused at a very young age, and I know that will stay with her for the rest of her life. I just wish there was a way to show her that she's worth more.

"Whatever, I'm with Bree," Court interjects, and the two high-five. "You just need to do it already."

"I will—eventually. I'm not in any rush and neither is Sebastian."

"Look, I'm sure he's telling you that, but do you really think that's the hundred percent truth? I mean, he is a guy after all."

"Well considering if it wasn't for him we would've already had sex, I'd say yes, he's a hundred percent," I blurt, wishing I could take it back the moment it leaves my lips.

"Wait, what?" Courtney's smile spreads. "You mean to tell me you've been willing to and he wouldn't?"

"That's exactly what I'm telling you," I huff. "I got a little carried away the night, well, you know…"

"When he flipped your bean." Bree's choice of words makes my stomach coil a little.

"Yes, that." I clear my throat. "Well, I might have asked for it—a few times—but he insisted I wasn't ready and has since refused to take the next step until he believes I am."

"Wow." Court sits back against the headboard, arms crossing over her chest as she considers my statement.

"Wow, what?" I ask after several seconds.

"Just wow." She continues to smile at me. "You've got that boy wrapped around your little finger, Tess. I'm not gonna lie, I thought his whole love confession might have something to do with wanting to get you into bed sooner, but learning you were already willing and he's making you wait." She shakes her head. "I'm kind of impressed."

"Um, okay." I chuckle, not really sure how to respond to that.

"I mean, Ant has talked about Sebastian's ways, and I gotta say the guy he described is nothing like the person he seems to be when he's with you. Kinda makes me jealous. I wish Anthony loved me enough to change for me."

"Y'all have made it official. That's something," I offer, ignoring my need to ask what kind of things Ant has said about Sebastian.

I think it's better that I don't open that can of worms. I trust Sebastian, and I trust what we share. I don't need to make something out of nothing.

"Yeah, I guess." She shrugs, picking at a string on her pants.

"What about you and Blake?" I turn my attention to Bree who seems to have retreated into wherever she's been most of the evening.

I don't miss the brief look of something dark that crosses her face before her easy smile falls back into place.

"We're good." She doesn't offer anything else.

"Just good, huh?" Court snorts. "Considering he never lets you out of his sight, I'd say he's either really into you *or* really possessive. My vote is for the latter. If you ask me, I think he's kind of scary."

"He has a temper, and he's kind of an ass." Bree brushes off Courtney's comment. "But he's only like that around other people. When it's just us, he's good."

"Okay…" I can tell Court wants to say more, but she refrains. The whole situation makes me feel uneasy, and yet I can't seem to put my finger on why.

I agree, Blake seems a bit controlling, but what Courtney seems to be suggesting runs deeper than that. I can tell by the way she's looking at Bree. I can also tell that Bree has no desire to discuss it any further with Courtney, so I quickly intervene.

"Okay, I've had enough boy talk. What do you say we go rent the new Channing Tatum movie?" I suggest, laughing when Courtney's eyes go wide and she grins at me knowingly.

"Girl, you know I can't resist my Channing." She giggles, flinging her legs over the side of the bed.

"I'm in." Bree follows suit, climbing off the bed seconds after Courtney does. "But first we need to order pizza. If I don't get some greasy food into my body, it's likely going to go into shock."

"Pineapple and Ham?" I ask, making my way into the kitchen to get the phone number to *Angelo's* from a magnet hanging on the fridge.

"You know it." Bree follows me in, grabbing a soda from the fridge.

"Don't get me that nasty shit." Courtney stops in the doorway leaning against the frame, her nose crinkling in disgust.

"Yes, I know—meat lovers for you," I call over my shoulder.

"Because we all know how much Courtney *loves* the meat." Bree snorts, leaning up against the counter.

I look from Courtney to Bree and then back to Courtney before all three of us burst into a fit of laughter. Once it starts, it's nearly impossible to stop. As soon as it passes and my laughter starts to die off, Courtney or Bree will start laughing again and pull me right back under.

This is exactly what I needed, a night with my girls. Some time for us to catch up, laugh, binge eat greasy pizza, and watch sexy men on television. It's something we don't get to do nearly enough anymore. We are all so busy with our own lives.

While I love my time with Sebastian, our quickly growing relationship feels almost too heavy at times. I mean, it's incredible, but it's nice to just let go of all of that for a while and enjoy a night with my two best friends.

With only a year and a half left before graduation, I'm not sure how many more of these nights we'll get.

TESS

The last few weeks have gone by in a blur. Even after over two months of dating, I still find myself sometimes wondering if all this is really happening. Sebastian has been nothing short of incredible and when I'm with him, I'm the happiest I've ever been.

It doesn't matter if were fooling around—*we still haven't gone all the way yet*—or if we're just sitting on the couch watching a movie, the butterflies in my stomach are always there. Even just thinking about him sends a swarm rushing through my belly.

He's consumed me. My thoughts, my dreams, my heart—every piece of me now belongs to him. I eat, sleep, and breathe Sebastian Baxter. And I wouldn't change one second of it.

Homecoming has been the highlight so far. Sebastian, of course, was crowned homecoming king and after accepting his crown led me onto the dance floor where we proceeded to share a slow dance in front of most of the school. It was only the homecoming queen, Heather, and her date, Jonah, with us on the dance floor and even with nearly all sets of eyes on us, I felt like there wasn't another person in the room.

That's what Sebastian does to me. He takes over all of my senses until nothing and no one exists except for him.

"Wow, Tess, you look..." Sebastian pulls me from my thoughts, and I turn away from the large windows in his formal living area just in time to see him enter the room, his eyes zeroed in on my bare thighs.

It's Halloween and because his Dad is in L.A. for the week and his mom is visiting her sister in Georgia, Sebastian decided to throw a huge party. I think throwing parties is Sebastian's way of giving his parents' a big ole middle finger.

Once he settled on a date for the party we agreed to dress up like characters from eighties movies, but since we chose to keep our costume selections a surprise this is the first time he's seeing me.

I opted to dress up as Alex from Flashdance and as such am wearing an oversized off the shoulder gray sweatshirt that hits me right around mid-thigh with only short black boy shorts underneath, black legwarmers, and bright red high heels. My long normally straight hair is teased in messy curls though I didn't go all eighties with it and kept my style more modern. I decided to pull the entire look together with some candy apple red lipstick just because.

I cover my mouth in an attempt to stifle the laugh bubbling in my throat when I get a good look at what Sebastian's wearing. If I'm being honest, Sebastian looks anything but comical. In fact, he looks even sexier than normal, if that's possible.

He's dressed in a light pink button-down shirt that barely covers the tidy whities he's sporting below. My eyes widen as I take him in. The clear definition of his man business making my lower belly clench tightly.

Certainly, he's not going to walk around like that all night?

Then again, I already know he is. Sebastian would probably walk around naked if he wouldn't get in trouble for indecent exposure. That boy is nothing if not comfortable in his own skin.

Averting my eyes, fearful that I might give away what seeing him like this is doing to me, I let my gaze travel along the rest of him.

His shirt is open at the top revealing a sliver of his perfectly toned chest. And his muscular legs are on full display with the exception of a pair of tall white tube socks that stop around the middle of his calf.

"Tom Cruise has got nothing on you." I shake my head slowly, unable to tear my eyes away from him.

"Fuck, yes. See, I knew you'd know who I was." He smiles in triumph.

"Risky Business is a classic. Who hasn't seen it?" I question, the idea absolutely absurd.

"I think you'd be surprised."

"I think you'd be surprised. That movie is more popular than you think," I argue.

"Not as popular as Flashdance," he says, gesturing to my outfit.

"I don't know about that." I shake my head in disagreement.

"Yeah?" I can already see the challenge in his eyes. "How about we make a little wager?" His smile turns wicked and he raises his eyebrows up and down as he stalks toward me, playfully shimmying his hips as he goes.

"Uh oh. I don't know if I like the sound of this," I tease, sliding my hand along the exposed part of his chest the instant he pulls me into him.

"I bet you that more people will know what movie you're from than what movie I'm from."

"And what do I get if I win?" I purr, pressing my body firmly against his as I grab a handful of his thinly covered backside and squeeze.

"Anything you want, baby." He smiles, trailing his tongue along my bottom lip.

"You have to give me my very own private Risky Business dance." I giggle against the kiss he presses to my mouth.

"Fine," he agrees. "But if I win," he whispers, deepening the kiss without finishing. He waits until he's made me good and flustered before pulling back. "Then you have to agree to let me strip you out of this little outfit and kiss this incredible body of yours—everywhere." He rakes his hand down my side and wraps the end of my long sweatshirt around his hand.

"Everywhere?" I swallow hard, not sure if the thought makes me more excited or nervous.

"Everywhere," he confirms, hoisting me up into his arms.

I instinctively wrap my legs around his waist, unable to resist the urge to grind downward when I feel how hard he is against me. A stiff groan escapes his mouth, and I swear it's the hottest sound I've ever heard.

"I've never wanted to lose a bet more than I do this one." I smile, claiming his mouth once more.

It isn't long until things have gotten pretty hot and heavy. Sebastian has me pinned against the wall in the formal sitting room, working hot kisses down the side of my neck when the sound of the doorbell echoes through the large house.

We both freeze, panting like we've just finished a marathon.

"Fuck!" Sebastian curses, slowly sliding me down his body until my feet are back on solid ground.

"How about you go splash some cold water..." I let my eyes travel down to his very clear erection, "...on your face," I continue with a slow grin. "And I'll get the door."

"Probably a good idea." He looks down and then back up at me knowingly.

"To be continued?" I offer.

"Fuck, yes." He kisses me once more before hightailing it toward the bathroom.

Taking a few deep breaths, I straighten my sweatshirt and make sure everything is covered before making my way into the foyer to let in the first arriving guests.

***

This party is so very different from the first one I attended at Sebastian's house back in August. I mean, the atmosphere is very similar with the addition to the costumes everyone is wearing, but there is a certain belonging I feel now that I didn't have the last time.

Sebastian is a social butterfly, rather than hiding out on the balcony upstairs he's working every angle of the room, always keeping me close beside him.

I smile freely and don't even bother looking over my shoulder. Knowing I don't have to worry about running into Dylan offers more relief than I thought it would, considering there's no way he would have the balls to show up here after what transpired a few weeks ago. I mean, unless he wants to repeat said events, which I doubt.

The night goes by smoothly, and I even find myself partaking in a little bit of drinking. It feels good to let loose a little and be an ordinary teenager. I know Sebastian's got me, and the thought makes me feel safer than I ever thought possible.

Just after midnight, I decide to go in search of Bree, wanting to get a picture of me, her, and Courtney together before Court and Ant call it a night—and by calling it a night I mean disappear upstairs.

I look all over the first floor and out back but can't find her anywhere. I decide to try my luck upstairs, humming happily to myself as I climb the back stairwell. I didn't realize how buzzed I had become until just now, and I can't help but giggle at myself when I stumble at the top of the steps.

My bubbling, drunk happiness quickly dies off though when I catch sight of Bree on the ground, tears streaming down her face as Blake hovers over her.

"What the fuck?" I blurt, my eyes bouncing back and forth between Blake and Bree.

"Tess." Bree quickly climbs to her feet, trying to wipe away the mascara streaked down her face.

"What the fuck?" I say louder, not paying any mind to my choice in language. Right now, *fuck* is the only word that seems appropriate.

"It's nothing," Bree quickly tries to explain. "I just fell. I've had too much to drink." When she steps toward me I can see the red welt across the left side of her face, and my entire stomach bottoms out.

"You fell or he hit you?" I grind out, my hands clenching at my sides.

"What?" Bree tries to act confused by my question, but I can see the truth in her eyes. That asshole put his hands on my best friend.

"Why don't you go back downstairs, Tess. This isn't any of your business." Blake steps in front of me, blocking my view of Bree.

"None of my business?" I question, shock turning into anger. "None of my business?" My voice intensifies tenfold. "You hit my friend, and you're telling me it's none of my business." I practically scream in his face, my heels allowing me to stand nearly nose to nose with him.

"I said, go the fuck downstairs, Tess." His voice is laced in warning, and he puffs his broad chest out like that's somehow going to scare me into leaving him here alone with Bree.

"No," I challenge, not planning to go anywhere. "Bree, go, now." I meet her gaze over Blake's shoulder.

"Tess." She's crying harder now, swiping angrily at her tears. "Please."

"She's not going anywhere with you." Blake takes a step forward, forcing me to take a step back. "If you know what's best for you, you'll turn around and not fucking say a word about this to anyone."

"Are you threatening me?" I plant my feet, unwilling to move another inch even when he tries to force me back again.

"Tess, please," Bree continues to plead.

"Shut the fuck up, you stupid bitch." Blake turns his face as he speaks to Bree.

The instant his face turns back in my direction, my hand lands against the side of his cheek, a loud smack echoing down the long corridor. I didn't even mean to hit him, but I'd be lying if I said it didn't feel good to do so.

I don't have time to prepare for what comes next. While I may be headstrong, my petite body is nowhere close to a match for Blake's muscular build. Grabbing my forearms, he squeezes so tightly that his fingers bite into my skin as he swings me sideways, and I hit the wall hard, my teeth jarring the instant the contact is made. Surprisingly, I somehow manage to stay on my feet.

"Stop!" I hear Bree seconds before my eyes find her, just in time to see Blake lay a hard backhand to the side of her face. She immediately stumbles backward, nearly losing her footing.

I don't know what comes over me. Maybe it's the alcohol, maybe it's the adrenaline or the sheer protectiveness I feel over my friend, but when I slide my high heel off my foot and swing it at Blake's head it's like I'm outside of my body watching someone else's actions.

It connects with his face just as he turns back toward me, the pointed heel tearing the skin below his eye. He retaliates instantly, slamming me against the wall, his forearm pressed firmly against my throat restricting my ability to breathe freely.

"You really shouldn't have done that, little girl." He smiles wickedly.

I have no idea where Anthony comes from or how much times passes, but it can't be more than seconds before he manages to pull Blake off me and pin him to the ground—after laying a few good punches to his face of course.

I stumble to the side, grabbing Bree's hand, and pulling her to me.

"Are you okay?" I wrap my arms around her and squeeze tightly.

She doesn't respond right away. I think she might be in shock. Honestly, I think we both are. But it doesn't take long before her body shudders against mine, and she breaks down in my arms.

I look up when I hear a commotion, finding Sebastian's eyes the second he reaches the second story landing. He looks down at where Ant has Blake pinned to the floor and then back up to where I'm holding Bree, seeming to piece it all together in a matter of seconds.

"I'm fine," I mouth, knowing his gut instinct is to come to me. "Get him out of here please." This time my words filter through the space between us.

He nods only once before him and Ant are dragging Blake down the stairwell, disappearing within seconds.

I sag forward into Bree relief the most prominent thing I feel right now. My alcohol buzz is long gone, as is my carefree, happy mood. What started out as a fun night took a dark turn I never saw coming.

It's in the few moments that Bree and I remain in the hallway alone that everything starts to fall into place. How withdrawn Bree has been. How hesitant she was to bring Blake around us. The black eye she had two weeks ago where she claimed to have walked into an open kitchen cabinet while walking and texting.

Like a lightbulb turning on, everything seems to come to life in front of me. Pulling back, I place both my hands on Bree's shoulders and wait until her gaze meets mine before speaking.

"How long?" I ask, giving her shoulders a light shake when she doesn't answer me right away. "How long?" I repeat, my voice thick with emotion.

"A couple months," Bree finally answers, unable to meet my gaze.

"A couple months?" I question, clearly upset to learn that one of my best friends has been getting knocked around by her boyfriend for weeks, and I'm just now finding out about it. "Why would you let him do this to you?"

"Because I love him." She shoves out of my grasp, crossing her arms protectively over her chest.

"You love him? He's been hitting you for two months, and you love him?" I hate how judgmental I sound, but I can't hide the fact that right now I want to kill that asshole.

"He has his moments. He's not always so bad."

"Do you hear yourself right now?"

"I don't expect you to understand," she bites out harshly. "Not everyone can be as perfect as you and Sebastian."

"This has nothing to do with me and Sebastian. It's not a competition, Bree. Blake hit you. He's been hitting you. How can you stand here and defend him right now?"

"Because I love him," she cries.

"I don't believe that for a second. Tell me the truth," I demand, knowing my friend a lot better than she's giving me credit for right now. "You can tell me." I soften my approach.

"I'm pregnant," she blurts, fresh tears streaming down her face.

"What?"

I expected a lot of things, but this certainly wasn't one of them.

"I was just telling him. That's what set him off. He blames me. Said if I didn't take care of it that he would." She sobs, trying to pull herself together. "I don't know what I'm going to do, Tess." The look she gives me damn near tears me in half.

"How long have you known?"

"About a month." She shrugs helplessly.

"You should've told me. I could've been here for you. I could've helped you." I'm pulling her back into my arms just as Courtney appears at the top of the stairs, her face flush and her breathing labored.

"Ant and Sebastian just dragged Blake outside. What the hell is going on?" she questions, dropping it the instant she gets at look at Bree's tear stained face.

Without hesitation, she wraps her arms around Bree from behind, sandwiching herself between the two of us.

It isn't until much later that everything calms down enough for Bree to tell us everything. The three of us are all sitting on Sebastian's bed, me and Court listening to Bree recount when the abuse first started and how things have spiraled from there.

By the end of the conversation, we're all mentally and physically exhausted. Bree falls asleep lying sideways across Sebastian's bed and Courtney follows closely behind, lying right next to her. I, on the other hand, feel wide awake. My mind can't shut out the image of Blake hovering over Bree while she cowered on the ground.

It makes me sick to my stomach to think that this has been going on right under my nose for weeks, and I was so preoccupied that I missed every single one of the warning signs. Guilt settles in my chest and wraps around my heart like a vice.

Even though I don't deserve to feel better, I go in search of the one person I know will give it to me anyway.

I find Sebastian in the kitchen, throwing away bottles, a pair of gym shorts now covering his bottom half. He turns when he hears me enter, opening his arms for me the second he catches sight of me.

"Hey." He pulls me against his chest, smoothing a hand over my unruly curls.

"Hey," I speak into his chest, breathing in his scent.

"How is she?" he asks, pulling back just enough to look down at me, the pad of his thumb tracing lightly across my cheek.

"Sleeping." I lean into his touch.

"And you?"

"I'm fine." I let out a shaky breath. "A little shaken up and a lot confused, but I'll be okay." I shrug.

"That motherfucker is so lucky it was Ant who found you and not me." He lets out a loud breath. "I swear to god, had Ant told me what happened prior to Blake leaving, he would've left in an ambulance instead of driving out of here himself."

"I'm glad Anthony knows you well enough to know how to play his cards." I smile sweetly. "Remind me to thank him later. The last thing I want is for you to end up in jail over someone like Blake. I still can't believe Bree." I shake my head slowly. "Out of all of us, she's the tough one. I never thought she'd be the type to let a man beat on her."

"Sometimes you don't always know what people are capable of, both doing and enduring. I'm sure she had her reasons. But she's done with him now, right?"

"As far as I know." I let out an audible sigh. "I can't see her going back to him after what happened tonight. Especially now that news of the baby is out."

"Has she said what she's going to do?"

"No, but I can't see her getting rid of it either. Bree may be hard on the outside but on the inside, she's one of the most loving people I know. I have no doubt she'll do what's right for her baby."

"I'm sure she will." Silence stretches between us for a long moment before he abruptly changes the subject. "We never did get to finish our bet."

He must have sensed my need to talk about something else because just as I thought it, he's offering me a much-needed distraction.

"We didn't, did we?" I smile up at him.

"How about we call it a draw and we both win," he offers, lowering his mouth to mine.

"Now that you mention it, I think you dancing around like Tom Cruise might just be the thing I need to erase this awful night from my brain."

"I'm more than happy to do anything my girl wants." He presses his lips to mine before speaking against them. "But that means you have to pay up, too." My body instantly flushes at his words.

"I think I can manage that." I slide my arms around his neck and let him pull me into his arms.

TESS

"Are you going to tell me where we're going now?" I watch a slow smile spread across Sebastian's face, but he only shakes his head side to side.

"You're going to have to wait and find out," he says, his eyes remaining on the road as we merge onto the freeway.

"You realize that I could get in big trouble for this. If my mom calls Courtney's house and finds out I'm not there, I'll probably be grounded for the rest of my life." I try to guilt him into telling me.

"Nice try." He chuckles, reaching over the middle console to squeeze my thigh. "But we both know your mom is working tonight, and if she needs you she will call your cell—not Courtney's house."

"You're really not going to tell me?" I whine, giving him my best pouty-lipped frown when he throws a quick glance in my direction.

"That's not going to work on me, Tessa Wilson. I know all your tricks." He laughs next to me.

I've been super nervous about this night away since Sebastian brought it up last week. With it being so close to

Christmas, he wanted us to have some time alone before we both became busy with family obligations, but up to this point, he's refused to tell me where exactly it is that we're going.

"You're no fun," I huff playfully, crossing my arms in front of myself.

"Oh, I'll be plenty of fun later. Don't you worry." He throws me a wink before his gaze goes back to the road.

My stomach tightens in both excitement and fear. I knew going in that tonight would probably be *the* night. We've been skirting around it for weeks, things getting a lot more heated between us after the Halloween party. At this point the only sexual experience I've yet to have with Sebastian is sex.

I'd be lying if I said I wasn't scared—hell, I'm terrified—but I think more than anything I just want it to happen already. I want to cross this last hurdle and feel like I can give myself to Sebastian freely without my virginity hanging over our heads.

We remain silent for the next several minutes, Sebastian humming quietly along with the music playing on the radio. It isn't until about forty-five minutes into our drive that I realize where we're heading, and the instant I do, a wide smile spreads across my face.

Sebastian chooses this moment to glance in my direction, chuckling when he catches my expression.

"Took you long enough." He snags my hand, wrapping his fingers around it.

"You're taking me to New York?" I ask in disbelief.

"I figured if you were going to plan your future around going to school here, you might want to experience it first." He falls silent for a long moment before adding, "I wanted to be the one to take you for the first time, that way the city will always hold a piece of us in it, something you can keep with you when we're not together." There's an air of sadness around his words, but I choose to ignore what that statement might mean for us.

I know our future is uncertain. With Sebastian's graduation less than six months away, I know there is still so much to figure out. I just can't bring myself to bring it up. And while I know Sebastian has been talking to a couple different schools that have shown interest in him playing ball for them, he's yet to really discuss it with me in any great detail. I think we're both hesitant to face what we know is coming.

A part of me is hoping that wherever the future takes us that we will find a way to make it work. I can't even entertain the idea that this will come to an end. When I think about *my* future, he's part of every single scenario. I'm just not sure if it's the same for him.

As much as I want him to choose me, to pick a school close by so we can be together, I'd also never forgive myself for holding him back should he choose to stay behind for my sake. So it's kind of a catch twenty-two. I can't win either way, so I've made a deal with myself not to think too much on it until that time comes.

"Hey." Sebastian squeezes my hand. "Where'd you go?" he asks, clearly picking up on my suddenly sullen mood.

"Nowhere. Sorry." I shake it off, forcing a smile to my lips. "I'm just—nervous," I admit, addressing another hot topic on my mind right now.

"There's no pressure here, Tess, you know that," he reassures me.

"No, I know. That's not it. I want to, Sebastian. I *really* want to," I say, knowing I don't need to say exactly what it is I want to do.

"It's normal to be nervous. And if you decide tonight's not the night, I'm not going to be upset. I planned this to spend time with you, not to pressure you into anything."

"I love you." The statement just leaves my lips without thought. I don't need to think about loving Sebastian or sharing the words with him, it's one part of our relationship that comes effortlessly.

"I love you more." He grins.

"Not possible."

"Very possible."

"You're delusional." I laugh, loving this back and forth banter we always share when one person tells the other they love them. It's like our thing now.

"Shut up and look." Sebastian chuckles, gesturing out the windshield where the city is now in full view.

"Wow." I lean forward, taking it all in.

"I still can't believe you've lived less than an hour from the city your entire life and you've never once been here."

"Never had a real reason to visit." I shrug. "Plus, Mom hates city traffic. Every time we've talked about coming here to see a play or visit the zoo, she's always talked me into going somewhere else. I think deep down the city just reminds her too much of my dad considering this is where they met."

"Makes sense. It was their place," he says. "And now it's going to be ours."

I smile, not realizing how much I wanted a connection to my parents' past until now. I love the thought that a place that once was so special to them will now be special to me and Sebastian. No matter what happens, he will always be the first person who pops into my head anytime I think of New York.

***

We arrive at the Westin at Times Square just after five o'clock. Sebastian reserved us a suite that is unlike any hotel room I've ever seen. Every window gives off an amazing view of the city. There's even a large window offering a breathtaking view from the jetted tub in the bathroom. Every inch of the room is pure perfection. I can't even begin to imagine what one night at a place like this cost. Something tells me I don't want to know.

After walking around the expansive space and looking in every nook and cranny, I reenter the main living space to find Sebastian standing next to the largest set of windows positioned in the center of the room, his hands shoved in his jean pockets as he looks out over the city.

My breath catches in my throat at how incredible he looks standing there, the beautiful city the perfect backdrop for someone like him. When he senses my eyes on him, he turns his head in my direction, a slow smile pulling at the corners of his mouth.

"Come here." He extends his arm, waiting until I'm securely tucked into his side before wrapping it around my shoulders.

"This place is incredible, Sebastian." I slide my arms around his middle, squeezing him tightly. "Everything is so beautiful. And this view—god, it's breathtaking."

"It is, isn't it?" I look up to find him looking down at me. "The most beautiful thing I've ever seen." His eyes bore into mine.

"I think you're looking at the wrong view," I tease, feeling squeamish under his gaze.

"I think you are." He grins, turning in our embrace so that are bodies are now pressed front to front.

Reaching out, he tucks my hair over my shoulder, letting his hand linger on the side of my neck.

"I can't tell you how amazing it feels to be here with you like this." His hand slides up my jaw before the pad of his thumb traces along my lower lip. "I love you so fucking much, Tess."

"I love you more." I smile when he shakes his head knowingly at me.

"What do you say we go see Times Square?" he suggests.

"I have another idea in mind." I wiggle my eyebrows suggestively at him.

"Don't tempt me, Tess. I brought you here to see the city, not the inside of this hotel room. But if you keep looking at me like that we'll likely never leave."

"I think I like the sound of that." I reach up and wrap my arms around the back of his neck, pulling his face down to mine. "Make love to me, Sebastian," I whisper against his mouth. "Right here, right now. I don't want to wait another second."

A groan vibrates from deep in his throat. He hesitates only seconds before his lips crash down on mine. It's slow at first, his tongue dancing lazily against mine, but it doesn't take long before the kiss morphs into something so intense I can feel it all the way to my core.

He slowly strips me bare, kissing each section of my body as the layers of clothing are removed—my shoulder, my collarbone, the swell of my breasts. The further down he goes the more the anticipation in my stomach grows.

Before Sebastian, before his touch and his kiss, I didn't know it was possible to feel like this—for my body to react so intensely to another person. It's like I'm an instrument and Sebastian knows how to play me with absolute precision, every note nothing short of perfection.

With shaky hands, I work the front of his pants open, swallowing up the deep moan that vibrates from his mouth into mine when I slide my hand inside the material of his boxer briefs and wrap my hand around his thick erection.

I work my hand up and down slowly, egged on by his reaction to my touch and how badly I can tell he wants this. Hell, I want it, too. I want it more than I think I've ever wanted anything else in my entire life.

No words can describe what Sebastian makes me feel, both emotionally and physically. To lump that together, to finally bring the physical and the emotional into the same playing field, makes everything feel that much more intense, that much more special, that much more incredible.

When Sebastian has finally rid himself of the rest of his clothes, he guides me onto the bed, my bare back coming to rest on top of the plush cream comforter. His eyes trail down me with so much heat I swear I can feel they're path burning into my skin.

His eyes are heavy, his breathing labored, and when he starts crawling up my body I feel like my heart is seconds away from beating out of my chest. The nervous butterflies in my stomach now feel like a large flock of birds, and my bottom lip feels raw from kneading it nervously between my teeth.

After rolling on a condom, Sebastian settles between my thighs, supporting most of his weight on his forearms that are positioned on either side of me.

"Are you sure about this, Tess?" His voice is strained as his heaviness presses against me.

"I'm sure." I nod frantically, wrapping my hand around the back of his neck to pull his face back down. "I'm sure," I say again, this time a whisper against his mouth before I press my lips to his.

Within seconds Sebastian is sliding inside of me—inch by painful inch— until I feel so full it feels like I'm being split apart from the inside out. Sebastian doesn't stop until he's planted all the way inside, pulling back to look down at me.

"God, you feel so perfect, Tess." He kisses me. "Tell me you're okay. I can't move until I know you're okay." He practically whimpers, like it's killing him not to move.

"I'm okay," I reassure him, crying out in both pleasure and pain when he pulls out and pushes all the way back in, in one swift motion.

"Tess."

"Keep going," I plead when Sebastian hesitates. "Please just keep going."

He repeats the same movement only this time he doesn't stop once he's buried inside me again. When he pulls out, he immediately pushes back in, working up a slow, steady rhythm. I swear I can feel every inch of him as he slides inside and then drags slowly out, working my body in a way I didn't know was possible. The pain and pleasure melding together until I can't tell where one ends and the other begins.

I don't know if minutes pass or only seconds—all I know is that the deep pressure inside me continues to build to an almost unbearable weight. Each thrust inward and each pull out has my eyes blurring and my mind unable to focus on anything but that feeling. A slow burn deep in my belly, something so intense I find myself having trouble even remembering to breathe.

"Sebastian." It's a strangled cry, void of any shame or embarrassment. I don't even mean to say anything, but as the pleasure starts to peak I find myself needing just to say something, needing to ground myself to the earth because I feel at risk of floating away.

"I love you, Tess. God, I fucking love you." Sebastian increases his speed, hitting me even deeper, causing another cry to rip from my throat.

"I love you. Sebastian…" I don't get to finish whatever it is I'm trying to say next because at that very moment everything reaches a head, and I feel like an explosion goes off inside me. My entire body convulses, and I grip Sebastian harder, drowning in the waves that crash over me again and again.

It's like the second I lose control Sebastian falls over the edge with me, groaning against my neck about how perfect I feel, how good I make him feel, how much he loves me. And then his chest is on mine, and he's struggling to catch his breath as we both come down from the highest of all highs.

It's in that moment, our sweaty bodies pressed together, Sebastian's heart beating erratically against my own, that I truly let myself embrace the power that this boy has over me. It used to terrify me, but now—after this, after feeling connected to him in a way I never have another human soul, I feel anything but scared. Sebastian was made for me and I for him—I've never been more certain about this fact than I am right now.

***

"What about that one?" I point at another building perfectly displayed from my view out of the bathroom window.

"I'm not sure about that one." His chest vibrates against my back as he speaks, his hands sliding up and down my bare arms.

The last couple hours have been the most incredible in my life. Being with Sebastian, giving him a part of me that I've never shared with anyone, was beyond anything I could've imagined in my wildest dreams.

Courtney and Bree had told me stories about their first times and other experiences beyond that, but nothing about sex with Sebastian was even close to what they had said. It was on an entirely different level altogether. But then again, that's the way everything is with Sebastian. Every feeling is intensified, every sensation heightened.

After we made love for the second time, Sebastian ran us a hot bath which is where we've been for the last twenty minutes or so, staring out at the incredible view. Eventually, I started quizzing him about the buildings that were within our view, surprised to find that he knows what almost every single one is.

"What do you say we get cleaned up, and I take you out for a nice dinner?" Sebastian speaks again, pressing his lips to the side of my neck. "There's this amazing little Italian restaurant just a couple blocks from here."

"I think that sounds perfect." I nearly groan at the thought of eating.

"Afterward we can walk around for a little while. I'd say we have at least an hour of sunlight left. Then maybe we can check out early and spend the morning in the city. What time is your mom expecting you home?"

"She works until six and then will probably sleep until three or four in the afternoon so we should be good until then. We'll just need to head back sometime after lunch maybe."

"Perfect." His hands slide down my arms and across my bare chest, causing my skin to prickle under his touch. "Let's go eat already. The sooner we do, the sooner I can get back here and plant myself inside of you again."

"You're insatiable." I giggle when he nibbles my earlobe with his teeth.

"Damn right I am, only for you, baby. I don't think I'll ever be able to get enough of you. This body," he slides one hand across my stomach and then lower, caressing me beneath the water. "It's like it was made just for me.

"I think you might be right." I instantly come alive under his touch.

"Tess," he groans into my ear, clearly egged on by my reaction to him. "If you keep riding my hand like that we're never going to get out of here." He nips at the flesh below my ear.

"I think that might be okay." My body takes over, seeking a need I know only Sebastian's touch can fill.

When he abruptly pulls his hand away and stands, water splashing over the sides of the tub, I instantly object.

"What are you doing?" I look up to see him wrapping a towel around his waist.

"I promised to show you the city, and that's what we're going to do. Even if it fucking kills me." He looks down at my naked body, heat in his eyes. "But when we get back, you're not going to be able to pry me off of you for the remainder of the night."

"You promise?" I smile innocently, making no attempt to get out of the tub.

"Baby, I do more than just promise." He smiles at me wickedly, grabbing another towel before extending his hand to me and helping me out of the bath.

***

"Well, what I tell ya?" Sebastian entwines his gloved fingers with mine as we make our way out of the restaurant and onto the rather crowded sidewalk.

"Amazing." I rub my overly full belly, not sure if I could feel any more perfect than I do at this very moment.

Unfortunately, due to the long wait for dinner, the sun has now set and we've lost what little hour of daylight we thought we'd have left. But the great thing about New York is it's even more alive at night.

Snuggling deeper into Sebastian's side when a cold breeze whips around us, he drops my hand and wraps his arm around my shoulders as he steers me to the right and then turns again about two blocks up.

The lights of the city illuminate the buildings, and even though it's after nine o'clock it could very well be the middle of the afternoon.

We spend the next two hours walking around, Sebastian showing me all the shops and famous landmarks I've only ever seen in movies. We spend a particularly long amount of time looking at all the billboards while Sebastian tells me about some of his favorite times visiting the city as a child. Of course, that was back when he lived in California and had to take a five-hour flight to get here.

"Do you miss it? California, I mean?" I ask when he falls silent next to me.

"Not as much as I used to." He shrugs. "Though I do miss the warmer temperatures. I hate the winter." He blows out a breath which instantly fogs from the cold.

"I don't know. I think I like winter—sometimes anyway. I love when there's a fresh snow and everything is covered in white. Snuggling up next to the window with a book and a cup of hot chocolate." I smile at the thought. "But I can see how someone who isn't used to the cold would not be as fond of it. I've lived here my entire life and still have a hard time adjusting when the weather changes." I pause, quickly adding, "Do you think you'll make it back to California someday?"

"Yeah," he answers without hesitation. "I mean, that is if you're up for living on the west coast." He nudges his shoulder against mine.

"Does that mean you're planning on including me in your future?" I say teasingly, but it's a question I've been dying to ask.

"There is no part of my future that I don't see you in, Tess." He turns toward me, resting his gloved hand on my cheek. "You are my future." He stares at me for a long moment before finally continuing, "For the longest time, I thought California was the only place I'd ever be happy. It was home and all I wanted to do was go back there. But that was before I met you. You're my home now." His words strike something deep inside of me, a reassurance I hadn't realized I needed until this very moment. "Do I want to go back someday; yes, I'd like to. But as long as you're by my side I'll be happy anywhere."

"Even if you have to endure negative temperatures?" I tease.

"Guess it just means we'll have to stay stocked on fuzzy blankets and lots of hot chocolate." He grins sweetly. "You're my home, Tess," he repeats.

"And you are mine." I smile up at him, my body choosing that exact moment to shiver.

"Come on, let's get you back to the hotel room and get you warmed up. It's freezing out here. Too bad we don't have any hot chocolate right now. Then again, I bet we can order some from room service."

"I can think of a few ways you can warm me up pretty quickly without any type of hot beverage," I tease, snuggling into his side as he leads us back in the direction of the hotel.

"Oh, trust me, Tess, so can I." Something wicked crosses over his face, and my stomach instantly twists in anticipation.

We can't get back to the hotel fast enough.

TESS

The weeks that follow our trip to New York are some of the happiest of my life. Sebastian has shown me the kind of love I only thought existed in romance books and fairy-tales. He's turned out to be the polar opposite of who I once thought he was and exactly what I had been missing in my life. But I'm also painfully aware that our days together could very well be numbered.

All I want to do is pause time, hold onto the moments with Sebastian while I can, but it seems like the tighter I try to grasp it the further out of my reach it slips. December turns into January and January into February with no signs of slowing down.

I've become one of *those* girls. You know, the ones who are so wrapped up in a boy that everything else just kind of falls to the wayside. Yeah, that's me. I know it. My friends know it. My mom knows it. We all know it, and yet there's nothing I can do to change it. Every second that I'm not with Sebastian feels like I'm suffocating. He says it's the same for him too, though sometimes I wonder if I'm holding on a little more tightly than he is.

"Hey." Bree stops by my locker just as I close it, pulling me from the inner turmoil that haunts me daily.

"Hey. Everything okay?" I ask, concern lacing my voice. It's not like Bree to just show up at my locker out of the blue, unless of course, something's wrong.

"Yeah, fine." She does a crap job of lying to me. "I just…"

"What?" I urge her to continue.

"I just ran into Blake." She lets out a slow breath. "With his tongue rammed down Ava Balinsky's throat."

"God, that asshole," I seethe, hating what he put Bree through and what he continues to put her through every day.

It's bad enough that in just four months she is going to be having his baby, and he has yet to even acknowledge it since everything went down at Sebastian's Halloween party. But to parade girl after girl in front of her face to purposely hurt her is low even for a guy like him.

He's lucky he's still able to walk around these halls freely after what he put Bree through. If it were up to me he would be in jail for putting his hands on my friend. But Bree being Bree, she insisted on letting things go. I think a part of her still loves him even after everything he did to her.

"It pisses me off that he thinks I even care who he kisses." She crosses her arms in front of herself. "Stupid bitch can have him. Maybe she'll get lucky, and he won't knock her around like he did me."

To someone outside looking in, Bree almost seems completely unaffected by the mess Blake has made of her life… Almost. She's always been a good actress, always putting on a show for everyone. But over the past few months, I've seen the holes in her exterior. She's still hurting over what Blake put her through, and then, of course, there's the baby and the fact that she's going to be a single mom at seventeen. If I was her, I'm pretty sure I'd have fallen apart a hundred times over by now.

"Who cares what he thinks." I give her a reassuring smile, slinging my bag over my shoulder. "You're way too good for him anyway, always have been."

"Someone needs to tell his ass that, knock him down a few pegs." She walks directly next to me as we make our way down the hall.

"Trust me, he already knows. Right now, he's just throwing a temper tantrum, showing his ass because he knows how bad he messed up. He's lucky Sebastian hasn't killed him after what hc pulled at Halloween."

"You're so lucky to have him," Bree interrupts before I can say more. "Sebastian," she clarifies. "The way he looks at you..." She trails off for a long moment, her right hand settling on top of her swollen belly. "What I wouldn't give to have someone look at me that way."

"Someday someone will," I promise. "You'll see."

"I doubt it. Who's going to want me after this?" She gestures to her belly. "I'm tarnished goods now."

"Don't say that. You are not. That baby is going to be an extension of you, and when you meet someone who loves you the way you deserve to be loved, he's going to love your child just as much."

"You're way too optimistic for your own good." She rolls her eyes, stopping outside of her math class.

"I can't help it. I just know things are going to work out—for all of us."

"I hope you're right." She gives me a half-hearted smile. "I gotta go. Mr. Jenkins will have my ass if I'm late again."

"Have fun." I give her a half wave before picking up the pace, dipping into my Economics class just as the bell rings.

***

"Oh my god, Tess, I just heard." Courtney slides down next to me at the lunch table where Bree and I are already planted. "LSU, that's incredible."

I'm instantly confused by her statement, but try to hide the fact that I have no idea what she's talking about.

"Sebastian must be over the moon right now," she continues. "A full scholarship. God, that man really does get everything he wants."

It takes several moments for her words to sink in and once they do, I feel like the floor is falling out beneath me. My chest tightens and suddenly I feel like it's near impossible to pull in a breath.

"Tess?" Courtney looks at me, her eyes wide in bewilderment. It takes a solid minute for realization to dawn, and the second it does all the color drains from her face.

"Oh god, you didn't know." She shakes her head from side to side. "Shit. Shit. Shit. Tess, I'm so sorry. I just assumed. I mean, Ant just told me this morning."

My earlier optimism that Bree had pointed out turns full circle, and my stomach knots with dread.

Sebastian got into LSU—a full scholarship?

The fact that Ant has known this long enough to share it with Courtney, and I had no idea only intensifies my feelings on the matter. It's one thing to find out your boyfriend has been accepted to a college a thousand miles away, it's another thing entirely to find out the news from someone other than your boyfriend.

"I knew he was applying." I shake off the panic I feel creeping its way in long enough to answer my friend. "I just didn't know he'd heard back." I try to brush it off like it isn't a big deal even though it feels like a *very* big deal to me.

"I'm sorry. I shouldn't have said anything."

"No, it's fine," I reassure Court, not wanting her to feel worse than I know she already does. "I'm sure he'll tell me about it later, probably just still trying to process it all." I force a smile.

"Yeah, you're probably right. Can you do me a favor and not say anything to Ant about me telling you?"

"I won't say a word to Anthony," I promise, knowing there's no way I'm going to be able to make the same promise when it comes to Sebastian.

When he finally makes an appearance a few seconds later I can't even look at him. Bree scoots down a seat to let him sit next to me, though honestly, I wish she would've just stayed put. It's easier to pretend like nothing's wrong when he's not sitting so close to me, his hand immediately finding my upper thigh under the table.

"Hey, babe." He kisses my temple, his gaze burning into the side of my face when I make no attempt to respond.

I want to be mature about this. I want to handle it rationally and not cause a big scene, but the longer I sit here the angrier I become. If LSU did, in fact, offer him a scholarship to play ball and he hasn't told me about it, it only means one thing. He's planning on accepting or worse, he already has.

There's no other explanation.

I knew this was coming. But with graduation just over three months away, I was starting to wonder if maybe he was reconsidering the schools he had shown interest in. I think a part of me was holding out hope that he simply wouldn't be able to leave me.

I know that's really selfish of me, but I can't help it. The thought of being here without Sebastian is just too much to even fathom.

"You okay?" Sebastian finally asks after several long moments have passed.

"Perfect," I grind out, turning to face him.

"You don't seem perfect," he observes, his voice low so only I can hear him.

"No?" I hate how sarcastic it comes out, but it's like the more seconds that tick by the more out of control I feel.

"No. You don't." His eyebrows draw together in confusion.

"Funny. I guess learning that my boyfriend is moving like twenty hours away has put a bit of a damper on my mood." With that, I push to a stand and quickly exit the cafeteria, dropping my still full tray into a nearby trashcan on my way out.

I can hear Sebastian's footsteps close behind me as I stomp through the empty hallway toward the back doors. I don't bother to turn around when he says my name. I just need to get out of this building.

Sebastian catches up to me the second the sun hits my face, his hand closing down around my forearm just as I suck in a deep inhale of cold air.

"Tess." He spins me toward him.

"Don't Tess me." I rip my arm out of his grip.

"I can explain," he starts, but I quickly cut him off.

"Explain what, Sebastian? How you purposely have been keeping things from me? How my best friend knew you had received a full scholarship to play football for LSU, and I didn't even know they were a serious contender?"

"You knew LSU was where I wanted to go."

"Yeah, because you mentioned it once—months ago." I swipe angrily at the tears that seem to come on without warning.

"Tess."

"Are you going to LSU, Sebastian?"

"I was planning on discussing everything with you tonight."

"Well, you can just get it over with and tell me now. I mean, you didn't wait to share the news with other people, so clearly it isn't some big secret."

"I only told Ant, and that's because I needed someone to bounce it off of. You're telling me that if you got a full scholarship to Columbia and accepting it meant we'd be separated that you wouldn't talk to Courtney and Bree first, get their opinions."

I hate that I know he's right. That's exactly what I would do. But that doesn't change how hurt I feel that I had to find out the way I did.

"So you're going to accept?" I question, the anger in my voice faltering.

"I don't want to leave you, Tess." He takes a step toward me. "But this is it. This is everything I've worked for."

"Are you going to accept it?" I repeat.

"I already have."

My eyes instantly go wide, and a rush of wind leaves my body like someone has just sucker punched me right in the stomach.

Deep down, the rational part of me knows this is a good thing. Sebastian's right, this is everything he's been working toward. He was just offered a full scholarship to play football at his dream college, and here I am souring the moment like a damn spoiled child. But at the same time, I can't help it. I can't help that I feel angry and hurt. I can't help that I want to scream and yell and make sure he knows how much I hate every second of this.

I stumble backward, not sure when the ground decided it wanted to swallow me up but willing to let it take me down either way. Before I can make it very far, Sebastian's arms are around me and I'm pressed firmly to his chest, his soothing voice soft against my ear.

"We'll figure it out, Tess. I promise. You're all that I care about, all that matters. I wouldn't be doing this if I didn't think it was the best thing for us. We can't hold each other back from doing what we've planned. As hard as it will be to leave you, I don't want to wake up five years from now and resent *you* for the choices *I* made. We can still do everything we want and be together at the same time. I'm not saying it will be easy, but I know we can do it."

"LSU is over a thousand miles away," I choke, letting my anger give way to the fear that is controlling it in the first place.

"I can come up on some weekends and holidays, it's less than a three-hour flight, and I can easily make that when time allows. And we'll talk on the phone every day," he reassures me, pulling back to meet my gaze. "I swear to you, Tess, no amount of miles is going to change my love for you. If nothing, it's only going to make me love you even more. And we'll cherish the time we get together more because we won't get it as often. I know we can make this work, Tess." He cups my cheek, the warmth of his hand soothing my cold flesh.

"I'm scared," I admit, swiping at the tears that continue to leak from my eyes, wishing like hell I knew how to stop them all together.

"I know you are, baby. I am, too. But I also know I need to do this."

"I know you do," I admit, letting out a deep breath. "And I love that you're determined enough to go after what you want head on. I just hate that your dream is taking you so far away from me."

"We still have some time to figure it all out, okay?" His eyes search mine for reassurance. "I'm so sorry that you found out this way, but I'm not sorry that you know. You were the only person I wanted to share this with, the first person I thought of when I got the call from the coach, but I also knew that telling you would be one of the hardest things for me to do."

"I'm sorry I made it even harder." Guilt tightens in my chest.

"Don't be. I should've just manned up and told you the instant I found out. Truth be told, I was scared. I'm still scared. But I know as long as I have your support, we can find a way to make this work. Just tell me I won't lose you over this."

"You're not going to lose me," I promise. "Ever."

He lets out a deep sigh and tightens his grip on me. "I want to spend every second I can with you. You're going to be so sick of me come June, you'll be ready for me to leave."

"June?" I question, assuming he had until at least August.

"Summer conditioning starts the first week in June."

"Wow. That's really soon." The reality of the entire situation sits like cinder blocks on my shoulders, weighing me down.

We have just over three months left before he leaves and suddenly the days between now and then feel like seconds ticking by on a bomb set to explode.

"It is. And I hate that we won't get to spend the summer together. But this is what it takes to play college ball. It's going to be demanding and time-consuming, but I'm up for the challenge. Who knows, maybe next year you'll decide LSU sounds a hell of a lot better than Columbia, and you can come be my own private cheerleader," he teases.

Truth be told, I'd be lying if I said I wasn't already considering it. While yes, Columbia is the dream, I honestly don't care where I go so long as I'm with Sebastian. I make a mental note to check out their admissions page later tonight.

"I think you're getting a little ahead of yourself," I retort, deciding not to rush into telling him anything until I know for sure that it's something I'm willing to do.

Could I see myself picking up and moving hours away from everyone and everything I've ever known just to be with Sebastian—yes. But I still have over a year before I graduate, and I know so much can happen in that time. I just need to slow down and remember to take it one day at a time.

"Come on. We should probably head back in." He drops a kiss to my forehead before turning to lead me back inside.

I didn't realize how cold it was outside until the stifling heat inside hits me like a brick wall the second we enter.

"Sebastian." I stop just inside, turning to face him. "Promise me that no matter what happens, you'll always be honest with me. No matter how hard the truth may be. I need to know that there won't be anything standing between us. If we're going to make this work, I need you to promise me."

"I promise, Tess. I promise a million times over." He pulls me back into his arms. "Don't overthink things. Just trust in this—in me, in us. We're going to be just fine. You'll see."

"I'm going to hold you to that," I say, smiling for the first time since all this started as I peer up at him.

"I hope you do." He grins, pressing a firm kiss to my mouth.

TESS

"Come on and just pick one already," Bree whines through the dressing room door where Courtney is currently trying on yet another dress.

Bree, who's less than five weeks away from giving birth, picked out her dress after trying on a whopping two. She settled on a light blue, knee-length number that's fitted in the bust and flows out over her belly. Even at eight months pregnant she looks gorgeous in it. Even though I can tell the pregnancy is wearing on her internally, externally she looks beautiful. Pregnancy really suits her.

"This is prom. It needs to be perfect," Courtney retorts, coming out of the dressing room wearing a floor-length red gown that does wonders for her complexion. She looks stunning. Then again, she looked stunning in the last twenty dresses she's walked out in as well.

"That one." Bree smiles, her feet stretched out in front of her as she lounges in one of the dressing room chairs, her hands splayed across her belly.

"Yeah?" Court questions, turning to look at herself in the floor-length mirror in the corner.

"Definitely," I agree, hoping maybe she'll actually take our advice this time.

I, like Bree, picked my dress pretty quickly, only trying on a handful before settling on the perfect one. It's a strapless pink gown that hits me about mid-calf. It's simple and elegant which is completely my style. I'm not nearly as flashy as my two best friends. Then again, I never have been.

"I think you're right." Courtney stares at herself for a long moment, nodding in approval.

"Thank god." Bree sighs loudly. "Do you see how swollen my feet are?" She holds up a flip flop-covered foot, her ankles about twice their normal size.

"God, I'm never having kids," Courtney says, shaking her head.

"Yeah, right," I disagree. "You say that now. Give it a few years."

Courtney starts to object but is quickly cut off when Bree abruptly announces, "I'm moving to California."

Not really sure where this is coming from, at first I'm not sure if I believe her. I can tell that Courtney is right there with me.

"Shut up." Courtney snorts.

"I'm serious. As soon as the baby is born. Honestly, I'm only staying that long because my doctor is here." She says, looking up to where the two of us are standing completely blindsided by her announcement.

"Wait, you're serious?" I question, my chest tightening.

"I am. I can't subject this child to what I grew up with. I won't. And honestly, I'm scared that if I stay here Blake will try to take the baby from me just out of spite. I think it's the right decision all around. My grandparents' have already cleared out a room for me and the baby and have talked to the local high school about me transferring for senior year."

"You're really leaving?" Courtney blurts, still not seeming to fully process the news.

"I am." Tears swim in Bree's eyes as she stands.

I can tell she's trying like hell to hold it together. She's cried more times since she's been pregnant than I've seen her cry during our entire friendship. I know it drives her crazy because she's never been one to show a lot of emotion.

"Trust me, the last thing I want to do is leave the two of you." She closes the distance between us, taking my hand in one of hers and Courtney's hand in the other. "But if I'm going to give this baby the best chance at a good life, I have to get it away from my mother and Blake. My grandparents' have already agreed to watch the baby during the day so I can go to school and graduate normally. I think this is the right choice all around."

"Bree." I fight back my own tears.

"You can't leave us," Courtney interjects, her voice swimming with emotion as well. "It's always been the three of us."

"And it always will be," She squeezes both of our hands. "I will come back and visit from time to time, and you guys can always come to visit me in California."

"But nugget." Court rests her free hand on Bree's belly. "We won't get to see him grow up."

"Yes, you will. I will send pictures, and we will see each other as often as we can. Besides, this isn't forever. This is just until I can establish myself on my own two feet and become stable enough to provide a life for this baby."

"I don't like it." I finally find my voice again. "But I get it. And I'm proud of you." I force a smile. "You're going to be an amazing mother."

"Thank you." The tears Bree has been holding back finally spill over and once they do, mine and Courtney's follow.

It's so hard to imagine my life without Bree in it. She's always been there, her and Courtney both. Now, not only am I losing Sebastian, I'm also losing one of my best friends—someone who is like a sister to me.

What started out as a fun, carefree day has morphed into an emotionally heavy and mentally exhausting one. By the time we leave the dress store just a few minutes later, all I want to do is go home and try to forget that next month is going to be one of the hardest I've ever had to face.

Unfortunately, Courtney insists we all go out to dinner afterward, so it's well after nine o'clock in the evening by the time she drops me off outside of my house. I throw her a half wave before making my way up toward the front porch, surprised to find Sebastian sitting on the steps waiting for me.

I jog toward him, knowing that after the day I've had he's the only person I want to see. That is until I spot the bottle of whiskey dangling from his fingers.

"Sebastian?" I question hesitantly, knowing immediately that something isn't right. "What are you doing here?"

"I didn't have anywhere else to go. I just couldn't stay there. I couldn't stay there another second," he mutters more to himself than to me, taking a long drag from the bottle.

"Hey." I take a seat next to him on the steps, angling my body to face him. "What's going on? Talk to me." I slide my hand across his shoulders.

"I can't do this. I can't fucking be who everyone thinks I should be. I'm going insane." He pounds on the side of his head with a closed fist, the abruptness of his actions cause me to jump slightly.

"Sebastian. You're drunk. Why don't you come inside and we can talk?" I suggest, not realizing how inebriated he is until this very moment.

"I don't want to fucking talk!" His voice echoes around us, his menacing gaze finding mine.

I can honestly say that I've never been afraid of Sebastian, but there's something scary about the way he's looking at me right now—his eyes full of rage and unpredictability.

"Okay, then tell me what I can do?" I try another angle, not really knowing how to approach him in this mind state. I've never seen him anywhere close to this drunk before, and it's clear something happened to make him want to drown himself in a bottle of whiskey.

"Unless you can somehow magically grant me new parents, there's nothing you can do," he bites, taking another long drink.

"What happened, Sebastian? Did your father do something?" I ask, knowing things haven't been easy for him on the home front recently.

Things have gotten much worse between him and his father since his parents learned that he had accepted the offer from LSU. Sebastian knew that losing the control over his future was going to be a tough pill for his father to swallow, but I don't think even he expected the backlash he's gotten because of it.

"Define *do something*?" he says flatly, staring straight ahead.

"Please talk to me?" I plead, wrapping my hand around his bicep in an effort to get him to look at me.

"What do you want me to say, Tess? That I'm the biggest disappointment in the world? How having me was the biggest mistake of my father's life? That he wishes I had never been born?"

I open my mouth to say something but can't find any words. I knew Jonathan Baxter was a piece of work, but this is a new low even for him. The anger I feel boiling in my chest only increases the pain I feel for Sebastian. How any father could say those things to his son is beyond me.

"Fuck. He's right, isn't he? I am a fucking disappointment," he adds bitterly.

"No, you're not. Don't say that." I quickly reposition myself in front of him, taking his face in my hands as I force him to meet my gaze. "You are not a disappointment, Sebastian, not to me. You are the most driven, talented person I've ever met, and I am in awe of you every single day. You make me want to be more like you. You make me want to fight for the things I want and believe that I can do anything. You did that, Sebastian."

"Did I?" His voice softens. "Because from where I'm sitting you're just another person in a long line of people I've let down."

"How did you let me down?" I argue, not letting him look away when he tries.

"I chose college over you?" He phrases it like a question.

"No, you chose to better *our* future by doing what's right for you right now. You're right to follow your dreams. You're not choosing anything over me, you're choosing it *for* me."

"If you believe that then you're even more delusional than I thought." His words are like a slap across the face, and I immediately let my hands fall away. "I chose it for me. Because that's what I do, I make everything about me."

"You're the least selfish person I know," I insist, not letting his attempt to hurt me get in the way of talking him off the ledge. He's trying to push me away, and I won't let him self-implode because of some bullshit his dad said to him.

"No, I'm not, Tess." He stands abruptly causing me to stumble backward a couple of steps. "I shouldn't have come here." He takes off through the yard toward his Jeep which I just now notice is parked across the street from my neighbor's house.

"Sebastian," I holler after him, following close behind. "Sebastian," I try again when he crosses the street and throws open the driver's side door. "What the hell do you think you're doing?" I make a grab at the nearly empty whiskey bottle, managing to catch him off guard enough to yank it free.

"What the fuck, Tess," he roars, grabbing for the bottle but missing it by a centimeter.

Launching the bottle as hard as I can, it hits the curb on the other side of the street and shatters into a million pieces.

Sebastian just stares at me wide-eyed for what feels like an eternity before the realization of what I just did seems to catch up to him, by which time I'm already trying to wrangle the keys from his hand.

"What the fuck, Tess," he repeats again as he rips his hand out of my grasp.

"Give me the keys, Sebastian," I seethe, doing everything in my power to pull his arm down so I can reach his hand.

"Get the hell off me," he growls, attempting to climb into the Jeep.

"You are not going anywhere right now." I practically crawl into his lap, still fighting to get the keys away from him.

"The fuck if I'm not." He lets out a roar before he's lifting me in the air and depositing me on the street in one swift movement.

I don't even know how he manages it. One minute I'm halfway inside the Jeep, the next I'm far enough away that he's able to swing the door shut without hitting me with it. I immediately make a move to open it again, but Sebastian quickly locks it seconds before the engine purrs to life.

"Sebastian." I beat on the driver's side window. "Please don't do this. Please," I plead, knowing half the neighborhood can probably hear me right now.

Running to the other side of the car, I manage to get the passenger side door open just as he pops the Jeep into drive. Realizing his mistake of not locking all the doors, he slams the vehicle back into park and turns his blazing glare on me.

"Get the fuck out of the car, Tess," he practically screams in my face.

I'm a little taken aback by the way he comes at me but quickly retaliate.

"NO!" I yell back twice as loud. "I'm not going to let you do this. I'm not going to let you push me away because of some fight you had with your father.

Newsflash—I AM NOT YOUR FATHER. I don't give a shit what he says about you, Sebastian. None of it is true. Do you hear me? None of it."

"Please, Tess. Just get out of the car. You don't know what you're talking about."

"Then tell me, Sebastian. Just talk to me."

"I can't!" His temper starts to slip. "Don't you see that! You would never understand."

"Why? Because I don't have a father," I bite, knowing full well that's not what he meant but letting my emotions get the better of me.

"Exactly, Tess." He throws his hands up in exasperation. "Because you don't have a father." His tone drips with sarcasm. "Just get the fuck out of the car so I can leave before I say something I can't take back."

"What? Say it. Say what it is you want to say, Sebastian," I press on, knowing I shouldn't, but I'm unable to stop myself.

This situation is spiraling out of control, and honestly, I have no explanation for why it even started to begin with. We've argued before, of course, but we've never fought like this. Nowhere even close to it. In fact, until tonight, I can't remember a time when Sebastian has even raised his voice at me, let alone yelled right in my face.

A part of me knows it's the alcohol talking, but it's impossible not to take every single word and action as a slice to my heart. This is not *my* Sebastian. This is not the boy who just yesterday looked at me like I was the only thing in the world he could see.

I have no idea who this person is, and that thought scares me more than anything else.

"Get out of the car, Tess," he demands again.

"I am not letting you drive like this. If I have to sit in this car all night I will, but I refuse to let you risk your life or someone else's because you insist on behaving like a lunatic. Grow up, Sebastian!"

"Tess," he warns, his voice low, "so help me if you don't get the fuck out of this car right now…"

"What, Sebastian?" I cut him off. "What could you possibly do to me that's worse than what you're doing right now? Do you even hear yourself?"

"Get. Out. Of. The. Fucking. Car. Tess." He punctuates each word.

"No," I repeat in the same tone.

"Then you leave me no fucking choice." With that, he pops the Jeep into drive and takes off like a bat out of hell.

I scramble to get my seat belt on, not for even one second considering that he would drive away with me still in the car. It just goes to show he's way beyond the point of talking down. It's clear he's not in his right mind, not even a little bit. I know deep down Sebastian would never put me in danger, but the fact that he's now speeding through town so drunk he can't keep the Jeep in his own lane tells me I made a huge mistake in thinking I could control *this* Sebastian.

"Please pull over, Sebastian. Please!" I plead, hanging on to the door when he takes a corner too fast and nearly flips us. I can feel the passenger side wheels come up off the ground seconds before they slam back down, causing the vehicle to bounce.

"Sebastian!" I scream, panic starting to set in.

This is it. It's all I can think. *This is how I'm going to die.* I can see it so perfectly. And yet, I wouldn't go back and change my decision to get into this car. If it means there's even a chance I can stop this insanity then it was worth the risk.

"Sebastian." I soften my approach, reaching out to touch his arm.

He jumps at the contact, flipping his gaze to mine. As if the reality of what is happening hits him like a ton of bricks, I can see the panic flash across his face seconds before the Jeep is screeching to a halt just on the outskirts of town.

I don't have time to think about myself or the fact that my heart feels like it's going to explode inside my chest from how quickly it's beating. All that matters is Sebastian. The way he crumbles in his seat, a sob tearing from his throat.

"Fuck. Fuck. Fuck!" he screams into his hands.

I don't know what to do.

Do I comfort him?

Do I let him get it out?

How do I fix this?

I don't even have time to answer my own question before I see the red and blue lights behind us. Sebastian seems to notice them the same time I do and when his gaze finally meets mine, I swear I can physically feel my heart splitting inside my chest.

"I'm so sorry, Tess. I'm so fucking sorry." It's all he has time to say before he's being removed from the vehicle.

Minutes later he's placed in handcuffs and shoved into the backseat of the police car while I'm forced to stand here and watch helplessly, knowing there's not one thing I can do to help him.

I don't think I've ever been more scared for someone in my entire life. But it's not only Sebastian that I'm scared for, I'm scared for me as well. I'm scared what this means for him. But more than anything I'm scared what this means for us.

TESS

"Please, Mom, you don't understand. I just need to make sure he's okay," I plead with my mom in the middle of the police station lobby, refusing to leave until I get to see Sebastian.

It's been nearly three hours since we were pulled over and Sebastian was stuck in the back of that police car, and I swear it's been the most agonizing three hours of my life.

"I just had to leave in the middle of my shift to come pick my daughter up from the police station. Forgive me, Tess, but I don't really care what you feel like you *need*," my mom retorts in a tone I've only heard her use a handful of times in my entire life. "I thought I raised you better than this. Getting into a car with someone you knew had been drinking. God, how could you have been so irresponsible?" She scolds me, not caring that we're on full display for anyone who cares to watch.

"You weren't there," I snap. "I was trying to stop him." Tears re-boil to the surface, and it takes everything in me to fight them down.

The words no more than leave my mouth when an officer appears through a door along the back wall leading

Sebastian into the lobby with Jonathan Baxter following closely behind.

"Sebastian." My feet are moving before I even process the action, but my effort to get to him is quickly cut off when my mom grabs my arm and pulls me backward.

"It's time to go, Tess." She attempts to pull me toward the door, but I'm having none of it, fighting her the entire way.

"Sebastian," I call to him, but he doesn't look up, his head turned to the floor, hands locked in front of himself. "Sebastian!" I raise my voice, my tone pleading and desperate.

My mom quickly steps around me, placing herself directly in the path between us, which also happens to put her face to face with Jonathan Baxter who looks down at her with a scowl on his face.

"Perhaps you should learn to control that daughter of yours," he suggests, his tone dripping with distaste as he moves to make his way past us, Sebastian on his heels.

"Me?" My mom whips around. "Your son is the one who got into a car drunk and put both his life and the life of my daughter in danger. I don't think you have any room to tell me what to do with *my* child."

"Well maybe had *your* daughter not pushed my son to his breaking point, he wouldn't have been drinking to begin with."

"What?" This time it's my voice that breaks the surface. "You're the one who pushed him to his breaking point!" I scream, the floodgates opening and tears now streaking down my cheeks. "You. No one else. So don't pretend like you give a shit about Sebastian because we both know you don't."

"I can see the apple doesn't fall far from the tree," he quips, his gaze bouncing between me and my mother. "Stay away from my son. I think you've done enough damage." This statement is thrown directly at me.

"Oh, you don't need to worry about that. There's not a chance in hell I would ever allow my daughter near *your* precious son ever again." My mom's voice cracks.

"Mom!" I object, my stomach bottoming out.

"I mean it, Tess. I trusted that boy." She points to where Sebastian is standing next to his father, his gaze still turned downward. "I trusted him with your life, and he repays me by putting you directly in harm's way. I won't have it. Never again." She takes a deep breath. "This is over." She gestures between me and Sebastian.

"You can't be serious!" I scream, feeling like I'm coming apart at the seams.

"Oh, I'm very serious." She turns back toward Sebastian who chooses this moment to look up.

One glimpse of his red swollen eyes and sullen expression, and I nearly hit the floor. I can feel my heart splintering off into a thousand pieces, and there's nothing I can do to stop it.

"We're done here," Jonathan says firmly, pushing the door open, and swiftly exiting the police station. Sebastian hesitates just long enough that my mother has time to say one last thing.

"You stay away from my daughter."

He nods only once and without saying a word, quickly turns and follows his father outside.

"Mom." I'm at my breaking point, the emotion so thick in my throat I can barely manage to get the word out.

"My decision is final," she says matter of fact. "Now, let's go."

***

"It's for the best, Tess," my mom says, shoving the car into park and shifting in her seat to face me. "I know it may not feel like it right now but it is."

"You don't know what you're talking about." I refuse to look at her, keeping my gaze locked out the passenger side window.

"Yes, I do, honey. You think I don't know what young love feels like?" She softens her approach. "I know how much you care for that boy, Tess, but after what happened tonight, there's no way I can continue to allow you to see him. He put your life in danger. Does that not say anything to you?"

"You don't know the situation, and you don't know Sebastian." I refuse to look at her.

"You're right, maybe I don't, but you are my daughter, Tess." She grabs my hand, but I quickly pull it away. "You can hate me all you want, but one day you'll see that I'm doing this to protect you. You are my world. You are all I have left of your father." The emotion that takes over her voice has my gaze finally drifting to hers. She swipes at a stray tear before continuing, "If something happened to you…" She trails off.

"Nothing happened to me, Mom. I'm right here," I reassure her.

"But something could've happened. Things could've ended much differently tonight than they did."

"But they didn't," I continue to argue.

"Tess, I love you. It's my job to protect you. Whether intentionally or not, that boy put you in horrible danger

225

tonight, and I simply can't take the risk that he'll do it again."

"Mom, please." My tears resurface in an instant. "I love him."

"I know you do. But, sweetie, he's leaving in a few weeks anyway. I think this is best all around."

"Best for you maybe. You're determining my entire life based on one bad choice. Sebastian is everything to me, Mom." My voice gets a little carried away as I struggle to reel in my emotion.

"Your entire life? I think that's a bit dramatic. You're only seventeen. Your life hasn't even really started yet. Trust me, one day this will all just be a distant memory. You don't see it now, but you will. One day when you have children of your own, you'll know I did this out of love."

"You can't keep me from him." The words seep out before I can stop them.

"I can. And I will. Even if that means I have to monitor you every waking minute," she warns.

"Good luck with that," I bite, directing all my anger at her.

"Phone." She holds out her hand. "Give me your phone, Tess," she continues when I just stare at her upturned palm.

"What?" I look at her like she has five heads. "I'm not giving you my phone."

"Yes, you are. Because I pay for that phone. So either you give it to me or I'll call and cancel your line. The choice is yours."

"Mom, please don't do this. Please," I sob, my hands shaking and my stomach so knotted I feel like I might vomit at any moment.

"You wanna threaten me, Tess, I will hand it right back to you. Now give me your phone."

I sit there for several seconds before finally digging my phone out of my back pocket, but instead of putting it in her outreached hand I throw it into her lap.

"Congratulations. I officially hate you," I spit, throwing open the car door and stomping toward the house.

I spend the rest of the night locked in my room pacing. My mom doesn't bother me. I think she knows right now is not the time. I still can't wrap my head around how quickly everything fell apart tonight.

Sebastian.

God, just the thought of how broken he looked at the police station makes my knees tremble beneath my weight. My strong, confident, carefree Sebastian was gone, replaced by a hollow shell that couldn't even look at me.

I know it only takes one night—one moment, one choice—to change the entire direction of your life. To take everything you thought you wanted or knew and jumble it into something almost unrecognizable. I experienced this first-hand the night I met Sebastian.

And now I'm terrified that this night—this moment, this choice—will change everything all over again. And not in a way that either of us ever saw coming.

***

I attempted to call Sebastian from the house phone the next afternoon while my mom was in the shower, but it kept going straight to voicemail. All I wanted was to hear his voice, to reassure him that no matter what my mom said nothing was going to rip us apart.

227

By Monday morning the knot in my stomach had grown substantially in size. I hadn't slept in nearly two days and couldn't stomach the thought of eating. I felt like my world was crumbling around me and had no idea how to fix any of it.

Sebastian never showed up for school, and his cell continued to go to voicemail. It was the same story on Tuesday. Again, a no-show. By Wednesday I'm running on fumes and just getting dressed for school feels nearly impossible.

When I walk into the building just after seven fifteen, I've all but given up hope of seeing Sebastian. So when I catch sight of him making his way down the hall, a rush of adrenaline runs through me and my body reacts as if on autopilot. I run to catch up to him, reaching him just as he stops in front of his locker.

"Sebastian." My voice is winded, my chest rising and falling at a rapid pace as I work to steady my raging heart.

I was prepared for a lot of things but when he turns to face me, I realize I couldn't have been less prepared for what I'm now looking at.

He looks like he's aged ten years in the past three days. His hazel eyes are dark and there are deep circles underneath. He looks as bad as I feel. Oddly, that makes me feel a little better. It means he's been just as miserable without me as I've been without him. For the first time since Saturday night, I feel a renewed sense of hope.

But that hope quickly comes crashing down around me.

"You shouldn't be here, Tess." There's an edge to his voice I didn't expect, and instantly my heart rate picks up speed kicking against my ribs like I'm in the middle of a marathon.

"What do you mean?" I blurt, hoping maybe I'm misreading the situation.

"I mean, you're not supposed to be here—as in with me," he says, turning his back to me as he fishes some books out of his locker. "Your mom was pretty clear."

"I don't give a shit what my mom says." I grab his arm, trying to force him back around. "Sebastian. Look at me."

"I'm sorry, Tess. I can't do this," he says, his back still to me.

"What?" I swear my heart stops beating altogether, a tingling sensation spreading down my face as everything starts to go numb.

"Your mom was right. I put you in danger. I could've killed you." He finally looks at me, and the distance I see in his eyes tells me he's already made up his mind. "This was good while it lasted, but I think it's time we face the reality here. This was never going to work out long term. I think it's easier all around if we just cut ties now and move on."

"But you promised me." I feel like the ground is going to open up and swallow me whole at any moment. "You promised we'd make it work. You promised."

"I shouldn't have promised something I knew I couldn't keep."

"You liar." My voice echoes down the hallway drawing the attention of several classmates as they pass by. Normally I hate causing a scene, but right now I really couldn't care less. "You're pushing me away because of what happened Saturday, but you don't have to. I love you, Sebastian. I know you would never intentionally put me in harm's way. Things just got out of hand, okay?" The desperation in my voice only portrays a small fraction of the panic I feel creeping into every pore.

"I'm sorry, Tess." He refuses to meet my gaze as he turns.

"Sebastian, please don't do this. Please." Tears pour from my eyes as I reach for him ,but he only shakes me off.

"I'm so sorry." His voice is so low I almost don't catch it and by the time I do, he's already walking away.

I'm not sure how long I stand there, my mind in disbelief, my body trembling in shock. *This can't be happening*, it's all I can think. I close my eyes willing myself to wake up.

Just wake up!

When I open my eyes and find myself staring down the same hallway which is now void of students, everything seems to hit me at once. Without thought, I turn and take off full speed through the hallway.

When I reach the exit, I don't stop. I push on, my feet pounding the pavement as I just run faster and harder than I've ever run before.

I don't know at what point my legs finally give out. All I know is one minute I'm moving and the next I'm lying flat on my back in my front yard, looking up into the bright cloudless sky.

My chest heaves up and down as I try to catch my breath. I feel like I'm suffocating. No matter how much air I pull in it never feels like enough.

It's not lost on me that this is a feeling I'm likely going to have to get used to.

Sebastian is my world, my air. I can't breathe without him. I can't survive without him. I can't imagine a world without his smile, his touch, the way he sounds when he tells me he loves me.

The thought of never hearing that again has me rolling to the side, letting go of the small amount of juice I managed to keep down this morning. I choke and gag, feeling like I might die at any moment.

Collapsing back onto my back, I feel like the sky closing down around me, trapping me in a world I no longer want to be a part of.

I close my eyes—seeing his face, his eyes, his smile. But even those are quickly replaced by what I saw today. The sadness, the pain, the wall that was so clearly placed between us when nothing used to exist in that space.

Every painful moment of the last five days seems to leak over into all the happy ones—tainting them, changing them, ripping my happiness away piece by piece until all that remains is a hollow feeling in my chest and an aching loss in the pit of my stomach.

TESS

It's funny how quickly your life can change. One minute I'm dress shopping with my best friends in preparation of my first prom, the next I'm sitting on my bedroom floor looking at my beautiful dress hanging on the back of my closet door knowing that I'll probably never get to wear it.

I have no intention of going to prom tonight, without Sebastian there's really no point. And considering he's done everything in his power to avoid me since our "break up" last Wednesday, I'm not really sure I want to see him anyway.

Okay, that's a lie. A big, fat, stupid lie that I've tried to convince myself of all day. Truth is, I'm terrified that if I go he won't be there or worse, he'll be there with another girl. Just the thought makes me want to throw up.

I shake it off, knowing there's no way he would do that to me. But then again, do I really know what he's capable of after this past week? For all I know he would flaunt some girl in front of me just to drive home the point that we're over.

I swipe at a tear that manages to escape my eye, angry with myself for not being able to just move on the way he seems to have.

It's like he just snapped his fingers and his world reset back to before we were together. I pass him in the hallway, and he doesn't even look up at me. It's like I never existed.

He rejoined his old lunch table, which has proven to be the hardest part of my day to get through. Watching him across the room laugh and cut up with his football buddies and various girls like he doesn't have a care in the world is some sick and cruel torture I shouldn't be forced to endure. After all, I didn't do anything to deserve any of this, and yet he has this way of making me feel like I brought it all on myself.

Hell, maybe I did.

I should've followed my gut a long time ago. The one that told me to steer clear. But even knowing what I know now and hurting the way I am, I can't bring myself to regret my time with Sebastian.

He may be putting on a good act, convincing everyone that he's happy and free once again, but I see through it. Because deep down I know Sebastian at his core, and I know this is his sorry attempt to make me hate him, to push me away. I wish it wasn't working... Or maybe I wish it was working better...

God, my emotions are so all over the place I can't even get a real grasp on how I feel anymore. But the one thing I can grasp, the one feeling that is the most prominent is sadness. I try to refocus it, hone in on the anger I know is building there behind the pain, but at the end of the day, it always comes back to the gaping wound in my chest where my heart used to be. The splintering pain that only seems to increase with each day that passes.

I wish I could turn it off. I wish I could find some sense of the person I was before Sebastian, but I'm not even sure that girl exists anymore.

I jump when I hear the doorbell ring, not expecting company. Slowly rising to my feet, I let out an annoyed groan when whoever is at the door rings it several more times in concession.

"Tess." I hear my mom call down the hall from the bathroom.

"I'm getting it," I grumble, emotion overwhelming me when I pull open the door to find my two best friends standing on my porch both dressed in pajamas.

Bree smiles and holds up the pizza box in her right hand, her belly so large she could probably balance the box on it instead. My gaze flips from her to Courtney, who gives me a wicked grin and pulls a bottle of vodka from her bag just long enough for me to see what it is before she shoves it back down.

"What—what are two doing here?" I question in disbelief, certain they would be getting ready for prom right now.

"Like we'd go to prom without you," Courtney retorts, pushing past me into the house, Bree fast on her heels.

"You guys," I start to object, closing the door behind them.

"Before you say anything," Bree turns toward me. "Just know that the last thing I want to do is go to prom looking like this." She gestures down to her belly.

"And the last thing I want to do is go to prom with Anthony. Jackass is lucky I haven't dumped him already." Courtney's statement surprises me, but I don't have time to comment before Bree cuts back in.

"So you see, you'd actually be doing *us* a huge favor by letting us just crash here tonight. Besides, this might very well be the last girl's night we have like this," she adds, an air of sadness to her voice.

I still can't believe that in just a few weeks Bree is going to be moving all the way to the other side of the country. It seems even more surreal that she's also about to become a mom. Things are changing so fast, and it's terrifying that I have no control over any of it.

"Hi, girls." My mom chooses this moment to come around the corner, her wet hair twisted up in a fluffy white towel.

"Hey, Mrs. W." Court smiles. "Hope you don't mind if we keep Tess company tonight," she adds quickly.

"Not at all." My mom smiles. "I think it's great," she says, turning her attention back to me. "Tess, baby, I'm running a little late. Would you mind throwing me a sandwich and some veggies in my lunch box."

"Sure, Mom." I nod, making my way into the kitchen with Bree and Court while my mom heads back to her bedroom to finish getting ready.

"So…" Courtney drags out, hoisting herself up onto the kitchen counter while Bree sets the pizza and snacks on the table. "How's everything with…" She points toward the back of the house where my mom is.

"Different," I admit, pulling open the fridge. I grab the chicken salad and the veggie tray, turning to set them on the island before continuing, "We haven't really talked about things since last Saturday. I think, like Sebastian, she just wants to pretend it never happened."

"I think you're lucky to have someone who cares so much." Bree steps up next to me, dropping the loaf of bread she got out of the pantry onto the island.

"I know." I let out an audible sigh. "It's just hard right now."

"And Sebastian? Any word?"

"Nothing." The tears form without warning, and once again I'm left trying to blink them down without allowing them to spill over.

Sensing my shift, Courtney is off the counter and on the other side of me in five seconds flat.

"Hey." She drops her arm over my shoulder while Bree wraps hers around my waist, both squeezing me. "At least you still have us," she offers, bumping her hip against mine. "And tonight, we're going to forget all about prom and boys. We're gonna catch a little buzz." Bree clears her throat at Courtney's words. "Okay, you and I are." Court grins, taking a small step backward. "Preggers over here is just going to have to observe and be jealous."

"I don't know if drinking is a good idea right now. You're likely to have a sobbing mess on your hands if you pump me full of vodka," I object.

"I think we're going to have a sobbing mess on our hands regardless. Better to have you a little inebriated." She winks. "And we didn't just bring your favorite pizza either." She stalks over to the table and dumps out the bag Bree set there moments earlier littering the table with chips, candy, and my absolute favorite—

cinnamon butter popcorn. "Did we do good or what?"

"I don't know what I'd do without you girls," I admit, feeling like I can breathe just a tiny bit easier.

"Lucky for you, you won't ever have to find out." Bree throws some veggies in a baggie and drops them into my mom's lunchbox just as I finish making her sandwich. "You'll always have us. No matter what," she states matter of fact.

"I'm gonna hold you to that ya know," I say, zipping up the lunchbox before turning to face her, taking her belly in my hands. "And this little one is going to be spoiled rotten by his aunty Tess, even if he is three thousand miles away."

"It won't be so bad," Bree says, looking down at my hands on her belly and then back up to meet my gaze. "You'll see."

"I still can't believe your ass is leaving us. Senior year just won't be the same without you," Courtney says, stepping up next to us.

All three of us share a silent moment where we just kind of take it all in. Each of us looking back and forth between the others, fully aware that everything is about to change and that this time—this moment—is something we'll never get back.

***

My mom left for work shortly after Courtney and Bree arrived. While she still hasn't given me my phone back, she's been pretty trusting that I won't go see Sebastian while she's at work.

I think she can tell by the way I've been sulking around the house that things haven't gone the way I wanted them to, but I have yet to actually confirm with her that we've officially broken up. In some weird way, I don't want to give her that satisfaction. Though I highly doubt she'd gain anything from it.

She's my mom, and I know she hates how badly I'm hurting right now. And while I still blame her in large part, I also know I can't stay mad at her forever. Deep down I know she's just doing what she thinks is right.

"So what's up with you and Anthony anyway?" I finally return to the comment Courtney made earlier.

Sitting in the middle of my bedroom floor with my two best friends, talking and laughing over the last hour, has dramatically improved my mood. Of course, the vodka and pizza helped, too.

I mean, don't get me wrong, the nagging feeling in the pit of my stomach is still there, but the buzz of the alcohol and the company makes it a little easier to ignore.

"He's been really distant recently," Court finally speaks after a long moment. "I honestly don't know what's going on with him. It's like ever since you and Sebastian broke up he's been making excuses not to spend time with me. Obviously, he's been sitting with Sebastian at lunch again. At first, I just thought it was the transition. You know, he felt like he needed to be there for his friend, but now I'm thinking it's something more."

"I'm so sorry, Court," I mutter, feeling suddenly responsible for her issues on top of my own.

"Don't you dare." She wags a finger at me, taking a long pull from the vodka before shoving it into my hand. "This is not your fault. Things haven't been that great with us recently if I'm being honest. I can't help but feel like if it wasn't for you and Sebastian being together, we would've broken up weeks ago. Now that you guys aren't," she gives me an apologetic look, "I can't help but wonder how much longer we have."

"I didn't realize you guys were having problems." I take a drink of vodka, cringing at the disgusting taste as it burns a trail down my throat.

"No one really knows." She shrugs.

"You know, for supposedly telling each other everything, we sure do keep a lot to ourselves," Bree observes, finishing off another slice of pizza.

Thinking over her comment, I can't help but agree. First, it was me, keeping my new relationship with Sebastian kind of hush hush in the beginning. Then it was Bree and the whole Blake/pregnancy fiasco, and now Courtney with her relationship problems. Seems we all have trouble opening up about certain things.

"Speaking of that." Court turns her gaze to Bree. "How's the Blake situation?"

"There is no situation. He's barely looked at me in months." She shrugs.

"It's for the best." I snag her hand, giving it a squeeze. "He's lucky he's not dead or in jail for putting his hands on you."

"I still don't know what the hell I was thinking." She shakes her head. "I didn't think I'd ever be that girl. It's funny how certain things can bring everything into perspective. I remember the first time it happened. He was drinking, got mad at me over something stupid, and ended up pushing me into a wall. He apologized afterward, promised he'd never touch me like that again. But then he did. It kept getting worse with each time that it would happen until eventually, I had lost all control over the situation. I knew I shouldn't, but every time he asked for forgiveness I granted it. I guess I just kept hoping he would stop because deep down I really thought I loved him."

"And now?" I ask.

"Now I know that what we had wasn't love. I've finally accepted that I can't bury my past by sabotaging my future. At least not anymore." She rubs her hand across her belly. "I can't change what happened to me when I was younger, but I can make the choice not to let it define me."

"I'm so proud of you," I speak the truth, amazed by how much Bree has changed over the past few months. It's almost like she's a completely different person with all my favorite parts of her still intact.

"It's crazy how much we've all been through together," Courtney adds, the moment seeming to catch up with her. "I can't believe this is the last time the three of us will be together like this. God, we've been inseparable since grade school, and now here we are on the cusp of adulthood."

"You still have senior year," Bree reminds her. "And you and Tess are going to be just fine without me. Besides, we can video chat all the time, and you'll be right there with me through it all." She picks my hand up and then grabs Courtney's, her eyes going back and forth between the two of us. "I love you girls so much."

"Me, too." I fight back the swell of emotion in my chest.

"Oh my god, stop already." Courtney pulls her hand back and swipes at her eyes. "I don't want to spend tonight crying." She quickly climbs to her feet.

"Then what do you want to do?" I ask, looking up at her.

"I want to..." She looks around the room, a smile pulling at the corners of her mouth when she spots my wireless speaker on my desk. "Dance." Her smile widens as she pulls out her phone and turns the Bluetooth on.

"Dance?" Bree snorts. "Will you look at me?" She gestures to her belly.

"You're pregnant, not dead. Now get your ass up." Court laughs, taking Bree's hand and pulling her to her feet. "It's prom after all. And what is prom without a little dancing."

Shaking my head, I manage to stand without swaying too much, not realizing just how affected I am by the vodka until now.

It's only seconds before some bubble gum pop song starts blaring from the speaker, and the instant it does we all three take one long moment to look at each other. It's like we're seeing how long the others can stay still before finally giving into to the ridiculously upbeat tune. Court breaks first, and before long we're all jumping and twirling around my bedroom like we don't have a care in the world.

This is exactly what I needed—to laugh, to dance, to remember what if feels like to just be one of the girls. And while Sebastian is never far from my mind, it's the first time in almost two weeks that I think maybe, just maybe, I can find the strength to get through this.

SEBASTIAN

"Sebastian." Tess's voice washes over me from behind, and I instantly feel like I've been sucked under a tidal wave. Water whips around me, pulling me further under the weight until I feel like I'm suffocating.

My skin prickles, my body all too aware of her nearness. I try to move, try to speak or even think, but the pressure continues to hold me under. It takes several seconds for me to find my way to the surface, able to suck in a deep shaky breath before turning to face her.

The second those blue eyes hit me, all the air leaves my body a second time, only this feels a million times worse than just hearing her voice. Seeing her face, seeing the pain and hurt so clearly etched in every single beautiful feature and knowing I put it all there is almost more than I can bear.

"I'm late for work." I hear my voice but it doesn't sound right. It's too forced, too panicked to come out as anything other than desperate.

"Oh." She seems surprised by my excuse, her eyes full of apprehension.

Fuck, why does she have to be so fucking beautiful?

All I want to do is reach out and touch her perfect skin, tuck a piece of her silky hair behind her ear the way I always used to, kiss those soft pink lips that have always been my undoing. All I want is her, and yet I insist on denying myself.

It's for her own good. It's easier this way.

But is it really? She looks so sad. How can any of this be good?

Because you crossed a point of no return, my inner voice continues to argue. I put her in danger, I hurt her, I did things I swore I'd never do, and now I have to suffer the consequences.

I'm not good enough for Tess, I never was. Staying with her will only result in me hurting her even more. Staying with her will eventually soil all the things I love about her until there are no parts left of the young innocent girl I fell in love with.

Pissed off at myself, I slam my locker closed and take off down the hallway without so much as another word.

I don't expect Tess to follow me. I expect her to let me walk away the same way I've been doing for weeks. So needless to say, I'm not prepared when she rounds on me again just as I reach my Jeep in the back row of the parking lot.

"You're a coward, you know that?" Her voice is eerily calm and when I finally turn to face her again her expression has morphed into something I never expected to see when she looked at me—hate.

She should hate me—I deserve it—but seeing the emotion so prominent on her face makes me realize how much I had hoped she never would.

"Tess." I sigh, running a hand through my hair.

I don't know how much strength I have left. I can feel myself caving more and more with every second that passes.

"No," she cuts me off. "Don't' you dare. Don't you dare blow me off with some lame ass excuse about working. God." She throws her hands up in exasperation. "How stupid do you think I am?" Her voice breaks at the end, and it takes everything in me not to pull her into my arms.

When I fail to say even one damn word she quickly continues.

"Tomorrow is your last day here." She gestures behind her to the school. "This is it. This is all we get. You're leaving in two weeks, Sebastian. Two weeks. Is this really how you want our story to end? After everything we've been through? You're just going to walk away after one incident and never speak to me again?"

I can see the tears brimming her eyes, but she manages to push them down. Thank fuck. I don't think I could handle her tears right now.

"I don't get it," she continues. "I don't get how you go from the sweetest guy I've ever met to the biggest asshole in the world overnight. Newsflash—I didn't do anything to you. So why are you treating me like I'm public enemy number one?"

I try to fight down my emotion, try to hold it in the way I have been since everything fell to shit, but I feel it boiling to the surface. I feel every ounce of anger and sadness locked inside threatening to pour out of me, and I'm not sure I have the ability to contain it any longer.

"Because I have to, Tess." My voice explodes between us, but she doesn't budge an inch, doesn't even flinch like somehow she knew it was coming. "Don't you fucking get it? I can't be around you. I can't talk to you or look at you without wanting to be with you, and I can't be with you. I can't."

"Bullshit!" she calls right back, her voice just as loud. "You CAN be with me. You're the only thing keeping us apart, Sebastian. You." She points at my chest. "You can make all of this stop—all of it—it's all in your hands."

"I'm not good for you, Tess," I start but am immediately cut off.

"Don't give me that *I'm not good for you* bullshit. You are good for me. You've always been good for me. So you made one mistake. So what! You're human. You're allowed. That's no reason to deny yourself the ability to be happy."

"You just don't get it, Tess. I could've killed you."

"But you didn't. God, why do insist on making this situation so much worse than it is? You didn't do anything to me. I'm alive and well. See! Do you see me?" she screams, eyes wide and voice strained as she gestures to herself. "What you're doing now—what you've been doing these past few weeks—is a million times worse than what you did that night. Maybe if you weren't so hell-bent on punishing yourself you'd see that."

"I don't want to see it, Tess." My tone is borderline crazed, my hands shaking uncontrollably. "I don't want to look at you anymore. I don't want to hear your voice or think of you every time I smell lavender. I don't want to see your eyes when I close mine or feel your smile against my neck like you used to do right before you'd kiss it. I don't want you to be the last thing I think of when I go to sleep or the first thing that crosses my mind when I wake up. I just want you to go away, Tess. I want you to leave me alone and let me forget you. Because it's fucking killing me. It's killing me." I stress the last sentence, not aware of the tears swimming in my eyes until I feel one trickle down my face.

"Sebastian," she chokes, her voice clogged with emotion.

"I can't do this, Tess. I can't. Your mom was right." I take a deep breath and let it out slowly. "She trusted me with your safety, and I betrayed her—and you. But it's not just about that night. It's what that night made me realize." I take both of her hands in mine. "You loved me so much you were willing to give up everything to be with me, including Columbia. And, Tess, I would've let you. I would've let you follow me around and live my dream never once considering what you were giving up for me. I refuse to do that to you. You deserve more, Tess. You deserve so much more, and even if it kills me I'm going to make sure you get it."

"I just want you," she sobs, the action splintering my already cracked heart.

"And I just want you. But I can't let you give up everything you've worked so hard for. I won't. I love you, Tessa Wilson. I love you like I've never loved another person in my entire life. But I have to let you go. I have to. I just need you to let me go, too."

"I don't know how," she whimpers, her shoulders shaking as sobs rake her body.

"Neither do I," I admit. "But I choose to believe that this is not goodbye forever. You are a part of me now, Tess, and no matter where life takes us or how much time stretches between us, that is one thing that will never change. You showed me what it means to be loved and to love someone—really love someone—and for that, I will be eternally grateful. I'm just sorry I couldn't say all this to

246

you weeks ago, but I'm saying it now. I love you, Tess. I love you so fucking much."

I lose the battle not to pull her into my arms. Within seconds she's against my chest, her tears soaking the thin fabric of my t-shirt as she clings to me like her life depends on it, and damn it if I don't let her. Because I feel it too, knowing that the moment she lets go my world is going to be a hell of a lot darker, and I'm just not sure I'm ready for that yet.

This isn't how I intended for it all to go down. In a way, I think I hoped by shutting her out she would grow to hate me which would make leaving her that much easier. Now I see how wrong I was. Having her hate me was never the solution. I should've just been honest with her from the start, told her the truth about why I pushed her away, but honestly, I don't know if I would've had the strength before now.

I'm not sure how long we stand there, wrapped in each other's arms, saying a silent goodbye that neither of us really wants, but I think both acknowledge that we need.

By the time we finally pull apart the parking lot is almost empty and there's a sudden heaviness around us, like the weight of everything has leaked into the very air we breathe.

Without a word, I help her into my Jeep and we make the quick drive to her house in silence. I make sure to park a few houses down when we finally reach her street, not wanting her mom to see her with me.

Tess stares out the window blankly for several long moments before she finally speaks, not once looking in my direction. "I don't think I can do this, Sebastian," she admits, her voice weak.

"You can, Tess. We can," I reassure her, not sure who the hell I'm trying to convince.

"I'll miss you every single day." She chokes on another sob working its way out of her throat. "Every day," she repeats, taking a deep shaky breath and letting it out slowly, her eyes still fixed out the window. "I love you." The last part is a strangled cry as she quickly climbs out of the Jeep and takes off down the sidewalk not once looking in my direction.

I watch her walk away, letting go of the emotion I've been fighting to keep in from the moment her voice sounded behind me. I cry for the girl I love, for her pain, for mine. I punch my steering wheel and curse myself until my voice is hoarse, and my eyes feel so heavy I don't know if I can manage to keep them open any longer.

I cry until I simply have no tears left to fall, and then I do the only thing I can do; I take one last deep breath and drive away. Leaving behind the only girl I've ever loved, praying like hell I made the right choice for not just her, but for me as well.

TESS

Six months later…

"Can you believe Mr. Jordan expects us to write a thousand-word essay over Christmas break? What the hell is wrong with that man?" Courtney complains as we make our way through the parking lot.

"What do you expect? He's notorious for giving out the worst assignments at the worst possible times. Are you really all that surprised?" I shake my head, stopping next to my car which is parked directly next to Courtney's.

It isn't much, a beat-up Jeep Wrangler that's nearly as old as I am. I worked full-time all summer to buy it, and even though I told myself it was because I liked Jeep's, deep down I know I picked it because it reminds me of Sebastian.

I named my old rusty girl Sara Beth. SB—get it? Sara Beth. Sebastian Baxter. Same initials. Even my Jeep is named after him, though I tried to disguise it by making it a girl Jeep. I really am pathetic.

The hard knot that forms in the pit of my stomach anytime I think of Sebastian rears its ugly head. It's the same feeling I get every time I think of him, which happens to be a lot considering it's been months since I've seen or spoken to him.

"Hello, earth to Tess." I look up to find Courtney looking at me with confusion.

"What?" I question, trying to refocus.

"What was it this time?" She crosses her arms over her chest and looks at me expectantly.

"What was what?" I play stupid even though I know it will do me no good. I give her a few seconds to really drive the point home that she can see right through me before finally answering honestly. "I was just thinking about Sara Beth," I say, resting my hand on the driver's side door.

"Oh, you mean the Jeep you named after Sebastian?" She gives me a pointed look, daring me to dispute it. When I don't, she quickly adds, "Ice cream at Luna's?"

Courtney is one of those who thinks ice cream solves everything. After she and Anthony broke up in July we practically lived at Luna's, an old ice cream parlor in town, for weeks. We still go there quite often. Too often really.

"It's like twenty degrees out here, and you want ice cream?" I chuckle, opening my driver's side door to throw my bag inside.

"When do I not want ice cream?" she asks sarcastically, tapping her foot on the concrete.

"Fine. One scoop." I cave, knowing at least this way I won't have to go home and sit in the deafening silence like I do every other night.

"Meet ya there." She squeals before quickly disappearing into her car.

Laughing, I shake my head and then climb into my Jeep. Turning the ignition, I'm met with the same familiar grumble I hear every time I start Sara Beth. I swear it sounds like she's cursing me for not just letting her rest.

Okay, so I'll admit I have this weird relationship with my Jeep. It's probably not the healthiest thing in the world but whatever. It beats spending my days in therapy which I tried shortly after Sebastian left for Louisiana. It didn't take me long to realize that therapy just wasn't for me. Plus, had I kept it up I probably would've ended up bankrupting my mother which is never a good thing.

I follow Courtney through the school parking lot and out onto the street, laughing when she attempts to make faces at me in her rearview mirror, half of her face cut off from my vantage point.

Courtney has been my saving grace, the one who has kept me from completely losing my mind over the past few months.

Sebastian leaving was hard enough, but then having to turn around and say goodbye to Bree and baby Jackson just weeks later made his absence even harder to deal with. Bree kept me busy, and I was able to throw all my focus into helping her prepare for the baby and the move. But once they were gone there was this eerie silence, an emptiness I just couldn't shake.

It all happened too quickly. One moment everything was one way, the next it all changed. Baby Jackson was born, and I was forced to say goodbye yet again. And not just to Bree but to her son, who I grew extremely attached to in the week before they left.

She was a natural with him out of the gate, just like I knew she'd be. Bree has always acted with her heart, searching for the love she was denied growing up. I think she needed Jackson more than she realized. He gives her something to sink that love into. Someone she can love unconditionally who will love her the same in return.

I don't hear from her as often as I'd like, but I know she's extremely busy with school and raising her son. The last time we spoke Jackson was on the cusp of crawling, though I'd say it will be a couple months before he actually nails it down. Because we always Facetime, I was able to see him in action—his little butt up in the air as he rocked back and forth on all fours.

He'll probably have mastered crawling and be walking by the time I talk to her next. It's scary how fast things are happening now. I have to remind myself sometimes to just slow down and look around me. Before I know it all of this will be gone.

I pull up next to Courtney in a street side parking spot and kill the engine to my Jeep. I take a deep breath in and let it out slowly, pushing down the sadness that seems to cling to me like a bad stench I can't seem to wash away.

Giving myself one last pep talk, I quickly exit the Jeep and join my best friend on the sidewalk. She may be able to see through the happy exterior I'm clearly faking, but she doesn't make a habit of calling me out on it.

I think she realizes that my smile acts as my armor, something I put on to protect myself, but it's also the very substance that holds me together. Without it, I wouldn't be able to get through most days. Even with it sometimes I'm not so sure.

And no matter how many times I try to secure the pieces in place, they always have a way of slipping when I least expect it. That's when thoughts of Sebastian creep in, the moments when I give in and let myself mourn the love I lost—love that still haunts me every single day.

Every corner I turn, every street I travel, every hall I walk—I see him everywhere. His eyes, his smile, his touch—these are all things that are embedded in my brain, tattooed on my skin, and etched into my heart.

***

"Tess?" I hear my name, but it takes a few seconds for me to register the voice.

When I glance up from the book in front of me I'm more than a little surprised to see Anthony standing directly next to the small table I'm currently occupying in the back of my favorite little coffee shop.

"Ant?" I question, dropping my paperback down onto the table as I stand and offer him a hug. "Wow. It's been a long time," I say, gesturing to the seat across from me which he quickly takes.

"Yeah, it has." He sets his coffee on the table in front of him, an awkward silence stretching between us before I quickly speak again.

"What are you doing here? Are you visiting your family for holidays?" I press.

It's so weird seeing him. He hasn't changed a bit. And just like that, I feel like I'm there all over again. Sebastian's face instantly flashes in front of my eyes, and it takes everything in me to shove the image down and focus on Ant.

"Yeah, I just came down for New Years. I'm actually getting ready to head back to campus." He takes a sip of his coffee, stretching his long legs out underneath the table.

"How's Boston? I bet it's amazing there."

Anthony got accepted to Boston College shortly after Sebastian was accepted to LSU. And while he didn't earn the full scholarship that Sebastian did, he still got lucky enough to play for their football team.

"It is. I love it." He smiles, the action easy and carefree.

God, what I wouldn't give to smile like that and actually mean it.

"That's incredible."

"I love living there," he continues. "Everything about Boston is so alive."

"I'd love to go there one day," I say, lacking anything of real interest to add to the conversation.

"You still planning on heading to the Big Apple in the fall?" he asks without missing a beat.

"If I get into Columbia, yes, that's the plan." I sigh, trailing my fingers across the top of my cup that's still ninety percent full of the hot chocolate I ordered nearly an hour ago.

"You will," he states like there's no question in his mind.

"Well, I wished I shared in your confidence but thank you." I shift in my seat.

Anthony and I have never been close. Even throughout my relationship with Sebastian and his with Courtney, we never shared a *real* conversation. Sure, we hung in the same circle, ate lunch together every day, hung out after every football game, but we never connected beyond him being Sebastian's friend and me being Courtney's. It almost seems strange sitting here with him, just the two of us, especially given how long it's been and everything that's happened.

"How is she?"

Ant's question comes straight out of left field but doesn't surprise me one bit. It's the exact same question that was on the tip of my tongue the second he sat down—*how is he,* but I fought the urge to ask.

"She's good." I relax back into my chair, taking a drink of my *not so* hot chocolate. "She just found out she got accepted to the University of Alabama."

"Alabama. Wow." He thinks over that for a long moment, taking a drink of his coffee before continuing. "Well… That's awesome. Good for her." I can tell there's more he wants to say, but for whatever reason, he decides against it.

"Yeah, she's doing pretty good. She misses you," I say, knowing Courtney would probably kill me if she knew I was telling him this. "Though I'm sure she'd never admit it."

"I know that all too well." He chuckles, like he's remembering something funny.

"Have you guys spoken at all?" I ask, already knowing they haven't.

Even after all these months, I still don't know the specifics of why they broke up. Courtney blew it off—saying he wanted to go into college unattached which is why he pulled away from her toward the end of his senior year—and before I could turn around twice she was sleeping with someone new.

I always suspected there was more to the story, especially given how quickly she forced herself to move on, almost like she was trying to prove a point to him. I've pressed her a few times, but she's never given me much more than that.

"No. I've text her a couple times but to be honest, life is pretty crazy right now. My course load is insane and as you know, I've never been one to excel in the classroom."

"Well, you always managed." I smile over my cup, taking another long pull of my drink.

"So, have you talked to him?" His question causes the thick liquid to catch in my throat, and I end up sucking it down the wrong pipe nearly spitting the sweet, chocolaty goodness all over the table.

"You okay there?" He eyes me curiously, not sure if he should get up and help or just let it run its course.

I hold a hand up as I sputter and cough. It takes me a full minute to clear my throat enough to speak again.

"Wow. Sorry about that. Wrong hole." I clear my throat again, trying to shake it off.

"I take it from your reaction that you haven't... Spoken to Sebastian, I mean."

"I haven't." The hollow feeling in my chest expands, and I feel like at any moment it's just going to swallow me whole.

Every time I talk about Sebastian I walk away feeling like I've lost him all over again. It's why I avoid speaking about him at all costs. But now that Ant's here—right in front of me, bringing it up—I can't help but want to know everything.

How was the season, is it over yet?

Did he get a lot of play time as a freshman?

Is he happy?

Does he ever talk about me?

Is he dating anyone?

The last question that filters through my mind makes my stomach twist, and heat floods my face and spreads down my neck. Just the thought damn near sends me into a full-on panic attack. My heart is drumming violently against my ribcage by the time Anthony speaks again.

"I guess I'm not surprised. I just thought... I don't know." He shakes his head like he's decided against saying whatever he was going to say.

"You just thought what?" I can't stop the question from coming out. Now that he's started it, I need to know what he was going to say.

"You and Sebastian were something special, Tess. It's been a while since we've spoken, and I guess I kind of thought he'd have wised up by now and realized that leaving you behind was a mistake." He gives me an apologetic smile.

"Yeah, well..." I knot my hands in my lap, feeling the heaviness and sadness of his words settle on my shoulders like a thousand-pound weight.

"For what it's worth, I think he made a huge mistake." I look up to find his gaze locked on me.

"You do?"

"You were the best thing that ever happened to Sebastian. I just hope he pulls his head out of his ass long enough to realize he's shit without you before someone else snatches you up."

"Thank you, Anthony. That means a lot coming from you. But I think it's safe to say that ship has sailed. He's been gone for six months, and I haven't gotten so much as a text message."

"I wouldn't be so sure," he says unconvinced.

"Well I am," I say, tears burning the back of my eyes just saying the words out loud.

Truth is, I knew we were over way before he left; him leaving only solidified this fact. He didn't even so much as say goodbye to me the day he left. He disappeared from my life without a trace, and if it weren't for the memories that haunt me daily, I'd almost think he never existed to begin with.

"I know we may not have always been the closest," Ant says, pulling my focus back to him. "But that doesn't mean that I wasn't rooting for you, Tess. You made my best friend tolerable for the first time…" He thinks about it for a moment. "Well, ever." He laughs.

"Well, for what it's worth, I was rooting for you and Courtney, too."

"Yeah, well." He shrugs. "You see where rooting for each other got us." A half smile plays on his lips before he quickly adds, "I guess I should probably get going. I just stopped in to grab a cup, and when I saw you over here I knew I had to come say hi."

"Well, I'm glad you did." I smile up at him as he stands.

"You take care of yourself, Tess."

"You too, Ant."

He nods, throwing me a half wave before spinning around and walking away. My eyes stay locked on him until he steps out onto the sidewalk and disappears around the corner, leaving me feeling even emptier than I did before his arrival.

TESS

I can't believe this weekend is prom. It seems like just yesterday I was preparing to go to this very dance with Sebastian, and now here I am an entire year later.

How has it already been a year?

It feels like just yesterday I was in the dress shop with my two best friends at the happiest point of my life. Bree was still here, Courtney and Ant were still going strong, and of course, I had Sebastian—the one person who tied it all together and made my life feel like a page out of a fairy-tale.

Of course, that was before everything fell apart—my last normal day before the ground got ripped out from beneath my feet.

Nothing has been the same since.

I stare at myself in the floor-length mirror on the back of my closet door, taking in the strapless pink gown that I purchased all those months ago. I shoved it into the back of my closet after everything happened and had yet to look at it since. But tonight, I don't know, I just felt like it needed to be worn.

Going to prom with someone who isn't Sebastian feels wrong on every level, but after some major convincing from Courtney, I decided it was time. It's time to let go, time to move on, time to stop letting a dress haunt me from the corner of my closet.

Tonight is the night I say goodbye to the girl who bought this dress and hello to the woman now wearing it. It's crazy how much older I look in just one year, how much older I feel. It's even crazier to think that in just a few short weeks I'll be packing up and moving to New York City.

I don't think I actually ever expected to get into Columbia, especially since it took them so long to contact me. But opening that letter, knowing that I actually did it, was probably the only real highlight of my senior year and even that happiness was muted by the fact that I wasn't able to share it with Sebastian.

"Hey, Tess." I hear my mother's voice just seconds before she appears in my doorway, her hand going to her mouth when she catches sight of me. "Oh my god, you look so beautiful."

"Thanks, Mom." I look back at myself, wishing I felt beautiful.

Pretty pink dress, just the right amount of makeup, my long brown strands pinned up on the sides and hanging down my back in thick curls; everything is as it should be, and yet it's such a stark contrast to what I feel inside. Inside I'm fighting the tightness in my chest and the voice in the back of my head telling me I can't do this.

Forcing a smile, I look back at my mom just as the doorbell rings, signaling Courtney's arrival. I insisted that she and I meet the boys at the restaurant so that I had an escape plan if I needed one. The last thing I want is to be stuck somewhere I don't want to be with no way of leaving.

"I'll get that," my mom practically sings, skipping toward the door.

Within minutes my mom has her camera out and she's snapping pictures like crazy, making me and Courtney turn one way and then the other.

Courtney, like me, opted to wear the prom dress she bought last year and never got the chance to wear since she and Bree skipped prom to be with me. I know she's been dying to slip into the beautiful floor-length red gown that looks like it was made for her for months, and tonight she finally gets to show it off.

I can tell she's excited about prom, and lord knows my mom is thrilled that I'm going; I just wish I shared in their enthusiasm.

By the time Courtney and I make it out the front door and down the yard, my mom has taken at least two hundred pictures and continues to take more from her place on the porch.

"Someone's excited." Courtney chuckles, gesturing toward my mom as we climb into the car.

"You have no idea." I sigh, closing the door and sliding my seatbelt in place. "I think she's just happy to see me getting out of the house and doing something normal."

"Can you blame her?" Courtney throws me a quick sideways glance before pulling out onto the road.

"It's been a hard year," I admit, letting out a slow breath.

"I know, which is why I'm so happy that you decided to come to prom with me. Ricky is really excited, too. I think he thought he was going to have to be mine and Dave's third wheel after Jess broke up with him."

When Courtney got the bright idea for us to double to prom, she pawned me off on her new boyfriend's best friend who recently split from his girlfriend. I guess it shouldn't bother me that I'm second choice considering I have no desire to go with him in the first place.

I should've stuck to my guns and not let her talk me into it, insisting that if I was going to go to prom I would just go stag, which is what I would've preferred. But per usual, Courtney just has a way of getting people to do what she wants. Though truthfully, I think she knew that either she needed to make it where I couldn't back out so easily, or I would've most definitely done so and probably opted to spend prom night vegging out in my pajamas.

"I couldn't imagine doing this without you, Tess," she adds, her voice falling serious. "With Bree gone and everything that's gone down this past year, we're all we've really got left."

"It seems weird, doesn't it?" I ask, my gaze locking on my reflection in the passenger side window. "How much everything has changed." I finish the sentence before looking back at Courtney.

"It is. But I don't want to think about that tonight. I just want to focus on being a wild, crazy teenager just one last time while I can still get away with it."

"Wild and crazy?" I sigh dramatically when she throws me a knowing look. "I knew I should have driven myself." I chuckle, thankfully starting to feel my nerves settle a little.

Who knows, maybe tonight won't be so bad after all.

"I don't know why I let you talk me into this," I grumble as Courtney shoves the car in park and kills the engine outside of *Dan Ruby's*, one of the fanciest restaurants in town.

Somewhere in the fifteen-minute drive over my anxiety had slipped back in and only mounted higher and higher the closer we got. Now that we're here, I'm feeling extremely uneasy and honestly a bit sick to my stomach.

"It'll be fine. You'll see." Court gives me an encouraging smile, reaching over to squeeze my hand. "Besides, it's not like you're going with someone you don't know," she continues. "You've known Ricky since grade school. Plus, he's really grown into his looks over the last couple years. Hell, if you pass on that I might go in for a taste."

"You're dating his best friend, remember?" I laugh, shaking my head at her. I swear Courtney always knows exactly what to say to pull me out of my head.

"Maybe I'll let Dave watch." She winks, laughing as she climbs from the car.

I'm still shaking my head as we approach the restaurant, not sure why I'm even surprised by Courtney's statement. Lord knows she probably meant it about messing around with Ricky and letting Dave watch. I wouldn't put it past her for a minute.

When she catches sight of the boys standing just inside the restaurant door, she turns to me and winks. "Yep, I would so let him watch."

Laughter bubbles out of my mouth, but the moment it breaks the surface I find myself suddenly face to face with the last person I expected to see. It instantly dies away, a large knot sticking at the base of my throat blocking anything from coming out at all.

Sebastian.

He's coming out of the restaurant just as we're about to go in and stops dead in his tracks the moment his eyes find mine.

I swear to god the very world shifts and suddenly I feel like the ground is moving beneath me, and I can't seem to figure out how to find my balance.

I don't know how much time passes. One second, two, maybe much longer. Time, along with everything else, seems to slow down around us, caging us in the moment.

I know it's him. I know he's standing right in front of me—those hazel eyes full of unreadable emotion as they hold my gaze—but my mind can't quite seem to process this fact. I feel like I've just entered the twilight zone and nothing around me feels like reality.

He looks exactly as I remember him and yet so different at the same time. His sun-kissed blond hair is lighter on the ends and slightly longer than the last time I saw him. There's also a thin scruff covering his jaw where he clearly hasn't shaved for the past couple of days.

His shoulders are broader, arms more muscular. He looks so much older, like he's grown up overnight. I can't stop my eyes from taking in every inch of him before looking back up to meet his waiting gaze.

"Oh my god, Sebastian!" I hear Courtney say next to me, jumping into action almost instantly. "What are you doing in town?" she asks, giving him a quick one-armed hug before stepping back.

This pulls his attention to her long enough that I'm able to take a few breaths and steady myself, feeling like I'm going to topple over at any moment.

"My cousin Lacey got married yesterday. I'm just here for the weekend," he says, shifting two takeout bags to his right hand, making me notice them for the first time. "So prom night huh?" He gestures between the two of us, his eyes only meeting mine for a fraction of a second before finding Courtney again.

"Yeah." She smiles, catching sight of Dave who signals her from the other side of the large glass door. "Speaking of which, I should probably get inside with my date," she says, turning toward me. "I'll give you guys a minute to catch up."

The next thing I know she's sauntering away, and I'm left alone with Sebastian.

I keep my eyes focused on the door long after Courtney has disappeared inside, not sure what I should say or do. How is it that a year ago Sebastian was the very air I breathed, and now I feel like there's no air to be found? My lungs scream for mercy, and only then do I realize that I've yet to actually take a breath.

I suck in a deep, controlled inhale, letting it out slowly as I try to gather my thoughts enough to actually speak.

"You look beautiful, Tess." Sebastian's words wash over me, and I swear every inch of my skin prickles when I finally meet his gaze again. "I'm sure your date won't be able to take his eyes off you tonight."

There's something there, something in the way he says the words that sends my heart galloping inside my chest and emotion clogging my throat. It's not long before the guilt sinks in too, though I have no idea why I feel guilty. Sebastian broke up with me. It's perfectly acceptable for me to go to prom with another boy—so why do I feel like I'm cheating him all of a sudden?

"Thank you." I fight back the sudden onset of tears I feel rushing to the surface, refusing to let him see how deeply the loss of him still cuts me.

What I wouldn't give to have him tell me those words as his date, to have him be the one taking me to prom, to know that it's his arms I would be spending the night dancing in. Knowing that I still want that so badly after everything is disheartening. Here I thought I was finally ready to move on, and now I'm realizing I'm still stuck in the very same place I was the day he broke things off.

"How are you? How's everything?" he asks, both of us stepping to the far side of the sidewalk to let a large group of people pass by us as they exit the restaurant.

"I'm okay. What about you? How's LSU?"

"Stressful. College ball is no joke. But it's good. It's really good."

"Well, then I'm happy for you," I force the words out, wishing like hell I could make them sound more believable.

Don't get me wrong, I want Sebastian to be happy, I really do. But the thought of him being happy without me feels like a betrayal I just can't quite stomach at the moment. Because try as I may, happiness is something that is simply out of my reach.

Sadly, I think I've accepted that I'll never be the carefree girl I once was. The one who gave away her heart to a boy like it had always belonged to him anyway. No smile will ever be as genuine as the one Sebastian always brought to my face. No one will ever make my heart beat like he does. No one will ever make me feel the way he makes me feel just by looking at me, which is exactly how I'm feeling right now.

"I should probably let you get inside." He switches his weight from one foot to the next.

There's something there—a flash of something dark behind his light eyes—

but before I can make out exactly what it means it's gone, making me question if I'm just looking for things that aren't actually there.

Truth is I want to know he's just as miserable as me. I want to know that right now he feels like he can't breathe—that walking away from me feels like the most impossible task and he simply can't do it—because that's exactly how I feel.

Unfortunately, I get none of that from him, not that I actually expected to.

"Yeah, you probably need to get that…" I gesture to the takeout bags in his hand, realizing I have no idea where he's heading with it. He could very well be on his way to a girl's house. The thought is nearly impossible to even entertain. "Wherever it's going," I add, heat flushing my cheeks.

He gives me a small smile that doesn't quite reach his eyes and then quickly steps past me without another word, and just like the moment I saw him standing in front of me, all the air is sucked from my body and I feel like I'm on the verge of suffocating.

An overwhelming panic starts to creep in and before I know what I'm doing, I spin around.

"Sebastian."

I don't even realize I've said his name until he's turning back toward me, his jaw hard and eyes full of so many different emotions it nearly drops me to my knees. I hesitate for only a second, but it's enough time for Sebastian to shut it down before I can say anything more.

"Bye, Tess." He gives me a curt nod, not allowing me to finish the thought before he's walking again.

I don't know what would have come out of my mouth next had he given me the opportunity to say anything anyway, but it's like a slap across the face just the same. I stumble back from the force of it.

Disappointment settles over me like a heavy blanket, and I let the weight of it hold me in place instead of going after Sebastian like I want to.

When he left me the first time, he told me it wasn't forever. He told me that it was just for right now and that one day we would find our way back to each other. With each day that has passed, my doubt over his sincerity has grown, but I refused to chalk it up to something he just said to make saying goodbye easier; because deep down, I've been holding onto hope that that wasn't the case.

Now that hope is crashing down at my feet, and I know I'm seconds away from losing it. I can feel it bubbling in my chest, constricting my throat, burning the back of my eyes. I struggle to suck in a breath, but I can't fill my lungs enough to get any relief.

It really is over.

I don't know why it's taken me until this very moment to finally wrap my head around it. Haven't I known it all along? Did I really believe that things would work out for us someday?

"Tess." The first of my tears spill over the moment I hear Courtney's voice. I turn just in time to enter her arms. "It's okay," she reassures me, securing me tightly against her. "You're okay," she chants over and over again until I feel the weight slowly start to recede and the fog begins to lift.

I don't know if it's one minute or ten before I take a deep breath and pull back to look at my best friend's face. She smiles sympathetically and uses the pads of her thumbs to wipe away the reminisce of tears from my cheeks.

"I'm okay," I say, letting out a slow, shaky breath.

I'm not sure if I'm trying to convince her or myself, but it feels good to say it out loud either way—like I'm telling myself that I don't have a choice. I *have* to be okay because there is no other option.

"I know. I know you are." She cups my face.

"He's taken so much from me already. I won't let him have this, too," I say, sniffing. It's easier to embrace the anger than let myself drown in the sadness.

"That's my girl." Courtney smiles. "You wanna head in or do you need a few minutes? I can buy you some time."

"No. No, I'm good." I take another deep breath in and blow it out. "How's my makeup?" I ask, wiping under my eyes.

"You're probably the only person who can cry crocodile tears and manage not to completely ruin their makeup in the process." She chuckles. "You look perfect."

"Thank god for waterproof mascara." I fan my face, trying to dry my eyes.

"Come on." Court grins, linking her arm with mine. "Ricky is looking mighty fine tonight. Might just be what you need to forget about what's his face," she jokes, leading me into the restaurant.

TESS

Given how this night started, I didn't expect it to be even remotely fun, and for once I couldn't be happier that I was wrong.

I didn't realize just how much this would help—allowing myself to just be a normal teenager. And while Sebastian never strayed from my mind, I was able to push him away enough that it didn't put too bad of a damper on my evening.

I even found myself enjoying Ricky's company a lot more than I originally thought I would. While we've known each other since we were little, we've never run in the same circle of friends and therefore haven't really had a ton of interaction. I was surprised by how funny and quick witted he is, managing to keep a smile on my face for most of the night.

And while there isn't that spark that exists between Sebastian and me, for the first time I think maybe I could see myself dating someone else. Not Ricky necessarily but just someone. And that thought feels better than I knew it could.

It means that even though I don't always feel like it, I am making progress. Second by second, minute by minute, day by day, a small part of me is letting go; even if deep down I'm not sure if I actually want to.

When I return to the corner table that Courtney and I—along with our dates and few other friends—claimed for the night, I feel dead on my feet. I don't ever remember a time when dancing took it out of me quite like it has tonight.

Stretching my legs out under the table I close my eyes for a brief moment, just needing a moment to take it all in. Maybe it's running into Sebastian earlier, maybe it's finally deciding that I just need to let go; maybe it's that tonight I've shown the first semblance of doing just that. But whatever it is, I feel absolutely emotionally drained.

"Here you go, Tess." My eyes pop back open at the sound of Ricky's voice, and I look up to find him standing next to me, drink extended in my direction.

"Thank you." I smile, taking the cup from him before watching him claim the seat next to me.

"I don't know about you, but I'm beat." He chuckles, relaxing back into the chair as he sips from his cup.

"I think I'm right there with you. How much longer does this thing go on for?" I ask, reaching for my phone in the center of the table and clicking it on to check the time.

When I catch sight of Sebastian's name on my phone followed by a string of messages; an uneasiness creeps up my back, and I stare at the device like it's grown legs and is about to start walking.

"I think another hour or so," Ricky answers, but his voice suddenly sounds so distant I barely even register the words.

Heat washes through me, feeling like someone just poured a bucket of scalding water over my head. It's several long seconds before I'm able to actually bring myself to open the message chat and the second I do, once again everything shifts.

Sebastian: *I'm sorry about earlier tonight. I'm sorry about a lot of things.*

Sebastian: *I hope you're having fun at prom.*

Quickly followed by—

Sebastian: *Okay, that's a lie. I hope you're having the worst time and you haven't been able to stop thinking about me just like I haven't stopped thinking about you.*

There's a twenty-minute gap between the last two messages, and when I reach the final one I enter a total and utter state of shock.

Sebastian: *I'm outside.*

I look up toward the door almost expecting to see him standing there. Of course, he's not there, but I can't help but look for him anyway.

He's outside?

I find my mind questioning if I read the message right, staring down at the device and then looking back at the door like the answer is somehow going to appear in front of me.

I find myself standing without actually meaning to, mumbling something to Ricky about needing to use the restroom before numbly making my way out of the gym and into the hallway.

Every step I take toward the parking lot becomes heavier, my head and heart battling it out with no clear victor in sight. My head tells me to turn around, to turn around right now and not let him do this to me. I was doing good, enjoying myself for the first time in a very long time. My heart, however, has other plans entirely. Because my heart belongs to the one person who's calling for it, and it's a call it cannot refuse.

The night air is warm as I step outside but I still shiver, running my hands up and down my bare arms trying to smooth out the sudden goose bumps that have broken out across my flesh.

It takes me no time to locate Sebastian because the second I look up he's there, leaning against the railing that runs the length on each side of the wide cement walkway.

I blink in rapid succession, my breath coming in short spurts as my chest rises and falls so quickly I wonder if I'm not hyperventilating.

He's dressed in the same faded jeans and black v-neck as before, only now an LSU baseball cap sits low on his forehead, casting a dark shadow over his eyes as he moves toward me. I can feel each step he takes, feel the air around me thicken the closer he gets. By the time he stops directly in front of me, I feel like I'm seconds away from succumbing to the weight of it all.

"I didn't think you'd come out," he admits, voice low.

"I'm not sure why I did." My voice shakes slightly. "What do you want, Sebastian?"

I finally meet his gaze, and what I see there has a year full of agony rushing to the surface. Every sleepless night, every painful day, every single tear I cried hits me all at once. One look and I'm reliving every single moment of the hell I've endured over the past year. And something about the look in his eyes tells me I wasn't alone in that hell like I assumed I was.

"I don't know." He shuffles his feet, looking downward like he's not sure what to say. I think it's the first time I've ever seen Sebastian Baxter look unsure of

273

himself. "I just—fuck, I don't know, Tess. This was supposed to be easy. I was supposed to come home, show up for my cousin's wedding, and then slip back out like I was never here. I didn't expect to see you, and I sure as hell wasn't prepared for how I would feel when I did."

"I'm sorry I screwed up your plans," I say bitterly, his words cutting right through me. It only confirms what I think I've known all along; he never had any plans to come back for me.

"It's not like that, Tess." He sighs, adjusting the ball cap on his head before shoving his hands into his pockets, his gaze finally meeting mine again.

"No? Then what's it like, Sebastian? Because from where I'm standing that's exactly how it looks," I bite, anger lacing my voice.

If he came here just to ruin this night like he's ruined so many other things, I swear I'll never forgive him. He can't keep doing this to me.

"I'm just trying to say that when I saw you it reaffirmed everything I've been trying to convince myself wasn't true for the last year."

"Which is what?"

"That I'm still in love with you." It leaves his mouth in a rush, and instantly I can feel tears stinging the back of my eyes.

"As if there was a doubt that you didn't?" I choke out. "Clearly we have very different views of this relationship because not loving you versus loving you was never even a thought that crossed my mind. Because I do love you. I love you as much as I did the day you left. And the fact that you're standing here telling me that you had convinced yourself that you didn't love me anymore speaks volumes, Sebastian."

274

"That's not what I meant. Nothing is coming out right." I can tell he's frustrated with himself, and yet he still can't seem to do anything but dig himself further into the hole he's currently burying himself in.

"Then perhaps you should've just let things *be* instead of showing up here in the middle of prom to tell me that you don't love me anymore." I swipe angrily at a tear that skates down my cheek. "You took away this experience last year, and now you've come back to finish the job. Why? Because you don't want me to be happy?"

"I do want you to be happy," he objects.

"Then you shouldn't have come here."

"I know. I know, okay?" His voice goes up a notch, and I can tell he's starting to lose his temper. "And I don't know why I couldn't just fucking stay away. But I just couldn't. Because I do still love you, Tess. Fuck, I love you so much it's fucking killing me."

"And it took seeing me on a date with someone else for you to reach this epiphany?" I stand strong even though everything inside of me wants to embrace what he just said.

"Of course not," he scoffs.

"Then what? What it is, Sebastian?" I square my shoulders in an effort to exert a strength I'm not sure I even possess. "It's been a year." My voice breaks, but I quickly recover. "A year, Sebastian! You leave me with promises that this isn't forever and then you disappear from my life without so much as a goodbye, and then a full year passes before I hear from you. And even then it's only because we ran into each other. How long would it have been if we hadn't, Sebastian, huh? How long would I have gone on not hearing from you? Another year? Two? Ten?

Did you ever plan on calling me, texting me, just checking in on me in general? Did I mean so little to you?"

"You mean everything to me, Tess!" This seems to be his last straw, and the words rip from his throat with a desperation I've never heard from him before. "You still do. Everything. I've spent the last year trying to convince myself that I didn't love you anymore because admitting to myself that I do, and I let you go, was just too painful. I thought I was doing okay. I thought I was living. But then I saw you and suddenly this fog lifted, and I realized that nothing had been right since the day I left. Not one fucking thing."

"Sebastian." I lose my battle, tears falling down my cheeks in quick succession one after the other.

"I didn't come here to hurt you, Tess." He steps into me, pulling me against his chest.

My anger evaporates so quickly it's like it was never there at all. I instantly melt into his embrace, breathing in his scent like it's the first time I'm smelling it.

"I came here because I just needed you to know that I'm sorry. I'm so sorry for everything," He continues.

"I'm sorry, too." I tighten my arms around his middle, realizing that memories have nothing on the real thing.

"I tried to stop myself from coming. I swear I did. But I knew if I didn't come that I'd regret it."

I don't dare look up at him, knowing I'd probably drown in emotion if I did. Instead, I savor the moment—the feeling of his arms around me—knowing there's no place I'd rather be than right here.

"Dance with me?" He finally speaks again after a long moment of silence. Sliding his hand under my chin he forces my face upward before taking my arms and wrapping them around his neck as he pulls my body flush with his.

"Here?" I question, looking around to see if there's anyone else around.

Given that the entrance to the dance is on the other side of the school, it's unlikely many people will have a reason to come back here, but the thought still makes me feel vulnerable and on display.

"Right here." He guides my head to lay against his chest and then slowly starts swaying to the music so far in the distance that I can't even make out what song it is.

Honestly, it doesn't much matter. We could be slow dancing to the most upbeat song in the world, and it wouldn't make a difference right now. Because this, being with Sebastian—feeling his heart pound against my cheek and his hand pressed to the small of my back—it's all I can see, feel, and hear. It's just him, just like it's always been.

I cry into his shirt, letting go of the emotion that has been bottled up so deep inside of me that I've let it consume me for the past year. I let go of the hurt and the fear and just let myself live in this one moment.

Because I know it's the only moment I'll get.

What is happening right now, no matter how intense, doesn't change the fact that nothing has actually changed. He's still going back to Louisiana, and I'm weeks away from moving into the city. If he didn't think we could make it work before, why would he think we can now?

I don't know how much time passes, how many songs flitter around us as we stand outside, arms wrapped around each other like we're both afraid to let go. At some point, we stop moving all together and go from dancing to just holding each other.

And while I wish I could hold onto this moment forever—bottle it up and never ever leave—like every moment before it this one passes too, and eventually we're left to face the reality that we have to let go. We have to let the world back in. We have to let go of the moment and let it become just another memory like all the other moments we've shared.

I'm the first to break the connection, letting my arms fall as I take a full step back and then another, needing to put a little distance between us.

Like he can sense me pulling away, more than just physically, Sebastian reaches for me, but I've already stepped far enough out of his grasp that he can't. Rather than moving, he stays rooted to the spot, like he understands this is just what I need.

"I can't do this anymore, Tess. I need you. I need you in my life. I need you in my arms. I feel like I'm dying a little more each day that I'm not with you. I know I said it couldn't work. I know I gave you a hundred reasons why ending us was the best thing for us. I was trying to put someone else's needs above my own for the first time in my life, and all it's done is backfire right in my face. If it's this hard to stay away from you then maybe staying away from you was never the right thing."

"Stop." It's the only word I can manage to push past the knot in my throat. "Stop," I repeat, knowing that if he keeps going I'll never be able to say no, and saying no is exactly what I need to do right now.

Had you asked me this morning if I were faced with the option to have Sebastian back what my answer would have been, I would have said *yes*—in an instant with absolutely zero hesitation. Because being with him is all

I've thought about for nearly a year. Being with him is all that has ever felt right.

But Sebastian didn't walk away from me because he didn't love me or some part of him didn't want to be with me—I can see that now more than ever. He walked away because he knew if he didn't that I would follow him. That I would give up everything and everyone to be with him. And he also knew that eventually, I would probably resent him for it.

These are all things he said to me nearly a year ago, and for some reason, it's only now that I seem to be listening.

"We can't." I finally muster the courage to admit it out loud and by the look on his face, he knew it was coming but I can still see it hurts.

Hell, it hurts me, too. Resisting Sebastian is like going against my very nature—like ripping my soul in two pieces, one that will never leave Sebastian and the other that knows it can't go with him.

"I know it won't be easy, but…" he starts.

"We can't, Sebastian. You live in Louisiana, and I'm moving to New York in a couple of months."

"You got in?" It's an instant shift, and the heaviness lifts slightly.

The pride in his eyes is enough to bring my tears back to the surface yet again. I didn't realize how much I needed his approval until this very second.

"I got in." I smile, letting the tears fall freely.

"Oh my god, Tess, that's amazing." Before I know it I'm back in his arms, my feet leaving the ground. "I knew you could do it." He squeezes me so hard that it's almost painful, and yet not nearly hard enough. "I'm so proud of you." The last part is a whisper before he finally lowers me

279

to my feet and takes a full step back, a sad smile etched onto his beautiful face. "So I guess this really is it huh?"

"I guess so."

He doesn't argue me on it or try to convince me that we can still make it work; I think deep down he knows it won't. How could it? College ball is a full-time job in itself. Add in his full coursework on top of mine and the fact that were over a thousand miles away from each other and it's clear to see that even if we tried, we'd only fail and probably be worse off for it.

"Fuck." He lets out a shaky breath. "I don't know if I have it in me to walk away from you a second time."

"I don't know if I have it in me to let you," I admit, wiping my eyes with the back of my hand.

"So then how do we do it?" he asks, emotion so thick in this voice I nearly lose my composure and throw myself back into his arms.

I don't know how I resist doing it. Honestly, I feel like every second that ticks by makes it harder not to do just that.

"We do it together," I finally say, letting out a deep breath.

"Together." He gives me a sad smile, tears filling his eyes. "I love you, Tess. No matter where life takes you, no matter where you go, I will always love you. If you meet someone new and get married, I'll still love you. If you have children with that man and go on to live the life you've always dreamed of, I'll still love you. I will love you until the day I die, and that's one promise I will never break."

"I love you ,too." It's the last words I utter.

I don't know how I force my feet to move. I don't know how I turn and not look back. I don't know how I manage to walk back into school. I don't know how I manage any of it and yet I do.

A year ago, I thought Sebastian and I would end up together some day. I thought when the time was right we'd find each other again and all the pain and heartbreak would've been worth it. Now, I walk away knowing that there's a very real possibility that I may never see him again. And that thought is both terrifying and freeing at the same time.

TESS

It's been fourteen months since the last time I saw Sebastian. So much has happened between now and then that I barely even recognize my life anymore.

I spent my last summer with Courtney, enjoying the last remaining weeks of our childhood before we were separated for the first time since we were in grade school. Saying goodbye to her proved to be one of the hardest things I had ever done. But it wasn't the hardest. That spot was and is still reserved for the one person who never strays far from my thoughts or my heart.

I wish I could tell you that Sebastian and I moved heaven and earth and found a way to be together, but that's simply not the case. Life is not a fairy-tale or some over the top romance novel where everything is some grand declaration of love. Life is real and painful, and sometimes love doesn't actually conquer all. And I've found a way to be okay with that.

He got moved into the starting quarterback position at the start of his sophomore year, and I've made a point to watch as many games as I can. In a way, it's almost like I'm torturing myself, but at the same time, I can't *not* watch. It gives me comfort to see him living his dream. It somehow makes it all feel worth it.

I miss him, I think a part of me will always miss him. But my life has changed so much sometimes it's hard to even remember the girl I used to be—or recognize the woman I've become for that matter.

It didn't take me long to settle at Columbia. From the moment I arrived, I felt closer to my dad than I ever had before. But being in the city also made me feel closer to Sebastian. I often find myself walking the streets, reliving the words he said to me when he brought me here years ago. I can still hear his voice like he's saying it now.

"I wanted to be the one to bring you for the first time that way the city will always hold a piece of us in it, something you can keep with you when we're not together."

I don't think he truly understood the magnitude of that gesture at the time, but it doesn't change the fact that his words still ring true every single day.

Freshman year went by in a blur. I finally picked a major after going undecided for the first two semesters, deciding to pursue a degree in finance. It's certainly not the choice with the most flash, but I wanted something practical, something I knew would be worth the effort and money when it was all said and done. Besides, I might also have a slight obsession with numbers so it seemed like the perfect fit.

I still talk to Courtney every couple of weeks. She's adjusting well to Alabama, having the time of her life or so it would seem. It's funny how different our experiences have been thus far, kind of a lot like high school.

She's out partying and hooking up with hot frat guys, really living up the entire college experience. Meanwhile, I spend very little time outside of the classroom, library, or my dorm room, preferring to lose myself in my studies rather than in a bottle of liquor.

It's not lost on me how very different we are, and yet how we've always just made sense. Like we balance each other perfectly. I'm the voice of reason, the one who talks Courtney out of the things she already knows she shouldn't do but probably would anyway. And Courtney is good at getting me out of my head and making me experience things I probably would never try without her encouragement.

I miss that in my life, her constantly in my ear pushing me out of my comfort zone. I'm sure some mornings when she wakes up with a wicked hangover in a guy's bed she has no recollection of sleeping with, she probably misses me, too.

I've managed to make a few friends over the last year but none have come close to what Courtney, Bree, and I have. Even with thousands of miles separating us we still have each other to lean on, and I'm confident that no matter where life takes us, we will always be there for one and another.

I don't talk to Bree quite as often as I do Courtney, but we still manage to squeeze in a Facetime session every few weeks. She'll tell me about all the cute things Jackson is doing now, and I'll tell her about my classes and anything new that's going on.

California looks good on her, as does motherhood.

She managed to graduate from high school on time and is now taking night classes and working part time during the day waitressing. I'm so proud of her for facing this head on and coming out on the other end a better stronger person.

Everyone has moved on to bigger and better things. Sometimes it's almost hard to wrap my head around how much everything has changed.

And that couldn't be more apparent than right at this moment, pulling into a town that now almost feels foreign to me.

I roll my window down, taking a deep breath of the air as it whips around me. Being back in Rockfield is like watching an old movie. I remember every road, every shop and sign, but I also pick up on things I never noticed before. Maybe it's because it's been so long or maybe it's because I was too focused on something else to really appreciate the little things that seemed to just blur into the background.

Like the smell of trees and fresh cut flowers, the sounds of nature, the peacefulness that comes with a sense of belonging. I don't know that I ever appreciated this place enough when I lived here, but now living in the city with the hustle and bustle of everyday life, a place like Rockfield is a breath of fresh air and a very welcome one at that.

I told my mom I wouldn't be in until tomorrow, so I'm not surprised when I arrive at her house to find her car gone. I know she's at work and probably won't be home until morning. Me being here when she arrives I'm sure will be a welcome surprise.

I don't get nearly enough time to visit and am ashamed to admit that even though I am just an hour away, this is the first time I've been home since Christmas. Considering it's now June, that's saying something.

Don't get me wrong, I miss my mom something fierce, but being here without Courtney and Bree—without

Sebastian—I don't know, it just feels wrong somehow. Like I'm an outsider now looking in.

I let myself inside the house and carry my suitcase to my old bedroom. Because I've opted to take some summer courses I only have two weeks off, only one of which I plan to spend here.

I was only able to get a few days off from work and while I know my mom was hoping for more time, a part of me is glad this is all I can give her. I mean, of course, I'd rather be here spending time with my mom than making coffees for people who don't even have the decency to look up from their phones when placing their orders, but being here brings too much to the surface. There are too many feelings and memories tied to this place. The less time I'm here, the better.

The instant I push my way inside my small ten by ten childhood bedroom I'm hit with a wave of nostalgia.

Of course, my mom hasn't touched it since I left, wanting to keep it exactly the same so when I come home on break I have my old room to come back to.

Looking around the small space, I take in a deep breath and let it out slowly, my eyes stopping on a picture still hanging from the mirror on my dresser. I know every single detail of the picture, but it doesn't stop me from dropping my suitcase on the bed, crossing the room and pulling it down, holding it gently between my fingers.

God, I remember that day so vividly. The picture is of Courtney, Ant, Sebastian, and me. We're all clad in swimsuits standing next to the lake behind Sebastian's house, wide smiles on all of our faces. Every set of eyes is looking directly at Bree who was operating the camera, except for one person whose eyes are trained directly on me like they always seemed to be.

Where the Night Ends

My chest swells and a thick knot forms in my throat. I quickly toss the photograph onto the dresser and walk directly out of the room. Knowing I can't just sit here and dwell in the ghosts of my past, I grab my car keys from where I left them on the coffee table and head outside to where my beat-up Jeep is sitting in the driveway.

I really don't have any place specifically to go, I just know I need to go somewhere. So when I climb into Sara Beth and throw her into drive, I have absolutely no destination other than away from here. And that's okay with me.

After thirty minutes of being on the road, I've only managed to sour my mood further. Making the mistake of driving past the high school and then the restaurant we all used to go to every Friday after football games, I let the memories wash over me, a part of me longing for a past I know I will never get back.

I don't know at what point I end up veering onto the winding wooded road toward Sebastian's house or why, but once I've started that way I can't bring myself to turn back. Even though I know he doesn't live there anymore, driving past the expansive property still gives me chills, like a part of him still exists there.

Forcing myself to turn around several miles after passing Sebastian's, by the time I make it back into town the sun is starting to disappear over the horizon, casting an orange glow over the streets and buildings.

I start to head back toward my mom's house, but then my stomach lets out a loud grumble and only then do I remember I haven't eaten today. And while I'm sure my mom has food at the house, I've been craving a pretzel bun sandwich from *Perfect Pita* for weeks, and since it's just a

287

couple blocks from where I am, I decide to make a quick left and head back that way.

When I pull up outside of the small sandwich shop on the corner, I park my Jeep at the back of the near empty lot and make my way toward the entrance. As soon as I reach for the door handle an odd sensation washes over me, and without thinking I look up, my stomach bottoming out the moment that I do.

At first, I think I'm seeing things that there's no way *he* could be here right now. But then he turns his face upward to assess the couple in front of him and a wave of nausea washes over me.

Sebastian.

I'm not sure how long I stand here, my hand suspended in mid-air but never actually reaching anything. I watch as he fiddles with his phone, swiping his fingers across the screen while he waits his turn, completely unaware of where I stand just a few short feet from him.

It's been a long time since I've felt as torn as I do in this very moment. Every part of me wants to go to him, wants to open this door and run into his arms—a place where I know everything will feel right. The other part of me knows I can't do that.

We've come so far and while I still think about him every day, I know that talking to him, looking at him, seeing that boyish smile and feeling the burn of his hazel eyes again will only upset the very delicate balance I have between my head and my heart. And I don't think I can do that to myself—not again.

So instead I just watch him through the thin pane of glass that separates us. Him unaware that I'm even here. Me all too aware, able to feel his presence in every single pore of my body.

I take a moment to appreciate him. His broad shoulders and massive biceps, the way the muscles strain against his gray t-shirt—no doubt from countless hours of conditioning, practice, drills, and games. His blond hair is covered by a backward baseball cap, and even from here I can see the week-old scruff he's sporting.

I swear to god he gets more attractive with every minute that passes. Seeing him on television, clad in his football gear, has nothing on seeing the real thing up close and personal. He really is a sight to behold.

It's so hard to believe that once upon a time I called him mine. Of course, that seems like another lifetime altogether. A time that would probably feel like it belonged to someone else entirely if it weren't for the pull in my chest—because despite everything that has happened my heart still knows where it belongs.

I watch him for several more seconds, a deep sense of longing lodged in my stomach. It takes everything in me not to pull that door open but somehow, someway, I manage to find the strength to slowly back away.

By the time I reach my Jeep my hands are trembling, and I feel like I've just run a marathon rather than walked just a few yards. My heart is beating so rapidly that I can feel my pulse pounding against my neck.

I take several deep breaths, slowly pulling air in through my nose and blowing it out of my mouth.

It's for the best, I try to reason with myself. And while I know I'm right, it doesn't make the act of not going to him any easier.

I don't make any attempt to leave the parking lot. While I blame it on the fact that I'm still too shaken up to drive, I know it's really because I want to see him again. Even if he doesn't know I'm here, I just want to look at him for a moment longer and wish that things could be different.

The longer Sebastian is in the restaurant, the more my inner battle rages and the harder it becomes to just sit here and do nothing when I know I could be seconds away from feeling his arms wrapped around me if I would just move.

My eyes stay glued to the front door, not once looking away. I'm so scared I might miss him that after some time I find myself wondering if I've even blinked. Then the gears in my mind start to shift, and I'm left arguing with myself for the next twenty minutes on whether or not that was actually even Sebastian inside or if it was someone who favored him and my eyes simply saw what they wanted to.

In fact, I've nearly convinced myself of this when he finally exits the restaurant several minutes later, hands shoved deep in his pockets and his face turned down toward the ground.

My breath quickens with each step he takes in my direction, and I swear I'm on the verge of hyperventilating by the time he rounds on a small sports car that I've not seen before, not feet from where I'm sitting. I watch him hesitate at the driver's side door, and then he turns in my direction.

I suck in a breath and hold it, afraid that even breathing will give away my position. Even though it's dark at this point and I know he can't see inside my Jeep, I still slink down in my seat.

He looks around, his eyes only grazing over my Jeep for a split second before he slowly shakes his head, looking a little unsettled, before finally climbing into his car.

I watch him drive away after the longest minute of my life, and the instant he does I'm pissed at myself. I punch the steering wheel, cursing at the top of my lungs at how stupid I am. He was right there—right in front of me—and I just let him walk away.

So what if things won't change? So what if it would be hard to say goodbye? Wouldn't it be worth it to see him, to hear his voice, to know that he's doing well? Wouldn't that have offered me some semblance of peace amongst the chaos?

Completely abandoning the reason I came here, I'm finally back on the road. Courtney's voice sounds through the phone held to my ear as she reassures me that I did the right thing.

I don't know if it was necessarily *right.* I mean, it sure as hell doesn't feel right, but I do agree with Court when she says that there's nothing good that could have come from me going to him.

"I mean, think about it, Tess," she continues. "Even if things were to go the way you wanted and you two would've ended up hanging out, where would that have left you tomorrow? Or the next day? Or the next? You've fought so hard to find your place without him."

"I know. I know." I let out an audible sigh, wishing the heaviness in my chest would lift so I could breathe without feeling like there's a thousand pounds weighing me down.

"Look, you're home right now, in the place where nearly every memory you have together is tied to. It's only natural that it feels harder when you're there. And then there's knowing that he's in town, too. Just know that if you go to him, you'll hate yourself for it tomorrow, and you know I'm right."

"You just love saying you're right." I chuckle, finally letting go of some of the tension winding tightly inside of me.

"Lord knows I don't get to say it nearly enough," she quips. "Just hang tight. You got two days with your mom and then you'll have my ass to distract you. And you know how good I am at that," she promises mischievously.

"I don't know if I'm down for your idea of distraction," I object. "But I really can't wait to see you."

"Me too. Don't forget you're picking me up from the airport at..."

"8 a.m," I cut her off. "Yes, I know."

"Don't be late, bitch," she teases.

"Late is not in my vocabulary," I spit back.

"I'll see you then," she says before quickly adding, "but if you need me between now and then just call me. Don't do anything you'll regret."

"You have my word."

"Love you, Tess."

"Love you, too." I smile before ending the call just as I pull up outside of my mom's house.

SEBASTIAN

Two Years Later…

"Come on, dude. Wake the fuck up." It's the first thing I hear the moment the morning sun stings my eyes. Throwing my arm over my face, I groan, stretching out my legs.

"What time is it?" I grumble, scratching my head as I peer up at Wilson, LSU's star running back and one of my closest friends.

We were lucky enough to get bunked together my sophomore year after my first roommate dropped out and moved back home. Wilson was just a freshman then, but we hit it off instantly. Since then we've pretty much been inseparable. He, like me, likes to play hard and work even harder, putting everything he has onto the field.

The one glaring difference between us is his drive to play ball professionally whereas I've chosen to walk away from it all together. I lost my love for the game a long time ago, and no matter how hard I tried I just couldn't seem to get it back. So I rode out my scholarship and declined to speak to any reps from the NFL when they came knocking.

Will thought I had completely fucking lost it. He's been dreaming of playing pro since he was little and can't see a world where someone else might not want the same thing. He'll no doubt go in the first round of the draft next year barring any crazy injuries. There's no way he won't. The kid is fucking magic on the field.

"It's fucking late, that's what time it is," he says, throwing a pair of dress pants over his shoulder. "Only you would be late to your own graduation."

It isn't until then that I remember what today is.

"Fuck," I groan, rolling to my side, the entire bottle of whiskey I killed last night burning the pit of my stomach.

Then I remember that my parents' flew in this morning, or at least they were supposed to, and my stomach lurches for another reason entirely. I haven't been home since two summers ago when I had yet another blow up with my father and he ended up kicking me out of *his* house.

Since then my relationship with my parents' has only gotten worse. Quite frankly, I'm surprised they even want to come to my college graduation at all. At this point, I think our relationship is beyond salvaging, so I'm not really sure why they even care. Then again, I'm sure it's nothing more than to save face. They'll take pictures and smile so they can brag to all their friends about what amazing parents they are.

Fucking pathetic.

"You can always stay here with me." I hear a female voice seconds before the bed shifts and an arm drapes over me from behind.

I glance over my shoulder to see bright green eyes, a pretty face, big red curls cascading over her slender shoulders, and while she's beautiful, I'm flooded with the same sensation I get every time I wake up next to a different woman—guilt and disappointment.

I slide her arm off of me and quickly sit up, holding the sheet in place as I do because I'm very certain I have no clothes on underneath. I look up to find Will fighting a smile as he slinks out of the room and into the adjoining bathroom, shaking his head.

"You better hurry the hell up!" he calls over his shoulder, laughter in his voice, seconds before the bathroom door slams shut, vibrating the wall.

"Last night was amazing," redhead croons as she slinks up behind me, pressing her bare chest against my back.

"Yeah, it was," I grumble out, running my hand over my face as I lean forward, elbows on my knees, still feeling the effects of the alcohol from last night.

When a few of the guys from the team, most of which are graduating today, suggested we spend the night at the bar just off campus celebrating, it sounded like an amazing idea. Now, well, now I'm wishing like hell I had taken it a bit easy. At this rate, I'll be showing up at graduation still drunk.

Glancing at the clock, I stand abruptly the second I register the time, the sheet falling from my lap. I hear an audible purr behind me but am too frantic to pay her even a second of attention. The ceremony starts in just over an hour, and I have to be there thirty minutes prior.

Racing around my room, I slip on a pair of boxers as I quickly gather the suit I plan to wear today, draping it over the back of the desk chair before turning to usher redhead out the minute she's dressed. I thank her for an amazing time, like I have so many other women before her, not even bothering to try to remember her name; I know I won't ever see her again.

I've watched countless girls walk out of my dorm room over the last four years, but every time there's only one girl I see... *Tess*.

I can't imagine she'd be proud of the man I've become or the fact that I've slept my way through half the student body just trying to fuck her out of my heart and my brain. It hasn't worked yet and I doubt at this point it ever will, but it doesn't stop me from trying.

Will exits the bathroom, successfully pulling me from my thoughts. I blink, realizing I've been standing in the same spot looking at the back of the door where redhead just exited for who knows how long.

I shake my head, quickly slipping past Will and into the bathroom. Hitting the shower and then shaving faster than I probably ever have in my entire life, I re-emerge within twenty minutes looking a lot more put together than I feel.

Will is decked out in a navy suit, his dark skin accentuating the white collar of his dress shirt making him look like he's already a rich NFL star. Hell, with the traction he's received already he might as well be.

"Bout time. You ready?" he asks, strapping a thick banded gold watch around his wrist before looking in my direction.

Even though he doesn't graduate until next year, he and the entire rest of the team, along with the coaches are coming to the graduation ceremony to support their graduating teammates.

"As I'll ever be." I let out a breath, waiting for Will to slip on his dress shoes before following him out into the hallway.

Graduation goes by in a blur of smiling faces and handshakes. I swear one minute the ceremony is starting and the next I'm climbing into my car, tossing my cap and gown into the passenger seat, getting ready to head to the graduation luncheon.

I didn't speak to my parents' during the ceremony, but at least they showed up. I honestly don't expect to see them at lunch, and I can't say I'm upset by it. They'd only end up making this day about my failures, about what I didn't accomplish that I should have.

I mean, fuck, I just graduated with a degree in Sports Medicine. Most parents would be satisfied with that, happy even, but not my parents'. More specifically, not my father. If it was up to him I would've followed in his footsteps—attended an Ivy League school and took over the practice from him someday.

He never accepted that I would do anything but that, and had I not fought so hard to get a scholarship, he might have actually gotten his way. Because then it would've been *his* school and *his* way or no way at all. Hell, he likely would've cut me off financially altogether had he not been so worried about what other people might think.

So, me being me, I burnt through more money in the last four years than I did the eighteen leading up to it. I maxed out credit cards on shit I didn't need and managed to drain the account he set up in my name to damn near zero. I wish I could say I was bigger than that type of behavior, that I wasn't stomping my foot like a child, but that simply wouldn't be true.

Just one of the many things I'm not proud of.

Catching my eyes in the rearview mirror, I take a long hard look at myself and wonder what Tess would think of me now.

She was always my voice of reason. She would have set me straight, told me to grow up and stop acting like a spoiled child, and I would have listened to her, too. But Tess isn't around anymore and even if she were, she probably wouldn't want a damn thing to do with me.

The women, the drinking, my clear taste for self-destruction is not likely something she would understand.

I ignore the nagging feeling in the pit of my stomach and try to focus on the road. I've been thinking about Tess a lot more than usual over the past few weeks now, and it's brought up a lot of unresolved feelings that I have.

Maybe it's because of graduation and knowing that all of this is coming to an end. Maybe it's because I'll be moving to California in just a few days having just secured an athletic assistant position working with one of the medical trainers at USC. I think I always knew I'd end up back there one day, but a part of me always thought it would be with Tess by my side. Maybe that's what it is. Maybe that's what has my insides in knots and my mind unable to focus on anything but the girl I left behind.

I know it sounds crazy, how someone can have such an effect on your life in such a short period of time. But in the almost year that Tess and I were together I learned a lot about myself and what I wanted out of life.

Truth be told, if it wasn't for her I probably wouldn't have had the courage to stand against my father and go after what *I* wanted. Not that she did anything specifically to drive that decision, but just being around her made me want to be more than what he wanted for me.

I wanted to be my own man, to stand on my own two feet and pave my own life. Tess made that feel possible.

There isn't a day that goes by that I don't think of her, that I don't wish things had ended up differently. There's been a hollow feeling in my chest since the moment I let her go, and no amount of women or booze could ever fill it.

Which leads me to the real reason why I'm so nervous about facing this next phase in my life because I think I'm finally realizing that I don't want a future without Tess. And that scares me more than I thought it could.

I try to push the thoughts away as best I can, slapping on a fake smile the second I enter the luncheon and working the room like I always do. But once the seed is planted it starts to fester, and by the end of the day, nothing has been able to distract me.

Not even my parents' showing up at lunch, which was a total shock, or the fact that for the first time since as long as I can remember my father actually shook my hand and treated me somewhat as an equal. Nope, not even that could stop the constant wheels from turning in my head.

My parents' left shortly after lunch, heading to Georgia to visit my mother's sister before flying back home in few days. If I wasn't already in a state of shock over the way they both behaved toward me, I certainly would've been watching them drive away in the same car together. I can't ever remember a time that my father has gone to Savannah with my mother. Add on the fact that he got into the car sporting the closest thing to a smile I've seen in a very long time, tells me there is definitely something going on with the two of them.

By the time I return to my dorm room hours later, having had a few drinks with the guys, the buzz running through my veins has only intensified my earlier thoughts of Tess. It's like once I open up and let the voices talk I can't get them to stop. And one voice is louder than all the others, the one that's been singing in my ears since the moment I looked out into the crowd at graduation and realized that the one person I wanted to see smiling back at me wasn't there. The voice that tells me it's time.

It's time to get my girl back.

I know I have a lot to figure out and a huge move coming u,p but for the first time in nearly four years something finally feels right, and I'm going to chase that feeling no matter where it leads me.

***

Stepping out of the airport into the bright sunlight, I take my first breath of New York air in over four years. God, I've missed this place.

After throwing my bag into the trunk of the cab, I quickly climb in the back seat, rambling off the address to the driver that I got from Courtney when I called her this morning. Funny, she didn't seem at all surprised to hear from me even though it had been nearly two years since the last time I checked in.

I try to keep my nerves at bay, but it's nearly impossible to do that the further into the city we get. By the time we reach the dorms where Tess lives, I feel like I'm seconds away from bouncing right out of my damn skin.

I can't remember a time I felt so nervous.

Okay, that's not true. But it's been years, and that night at Tess' senior prom feels like a lifetime ago. Just another thing I've tried to bury that has always found its way back to the surface. Just goes to show that some things are just not meant to be forgotten.

After paying the driver, I quickly exit the car, grabbing my bag before closing the trunk and turning toward the large four-story brick building in front of me. I take a deep breath in and then slowly let it out, trying to convince my feet to just fucking move already.

One step, two steps, three steps. I count each one as I make my way toward the front door. I've almost reached the sidewalk that wraps around the building when a sound I haven't heard in years whips around me, freezing me where I stand.

I'd know that laugh anywhere. The sweet airiness of it intoxicating as it dances around me.

I shift, my eyes seeking out the source, frantically searching until finally, finally after three long years, they land on the one thing they've never stopped looking for...
Tess.

Just the sight of her has all the air rushing from my body in an instant. She looks exactly as I remember and yet so different at the same time. Her long brown hair is now cut to her shoulders and there's a grown-up quality to her that wasn't there when we were kids. It makes me realize just how much a person can change over the years.

My heart constricts as I watch the smile spread across her face. It's the same smile I used to see my future in. The smile that used to make me weak in the knees. A smile that still does.

That is, until I follow her gaze to the man standing next to her—the man whose hand is wrapped around hers and looking down at her like she's all he can see. I know that look because it's how I used to look at her.

The realization of it all crashes over me, but before I have time to react, her blue eyes find mine and time seems to freeze me in the moment, paralyzing my ability to do anything but stare back at the love of my life, realizing that my worst fear may have just become my reality.

TESS

It's a beautiful day, one of those days where everything just feels right. The sun is shining brightly overhead, not a cloud in the sky, and the normally crowded campus is calm and relaxed; only students taking summer classes staying behind for the season.

Days like this don't happen often, at least not for me. Days where it feels like all the stars have aligned and there's a clearing in the distance where I can see all my hopes and dreams within my grasp.

Normally I would be one of the students heading to or from class, but this year I decided after two full years of classes not to enroll in summer courses. I'm already a full semester ahead of my other classmates and to be honest, I need the time off.

I stayed behind so Bennett could finish up some last minute coursework and then I'll be bound for the beaches of North Carolina for two full weeks of fun in the sun before heading home for a month to spend time with my mom and Courtney, who should be arriving in Rockfield a week before me.

Bennett talks excitedly about our upcoming trip, telling me all about his favorite restaurants and how he can't wait to show me where he grew up. I was apprehensive about joining him at his parents' house for the two-week trip when he first asked me, but since then the idea has grown on me. The more time I spend with him the more I forget about all the reservations I had when we first started dating six months ago.

He wasn't expected and a new relationship certainly wasn't what I was looking for, but after pursuing me for weeks I finally caved and agreed to a date. I mean, why was I so scared to date again anyway? Date… It was like the dirty, unspoken word that I avoided at every turn.

I guess deep down I believed that no one would ever fill Sebastian's shoes, that everyone would pale in comparison to the first boy who ever owned my heart. But slowly over time, I realized that I didn't need to fill the void left by Sebastian. I needed to embrace that it was a part of me and find a way to live with it.

So needless to say Bennett wore me down. Day by day with his warm smile and chocolate eyes, he broke down the walls that had once guarded my heart so fiercely. I don't know when my fondness of him morphed into something more. It was slow growing but the realization had hit me at all once, and I spent two hours on the phone crying to Bree over it.

It felt like a betrayal—like I was doing something wrong—but after a while, Bree finally made me see that I wasn't replacing Sebastian; I was simply letting him go. And hadn't that been what I wanted all along?

"I can't wait to take you out on the water. You're going to love it. I can't believe you've never been jet skiing." Bennett bounces next to me, his hand wrapped around mine.

I look up to see him watching me, a wide grin on his handsome face.

"You'll have to go easy on me." I return his smile, knocking my shoulder against his.

Bennett is one of those people who you just can't help but be attracted to. In addition to his obvious good looks— dark hair, warm brown eyes, a lopsided smile that shows off the smallest hint of two matching dimples, and a body that's toned and broad from the years he's spent surfing and sailing—he's also one of the most genuine people I've ever met. Nothing about him is complicated or hard. He wears his heart on his sleeve, and I never feel like there's anything he's keeping from me; no part of himself that he has hidden in the shadows.

"I will warn you," he continues, sliding his aviator sunglasses down on his face to shield his eyes from the sun, "my sister Brittany can be a bit of a handful. She means well, but I can't promise that she won't follow us around the entire time we're there." He chuckles, the sound vibrating deep in his chest. "She's done it since we were kids."

"I think it's sweet. I would probably do the same thing if I was her age and had a brother like you."

"She's a good kid but sometimes I just need some alone time, and I'm definitely going to want some this time around." He winks at me, and even though he's wearing sunglasses I can see the action clearly through the tinted lenses.

My cheeks flush and I quickly look away. I don't think I'll ever be able to talk about sex in a comfortable manner. I don't know why that is. Maybe it's because it feels like something that should only be discussed behind closed doors, or maybe it's because we've just recently become intimate and it just feels too new to really talk about out loud.

For the longest time, I didn't know if I'd be able to go through with it, sleeping with someone who wasn't Sebastian. It was something I struggled with for quite a while, and even after we did sleep together that first time I had a really hard time looking at myself in the mirror for a couple of days.

This entire process has been a really big step for me, and even though it's been difficult, I wouldn't take it back. Bennett has brought me back to life in a sense. His contagious smile and carefree attitude make me realize that sometimes you need to just give a little and not take life so seriously.

We've just rounded the corner of my dorm building when I feel the shift in the air. Goose bumps erupt across my skin and my stomach twists, a tight knot instantly forming. I don't understand the feeling right away. That is until I look up and find myself staring directly into a pair of bright hazel eyes, eyes I wasn't sure I'd ever see again.

"Sebastian?" I don't even realize I've spoken until his name is off my lips, thrown into the wind that seems to have picked up around us.

I stop abruptly, causing Bennett to stop next to me.

I feel disoriented, so caught off guard by his appearance that I'm not sure if it's actually happening or if I maybe fell and hit my head and am just dreaming this whole thing up.

"Sebastian?" I hear Bennett question behind me.

I don't have to look at him to know he sees what I'm looking at—or should I say who—though I doubt he would

306

have any clue who he is had I not said the name. He's only seen Sebastian once and that was in an old picture that he came across stuffed in the bottom of a desk drawer in my dorm room.

I can tell by the way his hand tightens around mine that even if he doesn't know for sure it's *my* Sebastian, he definitely suspects it.

Sebastian's eyes bounce from our adjoined hands to my face and back again, a slight tick in his jaw as he stands motionless just a couple of yards from us. I can see the struggle in his eyes, the uncertainty of what he should do next, but then he blinks and an easy smile quickly falls into place as he closes the distance between us.

"Hi, Tess."

It's just a statement, a simple greeting, and yet I feel like he's said so much more. I don't know how long I stand there, jaw on the ground, still trying to figure out if he's actually here.

I can feel Bennett's eyes on the side of my face, but I can't force a single thing to come out.

Bennett clears his throat and extends his hand to Sebastian, clearly seeing that I'm not going to introduce them anytime soon.

"Hi, I'm Bennett."

"Sebastian," he replies coolly, taking Bennett's hand on a firm shake before shoving both of his hands into the front pocket of his jeans as he rocks back slightly on his heels, eyes trained on my face.

"What are you doing here, Sebastian?" When I finally manage to push the question out it feels raw against my throat.

"I was in the area. Thought I'd stop by and say hey." He shrugs like it's no big deal. Just an old friend dropping by.

"You were in the area?" I repeat slowly.

"Was hoping maybe you'd have time to grab a bite to eat, catch up for a little bit." He ignores my question completely.

I open my mouth to respond but then close it without uttering a single word. Honestly, I don't know what the hell to say to that. And as unexpected as it is to find him standing in front of me, I also can't deny how incredible it is to lay eyes on him after such a long time.

He's just as perfect as I remember, maybe even more so. Sebastian always was the most attractive person I'd ever seen, still is. I feel guilty even thinking it with Bennett standing next to me, but it's true. I can't help it.

"I'm gonna run up and grab my bag out of your room. Why don't you take some time to talk to your friend?" Bennett offers, pulling my attention to him.

"Are you sure?" I ask, a thick knot in my throat.

"Yeah, of course. I still have a few things I need to take care of before our trip. I'll just call you later, okay?" He gives me a warm smile before pressing his lips to my forehead in a quick kiss.

Case and point why Bennett is so incredible. My ex-boyfriend shows up out of the blue and instead of being an asshole about it, he offers to give me some time to figure out what he wants and why he's here. God, he really is amazing.

"Okay." I force a smile when he pulls back.

"It was nice to meet you, Sebastian," he calls over his shoulder before taking off toward the entrance of my building, disappearing inside just moments later.

When I slowly turn back to Sebastian, his expression has morphed from carefree to something else entirely. He takes a shaky breath in, his nostrils flaring slightly.

"I take it that's your boyfriend?" The last part comes off more like a hiss than an actual word.

"He is," I answer shakily; it's not like it's worth hiding at this point.

"How long have you two been seeing each other?"

The last thing I want to do is have this conversation directly outside of my dorm building, so I quickly move to change the direction.

"What are you doing here, Sebastian? And don't give me that crap about being in the area because we both know that's not true."

"I just, fuck." He runs a hair through his messy hair, making it look even more perfect.

God, why does he have to look so good?

"I just needed to see you," he finally continues. "Can we maybe go somewhere and talk?"

I want to say no. I want to tell him to go away so I can pretend like he didn't just show up at the moment when I finally decided I was happy, determined to tear down everything I've built in his absence, but I simply can't do it.

Because at the end of the day, I still love him as much as I did yesterday, as much as I did a year ago, and two years ago and beyond that. Just because I have found some semblance of happiness doesn't for one second erase the way my heart beats against my ribs or the way my fingers itch to reach out and touch his silky hair. Even after all this time a part of me, a very large part still feels like he belongs to me and I to him.

"Okay." I finally concede. "There's a coffee shop just on the edge of campus. It's only about a five-minute walk."

"Sounds perfect." He waits for me to start walking before quickly stepping up next to me, slowing his long stride to match mine so that he can keep my pace.

We don't speak for most of the walk. It's clear to see Sebastian is just as in his head as I am in mine, both of us trying to sort through what we're thinking right now before having to sit down and actually speak it aloud.

"I graduated yesterday." He finally speaks just as we round the corner to the coffee shop where I've worked since freshman year.

"Wow. Congratulations. That's amazing. How do you feel?" I nod in thanks when he holds the door open for me before following me inside.

The smell of coffee instantly assaults my senses, and I take a deep inhale, having become one of my favorite smells over the last couple of years. I don't like to drink it, but the smell is incredible. I think it has a lot to do with the fact that the smell reminds me of my mom; she's always been a big coffee drinker.

"I'm not sure yet," is all he can get out before we reach the counter, and my co-worker Jill cuts in.

"Tess, what are you doing here?" Her long blonde ponytail swings as she talks. "I thought you were leaving for North Carolina with that hunky boyfriend of yours."

Sebastian shuffles next to me, clearly uncomfortable.

"We leave tomorrow." I try to sound as casual as possible despite the sudden flush of heat that has washed over my body.

"How fun. I'm so jelly. I would love to lie on a beach for a few days." Only then does she seem to notice

Sebastian, her eyes widening slightly as she takes him in. "And who's your friend?" Her voice completely changes as she asks me the question while looking directly at Sebastian.

"Sebastian." He gives her a megawatt smile, and I swear I can physically see her swoon a little.

"Where do you find these guys?" Jill asks playfully as she turns back toward me.

I offer her no more than a shrug and a "we go way back" before asking if I can have my usual chai tea with two sweeteners. Jill may be perfectly content standing here ogling over Sebastian until her little heart's content, but I'm rather anxious to have him to myself and find out exactly what has him coming all the way here to see me so unexpectedly.

Sebastian orders a coffee, black, and after paying for us both, grabs our drinks and follows me to a table in the far corner.

Sitting back in his chair, one hand on his leg, the other wrapped around his cup of coffee, he seems so lost in thought that I decide to speak first rather than waiting on him to start the conversation.

"So you were talking about graduation," I press, hoping he'll take the lead.

"I was."

Only then do I realize that I don't even know what he was studying. How sad is that? He hadn't claimed a major the last time we had actually spoken of college, and with everything that happened, it was honestly the furthest thing from my mind.

"What did you end up studying?"

"Sports medicine." He shifts in his seat, eyes never leaving mine.

"Oh wow. That's awesome." I feel cliché saying it, but I have no idea what the hell to say right now. Everything feels forced and unnatural which is unsettling considering I never felt anything but comfortable with Sebastian before.

"And what about football?" I quickly add when he doesn't offer a response.

"I had some interest going into senior year, but I wasn't interested in pursuing it."

"Oh." I don't know why but this surprises me. I knew football was never his end game, but I find it hard to believe anyone would walk away from the chance to play football professionally.

"I actually got a job offer as an athletic assistant for the medical team at USC. I'm supposed to start in a couple weeks."

"That's amazing, Sebastian, congratulations." I pause. "That's in California, right?"

"It is." He nods slowly, taking his first drink of coffee before setting it back down, his hand never leaving the cup.

"California," I let it roll off my tongue as I toss around what that means for him. "You always said you would go back there one day."

"Yeah, but when I thought about it I always saw you there with me."

I don't know what to say to that so I just sit here looking at him, my heart racing out of my chest, trying my best to control the tremble running through my hands.

"I miss you, Tess." Heat spreads over my face and down my torso the second the words are spoken.

"Sebastian," I try to interject.

"No, just let me get this out, okay?" He waits for me to nod before continuing, "I miss you every single day. Every moment was less because you weren't there to share it with. I've missed out on so much time and now, now I find myself unsure of how to move forward without you. I don't know how to explain it, but when I was up on that stage accepting the degree I worked my ass off for, the only person I wanted to look out into the audience and see was you. But you weren't there, and it made me realize that none of it means anything if I don't have you to share it with."

"Sebastian, please." My voice shakes, and I can already feel tears stinging the back of my eyes.

"The guy, is it serious?" He cuts me off.

"I mean, yeah, I guess it is." I sniff.

"Do you love him?"

"I think so." It takes me a long moment to force the words out. Why is it so hard to say what just an hour ago I thought I felt.

"You think so or you know so?" He crosses his arms in front of his broad chest.

"I mean, it's still pretty new."

"But you're going on a trip with him?" He continues to pound questions at me.

"We're going to spend two weeks in North Carolina with his family," I admit, guilt swarming me from every side.

Why the hell do I feel so damn guilty?

"So you're going to stay with his family for two full weeks, and you can't even tell me for sure if you love the guy?" He cocks a brow, frustration etched in every feature of his face.

"I mean, I do love him. It's just…"

"It's just what, Tess?"

313

"It's different, the love. It's different than what you and I had." He cringes at my use of past tense. "But he makes me happy."

"Good." He lets out slowly, clearly battling with what to say next.

"Why are you really here, Sebastian?"

"I told you. I'm here for you."

"So what then? You just show up after nearly three years and you expect me to drop my life and everything I've built here to what—go to California with you?"

"Well, when you put it like that." He blows out a breath, looking more conflicted with each moment that passes.

"I still have another year of school left. And I have friends here and a…"

"Boyfriend," he finishes my sentence.

"Yes and a boyfriend," I snip, letting my emotions get the better of me.

"I guess I didn't think this all the way through. I think… I mean, I guess I thought…"

"You thought you could just show up here, and we'd just pick right back up where we left off. God, Sebastian. Look at us. It's been three years and yet were still doing this same old song and dance. Maybe you've graduated and are ready to start the next journey of your life, but I'm not. My life is here. Nothing has changed for me. So unless you're here to tell me that you're moving to New York then we have nothing left to discuss."

"Would you leave him, your boyfriend I mean? If I were to move here, would you leave him and be with me?"

"Are you moving to New York?" I challenge, leaning back in my chair on a sigh when he doesn't answer right away. "That's what I thought."

"Fuck," he growls, pushing his chair back so it skids across the floor as he stands. "I shouldn't have come here."

And just like that he turns and storms out of the coffee shop, walking away from me yet again.

TESS

"Where the hell do you think you're going?" I'm on Sebastian's heels seconds after he steps out on the sidewalk.

"Just leave it, Tess."

"Leave it? You show up here announced after three years, lay all that on me back there, and then you just walk away?" I grab his arm, forcing him to stop and look at me.

"Tess," he warns, eyes anywhere but on me.

"Tell me what you want, Sebastian," I plead.

"You!" he screams. "Fuck, Tess, I just want you."

"But only the way you want me, right?" I bite back. "It's been three years, Sebastian. Three years," I stress. "You can't just show up here and demand that everything go back to the way it was. Life doesn't work that way." I soften my voice. "Did it ever occur to you that I miss you just as much as you miss me? That this has been just as hard for me? That I too always look for you first when anything happens? I still love you, Sebastian. I've never stopped. Not for one single second. But things are different now."

"Because of him?" he drags out.

"Because of me." I look down at where my hand is still on his arm, having not realized I hadn't pulled it back once he stopped.

I stare at our point of connection, my hand tingling all the way up my arm like an electric current that runs through him and into me. When I meet his gaze again I know he feels it too, and that makes what I'm about to say a million times harder.

"If you were moving to New York it would be a discussion I'd be willing to have. I'm not saying one way or the other, but I wouldn't rule it out entirely. I don't think I could even if I wanted to. But you're not moving to New York, Sebastian. You're going home, to California. And even though you might be willing to walk away from it out of desperation and fear of losing me, we're still in the same place we've always been. One of us not willing to let the other give up what they really want. I won't be the reason why you turn down a job I'm sure doesn't come around every day or the reason you stay in New York when all you've wanted for years was to go back to California."

"But it's just a state, and it's just a job. There are other places I can live, and there will be other jobs, Tess. But there's no other you." When he reaches out and cups my cheek, I swear every single emotion I've kept bottled inside comes rushing to the surface.

Love.

Anger.

Fear.

Pain.

They all bleed together in the most overwhelming concoction, and I can't seem to swallow them back down no matter how hard I try.

317

"I love you, Tess," he whispers, his other hand sliding around to the small of my back as he guides me toward him, pulling me flush against his chest.

I give myself one minute. That's it. Just one minute to breathe in his scent, to remember what it was to be held by him, to listen to his heart beating against my ear. Just one minute and then I know I have to muster the courage to say no.

I don't want to, though.

I wish I could say Bennett makes it easier, that knowing I have him makes the choice bearable, but it simply does not. Because Sebastian and Bennett are divided in my heart and in my mind; neither play into the decisions I make about the other because they are loved by two sides of me that will never touch. The part of my heart that beats only for Sebastian and then the other half that finally believes it's possible to love another, maybe not in the same way but no less just the same.

When I finally pull back, managing to put a few inches between us, tears are forming at the corners of my eyes. I blink rapidly hoping I can fight them down, but one look up at Sebastian and they topple over. I can feel my heart breaking all over again—the pain almost too much to bear—and a sense of panic washes over me.

I don't want him to leave.

I don't want to wait another month or year or longer to look at his face and feel what I feel looking at him now.

I don't want this to the end.

And yet, at the same time, I know it would never work.

I know he can read it all over my face, but it doesn't make the words any less difficult to force out.

"I'm sorry, but I can't."

When he blinks tears pool in his eyes, but not a single one falls.

"Go to California, Sebastian. Take your incredible job offer, and go home. Find happiness. Find love. Find peace. I want all of those things for you." And while I mean every word, the thought of him loving someone that isn't me is damn near crippling.

He takes a deep breath in and then slowly lets it out, resolve spreading across his face.

"Okay." The word is barely off his lips before his hands come up to cup my face on both sides. "I'll go to California. I'll take the job, and I'll live my life. But do not for one second think that this is me walking away again. I know what I want now, Tess. In fact, it's never been clearer. I've grown up a lot over the years, and I've learned some very valuable life lessons—as I'm sure you have as well. We're not the same kids we once were, and yet when I look at you, it's like I'm seventeen all over again; neither time nor distance has lessened my love for you. I've made my choice, Tess, and I choose you. I don't care if I have to wait five more years—

you are *my* girl, and I will wait as long as I have to."

"Don't do that," I croak. "Don't make promises you can't keep. You don't know what the future holds. You don't know where you'll be come that time. You might move to California and meet the girl of your dreams."

"I've already met her," he cuts me off. "And she's the most fucking beautiful thing I've ever seen."

"Sebastian."

"I'm serious, Tess. You are mine. You've always been mine. I don't care what you tell yourself or your boyfriend—facts are facts, and deep down you know who you belong to. This." He slides a hand to my chest and

319

splays his palm on top of my raging heart. "This knows who it belongs to. And when it's ready, when you're ready, I'll be waiting."

With that, he leans forward and presses a soft kiss to my cheek. I hold my breath, waiting, hoping that his lips will find mine next. I know I shouldn't want it. I know how wrong it is. But I can't help it.

Disappointment settles in my chest the instant he pulls back, followed by an immense wave of guilt.

What the hell is wrong with me?

I've finally found someone new, someone who makes me happy, and here I am willing to throw it all away for one kiss that will likely only succeed in hurting me further.

I know Sebastian says he'll wait, but I'm not entirely sure what he's going to be waiting for. I don't know what the future holds or where my life will go. And he can't promise me that he does either.

"Until then," he finally murmurs before stepping away.

I feel the loss of him everywhere, and it's deafening. My body pleads with me to bring him back. To pull him close and never let him go because he's right—

it knows where it belongs. *I* know where I belong.

But things aren't always so black and white.

I open my mouth just as Sebastian turns away, but nothing comes out. I watch him shove his hands into his pockets and tilt his head toward the ground, and for what feels like the hundredth time, I watch him walk away.

With each step he takes I want to call out to him, to stop him. But words and actions fail me.

Maybe it's because I'm afraid. I'm afraid to go there with him again only to have it all fall apart.

Maybe it's because deep down I know it would never work, and I don't think I could survive the loss of him a second time. In fact, I know I wouldn't.

Maybe it's because of the happiness Bennett has brought to my life over the past few months and that I'm not ready to walk away from him yet because what we have could be incredible—*could* being the operative word.

Or maybe it's a combination of all of these things that has me rooted to the spot, unable to stop Sebastian from walking away.

***

"I can't believe you told him where to find me," I seethe, repeating the same statement I've said several times since finding out Courtney is the one who gave Sebastian the address to my dorm. "You're supposed to be on my side here."

"I am on your side," Court objects.

"Then how could you just let him show up here and not even give me the slightest heads up about it?" I pace back and forth inside my small dorm room, unable to shake the nervous jittery feeling I've had since the moment Sebastian arrived.

"Because I didn't think he'd actually do it," she cuts in.

"And you didn't think I deserved to know that it was even a possibility? He showed up here to find me with Bennett, Court. Do you have any idea the position that put me in?"

"I'm sorry, okay? I just…"

"You just what?" I snap, directing my frustration at her when I know it's not her fault.

"I didn't want you to get your hopes up," she says almost apologetically.

"What is that supposed to mean?"

"It means that even though you don't talk about Sebastian anymore, I know you still love him. And no matter how much you wish you could deny it, had I told you he was coming and then him not shown up, a part of you would've been devastated."

I know she's right. Of course, I do. But that doesn't erase the sting I feel finding out after all this time that Courtney and Sebastian have been in contact behind my back. The fact that they've spoken at all since we parted ways leaves me with a sick sense of betrayal—even though neither of them really did anything wrong.

She claims it was just so she could tell Sebastian how I was. That he would call or text every few weeks just to check in. She says he always only ever talked about me, and he wanted to know everything I was up to each and every time they spoke. She said she could tell how miserable he was without me—how much he missed me—but she also said that eventually, the calls became less frequent.

What started as once a week turned into once a month and then once every three months to six months, and then he just stopped calling all together until recently.

I think that's the part that bothers me the most. The *why* he stopped calling.

"But he did show up, and yet I'm still devastated. So what did you really accomplish other than keeping something from me that you knew I'd want to know?"

"I really am sorry, Tess. I was just trying to help."

"Well, maybe next time you'll see that what would really help is knowing that I can count on you to have *my* back."

"Come on, Tess, don't be like that. Of course, I have your back. Why do you think I even took his calls to begin with?"

"I honestly don't know," I admit truthfully.

"Because I knew you'd want me to," she answers simply. "You loved him so much—hell, you still do. I knew the last thing you wanted was for him to worry about you, to be sad, and god, Tess, he was—he was so sad. So I did what I thought you'd want me to do. I tried to give him some peace. I tried to reassure him that you were doing okay and that you were getting by. I tried to help him heal, Tess. Can you honestly say you would've rather me turned my back on him?"

"No." I let out a loud breath, knowing she's got me there.

"Exactly, because at the end of the day all you've ever wanted is for him to be happy. How could I have turned my back on that knowing how much it meant to you that he find peace and move on? I knew that even if you didn't know I was talking to him that deep down you would've approved. I didn't just do it for Sebastian, Tess, I did it for you."

I don't really know how to respond to that. Luckily, Courtney isn't finished yet.

"Look, if you need to be mad at me, be mad at me. I get it. I should've given you a heads up that he asked for your address. I can see now that it would've been better for you to have been prepared and then disappointed rather than totally fucking blindsided. That's my bad. I really was just trying to help."

"I know." I sigh, my anger quickly dissipating.

"So tell me again everything that happened." I can hear the smile in her voice, knowing that I've forgiven her so easily, just she like she knew I would.

"I've already told you."

"No, you yelled at me and rambled off some nonsense about Sebastian and Bennett and having no idea what you were going to do, and then you yelled at me again." She chuckles.

"I did not yell at you."

"You did so," Court says matter of fact.

"Okay, maybe I did." I smile, shaking my head. "But you deserved it."

"That may be true, but it also doesn't change the fact that I still have no real clue what the hell happened. Stop leaving me in suspense and spill, woman!"

And just like that, it's as though nothing happened between the two of us. Courtney has this innate ability to know exactly what I need even when I don't. She also knows how to explain herself in a way that makes me feel like I'm the one doing something wrong, which certainly doesn't hurt her case when she's trying to talk herself out of a corner.

I guess at the end of the day it really boils down to the fact that I know no matter what the circumstance, Court wouldn't do something if she didn't truly believe it was the right thing for me. And I trust her. Sometimes it takes me a minute to get there, but she always has a way of making me see it in the end.

So, after taking a deep breath and sorting my thoughts, I start at the very beginning. Knowing if I have any hopes of processing what happened here today, I'm gonna need my best friend.

SEBASTIAN

One year later

I can't remember a time I've ever been this anxious. Okay, so that's not true. I can remember a time very specifically, and it was right around one year ago. Funny that both cases involve me going to see Tess and her having no idea that I'm coming—I'm starting to see a pattern here.

When Courtney called and invited me to Tess' graduation party at her mom's, at first I thought it was a fucking joke. I mean, her mom hates me, or at least that's what I thought at the time. And let's not forget that Courtney was very clear that the boyfriend is still in the picture and would most definitely be there. I'm still not sure what exactly that means for me.

Truth is—even had Courtney not invited me—I had still planned to track Tess down in the coming days. I meant what I said to her about waiting, and even though it's been difficult and I've found myself itching with impatience, I've managed to make it to the day when the excuses as to why Tess and I can't be together are over.

We've both graduated college and while I love my job, if Tess told me that she didn't want to move to California I'd give it up in a heartbeat. I've established enough experience that I'm confident I could find something comparable somewhere else if that's what I need to do.

The only thing I really didn't factor for was the boyfriend. I don't know why, but I didn't expect it to last nearly this long. The fact that it has is more than a little worrisome. In the back of my head, there is the voice asking me what I'll do if she chooses him.

I try to shake off the thought, not even able to accept it as a possibility, and turn my gaze back out the window of the cab. It's been so long since I've been to Rockfield, and while there is an air of familiarity as we drive through town, there's also so much that has changed.

I tried to talk Ant into coming with me; I'd feel a lot better if I had someone to talk me down from the ledge I'm currently teetering on. He's been staying in California with me the last few months, and while I could tell he wanted to come, I think he was hesitant to see Courtney again. I think he's been just as hung up on her as I've been on Tess. Together we're just a bunch of sorry ass saps. It's pretty pathetic really.

Nervous energy bubbles in my stomach, and I have a hard time sitting still in my seat. I want to regret my decision to do this, convince myself it's a bad idea and have this car turn around right now before I do something I'm going to regret, but I can't. I can't because I know at the end of this I'll finally have my answer.

Will she or won't she?

I'm done playing the games of our past. I'm done with the back and forth and the excuse that always seems to plague us—*we're in different places in our lives*.

Well, not anymore. We are finally—for the first time since high school—on the exact same page. We've graduated college, both completed degrees at the school of our dreams, and now all that's left is to decide if she's coming to California with me or if I'm going to be packing up and relocating; something I'm more than willing to do if it means I get to be with Tess.

When the cab slows outside of Tess' mom's house I feel like I'm on the verge of having a heart attack. My chest throbs and my heart is beating so rapidly against my ribcage it's a fucking wonder it hasn't exploded yet.

There's so many more factors than just seeing Tess. There's also the other dynamic. The fact that a lot of our old friends will be here, as well as her boyfriend, and of course her mom; though, I'm not quite as worried about the last one—at least not anymore.

I knew there was no way I could come back here without first making peace with Elizabeth. It was a long overdue phone call, one I should've made nearly five years ago. Even though it took me that long to make it, Tess' mom seemed to understand.

I knew at the end of that phone call that should Tess choose to be with me, her mom would fully support her daughter's choice. I know she could tell how much I still love Tess. I think at the end of the day the most a parent can ask for is that their child finds the love and happiness that they've always dreamed they'd find. Well, a good parent anyway.

It takes a few seconds but after a couple deep calming breaths, I finally manage to pay the cab driver and climb out of the car on shaky legs.

As I make my way up the sidewalk I'm accosted by so many memories of my time spent in this small ranch. The first night I came here and how I'd barely watched the movie Tess had put on, spending more time with my eyes on the girl who was next to me. How I used to sneak over after Tess' mom left for work; the nights that I would hold her until just before the sun peeked over the horizon and then I would slip out before her mom returned home.

Those are some of my favorite memories, the ones where it was just Tess and me. We would lay in bed for hours just talking about everything and yet nothing at all at the same time. She brought me a peace I hadn't realized at the time I was looking for, a sense of belonging. Tess was my home... She still is.

I force my feet to keep moving, one after another until I've rounded the small house and the backyard comes into view. There's more people than I expected—at least thirty or more—and the entire yard is set up like you would expect any summer cookout/party to look. Picnic tables line the back of the house with another table set up to the side covered in different foods—burgers, corn on the cob, fruit salad, and tons of other things.

There are two sets of cornhole boards set up at the back of the small yard, a group of people corralled around them as they toss bags and drink from beer bottles and blue plastic cups.

Suddenly wishing I had brought some food or drinks just to have something to hold, I shove my hands into my pockets and let my eyes wander the yard in search of Tess, staying far enough back that I don't draw attention to myself. What I find instead is Courtney, and before I can even move she's closing the distance between us.

"You made it." She gives me a nervous smile, stopping directly in front of me. "I wasn't sure if you would."

"Honestly neither was I," I admit, rocking back on my heels. "But I didn't know when I'd get the chance to see her again, and I didn't want to wait until it was too late."

"Well, I'm glad you're here."

"I wouldn't be if it wasn't for you. I know Tess was pretty upset with you when you gave me her address last year. I can't imagine that she'll be very happy when she finds out you're the one who invited me. So I just want to say thank you again—for everything."

"I wouldn't have done it if I thought there was another way. I don't like sneaking around behind my best friend's back like this."

"I know. And I appreciate everything you've done for me. You really are an amazing friend. Not just to Tess, but to me as well."

"Just remember that when I'm friendless after Tess realizes I had a hand in you being here," she quips, a smile tugging at her lips.

"Any news on the job front?" I ask, knowing that will significantly hurt my chances if she's already committed to something.

Courtney shakes her head slowly side to side before answering, "I will tell you that she's had a couple offers in the city recently, but has yet to accept a single one. I think her hesitance comes from you, though she's yet to actually admit that to me."

"And the boyfriend?" I question, arching my brow at her.

"He accepted a job last week—in New York City. I don't know what that means for Tess, but I do know she's been acting very restless the past few weeks. Again, something I'm fairly certain has to do with you."

"I told her I would wait until she graduates."

"And now she has," Courtney interjects.

"Which is why I'm here."

Courtney opens her mouth to say something else, but then quickly snaps it shut when she sees Tess emerge from the house at the very same moment I do, her douche bag boyfriend following directly behind her.

"Shit, I'm gonna go hide now," Courtney whispers. "Good luck," she quickly adds before slinking off into the crowd before Tess has a chance to see us together.

I watch Tess stop and talk to a handful of people on her way to the far side of the yard where I see Courtney now standing next to Bree, a child—who I presume is her son, running circles around the two of them.

The little boy is laughing hysterically, his little giggles echoing across the space, but when Tess swoops down and hoists him over her shoulder, he squeals and laughs even harder. She spins him around a few times before finally lowering him to his feet, clearly becoming dizzy in the process.

I can't help the smile that stretches across my face as I watch her with the little boy. Visions of her playing in the backyard with *our* children flash through my mind and it's honestly the best fucking motivation to do what I know I have to.

I take a deep breath and finally step fully into the backyard, ready to take what I came here for. Tess.

My plan quickly gets thwarted when Timmy and David, a couple of guys from high school, stop me just a few feet from where I was previously standing. We shoot the shit for a minute or two before I finally manage to excuse myself, my eyes locking on Tess once more.

I've almost reached her—so close that less than ten feet separate us—when the world seems to come to a screeching halt, my legs right along with it.

The next several moments happen in slow motion, like they're being captured in snapshots, each one a still frame.

Snap—the boyfriend asks for everyone's attention.

Snap—he says something that sounds an awful lot like what I was about to say. Love of his life, not able to live without her; every word is muffled by the white noise suddenly ringing in my ears.

Snap—he's lowering himself down onto one knee.

Snap—there's a ring box in his hand.

Snap—he's opening it, saying what I can only presume is *will you marry me*. By this point, I've completely stopped processing the actual words being spoken.

Snap—Tess raises her hand to cover her mouth, her beautiful face contorted in surprise.

Snap—she hesitates, a blush running up her neck and onto her pale cheeks.

Snap—she swallows hard. I watch the way her throat bobs as she does.

Snap—she nods yes.

Snap—he slides the ring on her finger.

Snap—her eyes find mine and every ounce of color drains from her face.

TESS

My heartbeat is the only thing I can hear. The constant thudding against my ribcage echoing through my ears, making everything sound distorted and far away.

I don't know how it happened. One minute Bennett is down on one knee, the next my head is nodding yes. I don't think I even processed what he was asking before just reacting the way I thought I should have, given that every single set of eyes were on us.

Did I really just say yes?

My stomach twists violently and suddenly every single thing in my stomach threatens to come back up.

I quickly look for an escape, my eyes darting toward the house; only the house never comes into view. Instead, they land on the last person that I would want to witness what is currently taking place in the middle of the backyard.

The minute his hazel eyes find mine—the shock and anger so evident—it steals my breath. My legs wobble, and I nearly lose my footing.

I want to go to him but before I can move even a muscle, Bennett is pulling me into his arms, and applause breaks through the static in my ears.

What the hell is happening right now?

I feel so disoriented I can't seem to process a single moment of it. I'm in my mom's arms next, followed by Bree who squeezes me excitedly. The second she releases me I immediately turn back to where Sebastian was just moments ago, only this time he's nowhere to be found.

Did I just imagine he was there?

It isn't until I catch sight of Courtney's face that the reality seems to catch back up to me. She looks torn between crying and vomiting which sends off warning bells in my head.

Bennett steps up next to me, dropping his arm around my shoulder making me feel weighted to the ground. I keep my gaze focused on Courtney, learning everything I need to know just by the expression on her face.

Suddenly I feel like I'm on verge of suffocating. I can't pull enough air in, and tears prick the back of my eyes.

Knowing I need to hold it together, at least for a little while, I fight down the panic I feel clawing its way up my throat and force the best smile I can muster.

***

The sick feeling in the pit of my stomach only intensifies over the next hour. Courtney doesn't say a word about Sebastian, and neither do I. I know with complete certainty that she had a hand in his being here, I just don't know why yet.

And then there's my mom. While I know she really likes Bennett and she seems genuinely happy about this entire ordeal, I can sense something is off with her and yet I can't pinpoint what.

With her eyes constantly on me, as well as Bree's and Courtney's, it's like they're just waiting for me to breakdown, like they know it's coming. I feel scrutinized and on display, and yet a part of me feels like maybe it's just all in my head. My mind twisting reality to match the guilt and uncertainty in my heart.

The same question I keep going back to over and over is if Bennett had asked me when it was just the two of us, would I have said yes? The fact that I can't answer that with complete certainty is nagging at me, and I can't seem to swallow it down no matter how hard I try. And the one thought that plagues me over and over again is becoming harder to ignore.

I have to get out of here.

With each moment that passes, I feel more on edge, more tense, more emotional. I feel like I'm seconds away from splitting apart at the very seams which hold me together.

"I'm gonna run to the bathroom," I finally say to Bennett, who has yet to leave my side since the whole proposal fiasco. "I'll be right back." I force yet another smile before ducking out from underneath his arm.

Before anyone can say anything, I take off into the house. I stumble through the kitchen, my feet feeling like they've been weighted by heavy cinder blocks. Each step feels harder to take than the last, but I still manage to propel myself further.

The next thing I know I'm through the front door and out onto the front porch, leaning forward with my hands gripping my knees as I struggle to suck in air. I've never had a true, full blown panic attack before, but I have very little doubt that this is exactly what is happening right now.

My senses feel under attack, my lungs unable to pull in enough air, my heart beating so erratically I feel on the verge of a heart attack; the smell of copper strong in my nose and the taste of it heavy on my tongue.

When I look up to see someone sitting on the curb directly in front of the house, I know instantly that it's Sebastian. I can tell by the width of his broad shoulders and the sun-kissed blond hair that blows in the light breeze.

The panic starts to recede the instant I realize he's still here, and while the thought is unsettling as to why that might be, I can't pretend it's not true. Without thinking I find myself walking toward him. One small step and then another until I'm standing just a foot behind him, watching his shoulders rise and fall with each breath he takes, his knees pulled up and arms draped over them.

"I thought you left." My voice sounds small, weak, and I hate every second of it.

"I've been sitting out here waiting for you, but I gave up that you were coming out about twenty minutes ago," he responds, his tone flat, eyes fixed straight ahead; not seeming the least bit surprised by my appearance. He lets out a slow exhale and then adds, "I'm waiting for my cab to get here to take me to the airport. Don't worry, I'll be out of your way shortly."

"You're leaving?"

He lets out a laugh, but it's not the carefree sound I'm used to. There's something sinister about the sound, something dark.

Without saying anything else, I slide down next to him, mirroring his posture. He makes no attempt to look at me, and I try my best to keep my eyes directed forward as well. I would guess a good ten minutes have passed before I finally get the nerve to speak again.

"Why did you come here, Sebastian?"

"You know why." He glances at me out of the corner of his eye. "I meant what I said to you outside of that coffee shop. I've been waiting for you. Though it would appear I've been alone in this venture."

"You knew I had a boyfriend," I weakly argue.

"Trust me, I'm all too aware of your *boyfriend*. But I'm also aware that you said you loved me; here I thought that was still true." His voice shakes slightly and only then do I realize how distraught he seems, though he's doing his damndest to hold it together.

"I do love you." I lay my hand on his forearm, jumping slightly when he pulls away from my touch.

"If you loved me you wouldn't have said yes." He shifts inward to face me straight on, and the hurt in his eyes knocks the wind right out of me. It's like taking a punch to the stomach; I will the air in, but my lungs have no capacity for it.

"That's not fair," I finally manage to croak out.

"I don't give a fuck what's fair anymore, Tess. It's always been an excuse. I'm starting to realize you're never going to stop making excuses, and I'm just simply wasting my time at this point," he seethes, quickly pushing to his feet.

"Don't do that. You know that isn't true," I object, resisting the urge to reach for him when I stand as well.

"Bullshit, Tess." He spins on me. "You're never going to forgive me, are you?"

"What are you talking about?" I question, confused by his words.

"I'm talking about the fact that five years ago I broke your heart and your trust, and deep down you're still holding onto that. If you weren't you wouldn't have turned me away when I showed up at your prom. You wouldn't have denied me when I came to you last year. And you sure as hell wouldn't have just agreed to marry another man. Admit it, Tess, you just can't let it go."

"That's not true, Sebastian."

"Don't fucking lie to me!" he roars, causing me to stumble backward slightly. "Don't fucking lie to me, Tess," he repeats more calmly. "I know I fucked up. I know letting you go was the biggest mistake I've ever made. But fuck, Tess, I was just a kid. A kid who was trying like hell to do what was right by you. It wasn't until that night at prom that I realized how stupid I'd been."

"You mean after you realized that I was going to prom with another guy. Or do you think I'm so blind I can't see where your actions are stemming from? It's jealously, Sebastian. That's the one thing that's always fueled you. You don't want me. You discarded me so easily, and yet the second you see me with someone else it's like you can't live without me. So what is it, Sebastian, huh?"

"This has nothing to do with anyone but you and me. Yes, realizing that you had a date to prom—that you were going with someone who wasn't me—was a hard pill to swallow, and maybe I didn't handle that situation the way I should have, but that's not why I came for you that night. And it sure as hell isn't why I showed up at your dorm last year. I didn't even know you were involved with anyone. I know I'm the one who started all of this when I let you go the first time, but the only person who's been keeping us apart is you. I tried to keep my distance, fuck—for years I tried. But I kept coming back to you, Tess. You are it for me. You've always been it for me."

"Sebastian," I try to speak but he quickly cuts me off.

"I want you to think long and hard about what you say to me next, Tess, because this is it for me. I'm done. I'm done chasing you. I'm done putting my life on hold waiting for you to decide you want to be with me. I'm done with this game, Tess. I'm just done."

"I'm not playing any games, Sebastian."

"You know what, I honestly believe that you believe that. I can tell by the way you look at me that you still love me. But you've put up this guard. I broke your heart, and so you've built a wall to keep me from it."

"The timing just wasn't right, we agreed."

"No, I blamed it on timing once when I was trying to do what I thought was right. After that you ran with it, and it's been your crutch ever since. Now, when you finally have the ability to choose me—to be with me—you agree to marry another man."

"I've been with Bennett for almost two years. It's not just you and me. There's another person to consider here. A person I care a great deal for. It's not as black and white as you seem to think it is."

"But it is, Tess. It is black and white. Either you love me or you don't. Either you choose me or you don't." He throws his hand up in frustration. "I can't fucking do this anymore, Tess. I can't keep running to you only to have you push me away again. I need to know now—without question—do you truly intend to marry that man?" He gestures toward the house where Bennett and all my other friends and family are gathered out back, completely oblivious to the life-altering decision staring me right in the face.

"I don't know what you want me to say." I fight back the tears I feel burning the back of my eyes.

"I want you to say no, Tess. I want you to tell me that you don't want to marry him. I want you to tell me that you want to marry me, that you love me."

"I do love you," I choke, emotion thick in my throat.

"But you love him more, is that it?"

"I didn't say that."

"You didn't have to." He shakes his head. "You saying yes was all the proof I needed."

I want to argue it. Tell him I only said yes because he put me on the spot and I didn't see a way I could say no, but I refrain because truthfully a part of me really did want to say yes. Bennett is a wonderful man and unlike Sebastian, he's never hurt me. He's supportive and reliable and all the things I had hoped to find in a person one day.

But the one glaring problem, the one thing that has always kept my heart at bay is that he's not Sebastian.

"I just need some time," I plead, my heart and my head clashing against one another.

My head says Bennett—he's the smart choice, the safe choice.

My heart says Sebastian, knowing there's no way anyone will ever make me feel the way he does. But I know what comes along with loving someone so intensely—you lose a part of yourself in the process.

"I've given you years, Tess."

"Sebastian."

"No," he immediately cuts in, "I can't do this. I can't fight my way past a wall that you keep building faster than I can tear it down. Either you tell me now that I'm who you want—that this is what you want," he gestures between the two of us, "or I'm going to walk away, and you'll never see me again." He waits a long moment before adding, "choose."

"I can't. I can't just make a spur of the moment decision that will not only effect my life but the life of a man who is completely innocent in all of this. Bennett doesn't deserve what you're asking me to do, not like this. Please just give me some time."

He stares at me for a long moment, the anger long gone, the sadness a distant memory, all that seems to remain now is acceptance. And that's how I know there's nothing more I can do.

I either choose him or I choose Bennett, and truthfully, I'm not ready to choose either. I've never felt so split, so torn between two things in my entire life. It's like I'm two completely different people. The girl who loves Sebastian and the woman who loves Bennett.

No matter what choice I make, no matter what I do— someone loses. I lose. I can't see a clear path, and yet I also can't deny that out of the two there's only one person I can't see myself living without for the rest of my life, and that person is standing right in front of me, asking me to choose him. And yet, for the life of me, I can't force the words out.

"I really hope the two of you will be happy together, Tess." He lets out a slow breath, struggling to meet my gaze.

Seconds later a cab pulls up onto the curb next to us, slowing to a stop. And only then do I realize that this is really it. This is the moment that will define my entire future. And while the magnitude of what is happening is not lost on me, I still can't seem to force out the words I know deep down I want to say...

Stay.

He reaches for the car door, throwing one last look over his shoulder—his eyes meeting mine for a fraction of a second before he's uttering the words I've heard more times than I care to admit, and yet their effect on me never lessens.

"Goodbye, Tess."

I don't remember him climbing into the car. I don't even remember the car driving away. All I know is that when Courtney yells at me from the front porch what feels like several minutes later, I'm still standing on that curb, watching the love of my life drive away as if the car is still in view—knowing this time Sebastian has no intention of ever coming back.

TESS

It's been a week since the graduation party at my mom's—a week of restless nights and a sickening knot in my stomach that has only gotten worse as the days pass. I wish I could say that I found peace in my choice, happiness even, but I can't seem to muster that feeling no matter how hard I try.

Bennett returned to the city the day after the party to start the process of moving into the studio apartment he leased—the apartment I'm expected to move into as soon as I get the rest of my things from my dorm moved over.

It's taken me a lot longer to pack than either of us anticipated. I just can't seem to get the motivation to move any quicker. I feel torn, depressed—uncertain of every single thing that stands before me.

I haven't been able to commit to a job. I don't know what it is, but nothing feels right. Bennett says not to worry that all of it will come with time and he can cover the bills until then. He still thinks my inability to accept a position comes down to how I feel about the companies that I'm interviewing with. God, I wish it were that simple.

Honestly, I've received two amazing offers and would normally be ecstatic to accept either one, but I just can't seem to do it. I've picked up the phone more times than I can count to make the phone call, the one where I accept a job and finally settle on a path, but every time I hear the ring on the other end of the line, I panic and hang up.

Working on packing the contents of my desk into the last box, I look around my dorm room and wonder where the last four years have gone. My roommate, Joanie, moved out last week and now that the last of my things are being packed away the room is completely bare.

I let out a deep sigh, the sound echoing around me. What I wouldn't give to rewind time—experience this all over again—and yet at the same time I'm so relieved that it's finally over. There's such a contradiction of emotions raging inside of me.

Reaching into the last desk drawer, I pull out some random pieces of paper with notes and reminders scribbled on them, some pens and post-its, but when I reach the very bottom I pause, every muscle in my body tensing.

Staring up at me is a much younger version of myself, one with a wide smile and happiness in her eyes. I forget what it feels like to be that girl. It seems like such a lifetime ago. Next to me in the picture is Sebastian—we're laying on my bed, the camera outstretched above us. Instead of looking at the camera too, his eyes are locked on me, a wide smile on his lips.

With shaky hands, I retrieve the picture from the drawer and run my finger along the outline of his face. I remember the day this was taken. It was during winter break and Sebastian and I had holed ourselves up in my room for a week straight, him only leaving when my mom came home and coming back the second she left.

That was hands down the best week of my life.

It's strange how it took seeing this picture to remind me that it ever even happened. A memory I once held so dear, pushed into the back of mind and discarded like so many others. I stored it all away—every moment, every kiss, every touch. I couldn't bear to relive any of them because if I did I would have to remember what I lost, and that was something I simply couldn't do.

I turn the picture over in my hands, the inscription on the back causing tears to well instantly behind my eyes.

My everything.

It's only two words and yet those two words say more to me than anything else ever could. Because it reminds me of what that meant back then.

I close my eyes and let it all come back. Every single piece of the past I stored away. I let it flood through me, pulling me under until all I can see is Sebastian. All I can feel is Sebastian. All I want is Sebastian.

The last five years disappear and suddenly I'm there again—to the night where it all began. I can see everything so clearly—hear the noise of the party going on downstairs, feel the warm breeze on my face. And then I hear his voice, and my eyes shoot open.

Like being doused in cold water, the fog I've spent the last five years living in lifts and everything comes into focus. Bennett. Sebastian. My past. My present. My future.

I know what I want. I think I've always known.

Sebastian was right. I let fear rule my choices. Even though I couldn't see it at the time, it's now staring me right in the face—the truth that I've fought so hard to deny.

Shoving the picture into the back pocket of my jeans, I quickly empty the rest of the drawer into the box and tape it up haphazardly, only half paying attention to what I'm doing.

My mind is set on the task ahead. I don't have to worry that I'll chicken out or that I won't be able to find the strength to do what I know needs to be done. I know I will. Because for the first time in a very, very long time, I'm prepared to fight for what I want instead of hiding from it.

***

Within an hour I have the last of my boxes packed into my car and am making the twenty-minute drive across the city to Bennett's apartment. It's crazy to think that after four years of living in New York that I can still manage to fit every belonging I have in the hatch of my run down old Jeep. I think I'm leaving with less than I came with, though I'm not sure how that's possible.

Bennett meets me out on the street within moments of me pulling up to the curb prepared to help me carry my stuff upstairs. Jumping out of the driver's seat, I stop him just as he rounds the back of my Jeep.

"I'm not staying." I'm surprised I'm able to push the words out without my voice shaking.

He misunderstands.

"Okay, well let me carry this up first," he offers, his hand freezing mid-air when the next rush of words leaves my mouth.

"No, Bennett. I mean, I'm not staying here. I'm not staying in New York." He drops his hand and looks at me, eyebrows drawn in confusion.

"I don't understand." His warm chocolate eyes hold my gaze and even though I know I'm doing the right thing, my heart is still breaking for what that means for Bennett—for us.

"I need you to understand that this was real for me—all of it. I wasn't prepared to open my heart to anyone when you stumbled into my life. I tried to fight against it, tried to resist you, but you made me love you anyway; even when I didn't want to. I didn't realize it back then, but I needed you more than I would've ever thought possible. You became my rock, my strength. You held me up when I didn't have the strength to do it myself, and you never once asked me for anything in return." I pause, letting out a shaky breath.

"But no matter how much I love you, no matter how much I wish I could be your wife someday—I just can't."

"What are you saying, Tess?" The question is an automatic response. I can tell by the look on his face he still hasn't fully processed what I'm doing.

"I'm saying I can't marry you, Bennett. I can't be with you, not in the way you deserve. You deserve a woman who will give you her whole heart. A woman who will love you more than anything in this world. A woman who will never have to split her love between you and someone else. I can't stay here and pretend to be that woman anymore. Because the truth is I gave my heart to someone when I was sixteen-years-old, and I never got it back." I swipe at the tears now falling down my cheeks. "I'm so sorry, Bennett. I'm sorry that I made you believe I could give you something I can't. I'm sorry that I made you promises I'm now going to have to break. I'm just so, so sorry." My bottom lip quivers as I speak.

I know I'm the one doing the hurting here, but that doesn't mean it doesn't hurt me to do it. It doesn't mean that the part of me that loves Bennett isn't already mourning the loss of him. No matter how sure I am about what I want it doesn't change the fact that I've loved the man standing in front of me for the better part of almost two years, and I'm going to miss him horribly.

"I-I don't understand. Why did you say yes? Why did you agree to move in with me? Why do any of it if you were just planning on leaving me anyway?"

"I wasn't planning for this. In fact, it's something I hadn't decided until earlier today. I meant it when I said yes. I do love you, Bennett."

"If you loved me you wouldn't be doing this right now." The first sign of anger sparks in his voice.

"It's not that simple," I try to explain.

"Sebastian," he cuts in, his eyes full of questions and hurt.

There's nothing I can do or say, I know the truth is written all over my face.

"How long has this been going on? Have you been seeing him behind my back?"

"Of course not. I would never do that to you. It's not something that's been going on for a certain period of time, more like something that I buried and refused to face. I know it's hard to understand, and I'm sure right now you probably hate me, but please know that at the end of the day I'm sparing us both. I never could've made you happy, not truly, not when my heart exists somewhere else."

"I don't know what to say." Bennett takes a step back, shaking his head like he's still trying to process it all.

"Don't say anything. Just let me go." I reach out and take his hand, turning his palm upright before depositing the engagement ring he gave me into it. I close his fingers around the ring and mine around his hand.

He looks down at our point of contact and then back up to my face, the emotion so evident in his eyes that I nearly lose my ability to go through with this. It's hard, saying goodbye to someone like Bennett, knowing the pain and shock I'm sure he's feeling. But at the end of the day, I know this is the right thing for both of us.

He opens his mouth like he wants to say something—maybe even try to convince me to stay—but then he closes it without a word. The moment stretches on for what feels like forever, his brown eyes locked on mine, a mixture of both anger and sadness behind them.

"Go," he finally says, pulling his hand away from mine.

"Bennett."

"Go, Tess." He raises his voice, a slight shake to it. "Don't make this any worse than it already is. Just leave. Please."

I bite my bottom lip, willing myself not to say another word as I nod only once and silently back away, slipping into my Jeep seconds later.

I wish I could say it was easy—pulling away from that curb—watching a man I agreed to marry just one week ago disappear in my rearview mirror, knowing I'd likely never see him again. But it wasn't. In fact, it was one of the hardest things I've ever done.

Nothing about any of this is easy. And while I've gotten through the part I was dreading the most, there's still the matter of Sebastian and the worry that maybe I'm too late. Maybe last week was his breaking point and I pushed him too far. Maybe this is all for not. Maybe…

And while that thought sparks fear deep inside me, I also know that I'll never forgive myself if I don't at least take the chance.

***

"You're sure about this?" Bree looks up at the apartment building and then back to where I'm sitting in the passenger seat of her car.

I arrived in California two days ago. After realizing that Sebastian had changed his phone number and Courtney had no idea what his address was, I had to resort to contacting his mother. To say that was an unpleasant conversation is quite the understatement, but at the end of it, I did manage to get Sebastian's address out of her; though truthfully, I didn't think she was going to give it to me.

Now, sitting next to Bree, looking up at the brick six-story building in front of me, I realize that making that phone call was nothing compared to what I'm about to do now. My stomach is a mass of nervous knots, and I swear my hands have never sweated so much in my life. My nerves, which I thought couldn't get any worse when I woke this morning, only intensified on the hour drive down from where Bree lives.

I'm an absolute total wreck. It's not lost on me that this is very possibly the way Sebastian felt when he came to me. I just hope this visit will end up with a different result than his previous two.

"I'm sure," I finally manage to answer Bree's question, letting out a slow breath as I look back in her direction.

She gives me a warm smile and reaches out to pat my leg. Everything about her is so motherly now. From the way she acts to the way she looks, you would never guess that just five years ago she was a wild child who rocked a

349

red bob and always sported thick black eyeliner and short skirts.

There's no trace of that girl anymore, at least not on the outside. Her red hair is now back to her natural brown and hangs a few inches past her shoulders. She usually keeps it tied back in a low pony, but today she has it down and wavy. She's traded in her dark eyes and bright lips for more neutral tones and clear lip gloss, and her short skirts have been swapped for cute jeans and flowy tops.

But even with all that, even with how much she's changed and grown, I still see little pieces of the old Bree that shine through. She might have grown up and traded in her bad girl ways, but she is still the same spitfire she's always been; she just reins it in more now.

"You can do this, Tess," she reassures me. "Just walk up there, knock on his door, and tell him you love him."

"Just like that." I laugh nervously. "You make it sound so easy."

"He loves you, and you love him. If you both focus on that it should be easy."

I nod, mustering a small smile. "I hope you're right."

"Only one way to find out." She looks up at the building and then back to me. "Go, you got this."

"You'll keep your phone on you in case I need you to come back?" I ask for the tenth time.

"Yes, now stop stalling and go."

"Okay." I let out another deep breath before pushing open the car door and climbing out, Bree shouting words of encouragement my way until I close the door.

The walk up to Sebastian's apartment is like a blur. By the time I reach his door my entire body is shaking, and I'm fairly certain that had I eaten anything today it would now be on the shiny hallway floor rather than in my stomach.

I take a deep breath in and slowly let it out at least five times before I manage to reach out and rap on the door with my knuckles.

I can hear movement inside almost instantly followed by the sound of footsteps, each one getting louder the closer they get to the door. My breath lodges in my throat, and I squeeze my hands together in anticipation.

This is it.

This is what everything has led up to.

This is the moment of truth.

SEBASTIAN

"Tess?" I hear Ant say seconds after he pulls the front door of my apartment open.

At first, I think I'm hearing things; there's no way he just said what I think he said, but then he opens the door wider I damn near hit the floor at the sight of her.

Tess…

She looks so fucking beautiful in a pale yellow sundress, her hair falling around her shoulders. The sight of her takes my breath away, as cliché as that sounds.

I'm standing in the kitchen which is open to the rest of the apartment, unable to move a fucking muscle. I feel paralyzed, in complete and utter shock. Seeing her standing inside of my apartment is absolutely the last thing I expected.

"Hi, Ant." She gives my friend a small smile, purposely keeping her gaze on him as he closes the door and joins her in the living room.

"What are you doing all the way out here? I thought you were still in New York." He gives her a quick one-armed hug, meeting my gaze over the top of her head.

"I've been at Bree's the last couple of days. She only lives about an hour north of here."

"I didn't realize she was so close," he quickly adds.

"Neither did I." Her gaze darts around nervously.

She couldn't look more uncomfortable if she were standing on a rug of hot coals. It's painfully obvious that she's terrified to be here right now. She looks around the space, her eyes touching my face for only a brief moment before she sets her gaze back on Anthony.

Ant looks almost as uncomfortable, glancing at me and then back to Tess who knots her hands in front of herself, not saying anything else.

The tension in the room so thick it's damn near suffocating.

"Uh…" Ant rocks back on his heels, finally breaking the awkward moment. "I'm gonna…" He looks between the two of us. "I'm gonna take off for a bit, let you kids catch up." He shoots me a knowing look before grabbing his wallet and keys off the breakfast bar. "It was good seeing you, Tess," he calls over his shoulder as he makes his way toward the door.

"Yeah, you too," she offers, watching him exit the apartment without another word.

It feels like an eternity from the point that the door latches closed to when her gaze finally finds mine, by which point I've grown extremely anxious.

"I didn't know he was staying here." Out of everything she could say, I didn't expect those words to be the first out of her mouth.

"Yeah, he's been here a few months." I shrug, not sure what else to say.

"It must be nice, having a familiar face around I mean. Does he plan on staying in California permanently?"

The last thing I want to talk about right now is Ant, but I force myself to answer her anyway.

"I don't think he's a hundred percent sure at this point."

"I see." She looks around the apartment, doing everything she can to avoid my gaze.

As much as I want to let her work her way into telling me whatever it is she's doing here, if I have to exist in this awkward in between stage for even a second longer I just might fucking burst.

"What are you doing here?" I don't mean for it to come out as harshly as it does. It leaves my mouth on a rush, and I immediately suck in a sharp breath preparing for her answer.

"I needed to see you," she offers apologetically.

"How did you even know where to find me?"

"Your mom."

"You called my mom?" I can't help the impressed grin that pulls at my mouth, but it does nothing to quell the uncertainty inside me.

She shrugs. "You didn't give me much of a choice."

"I didn't realize you needed a choice," I answer truthfully. "I thought you had already made yours."

"You changed your phone number," she observes, hurt evident in those beautiful blue eyes of hers.

"We said all we needed to say. I walked away ready to leave you behind, but in order to do that, I had to make sure that I made a clean break. No way to contact you or you me—no more of the back and forth. It was the only way I could think to even give myself a fighting chance."

"And is that what you still want? To leave me behind?" She shuffles from one foot to the other, clearly very nervous.

354

Fuck—I'm nervous, too. My heart is pounding relentlessly against my ribs, and I swear I haven't taken a real breath since she walked in the door.

"You didn't give me much of a choice," I bite, crossing around the kitchen counter to stand at the edge of the living room just feet from where Tess is.

"That's not what I asked." She shakes her head, taking a hesitant step toward me. "Do you still want to leave me behind?"

"What does it matter, you're with someone else?" I grind out, my entire body tensing as she takes another step and then another until she's standing just a foot in front of me, her eyes locked on mine.

"What if I weren't, would it make a difference?" My heart beats even faster. Every single thing that ran through my mind the moment I laid eyes on her now seems within my grasp, and yet I'm hesitant to accept it so easily. We've done this song and dance before, and the last thing I want to do is get my hopes up and think she's offering something that she's not.

"That depends, are you still planning to marry…" I pause when I realize I don't even remember the fucker's name.

"Bennett," she clarifies.

"I don't care," I snip, growing even more impatient.

"No." She shakes her head softly. "I'm not going to marry him."

"And does he know this?" I question, a tight knot forming at the base of my throat.

"He does."

She takes another step, leaving just inches between us. She's so close I can smell her sweet scent, hear the sound of her shallow breath, feel the tension seeping off of her.

And yet not one part of our bodies is touching, a fact I'm acutely aware of.

"Now answer the question," she adds. "Do you still want to leave me behind?"

I take a deep breath and let it out slowly, thinking over my response before actually speaking it.

"I never wanted that. Not ever. But I didn't see another way."

"You were right when you said I was scared. I was, I still am. But I finally realized that living a life without you was a hell of a lot scarier than the risk that I might lose you again."

"What are you saying, Tess?"

"I'm saying I love you. I'm saying that not a day has gone by that I haven't thought about you. I'm saying that you've been with me—a part of me—since that first night on that balcony. I gave you my heart back then Sebastian, and I don't ever want you to give it back."

"I never planned to anyway." I grin, allowing my fingers to brush down her forearm, her skin prickling under my touch.

"I'm sorry it took me so long to find my way back to you," she whispers, eyes welling with unshed tears.

"I'm sorry I let you go to begin with." I bring my hand up to cup the side of her face, feeling the overwhelming urge to pinch myself to make sure this is real.

"Don't ever do it again okay?" She half laughs, half cries, the sound coming out a little jumbled mess of emotion.

"Never." It's the last word off my tongue before my lips land on hers.

It's soft and hesitant at first, but then quickly morphs into something else entirely. Tess has a way of lighting my body on fire, and feeling her mouth pressed to mine for the first time in over four years has my entire body engulfed in the burn. I relish in the pain, in the pleasure, in the unspoken promise the kiss holds.

I put it all out there. I bleed everything I am into that kiss, willing Tess to feel how much I love her—how much I've always loved her.

I never expected Tess. Not five years ago, not a year ago—not today. I never planned for her to change my life the way she has. I didn't expect it or want it, but the moment I touched her, tasted her, felt her heart beating against mine; I knew there was no going back. I had no idea just how right I had been.

I pull Tess closer, kiss her harder, afraid that the moment I open my eyes she'll be gone; that this will have all just been some cruel dream, and I'll wake up to find myself staring at the same painful reality that I was yesterday. That I've lost her forever.

Only I know that's not true. I can feel it in my bones, in the way blood pumps through my veins, in the trail of heat Tess' touch brings to the surface; I know it's real. And while it's still hard to wrap my head around—I know she really is here, touching me, kissing me, whispering she loves me against my lips.

It's everything I've dreamed of since the moment I lost her. Only now I appreciate it all a little more. The sweet noises she makes when my tongue slides against hers. The way her fingers tangle in my hair. The way her body responds to me as if it were made for my touch. All things I took for granted before. All things I overlooked because I thought they'd always be there. These are the things I've missed most of all.

When we finally break apart, my forehead resting against hers, our breathing labored and hearts clamoring, there are no words left to speak. Even after all this time, Tess still knows me better than anyone has ever known me. And right now, she knows that every single word I've said to her over the past couple of years has been true. I know she can feel it— she can feel me, just as I can her.

It's strange to go from the lowest of lows to the highest of highs in the matter of minutes, but that's what Tess has always done to me. I wish I could say it scares the hell out of me to have a person hold so much power over me, honestly, it probably should. But in this moment, with Tess pressed against me—her blue eyes boring into mine, her soft hair on my fingertips—fear is the absolute last thing I feel.

Maybe it's because I'm a glutton for punishment. Maybe it's because I truly believe that Tess is the person I'm meant to spend my life with. Or maybe it's because no matter the outcome, having Tess even for a short time is better than not having her at all.

Every moment, every touch, every kiss is a blessing that I will never take for granted. Because at the end of the day I know what it means to live without her, and I never intend to do it again.

TESS

I've dreamt of this moment—wished for it, prayed for it—but never truly believed it would ever be again.

Sebastian is sitting next to me in the sand, his jeans rolled up to his knees as the water washes up over our feet.

We've been sitting out here for hours. At first, we talked—a lot. We talked about college and friends. We talked about Bennett and some of the girls of Sebastian's past. It wasn't an easy conversation, but it was a necessary one. In order to fully put the past behind us, we had to lay it all on the table. The more we talked the more we seemed to understand the other person's stance on things.

I understood why Sebastian did what he did all those years ago. That he was trying to do what he thought was right. In a lot of ways, I think he feared he would hold me back when in reality he was always the one who propelled me forward.

He understood why I spent years trying to convince myself that I didn't need him, that I didn't love him. Truthfully, I didn't even realize it was happening. I didn't see it at the time, but every move I made was an intentional one; one that placed me further away from

Sebastian and therefore further away from the pain I knew he was capable of inflicting.

All those wasted years. All this time we could've been together. I want to regret it. I want to hate myself for making the choices I did, but I simply can't do that. Because had we forced it, had we stayed together through time and distance, there's no telling where we would be now.

Don't get me wrong, there are certain things I regret. Hurting Bennett. Hurting Sebastian. Hurting myself. But I'd do it all over again if it meant that this is where I would find myself at the end of it all, sitting on this beach with Sebastian by my side.

Beyond all the hurt, beyond all the arguments and doubts, one thing has always remained true even when I was too stubborn to see it. Sebastian was never a choice. It wasn't a matter of choosing him or not choosing him; I had already given him my heart years ago. I just needed to open my eyes wide enough to see it.

"So..." I say, watching another wave wash up on the shore, the water barely reaching my feet before being pulled back in.

"So..." Sebastian repeats next to me, bringing a smile to my face.

"What do we do now?" I ask, flipping my gaze to him.

I have every intention of adding to the question, but the instant my eyes find his everything else just vanishes in the light breeze that dances around us.

I swear I've never seen a more breathtaking sight.

Sebastian, his face cast in a beautiful orange glow from the setting sun. It's in this moment that I realize something I wish I would've realized a long time ago. It doesn't matter what happens next. As long as this man is by my side I will take whatever life throws my way.

"No idea." Sebastian chuckles next to me, wrapping his arm around my shoulder as he pulls me closer. "I guess we'll just have to see where the night ends."

And just like our past, so begins our future. A promise of what's to come. A reminder of what has passed. And even though days ago I thought our love story was over, I know now that it's really only just beginning.

Because it's not about where the night begins. It's not about the struggle or the uncertainty along the way. It's not about the past or the years we spent hurting each other.

It's about where we end up after it's all said and done. It's about sitting here with Sebastian on this beach knowing that I will never love another person the way I love him.

It's about knowing that this time it's forever…

It's about where the night ends.

TESS

Six months later...

"There you are." I hear Sebastian's voice seconds before his arms wrap around me from behind. "I've been looking all over for you. It's freezing, what are you doing out here?"

I take a moment to appreciate his scent that instantly engulfs me, breathing him in deeply before responding, "Hey." I lean my head back against his chest and look out over the expansive lake that sits at the back of the Baxter property.

It's the first time I've been here in years, and so many memories have come rushing to the surface in the twenty minutes since I found myself standing on this dock.

"It's so beautiful out here this time of year." I sigh in contentment, loving the way the moon hits the frozen water just right, making the lake look like it's speckled with diamonds.

"It is," Sebastian agrees, running his hands up and down my arms in an effort to warm me. "Still doesn't explain why you disappeared on me." His lips brush the spot just below my ear. "Had enough Baxter family fun have you?"

"How you ever grew up with parents like that I'll never understand," I admit, turning in his embrace to look up at him.

"Please. Those two people in there are nothing compared to what I grew up with."

Sebastian's parents, at some point while he was away at school, seemed to have rekindled a relationship they had long since lost. While they are still nearly unbearable to be around, it's clear to see that life in the Baxter home is a lot better than it used to be. And I know how much that means to Sebastian. It's been a long and messy road, and while I don't think they'll ever be the type of family Sebastian deserves, I think it's enough for him that they're at least trying.

"Even still, if I have to listen to your mother tell me one more time that I don't have the body for a strapless wedding dress, I might end up stabbing her in the forehead with my dinner fork."

At this Sebastian laughs, a deep rumble vibrating through him. It instantly brings a smile to my face. It's my favorite sound in the world.

"Well, you better get used to it. In just a few short months you will be an official Baxter, and old mom and pop up there will be your family." He gestures up toward the house.

"Can I reconsider?" I joke, earning me a quick squeeze to my side.

"Not a chance. No take backs." He tightens his grip around my waist and pulls me closer. "I've been waiting years to marry you, Tessa Wilson. There's no way I'm letting you slip through my fingers now that I'm so close."

"Then perhaps the next time your parents' invite us up for a long weekend we should reconsider," I tease.

"Speaking of which, I wonder how your mom is doing in there. Some daughter you are, throwing her to the wolves like that."

"Please. My mom can handle her own. Besides, Jeff is in there with her. He'll make sure my mother doesn't kill yours. I mean, at least I think he will." I laugh at the thought.

"Remind me again how we ended up with all of them in the same house?" He chuckles in response.

"I have no idea. They must all have a death wish." I shake my head. "I just can't believe my mom brought her new boyfriend over here. I guess she figures if he can handle a night with your parents' then he's a keeper." I reach up, wrapping my arms around Sebastian's neck.

"Well, if I had to guess, I'd say he's passing with flying colors." He leans down and lays a light kiss to my lips, smiling against my mouth. "I remember the very first time I brought you out here." He changes the subject.

"Me too." I pull back slightly, grinning up at him. "Thought you were gonna get lucky."

"Oh, I did get lucky."

"That's not the way I remember it."

"Are you kidding me? I got to hang out with the most incredible girl I'd ever met, watch her drink whiskey like a boss, and then spent two blissful hours watching her sleep—all the while thinking how I'd never seen anything more beautiful in my entire life. If that's not getting lucky I don't what is."

"Are you trying to butter me up, Mr. Baxter?" I pull him down for another kiss, letting my lips linger against his.

"That depends, is it working?"

"Keep talking and we'll see," I tease, dragging my tongue along his lower lip.

He pulls back just enough to look down at me, his hand reaching up to tuck a strand of hair behind my ear—something he's always done. "I love you, Tess."

"I love you more," I practically cut him off.

"Not possible," he argues, continuing the tradition from when we were teenagers.

"So possible," I retort.

"Don't argue with me, Tessa," he warns, his eyes playful.

"Don't argue with me, Sebastian." I give it right back to him, laughing when he swoops me up and cradles me to his chest, nuzzling his face into the crook of my neck.

"Thank you." He suddenly falls serious, his hazel eyes locked on mine.

"For what?" I question, confused by the abrupt shift.

"For spending Christmas in this shit show. For moving to California with me. For agreeing to be my wife. For making me the happiest man in the entire world. The list goes on and on." He kisses the tip of my nose. "I imagined this life, being with you like this. For years I dreamt of it, prayed for it, but I don't think I ever really thought it would actually happen. Being here with you like this, remembering how it all started and how far we've come, it just makes me appreciate it all that much more."

"Me too," I agree, my voice shaky, emotion bubbling inside my chest.

"What do you say we ditch the wedding? Let's get married now," he suggests, a wide smile spreading across his handsome face.

"What do you mean now?" I choke.

"Tomorrow. Let's get married right here on this dock. Just you and me."

"I'm pretty sure Bree and Courtney would kill me," I object, convinced he's not actually serious.

"Well, they can try, but they would have to get through me." He shifts, slowly lowering me to my feet. The instant they hit the dock his hands are cupping my face. "I'm mean it, Tess, let's do it. Why wait?"

"You're serious?" I finally manage to speak after a long moment.

"I am. I don't need anyone to show up but you. All I want is for you to be my wife, and I want it now. Hell, I'd marry you this very second if I had someone who could perform the ceremony."

"Sebastian," I start, but he instantly cuts in.

"Over six years ago I fell in love with you on this very dock. I fell in love with your smile and your laugh, with the way you viewed the world like everything had beauty and purpose in it even though you had no reason to believe it so. I fell in love with you right here, and I've only fallen harder every day since then. Marry me, right here, where it all began. What do say, Tess?"

"I say you have some phone calls to make, and I have a dress to buy." It takes a moment for my statement to register, but once it does that incredible smile of his slides into place.

I squeal when he lifts me off my feet and spins me around, our fogged breath clouding the air around us as we laugh and kiss, losing ourselves in the moment.

An outdoor wedding on a dock overlooking a frozen lake in the middle of winter would not have been my first choice, but looking at Sebastian—seeing the sheer happiness etched into every feature of his face—I can't imagine doing it any other way.

Because at the end of the day, all that really matters is Sebastian, becoming his wife, spending my life with him. It's all I've wanted from the moment he took my hand on that balcony over six years ago.

Sebastian pulls my mouth down to his, delivering an earth-bending kiss before lowering to my feet. "Tomorrow can't come soon enough," he mutters against my lips.

Melissa Toppen

Where do I even begin…

Thank you for taking the time to read Tess and Sebastian's story.

This entire journey was such a roller coaster of emotions for me. To be reminded what it means to love with such reckless abandon, to remember how it feels to give your heart for the very first time, proved to be one of the most rewarding and challenging writing experiences I've ever had. I spent weeks buried in Tess and Sebastian's story and when I finally resurfaced, I found myself looking back on my own past with an appreciation that I had long since lost.

I gave my heart to a blond-haired, blue-eyed boy when I was just sixteen-years-old, and I thank God every day that he never gave it back. To that boy, my now amazing husband, I love you. Even when I can't stand you, I love you. Thank you for being you. Thank you for loving me. Thank you for being such an incredible father to our two amazing children. My life is full because you're in it.

To my street team—Melissa's Mavens—I'll never be able to thank you enough for everything you do for me. I am truly blessed to have you all in my life and am so proud to call you my friends.

To Angel—sometimes I think you work harder for me than I work for myself. I don't know how I was lucky enough to find you, but now that I have you're stuck with me forever!!

To Alex, Avelyn, Jaime, JC, Allison, and Reagan—the Horsemen—I am so incredibly lucky to have all of you in my life. Thank you for always being there when I have questions and need advice. Thank you for being my friends. I love all of you to the moon and back!

To my beta and proofreaders—THANK YOU! Thank you for dedicating your time and effort to make Where the Night Ends the best it could be. You are all a gift and deserve more thanks than I could ever give you!

To Judi Perkins of Concierge Literary Designs—Thank you for making the perfect cover for Where the Night Ends.

To my editor and all around bad ass, Silla—thank you for always understanding my vision, and doing everything in your power to make my work the best it can be. It means so much to me that I have someone like you that I can trust and rely on.

To my readers. Thank you from the bottom of my heart. I don't know what else I can say but thank you. This is for all of you. This is for every single person who has stood behind me, supported me, and given me the opportunity to live out my dreams every single day. None of this is possible without you.

All my love,
-Melissa

www.mtoppen.com
www.facebook.com/mtoppenauthor
www.facebook.com/melissatoppen
www.goodreads.com/mtoppen
www.twitter.com/mtoppenauthor
www.tsu.co/mtoppenauthor
www.instagram.com/melissa_toppen
www.pinterest.com/mtoppenauthor
www.amazon.com/author/melissatoppen